GODINE DOUBLE DETECTIVES
Robin W. Winks, General Editor

THE ROCKSBURG RAILROAD MURDERS

THE BLANK PAGE

Two Mario Balzic Mysteries

K. C. CONSTANTINE

With an Afterword by Robin W. Winks

A Godine Double Detective

DAVID R. GODINE, PUBLISHER · BOSTON

Published in 1982 by

DAVID R. GODINE, PUBLISHER, INC.
306 Dartmouth Street
Boston, Massachusetts 02116

Library of Congress Cataloging in Publication Data

Constantine, K. C.
   The Rocksburg railroad murders; The blank page.

   (A Godine double detective)
   1. Detective and mystery stories, American.   I.
Constantine, K. C. The blank page.   II. Title.   III.
Series.
P S3553.0524A6 1982   813'.54   81-47322
I S B N 0-87923-408-3   A A C R2

Printed in the United States of America

THE ROCKSBURG
RAILROAD MURDERS

Even with the hand-talkies, it took Chief Mario Balzic a half hour after the game to get the auxiliary police coordinated. Maybe more people were coming to high school football games, or maybe more were coming to Rocksburg High's games, or maybe Rocksburg's narrow streets were never intended to handle this kind of traffic, or maybe there were just too damn many saloons too near the high school field.

Whichever it was, it left Balzic surly, distracted, and thirsting for a beer. He stepped into Evanko's Bar and Grille, hoping for a quick draught, and walked instead into a fist fight between two drunks whose high school football careers had ended at least twenty years earlier and who had started out reminiscing and ended up swinging over the cause of Rocksburg's forty-to-six loss. It took Balzic a half hour to get that straightened out, doing it by buying drinks all around to pacify Mike Evanko to keep him from pressing charges, and by seeing to it that friends of the fist fighters got some coffee into them and gave their word that they'd drive them home.

Back out on the street, traffic seemed worse than before Balzic had gone into Evanko's. Then the auxiliary at the corner of Amelia

Street and Eurania Avenue quit communicating and it took Balzic fifteen minutes to get there to find out why.

"Something's wrong with it," Henry Adamchik, the auxiliary, said, holding the radio up to Balzic's ear and shaking it.

Balzic jerked it out of his hand and fiddled with it. "Here, take mine," he said after an exasperating minute trying to make the other one work. "I'll go back and use my car radio."

On the way back to his cruiser, Balzic looked up at the clear black sky and said, "Bad enough you let somebody invent football, but you weren't satisfied with that. No, you had to let somebody go and invent cars, and then radios, and then, Jeezus Christ Almighty, you had to stick me with auxiliaries yet. . . ."

It was eleven-fifteen before the flow of cars approached the usual level of traffic for that time of night on a Friday, and eleven-twenty before Balzic told the auxiliaries to pack it in. He headed his cruiser down Bencho's Alley and threaded his way through a half dozen more alleys before turning onto Delmont Street to his home. Once inside, he headed straight for the refrigerator and a beer.

On the kitchen table was a note from his wife, Ruth, telling him that she'd given the girls permission to go to Valleta's Drug Store after the game, but that they were to be in no later than midnight. The note also said his mother had had a good time at the Eagles' bingo and won a set of dish towels.

Balzic opened the beer and set out a plate. He cut up some provolone and quartered a banana pepper, filled the plate with them, and went into the living room, taking a long drink of beer before setting the dish on the coffee table and turning on the television. With a little luck he thought he might be able to catch the last inning of the Pirates' game out of Saint Louis.

There was another note on the coffee table with a snapshot beside it. The note said: "Hey, Mario, big shot. What you think this? Next time you holler hippeys, you think this over. You look pretty funny. No?" It was his mother's barely legible script.

The snapshot was of himself. There he stood, grinning with the arrogance only being eighteen can muster, thirty pounds lighter, hair slicked back in a duck's tail, wearing a one-button jacket down to his knees and trousers pulled up by inch-wide suspenders to a point just below where his ribs joined and then ballooning out at the knees and coming to rest in a tight circle on his spade, suede shoes. Completing the outfit were a floppy, polka-dotted bow tie and a key chain that nearly touched his shoe.

"Brother, if I wasn't a mess," he said.

He turned the faded snapshot over and looked closely at the smudged date: June 4, 1942, the date of his senior class picnic. He remembered the date very well. The next day he had enlisted in the marines.

He chuckled ruefully and, tossing the snapshot on the table, drank some more beer, and mused for a moment about taking his mother to the courthouse to give a lecture to District Attorney Milt Weigh about social customs, particularly in matters of dress. Weigh needed somebody to lecture him about that at least as much as Balzic needed to be reminded of it; to Milt Weigh, anybody who didn't wear four-dollar ties and calf-high socks had to be doing something suspicious.

Balzic chuckled again, thinking about all the things Weigh didn't know and about how Weigh managed to sustain the impression that anything he didn't know wasn't worth knowing.

The sound of the television interrupted his thoughts. He got up to adjust the set and then settled back in the recliner the girls had bought him last Christmas to watch the Pirates and the Cards. Instead of the game, he got the last minute of a post-game interview and the beginning of what would have been the eleven o'clock news.

He had just kicked off his shoes and put his feet on the coffee table when the phone rang. He swore in Italian and Serbian and was still swearing as he hustled into the kitchen to lift the receiver before it woke either his wife or mother.

"Balzic."

"Royer, Chief."

"Yeah, Joe—oh, wait. Don't tell me you're sick or something and can't make it tonight. Please don't tell me that."

"What do you mean sick? Where the hell you think I'm calling from?"

5

"You at the station?"

"Hell yes, I'm at the station."

"Jesus, is it after twelve already?"

"Five minutes after."

"Oh boy," Balzic said, sighing. "I just got back from that damn football game. You never saw such a mess. So what's up?"

"Angelo just called in."

"So? Angelo's always calling in. Angelo can't find straight up without calling in."

"He got a reason this time," Royer said. "He found a guy up on the train station platform with his head caved in. Dead."

"Did he get hit by a train, or what?"

"No. Angelo wasn't making too much sense, but from what I gather, somebody beat the shit out of him."

"I'll be right down. You call Weigh's office?"

"Not yet."

"Well, call him, for crissake. I'll be down the train station."

Balzic gulped down a piece of cheese and some of the pepper as he was putting his shoes back on. He took another gulp of beer, grabbed another piece of provolone to eat on the way, and was starting out the door when his daughters came up on the porch.

"Hi," he said as he hurried past them. "You have a good time? And what are you doing coming in this late? You know you got school tomorrow."

"Tomorrow's Saturday, Daddy," Emily, the fourteen-year-old, said.

"Besides, Mother said it was okay," Marie, the fifteen-year-old, said.

"I'll talk to her about that tomorrow," Balzic said, getting in his car. He got back out to say, "Hey, put that plate of cheese and peppers back in the ice box, will you? And turn the TV off, okay?"

"It's a refrigerator, Daddy," Emily said.

"You know what I mean. And if your mother wakes up tell her I had to go out. Urgent, got it?"

"Yeah, we got it," Marie said with a sidelong glance at her sister.

"Good night, kids," Balzic said, spinning the wheels backing out of the drive.

6

"Talk about hot-rodders," Marie said.

"Hey, come on," Emily said. "We can watch Humphrey Bogart. He's on channel four."

Balzic had parked his Chevrolet on the State Street side of the Pennsylvania Station when he spotted Angelo Seretti's cruiser. The ticket office was deserted, and he went through the tunnel and up the steps to the platform. Patrolman Angelo Seretti was trying his best to look professional, but the color of his face gave him away. Frank Bennett, the station master, stood beside Seretti, his face more ashen than Seretti's.

"Where?" Balzic said when he approached them.

"Over there," Seretti said. "Under the bench."

Balzic hustled to the bench and went down on one knee. For a second he thought he was going to lose the little beer and cheese he'd gotten down. "Good Christ," he said. He stood up and walked back to Seretti and Bennett. "Get on the horn, Angelo, and tell Royer to get the coroner and the state boys."

"The D.A.'s office, too?"

"He already called them. They should've been here by now. Go on, Angelo."

Angelo, flushing over his hesitation, turned quickly and broke into a run toward the steps.

"Did you know him, Mr. Bennett?"

Bennett nodded, a lock of his gray hair falling over his eye. "So did you," he said, his voice barely above a whisper.

"Who was it?"

"John Andrasko."

"You're—you sure?"

"Yes, I'm sure. John's been riding the eleven-thirty-eight to Knox every night for eight, ten years. I've sold him enough passes. He just bought a new one tonight, as a matter of fact."

Balzic walked back over to the body lying half under the bench. "Good Christ, John, I'm sorry." He was almost going to say he was sorry he hadn't recognized him, but the beer and cheese started

7

coming up, and he just got his face over the edge of the platform in time. He coughed and gagged a couple more times before he wiped his mouth with his hanky. Spitting didn't get rid of the taste.

He was going back to Bennett to ask some other questions when he heard the shoes on the steps coming up.

Milt Weigh, the district attorney, came up, his breath heavy with the smell of gin. He was followed by Sam Carraza, his chief of detectives, and by John Dillman, another county detective. Carraza and Dillman both were raw-eyed and breathing heavily.

"Hello, Milt," Balzic said, nodding to Carraza and Dillman. "I think I ought to warn you guys, be ready to lose all that high-price stuff you been drinking."

"Balzic," Weigh said by way of greeting. "An ugly one?"

"Ugliest one I've seen since Tarawa. Over there. Under the bench."

Weigh, Carraza, and Dillman set off toward the body. The two detectives took a long look, but Weigh recoiled. "My God," he said and immediately turned away and came back to Balzic. "My God," he said again.

"Yeah," Balzic said. "I lost about half a beer, so if you're thinking you're going to lose your gin, don't hold it in on my account."

Weigh took a couple of deep breaths. "What do you have?"

"Just a name so far. John Andrasko. I've known him since I was a kid. Mr. Bennett here had to tell me, though. Says he just bought a pass from him tonight. But I'm really taking his word for it. I haven't gone through his pockets yet."

"Dillman?" Weigh called out.

"Yeah?"

"Check his pockets."

"I'm doing that."

"What's the station man say?" Weigh said.

"Just what I told you. Says he sold John a pass tonight and that he's been riding the eleven-thirty-something every night to Knox for eight, ten years."

"He didn't say anything else?"

"I didn't get a chance to ask him."

"Well, let's go ask him."

They walked back to where Frank Bennett was sitting and kneading his palms.

"Mr. Bennett," Balzic said, "this is Mr. Weigh, the district attorney."

"How do you do, sir," Bennett said.

Weigh extended his hand and Bennett shook it feebly.

"I'd like to ask you some questions, Mr. Bennett."

"Go ahead. I doubt that I can tell you much, though," Bennett said.

"How did you learn about this?"

"Fireman from the eleven-thirty-eight came down and told me."

"What time—I mean, was this fellow Andrasko a regular?"

"Yessir. The only one. Been riding for years. Ever since he took the job over at Knox Steel. Eight, ten years at least. Longer, maybe."

"Did you see anybody else?"

"Nossir. Nobody. Of course that doesn't mean anything. There are lots of ways to get on this platform. You can come down State Street Extension from the other side over there, or you could walk up the tracks from either direction. Going past me is only one of the ways. But nobody went past me since eleven tonight except John. He bought his pass and we talked a bit."

"What time was that?"

"Well, on nights when John just comes in, he gets here about eleven-thirty, but on nights when he buys his pass, he generally comes in about eleven-twenty and we shoot the breeze. Nothing important. We just talk. He was a nice fellow."

"How does he usually get here?"

"He walks. John doesn't like to drive. Never has. I guess that's why he's one of the few people left who still ride the trains."

John Dillman walked up then, holding everything he'd found in John Andrasko's pockets: a thin billfold, a ring of keys, a package of chewing tobacco, a pack of twisted Italian cigars, and four dollar bills and three dimes. "This is it," he said.

"Mr. Bennett," Weigh said, "you said he bought a pass tonight. How much money, if you know, would you say he might've had?"

9

"Well, he paid me with a twenty-dollar bill, as he always does. That money you're holding there is the change I gave him. Should be four dollars and thirty cents. Month pass to Knox costs fifteen-seventy."

"Mario," Weigh said, "I assume your people have contacted the state police."

Balzic nodded. "They should've been here by now."

"Mr. Bennett, are you positive nobody else went past you tonight?"

Bennett nodded slowly. "Yessir. But I've already told you that doesn't mean anything. I mean—no disrespect, Mr. Weigh—but somebody had to get up here tonight, and they didn't come by me."

"Here come the state boys," Dillman said. "Looks like they brought half the barracks."

Lieutenant Phil Moyer, in plain clothes, followed by Sergeant Ralph Stallcup, led a contingent of seven troopers up the steps onto the platform. One of them carried a camera and immediately began photographing the body of John Andrasko from a variety of angles. The rest of them, with no direction from either Lieutenant Moyer or Sergeant Stallcup, fanned out over the platform and began examining it. Moyer ordered them off the platform after about ten minutes, and they started to make their way up and down the three sets of tracks.

Moyer and Stallcup listened as Frank Bennett repeated what little he knew about John Andrasko and the events leading up to the discovery of the body by the fireman from the eleven-thirty-eight to Knox. Moyer went through the effects found by Dillman, verifying the amount of money with the amounts Frank Bennett gave as the price of the pass and the change given.

"Mario," Moyer said, "what's it look like to you?"

"Looks to me probably what it looks like to you. Somebody either had a grudge or else that somebody's off his rocker. Nobody does that kind of job for any other reason that I know of. It sure wasn't for money, unless he was carrying a wad nobody knew about. But a guy like John, well, he was too steady. Too regular."

"You knew him?" Moyer said.

10

"Ever since I was a kid. Went all through school with him. We were in the same room most of the time."

"Wasn't there anything irregular about him?"

"Not that I knew about. He married a little late, I suppose. No. I can't even say that. He just didn't get married as early as the rest of us is what I meant to say."

"Gambler?"

"Not that I know of. No. He watched his money pretty close even when he was a kid."

"What did he do for a living?"

"He was a millwright over at Knox Steel. Before that I think he worked for one of the big steel outfits down the river. I'm not really sure."

"Ever in trouble?"

"Hell no. John was as straight a guy as everybody ought to be. If everybody was like him, you and me'd be looking for sensible work."

"From what you say, it looks like we can rule out a grudge job."

"Oh, I wouldn't do that. Not just yet anyway."

"Why not?"

"Well, as far as I know, John was a straight, regular guy. But that doesn't mean there wasn't somebody around who thought he was a prick. I just said I've known him most of my life, but I wasn't a drinking buddy of his or anything like that. He may have had a side to him he never showed me. For one thing, I've never even seen his wife. He kept pretty much to himself."

"Where'd he live?"

"He bought a small farm years ago about three miles out of town. North, on 986."

"And you say he rode the train every night to get to work?"

"That's what Mr. Bennett says."

"So how'd he get from his place to here every night?"

"I think I can answer that for you," Frank Bennett said. "John walked. He was a great believer in the virtue of walking."

"Why?"

"Said it kept him in shape."

11

"He had a driver's license. It's right here," Moyer said, pulling it out of Andrasko's thin, black wallet.

"Oh, he could drive all right," Bennett said. "But he hated to. Never drove unless he absolutely had to. Just to go shopping for groceries and for things he needed for the farm."

"So he walked in here every night? More than three miles? In bad weather, too?"

"Yessir. Every night. Rain, snow, whatever. He walked."

"Well, hell," Moyer said. "Look here. He's got two vehicle registration cards. One for a Ford pickup and this one's for a Ford sedan. Why the hell's a guy who hates driving have two vehicles?"

"He said he needed them," Bennett replied. "Many's the time he wished he didn't need them, but then he'd just shrug and say what's the use. America was car-crazy, he used to say."

"Lieutenant?" one of the troopers walking the tracks called out. "Think you better come have a look at this."

Except for Frank Bennett, everybody on the platform set off toward the trooper. He was standing under the State Street bridge, and when they got to him, he flashed his lamp on the gravel near one of the rails between two ties. The light reflected off the fragments of a Coke bottle. Moyer squatted and took a pen from his inside pocket and lifted the neck of the bottle. It was the largest piece.

"Looks like we got the weapon."

"Which means that whoever did it went across the tracks and up the steps to State Street and then dropped it. Or threw it. Must've been thrown. I doubt it would've broken from that height, just being dropped."

"And I'll just bet if somebody took the trouble to throw it, he also took the trouble to wipe it clean," Moyer said.

"One thing's sure," Stallcup said, "he had to have a lot of blood on him."

"Well," Moyer said, standing, "get everything measured off and get the photographer. And get the plastic bags. I want as much of this bottle as we can get."

"Beaten to death with a Coke bottle," Milt Weigh said. "My God."

"Hell of a thought, ain't it?" Balzic said.

12

"Well," Moyer said, "I think that's about all we can do until we get some daylight. The coroner showed yet?"

"That's probably him now," Balzic said. "Behind the ambulance."

"That only leaves one thing," Moyer said. "Who wants the pleasure?"

"What are you talking about?" Milt Weigh said.

"The next of kin, Mr. Weigh. You want to give them the good news?"

"I'll pass that if you don't mind."

"How about you, Mario?"

"Yeah. I guess I'm up for this one. Rather do it alone."

"Hell, be my guest. And see what you can find out."

"Well, I'm not going to ask any questions. I'll nose around, but tonight ain't the night for asking questions."

"Why not?" Milt Weigh said.

"Well, if you want to ask them, Milt, you're welcome to come along and do the asking."

Weigh thrust his hands into his coat pockets. "I'll take your word for it."

"You'll let me know. Right, Mario?" Moyer said.

"Yeah, sure," Balzic replied, clearing his throat and spitting. "See you, gentlemen." He turned to leave the platform as the county coroner, Dr. Wallace Grimes, was placing a stethoscope on John Andrasko's chest, confirming what was obvious.

Balzic had trouble finding the Andrasko place and had to stop at a house to ask directions.

"You passed it," the lady said after she saw Balzic's ID. "It's the next place down."

"You a friend?"

"I know them, if that's what you mean."

"Do you know if Mrs. Andrasko has any close friends around here?"

"Something happen bad?"

"Yes, ma'am. Do you know—"

13

"Oh, I guess I'm about the only one she talks to. You want me to come along?"

"No, but I might have to come back for you. They have kids?"

"Oh yeah. They had two, and she had one from before. It's that bad, huh? Was it to him? John?"

"Yes, ma'am."

"I always said he was going to get hit by a car some day."

"Well, thank you very much, ma'am. If it's necessary, I can count on you to come over there?"

"Sure. That's what neighbors are for, ain't they?"

"Fine. Thanks again," Balzic said and hurried over the grass to his cruiser.

When he found the drive and pulled into the Andrasko place, all the lights were off, save one upstairs. "Damn," he said and sat in the car for a minute after he turned off the ignition. He tried to arrange what he wanted to say. There was no good way he knew. But then there never had been. He just wished they were awake. It always seemed worse to have to wake the people up.

"Just a little help," he said as he got out of the car. He looked up at the stars and said it again and then made his way onto the porch. In the rear, a dog started growling.

He had to knock three times before a light came on downstairs. He took his ID out and waited.

A light came on above him, and he stepped back, so whoever had turned it on could get a good look at him.

"Who is it?" a woman's voice said.

"Mrs. Andrasko? I'm Mario Balzic. I'm the chief of police in town." He held his ID folder up to his cheek so that the badge and his picture showed.

The inside door opened. Mrs. Andrasko pushed open the screen door enough for her to show half her face. Her sleep-wrinkled confusion was already starting to turn to panic.

"What—what's the matter?"

"Mrs. Andrasko, it's about your husband. May I come in, please?"

"Oh God, what happened? What's wrong?"

"Let's go inside, Mrs. Andrasko. Please."

She backed away from the door, her hands covering her mouth.

14

Balzic stepped inside and took a deep breath. "Mrs. Andrasko, I'm very sorry. I've known John all my life."

"Oh God, God, God," Mrs. Andrasko said and slumped onto a misshapen ottoman.

"He's dead, Mrs. Andrasko," Balzic said, going down on one knee to stop her from falling, in case she fainted. She didn't faint, but she began to sob from deep in her throat, and then she began to wail, rocking back and forth on the ottoman, her hands pressed against her face until the tears ran over her fingers and down her wrists.

"Hey," a boy's voice said behind Balzic. "Are you hurting my momma?"

Balzic stood. "No, son, I'm not. I just had to be the one to tell her."

Mrs. Andrasko threw out her arms, and the boy rushed into them.

"My Billy, my little Billy," she sobbed, pulling the boy to her and kissing him.

"What's the matter, Momma?"

"Oh God, Billy. Daddy's gone, Billy. Daddy's gone."

The boy looked bewildered, but he did not cry. His eyes went from his mother's raw grief to Balzic's somberness.

"He's dead, son," Balzic said.

"Who's dead?" a girl's voice said.

"Oh God, Norma, come to your mother," Mrs. Andrasko said, and the girl, taller and two or three years older than the boy, stepped quickly to her mother's side. She began to cry at once, and in the next second the boy began, too.

Balzic thought his skull would burst. There was no sound like it, and as many times as Balzic had heard it, he had never gotten used to it. This time, because he'd known John Andrasko, he had to bite the inside of his cheeks to stop himself from crying.

He turned away and looked around for the kitchen. He was suddenly very thirsty. He found the kitchen in the rear of the house, and as he turned the tap and looked for a glass, he could hear the dog growling on the other side of the kitchen door.

He drank and let his eyes wander over the kitchen. Aside from a stack of glasses and spoons in the sink, it was tidy and clean. A jar of peanut butter sat open on the corner of the table, and a knife with

15

some peanut butter on it lay beside the jar. It was a small room, but orderly, and there was no smell of grease.

He finished the glass of water and leaned against the sink, and then, just as he was about to put the glass in the sink, he saw the cartons of Coke. They were between the back wall and the refrigerator. Two six-packs contained empties, and the top one in the stack had two empties in it. He stepped quietly to the refrigerator and opened it as gently as he could. Inside, on the bottom shelf of the door were four full bottles of Coke. He closed the refrigerator and shook his head. "What the hell am I thinking about?" he whispered and went back into the living room.

Mrs. Andrasko was still sitting on the ottoman with her arms wrapped around her children. They were all still sobbing.

"Mrs. Andrasko, would you like me to call somebody? A relative maybe. A neighbor?"

She shook her head no.

"A priest then?"

"No—yes. Father Marrazo. Call him."

"Where's the phone?"

Mrs. Andrasko nodded toward the kitchen, and Balzic found it on the wall. He dialed the station and got Royer. "Do me a favor, Joe, and get hold of Father Marrazo. Tell him to get out here to John Andrasko's place to sit it out with the family. It's on 986 North, about three miles. I'll leave my lights on in the drive."

"Rough one?" Royer said.

"Next one I'm saving for you."

"Is this Father Marrazo out of St. Malachy's?"

"Yeah, but he won't be there. He's playing cards in Muscotti's. I'd call myself, but I forget the number, and I want to look around out here anyway. I'll be here till he gets here. And oh—listen. Whoever answers down there might try to give you the noise he ain't there. But tell them I said he is and I need him."

"You do?"

"Almost as much—never mind. Just tell him to get his ass out here. Probably give him the good excuse for getting out of the game anyway. Any calls?"

"None for you."

"Good," Balzic said, hanging up, and in spite of himself, found his eyes fixed on the cartons of Coke between the wall and the refrigerator.

He rubbed his eyes and went back into the living room. He watched Mrs. Andrasko for another moment, her arms still pulling her children to her, her sobs now almost a croon, and then stepped quietly through the front door onto the porch.

He lit a cigarette and went down to the cruiser to wait for the priest. He sat for a minute inside the car with the door open and then tossed the cigarette on the ground, got out, and started walking toward the rear of the house.

Set apart from the house about thirty yards was a small barn and beside that was a wide, low building that looked like a garage. The gravel drive forked: one fork led to the barn and the other to the low building. Balzic took the second fork as he heard the dog start growling again.

"Aw, shut the hell up," he said, hoping that the chain he heard being dragged about was both short and sturdy.

The doors on the low building were the sliding kind and without locks. He pushed the nearest one back and stepped inside, taking out his pencil flashlight and shining it around.

Parked near the opposite wall was a dusty Ford pickup. The bay where he had come in was empty, and in the middle bay sat a small Allis-Chalmers tractor. Behind the tractor and hung on the back wall were implements, tools, cans, drums, ropes, chains—most of the things necessary for operating the farm. There was about it all the same care and order Balzic had seen in the kitchen.

Balzic thought almost at once of the vehicle registrations Lieutenant Moyer had found in John Andrasko's wallet, the registrations for a Ford pickup and a Ford sedan. He thought also about the woman he'd talked to down the road and what she'd said about the children the Andraskos had—two of their own and one of hers from before.

"Well," Balzic said aloud, "somebody's driving that car."

He was walking back to the cruiser to call the station again when he heard the tires and saw the headlights of a car as it pulled off

17

Route 986. It slowed just briefly, then picked up speed and came on, sliding to a stop scant yards from the rear of the cruiser.

Balzic doubted that it was Father Marrazo—the priest didn't drive like that—and he was sure it wasn't when the driver kept the engine running and the lights on.

"Hey, mister, would you mind moving your car?" a young voice called out.

Balzic walked quickly to the car window and put his pencil light in the driver's eyes. "I'm a police officer," Balzic said.

The driver was a youngster, sixteen, seventeen at most—thin, with a bad case of acne.

Balzic took out his ID and shined the light on it for the boy to see. "Who are you, son?"

"Tommy—Thomas Parilla."

"What are you doing here?"

"What am I—I live here," Tommy said. "What are you doing here?"

"You Mrs. Andrasko's boy?"

Tommy nodded. "What's the matter?"

"I'm sorry to be the one to have to tell you, son, but your father's dead." Balzic knew as soon as he said it that it did not sound right, but he had not prepared himself for telling anybody else.

"My father's been dead a long time, mister," Tommy said. "He went away a long time ago. You must be talking about John."

Balzic tried not to change his expression. "Yes. I guess I am."

"My mother inside?"

"Yes. She's with the kids."

"Well, you still have to—I mean, would you please move your car? I have to put this one in the garage."

Balzic moved the cruiser and then watched Tommy wheel the Ford sedan around him, skidding on the gravel. He hit the brakes hard in front of the garage door, jumped out while the car was still rocking, and opened the door. The boy put the car in, then came out and shut the door, moving, Balzic thought, no differently from the way any other boy his age would move when he'd come home too late with the family car.

Balzic watched the boy go into the house through the kitchen door, then backed the cruiser down the drive and opened the door and turned on his lights so Father Marrazo could see him from the road.

He took out his notebook and made an approximate chronology:

> 11:20–11:38 killed, not enough noise for Bennett to hear
> 12–1 with Weigh and state boys
> 1:15 told wife
> 1:30–35 kid comes home in Ford sedan, could care less

He put the notebook away and sat wondering whether the boy had left the keys in the car. Or was it key? Andrasko had had a key ring. Balzic hadn't looked carefully at the key ring, but something told him that among the dozen or so keys, there had been three or four ignition or trunk keys. Could it have been about something as simple as that—an argument over taking the car out? Well, he thought, it's happened for less likely reasons.

He was debating whether to check the car for the key when Father Marrazo's car turned into the drive and stopped behind the cruiser.

"Hello, Father," Balzic said.

"Mario, old friend," the priest said, getting out of his car. "Old friend—old nuisance. I was twenty-one dollars ahead when your call came. Why do I love you so much, Mario, can you tell me that?"

"For the same reason I love you," Balzic said. "Nobody loves like one coward loves another."

"Sounds like that came out of a book, Mario."

"If it did, Father, then it was a book you read."

"You heard it from me?"

Balzic nodded, and then told the priest why he'd called him.

"Ah, well," the priest sighed. "The family's inside, I suppose."

Balzic nodded.

"How are they taking it? Very hard? Of course, how else?"

"Three of them are. There's one that could care less."

"Tommy."

"You know him?"

"Yes, I'm sorry to say that I do. Strange kid. He lies in confession just to provoke me. For no other reason. Very full of spite and

19

resentment, but as much as I've tried to find out why, I've never been able to get anything out of any of them. Well," Father Marrazo said, stretching and yawning, "I guess I better get in there. Would you like to join me, Mario? Then maybe afterward, after we get them all to bed, we could find something to drink someplace."

"Muscotti's will still be open."

"The name's familiar. Is it a local establishment?"

"Well, I'm not going in with you, Father, but I'll tell you what. After I go back to the station to check on something, I'll drop in there and save you a seat. How's that?"

"Sounds fine. Depends how quickly I get them calmed."

They said good night, and Balzic could see the priest going inside as he wheeled the cruiser out onto 986 and headed for the station.

Balzic heard the commotion as soon as he opened the cruiser door in the city hall parking lot. Somebody inside was having a shouting match. There was no mistaking Joe Royer's voice, but three or four other voices kept getting mixed up with John Dillman's and Sam Carraza's. By the time Balzic got to the landing outside the station, he was wishing he had just gone on to Muscotti's and had a couple of cold ones.

Inside, at the desk, Carraza and Dillman were trying to herd a crew of the bearded, beaded ones Balzic recognized as the leaders of The Community Store, the local answer to the hippie question. Milt Weigh had been trying for months, ever since he'd been sworn in, and with monotonous failures, to bust them on a narcotics charge. As far as Balzic was concerned, their only crime was that they looked like hell and that they had been naive enough to believe they could open their place on State Street and be left alone. Balzic took a deep breath and went inside.

"What the hell's going on, Joe?" Balzic shouted over the uproar.

Royer motioned him behind the counter and then led him into one of the cubicles in the rear.

"Our hero's done it again," Royer said, lighting a cigarette wearily.

"Weigh?"

"Yeppie. Only this time it's because they gave him a lot of static

20

when he and Carraza and Dillman went in to find out if they saw anybody coming down State Street. So naturally he wants them booked for surety of the peace and Christ knows what all else."

"Naturally they don't know what anybody's talking about."

"Naturally," Royer said. "But that ain't the best part. The best part is, our hero wants us to lock them up down here. He don't have the space out at Southern Regional, he says. Turns out he got four of them in there from a bust he made last night. Sometimes I think he ought to get married, then maybe he'd have something better to do at night than go around busting these goofballs."

"Well, let's go see what we can make of it," Balzic said. "If we're lucky, maybe we can send them all back to their store. The thing that pisses me is, one night Weigh's going to go in there and somebody's going to get hurt."

Balzic went back out to the counter and hammered on it with the flat of his hand. "Sam, you turning these people over to me?"

There was silence for a second as the bearded, beaded ones interrupted their shouting to look at a new target for their rage. One of them started shouting "Pig," and Balzic bounded around the counter and slapped him with a cupped palm so its sound was more impressive than its sting.

"Next person opens his mouth gets the same, only harder," Balzic said, taking in Carraza and Dillman in his warning glance. "Now, Sam, I'm going to ask you again—you turning these people over to me or not?"

Carraza nodded.

"On what charge?"

"Surety of the peace, resisting arrest. Those two'll be enough."

"All right, Sam. You turned them over. Good night."

"Not so fast, Mario—"

"I said good night, Sam. Good night, John."

Carraza looked at Dillman, and they both looked at Balzic. Dillman started to swear under his breath, but he and Carraza left.

Balzic turned to the group now in his charge. None had moved since he'd slapped the one who'd been shouting pig. "Okay, men," he said, "this is my 'Community Store,' and in my store we don't call names, we don't shout, and we don't shove. The sooner you

21

understand me, the sooner I understand you. I already got a pretty good idea why you're here, but I want one of you—and just one—to tell me why you think you're here."

Balzic took off his raincoat and suit coat and sat on a bench near the front door. "I got time," he said.

"Put it on him, Charley," one of them said.

"Yeah, Charley, give him the news," another said.

Charley stepped forward. He was very tall, barechested under a fringed leather vest, and Balzic could see he had spent some time doing something physical, probably playing football.

"Okay, Chiefey, it's like this—"

"I said we don't call names in my store."

Charley looked for a moment as though he would call some more names just to save face. Instead, he said, "Okay, Chief, it's your store. No names, But you know why we're here. That D.A. had the heat for us ever since we set up our place."

Balzic nodded. "But why tonight?"

"I don't know, man. He come in there with his deputy sheriffs looking for Robin Hood or somebody. He don't ask three questions in a row that make sense, man, and the next thing he's telling the deputies to book us. So naturally there got to be a little scuffling. Maybe we did some shoving and bad-mouthing, but that pi—that dude just steady won't let us be, man. He's put the bust on us three times in the last lunar, man, and he still ain't found nothing."

"And tonight he came in and you thought it was going to be more of the same, is that it?"

"You got it, man."

"So you started hollering and shoving before you found out what he was really after?"

"No, man, it wasn't like that. I mean, he really didn't ask nothing that made sense. Like the only thing I heard him ask was did we see somebody coming down State Street at such and such on the clock, man, and I ask you—what kind of shit is that to put down? That's the freakiest excuse for a bust I—"

"It so happens he had a reason for asking that question," Balzic said. "I admit, the chances are probably six to five, he asked it in every wrong way, but he was on the square when he asked."

"Well, hell, man, lots of people come up and down that pavement. Nobody ever told me we were on the payroll to play cops and robbers for his store. What are we supposed to do—check ID's on everybody that trots on by our front door?"

"Think a minute, Charley," Balzic said. "How many places are open on State Street after nine o'clock? Besides yours?"

"None, man. At least I don't think any."

"Okay. So then where else is the D.A. supposed to go to ask if not your store? See what I mean?"

"Yeah, I guess."

"I admit, understand, that Mr. Weigh, if I know him, probably had something else in mind when he came in your place. Maybe he even stood out on the street and told himself that he was only going in to find out the answer to that one question, but when he got inside, other things got into his head. I know brother Weigh a helluva lot better than you do." Balzic paused. "By the way, *did* you see anybody coming past your place, say between eleven-thirty and twelve?"

"Aw, hell, man. I wasn't paying no nevermind. People come, they go. If they don't stop and get commercial in our place, we don't pay them no nevermind."

"Well, if you think of anybody, let me know, will you?" Balzic stood and put his coats back on. "If anybody asks you, I'm releasing you due to a lack of sufficient evidence to warrant arraignment. You want a ride uptown?"

"You letting us go, man?"

"Make sure you put that in the log, Joe," Balzic said. To the bearded ones he said, "Well, I sure as hell ain't letting you sleep here tonight. You go find your own place to sleep. You want a ride or not?"

"No, man. We'll use our feet," Charley said, leading the others out the door.

"So much for that," Balzic said.

"Weigh'll shit," Royer said.

"So? Let him. He makes my ass tired, busting those kids all the time. If he wants them locked up so much, he can just haul them down to the magistrate's himself. He makes half the bust and then

23

expects us to do all the paperwork. I'm tired of that. Then he goes around making speeches to the P.T.A. and the ladies clubs talking about the drug problem right here in old River City. He got so many old ladies fired up now it wouldn't surprise me if they started marching down Main like those temperance biddies used to do. My mother used to tell me about them."

"Your mother told you?"

"Aw, go pound sand," Balzic said. "Anybody wants me, I'll be in Muscotti's. By the way, the coroner call yet?"

"Uh-uh. You want me to call if he does?"

"Nah. I'll hear what he has to say soon enough."

Balzic was finishing his second draught when Father Marrazo, wearing a sport shirt and tan raincoat, joined him in the back room. The poker game was down to four players and, as usual for this stage of the night, had turned moodily mechanical. Nobody invited the priest to play, even though earlier he had taken more than his share of their money.

"You get things calmed down out there?" Balzic said.

"As well as can be expected," Father Marrazo said. "Are you buying?"

"Sure."

They went out to the bar, and Balzic motioned to Vinnie the bartender, who was preoccupied with a crossword puzzle, to bring a round. "Put it on my tab," Balzic said.

"You going to pay that someday?" Vinnie said.

"It's not the end of the month."

Vinnie snorted. "The end of the month. The national debt you're running up." He brought the beers and stood there, grinning at Balzic.

"Put in a good word for me, Father."

"As soon as I see the police department's check for Catholic Charities, I'll be happy to."

"Don't hold your breath, Father," Vinnie said, taking a check out of a cigar box from under the cash register and adding some figures to it.

"Behold the miracle of perseverance, Father," Balzic said, nodding toward Vinnie. "He flunked arithmetic eight years in a row in school, then he drops out, and now he's the richest bartender in the county."

"Quit it, willya," Vinnie said. "You make my chest hurt when you lie like that."

Vinnie went back to his crossword, and Father Marrazo and Balzic drank in silence.

"Anything new?" Father Marrazo said after a minute.

"Nothing much. Our esteemed D.A. made a bad bust and tried to get us to do the pencil work on it, and I sent the people home. He'll be three shades of purple tomorrow, but that's tomorrow."

"Did it have to do with John?"

"Only if you don't know the D.A."

"I don't understand, Mario."

"Well, he figured that whoever did it had to come down State Street, which might make sense if there was only one direction on a map or only one street in this town. The state boys found a broken Coke bottle with blood on it on the tracks under the bridge on State, so apparently Weigh figures whoever dropped it there had to keep on coming down the street. The only place that's open in that stretch at that time of night is the hippie joint—"

"The Community Store?"

"Yeah, so him and his two top honchos, Dillman and Sam Carraza, went booming in there, and before anybody made any sense, the kids were hollering and shoving, so Weigh busts them. Then he remembers his lockup is overcrowded, so he tries to dump them on me. To make the story short, Father, I wasn't in the mood to wake up a magistrate to file the information. I mean, it was his bust, he could take care of the whole thing or nothing.

"But what burns me is, Weigh's got his head full of drug propaganda, and he thinks those kids just naturally have to be pushing something. He's tried three times in the last month to bust

25

them, and he comes up zero every time, and tonight, instead of trying to find out something, he hauls them in. He doesn't even have sense enough to think that whoever did Andrasko in could've gone three other ways after he dropped the bottle off the bridge. Ah, what the hell. So how'd it go with the wife?"

"Needless to say, she's taking it very hard, and the children are upset because she is. I doubt that the truth of what's happened has sunk in as far as they're concerned. But I managed to arrange for the funeral. And that relieved her. Not much, but enough."

"What about the boy?"

"Tommy? He's a puzzle, as I told you out there. But I really know very little about him."

"All I know is he didn't even blink when I told him. I may as well've been telling him it was going to rain. All he wanted me to do was move my car so he could get his car in the garage. That's right before you showed, and I didn't get a chance to look how many keys he had with him."

"What's that have to do with it?"

"John had a key ring on him, but I didn't get a close look at it. Plus, he had the owner's card for the car the kid was driving and another one for a pickup. Then Frank Bennett—he's the station master—he tells me that John hated to drive and didn't really like cars. Told Frank he thought America was car-crazy or something like that. And the way the kid wheeled in there—well, he's like most kids with cars."

"Uh, Mario, correct me if I'm wrong, but I'm beginning to get the impression that you suspect him."

"At this point, Father, I suspect everybody, and if I didn't know you were down here earlier playing cards, I'd be asking you where you were around eleven-thirty, eleven-forty-five."

"Are you serious?" The priest laughed lamely.

"Of course." Balzic laughed and nudged the priest's elbow. "You got that dark complexion, that black hair, dark brown eyes—distinctly a Mediterranean type. Everybody knows wops are the only people who kill other people. What're you—kidding me?"

26

"For a moment—"

"Ah, come on, Father."

"But then you, uh, you really are serious about suspecting the boy?"

"Well, Father, it's like this. Contrary to what all the law-and-order nuts holler about, most people who kill other people know those other people. In fact, if you broke it down—and don't take my word for this. Write a letter to J. Edgar Hoover—he'll tell you. If you broke it down, you'd find most murders happen in the great red, white, and blue institution, the American home. Break it down even tighter, and most of them happen within twenty-five, thirty feet of the kitchen stove.

"Those ones that hit the front page, the Mansons, the Specks, the Whitmans, they're the exceptions. That's why they're front page. Hell, even the so-called gangland style—to use the newspaper language—even those happen with people who know one another. Not necessarily the guy who pulls the trigger. But the guy who paid the guy to pull the trigger, he knew the guy that got it, otherwise what the hell'd he have him killed for? He picked his name out of a phone book? No way. The guy did something to him, which means they had to be close enough at one time or another to be in a position for something to get done."

"You still haven't answered my question," Father Marrazo said. "You suspect the boy?"

"Well, naturally. But that's just my inclination. I don't suspect him at this point anymore than I suspect the wife. It's a general thing.

"Look," Balzic went on, "I've been a cop here for twenty-five, going on twenty-six years. Now this is here. Rocksburg. This isn't New York or Chicago or Philly. This isn't even Pittsburgh. But right here, in all those years, I only remember four murders where the victim had no connection with the murderer. And every one of them happened in a holdup. There was that old lady in the grocery—Mrs. Manfredi. All we know about that one is somebody heard a shot, we answered the call, and there it was. Cash drawer open, no prints, one twenty-two-caliber bullet. Never even arrested anybody for that one.

27

"Then there was the watchman out at the Sears warehouse about six years ago. Two thirty-eights in the chest. Whoever did it panicked and didn't even take anything. No arrest on that one either.

"Then about four years ago, there was the Southwest Commercial Bank. You remember that one."

"I do indeed. I gave the sacrament and heard the guard's confession."

"Okay, so there were two dead on that one. Case closed. Then two years ago this July, there was the payroll robbery over at the ready-mix plant. One clerk tries to be a hero, and there he goes. Three arrests on that one, no convictions."

"No arrests were ever made on those first two you mentioned?"

"Uh-uh. How? That's the point. If you don't have some way to connect the victim to the murderer, how you going to grab somebody who just walks in trying to score some money? There's only a couple of ways: either you have a witness or else you get a talker. In the first two we had neither. In the last one, we had six witnesses, but when we arrange the lineups, not one of them puts a solid make on any of the three guys we busted. What galls me about that is I know as sure as I'm standing here those three did it. But they knew we didn't have a make, so we couldn't break them, and I'm here to tell you, Father, I used everything I knew. The only thing I was able to do was get them out of town."

"How did you do that, I mean, if you couldn't prove anything—"

"I'll tell you how, Father. I told them one by one if I ever saw them again, I'd kill them and plant a gun on them."

"You actually told them that?"

"That's right, Father. So even if you and me both know me better than that, these guys must've thought I wasn't just making funny noises. They're not around, Father, that's all I know."

The priest shook his head and sat silently for a long moment, looking wide-eyed at his beer. Then he shook himself and said, "Uh, to get back to what I asked you—"

"Do I suspect the boy, right?"

"Yes."

"In a word, Father, naturally. The way he was driving, the time he came home, the way he reacted when I told him, plus when I was in the kitchen getting a drink of water, I saw a couple cartons of Coke. None of those things by themselves mean all that much. I mean, hell, most kids are car nuts and drive too fast, and who doesn't drink Coke? But it was what he said about his own father that got me."

"His own father?"

"Yeah. I said something like, 'I hate to be the one to have to tell you, but your father's dead,' and he said, 'My father's been dead a long time, mister.' And then he said, 'He went away a long time ago.' Those were his exact words."

"Well, what do you infer from that?"

"I'm not sure. It's just funny, Father. People use all kinds of ways to say somebody's dead. You know that better than I do, but did you ever hear anybody say that somebody *went* away? Passed away, yeah. Passed on. Stuff like that, but 'went away'? I never heard it before, did you?"

"No, I can't recall hearing it put exactly that way, but maybe I have and never paid any attention to it. But I can't see what you're getting at."

"I don't know for sure. There's just something about saying somebody's dead in one breath and then saying that somebody went away in the next. That, plus where John was killed. I mean, a train station is a place where people are always going away. And I'll spare you the details, Father, but John wasn't just killed. Whoever did it literally beat his face to nothing. Like he was trying to wipe out his face."

"You mean so it could look like anybody."

"Yeah. Or coming at it from another direction, like it could look like somebody else." Balzic thought a moment. "It was like, uh, whoever was doing it to John maybe wasn't really doing it to John."

"Mario, you're the policeman, and I'm sure you know what you're talking about more than I do, but from what you've said so far, that is a very fragile connection you're making. I mean, just because the boy used that phrase—'went away'—and because the man was killed in a place where people are always going away, I think you said—that seems a really tenuous association. After all, people are not only always going away in train stations. They're also always coming back in them."

"Oh, that goes without saying. I know it's a delicate proposition. But you asked me, remember? You asked me if I suspected the boy, right?"

The priest nodded.

"Well, if I tell you I do, then I got to give you some reason. And that's what I just did, give you a reason. Hell, I might be ten miles wide. Who knows? It could be anybody for any reason. I'm just telling you that when somebody gets killed, I just naturally start thinking family, and until somebody comes up with something different, I'll keep on thinking family. Speaking of which, what all do you know about them, the whole family I mean?"

"Very little. Mrs. Andrasko and the younger children were very regular in church and confession and catechism and so on, but John was a Christmas-Easter Catholic. The boy, Tommy, came irregularly to mass and was the same about confession. And as I told you before, when he did come, he told me the most improbable lies, and, again as I said before, I had the feeling he did that purely to provoke me."

"Like what kind of lies?"

"You know I can't tell you that, Mario."

"Tell me that when you're wearing your collar, Father. Don't tell me that when you're wearing what you got on."

"Mario, I believe you're serious."

"Damn right I am."

"I'm sorry, Mario, but regardless of the clothes I'm wearing, I can't tell you what was said."

"I remember seeing a movie about that once. Montgomery Clift played the priest, and who the hell was it played the cop?"

"Karl Malden."

"Yeah, you got it. Tell me Father, did you believe Clift?"

"Yes. He was one of my favorite actors."

"Well, I thought Malden came on a little too strong. Course he was playing a Canadian cop. Maybe that's the way they are up there."

"Are they different here?"

"A cop's a cop, is that it, Father?"

"I tend to think so."

"An Irish priest is the same as an Italian priest then, right?"

Father Marrazo smiled, but said nothing.

"Okay, Father, have it your way. I can probably make a pretty good guess what the kid lied about anyway."

"You'll not get me that way, either."

"I'm not trying to, honest. But I'll just bet the kid came in and said he was making it with some older ladies in the parish."

Father Marrazo stared into his beer.

"You're a pretty good actor yourself, Father. I'll bet you been studying all the movies Clift was in."

"Never mind that. Where does this theory get you?"

"Same place I was before. It doesn't get me any place. Too much has to be checked out. There's the thing about the car keys, and somewhere there has to be some bloody clothes. The state boys might even come up with a palm print on the neck of that bottle, or they might come up with a witness who saw whoever it was coming or going. There are lots of possibilities, Father. Until somebody comes up with something solid, all I've got are theories."

"I meant to ask this before, Mario, but why aren't you out looking for these possibilities yourself?"

"The state boys are better at that stuff than I am, for one. They got more eyes, more ears, more legs, more equipment. Besides, my tail's dragging."

"Something tells me those aren't the reasons," Father Marrazo said quietly.

"Okay. So I lie," Balzic said. "The fact is when the state boys come in and the D.A.'s in, then I'm out. It's been that way as long as I can remember, and I don't see anything happening anywhere that's going to make it change."

"Bitterness corrodes the soul, Mario."

"You said that in church last Sunday."

"Well, it's still fresh in my mind, I suppose."

"If it's any consolation to you, Father, I was with you all the way in that homily of yours. I just sat back there shaking my head, thinking, yeah, brother Balzic, that's exactly what it does. It corrodes the soul."

"But you got nothing else from what I said?"

"The forgiveness you mean? Sure, I read you on that. I know

31

that's the way. But my guts don't know it, Father. Only my head."

"Mario, why don't you go home and get some rest?" Father Marrazo stood up as though to leave. "We'll talk about this some other time."

"Are you kidding, Father? I saw him tonight. You only had to deal with the widow, which wasn't any picnic, I know, but I saw him. I won't be able to sleep for two, three days."

The priest nodded. "Well then. How about another beer?"

"Now you're talking. Hey, Vinnie, once more here, and keep them coming."

"Sure, sure," Vinnie said. "And put them all on the national debt, too, I guess."

"How else you going to cheat me?"

"Oh, funny," Vinnie said. "Your friend here's a real funny man, you know that, Father? I'll bet you didn't know that."

"Vinnie, now that this has come up," Father Marrazo said, "I've been meaning to ask you when draughts went up to twenty-five cents."

"They didn't."

"Well, my friend, earlier tonight, I gave you a dollar for a draught and you brought me three quarters change."

"Oh, Father, now wait. I must've been thinking about something. I would never try to hustle you."

"Not so it was obvious," Balzic said, laughing.

"Tell you what, Vinnie. You send me a generous check for Catholic Charities, and I won't remember a thing."

Vinnie shook his head. "My old man told me. How many times he told me. He said you hustle a priest for a nickel, you're going to get hustled for a fin. Don't hustle priests, he said. Be smart. *Be* a priest, he said. *Then* you can hustle...."

Balzic stayed with Father Marrazo until three-thirty and then drove to the station. Joe Royer was alone behind the counter, drinking soup from a vacuum bottle.

"Coffee's on, Mario, if you want some."

Balzic shook his head no. "Coroner call yet?"

"About five minutes ago. Nothing except what you probably know. Said he'd give us a typed report about ten or so today. Only thing he did say was whoever did it was either strong as hell or mad as hell."

"Why's that?"

"Said practically every bone in his face was broken. Must have been—"

"Never mind what it must've been," Balzic interrupted him. "You knew him, didn't you?"

"Andrasko? Yeah, slightly."

"Ever hear anything wrong about him?"

"I never heard anything about him," Royer said. "When I was on a beat, I used to see him hoofing it in. I'd say hello, he'd say hello, we'd both say something about the weather, and that was that."

"Nothing else?"

Royer shook his head and poured himself another cup of soup from his vacuum bottle. "Nothing. John Q. Citizen. Up and down."

"Ever hear about a guy named Parilla?"

"Which one? There's about three dozen."

"I don't know which one. All I know is Andrasko had a stepson named Tommy Parilla. He's about sixteen, seventeen."

"So?"

"So among other things, the kid was driving Andrasko's car tonight. He didn't come home until one-thirty or so, and when I told him about John, the kid didn't say a goddamn word. Just asked me to please move my car. Which reminds me. I got to call the state boys."

Balzic dialed the state police barracks and asked for Lieutenant Moyer.

"Yeah, Mario," Moyer said. "What did you come up with?"

"Not much. Listen, you got Andrasko's effects handy?"

"Right here. I've been sitting here looking at them. Not much to look at."

"Well, take a look at the key ring. How many car keys are there?"

"I count two ignition keys and one trunk key. All Fords. Why?"

33

"His stepson was driving his car tonight. Came home about one-thirty. I wanted to check out the key he was using, but I didn't get a chance."

"How'd the kid look?"

"Like his stepfather died every day of the week."

"Oh? No emotion at all?"

"None."

"How about the wife?"

"Hysterical. I called a priest to stay with her for a while. He said she was all right as soon as he made the funeral arrangements."

"But the kid was a stone?"

"All he said when I told him was his father was dead a long time. Then he said something struck me. He said something like, my father went away a long time ago."

"What do you figure from that?"

"I don't know for sure. Just didn't sound right somehow. But what did you come up with?"

"We verified the Coke bottle as the weapon. I sent most of it off to Harrisburg, but I gave one piece to the coroner and had him take it up to the hospital to check blood types. No question about it. But all we got by way of a quick check for prints was one lousy smudge on the neck of the bottle. I sent it off to Harrisburg purely for routine, because between you and me, I don't think they're going to find a thing."

"You didn't check the houses north on State Street?"

"We didn't, and we won't until after eight this morning. That's all I need to do, is start waking people up. You know what they'll remember—that we disturbed their sleep."

"You want me to spell your men down at the station? Starting with the daylight shift?"

"Not for today at least, Mario. We got a lot more looking to do down there as soon as we get some light. I left a man there tonight. It's roped off. Let's just wait for daylight, okay?"

"Whatever you say."

"Okay, Mario. See you in the morning."

"Right," Balzic said and hung up.

34

"Anything?" Royer asked.

"Nah. Just a confirmation on the weapon." Balzic started looking through drawers. "Where the hell's the cards?"

"By the switchboard. I was playing solitaire a little while ago. You want to play some gin?"

"Yeah. How much I owe you?"

"Four something."

"That much? Jeez, I better start paying attention."

"I got the slip right here in my wallet, if you don't believe me."

"Oh, I believe you, Joe. I believe you. I just don't believe I could've lost that many hands in a row. Not to you."

"Aw shut up and deal. I got to wash out my thermos."

"Shut up and deal. Listen to you. By six-thirty you'll be screaming to play double or nothing," Balzic said, shuffling the cards. "Why in hell don't you guys spring for a new deck once in a while? This deck's been here since time."

"We're waiting on you, Chief—Sir. Nobody around here remembers the last time you sprung."

"Oh, you'll be sorry for that, Sergeant, insinuating that I'm a little close. Are you ever going to be sorry for that."

They played until six-twenty.

"How do we stand now, Joseph, old buddy, old pal?" Balzic said with a broad smirk.

"I owe you two dollars and seven cents, that's how we stand."

"That's what I've always tried to tell you. Straight shooters always win. Well, I got to go. Nice playing against you, Joe."

"Wait a minute. Where the hell you got to go?"

"I got to go home and get cleaned up, for one thing. I been wearing these clothes since yesterday morning, and I'm starting to smell myself. If that's all right with you?" Balzic said, putting on his suit coat and raincoat and heading for the door. "Who's on the desk today?"

"Stramsky."

"Well, tell him what Weigh tried to pull last night, and tell him when Weigh calls to be polite. Polite but dumb. See you."

"You think Weigh'll call?"

35

"Oh, he'll call all right. You can give twenty to one on that," Balzic said and stepped outside just as the sun was breaking over the roof of the A&P. He stood on the steps for a moment, feeling the cool of the night being burned away, and when he got in his car he indulged himself in a wish to live in a place where every morning of the year he could count on the sun to burn off the night's damp chill.

When he got home, Balzic found his mother sitting at the kitchen table in her flannel gown sipping hot milk.

Balzic bent down and kissed her on the cheek. "S'matter, Ma, can't sleep?"

"Ah, no good last night. All night getting up for the bathroom. Six, seven times. Go back, snooze little bit, then up. Up, down, all night. Where you was last night? I no hear you come home, what's the matter?"

"Something happened, Ma. You make any coffee?"

"Not yet. I no have time." Mrs. Balzic started to laugh. "Hey, Mario, ain't that funny? I'm up half the night and don't think I got time for making coffee. Ah, I don't know, Mario. Every day more, more get tired. Pretty soon die, I think."

"Quit talking like that, will you. You ain't going to die."

"Mario, don't be stupid. I don't raise you up be stupid. Everybody going to die. Soon, late—what the heck you think? I going live forever?"

"I know all that, Ma, but I don't like to hear you talk about it, that's all. Where's the instant?"

"Same place always, Mario. How long you live here?" Mrs. Balzic stirred her milk and watched her son moving around the room, filling a small enamel pan with water, setting out a cup, and putting a spoonful of instant in it, stripping off his tie as he turned up the gas.

"Somebody killed last night, Mario?"

"No, Ma."

"Mario, you my bones and blood and your father's, too, and you can't lie no good ever since you was little boy. Who killed?"

"John Andrasko, Ma," Balzic said, hoping she'd drop it.

"Accident?"

"No, Ma."

"How? Murder? Mario, no. Murder? Say no."

"Yeah, Ma. And now if you don't mind, I don't want to talk about it, okay?"

"Oh, yoy-yoy, that no good, Mario. Who want kill John? My God, I know since little boy. Since born. I know mother, father, grandmother, grandfather, both sides. My God, Mario, you was grew up together, no?"

"Yeah. That's right. I knew him most of my life, I guess. But not too well, Ma. We weren't close. I just knew him."

"That's why don't sleep."

"There was a lot of work to do, Ma. You can't just quit when something like this happens, you ought to know that by now."

"Don't be mad for me, Mario. My ankles hurt too hard already. I'm just old lady talking too much, okay?"

"I'm not mad, Ma. I just don't want to talk about it, all right?"

"Okay, Mario. Hey, kiddo, water's boil."

"I hear it, Ma. I hear it."

Balzic poured the water into the cup, stirred it for a moment, then sipped it standing by the sink, screwing up his face from the heat.

"Wait, Mario. It's too hot."

"I don't have time. I want to get cleaned up before the girls get up. Else I'll never get into the bathroom. Hey, I hear you did okay at the bingo."

"Ah, some towels. Two times I need one more corn for ten dollars once and next time for fifty dollars. But I see lots people. Even friends. Not too much time left for see friends."

"Will you quit talking like that? I can't stand it—never mind. I'm going to the bathroom. If anybody calls, tell them I'll call back. Okay?"

"All right, Mario. All right. No more, okay?"

Balzic gulped down some more coffee, kissed his mother again, and then showered, shaved, and changed clothes just in time. The girls were up and prowling, morning surly, alternately grimacing and giggling in their adolescent conspiracy against the world.

Balzic kissed both on the cheek as he passed them in the kitchen. "Why don't you two do something about night football games?" he said to them in passing.

"What's for breakfast?" Emily said.

"Mother wants to talk to you, Daddy," Marie said.

"What's wrong with night football games?" Emily asked.

"Mornings is what's wrong with them," Balzic said. "Isn't your mother up yet?"

"She's awake, but she's still in bed."

"She sick?"

"Uh-uh. Just sleepy."

"I probably won't be around much today," Balzic said, "so have a good day."

"You too, Daddy," Emily said.

"Ditto," Marie said.

"Ditto," Balzic mimicked her, hurrying into the bedroom. "Come on, sleepy, time to get up. You can't lounge around all day."

"Oh, Mario, I'd like to sleep and sleep," Ruth said. "The girls up?"

"Yeah. Ma's up, too. Said she was up half the night. She okay at the bingo last night?"

"She seemed like she had a pretty good time to me. But I know she had a rough night. That's what I wanted to ask you. Maybe I ought to take her to Dr. Wilson's this afternoon."

"She won't want to go. What do you think?"

"Oh, yes she will. Just let me talk to her a while," Ruth said, pulling the pillow under her chin and turning on her side. "And where were you last night?"

"Ask Ma. I told her already, and I don't feel like talking about it. I'm going to be talking about it all day every place else. I'd like to be able to give it a rest here."

"It wasn't an accident, was it?"

"No. Listen, babe, I got to get moving. I'll call you around noon, let you know about supper, okay?"

"Okay, Mario. If I ever get awake."

Balzic leaned down and tried to kiss Ruth on the mouth, but she

38

turned her head and buried her face in the pillow. "God, Mario, my mouth tastes like yuk. It must smell worse."

"So? What's a little smelly kiss between friends?"

Ruth pushed her face deeper into the pillow, and Balzic kissed her on the neck. "Have it your way, garbage mouth," he said, and squeezed her ear. "See you, hon."

"Bye," Ruth said dreamily.

It was eight-fifteen when Balzic pulled into the train station parking lot on the lower side near the freight office. There were only four other cars in the lot, and one of them Balzic recognized as an unmarked state police cruiser. A man and woman were arguing with the man in the freight office about something; except for them, no one else was around.

Balzic headed into the tunnel and up the steps to the platform where a raw-eyed, yawning state patrolman was rocking on his heels. The patrolman was new to Balzic. He went over and flashed his ID.

"Lieutenant Moyer been around yet?"

"He should've been here. I was supposed to be relieved ten, fifteen minutes ago," the patrolman said. "Damn," he added, "if this isn't the dreariest place at night I've ever seen. You look at this place for a night and you start believing the railroads are in trouble."

"Yeah," Balzic said. "Even when nothing happens it's ugly enough to make you think something's going to."

"There's the lieutenant now," the patrolman said, nodding toward the opposite side of the tracks.

Lieutenant Moyer got out of an unmarked car as three marked cars of the Pennsylvania State Police pulled in behind him on State Street Extension. Moyer waited by his car until eight troopers from the other cars gathered around him. He talked to them briefly, gesturing and pointing. All but two of the troopers set off in different directions, and those two followed Moyer across the tracks toward the platform.

"Morning, Mario. Dunn. See anybody last night?"

"No sir," Patrolman Dunn said. "Only the station master."

39

"Figures," Moyer said. "You can go."

"Yessir," Dunn said and left, trying vainly to stifle a yawn.

"Mario, something tells me this one is going to be a real corn bender."

"I'm inclined to agree with you. We'll know after your boys talk to the people."

"Yessir, I just got a feeling about this one. We're going to walk and talk and walk some more, and we're still not going to know anything." Moyer walked around the bench where John Andrasko's body had been found. Moyer looked down at the chalked outline and the patch of dried blood that was longer and wider than the chalked outline. "Ever notice, Mario," he said, "how fast the chalk washes away and how long it takes for the blood to wash away?"

"I try not to think about it."

"First rain, this chalk'll be gone. Come back three months from now, you'll still be able to see this blood." Moyer stepped around the blood and came near Balzic. "Any more thoughts about the kid?"

"No. Nothing worth talking about."

"Don't kid me. I can see it in your eyes."

"Well, it's just a feeling. But I still want to run down some papers."

"Mario, I think you're going to wind up chasing your tail about the kid. I can't stop you from thinking, but—well, I can see from the way you're not listening to me that I'm really getting through. Go on and run down your papers. I'm not going to do anything here but get a blister on my brain until my boys get through. Go over the platform again and up and down the tracks, but I don't think we're going to find a damn thing. Why the hell am I getting these blanks about this thing? Can you tell me that?"

"Can't tell you why you are, but if it's any consolation, I feel pretty blank myself."

"No consolation. One pessimist on a job is enough."

"I'll give you a call around noon. Sooner, if I learn anything." Balzic started off the platform with a wave but turned back. "Guess

40

I ought to tell you that Weigh and his horses busted five people over this thing last night, and I turned them loose, so don't be surprised if he comes up and throws a hook in your ear about my incompetence."

"Who had reasons?"

"We both did. He probably thinks he had the best damn reason in the world for busting them, but then he didn't want to do the rest of the work, so I said the hell with him and let them go. I'll settle it with him soon enough, but I thought I ought to warn you." Balzic turned and left without waiting for another question.

He drove through the alleys to the rear of the courthouse, parked in the back lot, and, once inside, tried unsuccessfully to duck the courthouse reporter for *The Rocksburg Gazette.*

"Morning, Chief," Dick Dietz said. "Little early for you, isn't it? I mean especially today."

"What's so special about today, Dietz?"

"Nothing's today. That's just it. It's Saturday. Criminal court session ended yesterday. Civil session starts Monday. You aren't by any chance involved in a civil proceeding?"

"Not likely," Balzic said, looking at his watch.

"Then could it be you're here to find out something that has to do with what happened last night?"

Balzic edged closer to Dietz and lowered his voice, even though no one was close enough to hear what he might have said in a normal tone. "You know something, Dietz? You make my ass tired, and you know why you make my ass tired? Cause you're always trying to chisel information instead of just coming out and asking for it. And as far as last night goes, you got all the information you're going to get when your people made the phone calls they make every night."

"Aw, come on, Chief. There's no need to get touchy now. Not at your age. Besides, I've already got the best news of the day from the district attorney. I just thought you might perhaps be down here to, let's say, reconcile your differences with him. Any possibility of that?"

41

Balzic backed away and headed for the drinking fountain beside the door to the office of the clerk of courts. When he finished getting a drink, he looked up and saw Dietz standing beside him. "Get lost, Dietz," he said, "before I forget what I get paid for doing."

"Wouldn't you like to know what Weigh had to say about last night?" Dietz said, smiling.

"Not particularly."

"Well, among other things, Weigh said that he was upset over the manner in which the investigation was being conducted. He said, in effect, that anyone could see that the murder was the work of either a lunatic or a drug addict."

"Naturally, he told you that in strictest confidence."

"Well, of course, he wouldn't want me to use those words for the record, which is understandable considering his position. He will have to prosecute, and he wouldn't want an adverse-publicity charge to be thrown against him during the trial."

"Naturally," Balzic said, looking again at his watch.

"Do you have any comment about what the district attorney said?"

"Yes. But strictly off the record. You make my ass tired."

"Careful, Chief. This is my beat too, remember."

"Why don't you quote me the Bill of Rights, freedom of the press and all that horseshit."

"If I thought it would do any good, I would."

Balzic looked again at his watch. It was eight-fifty. He left Dietz standing by the water fountain and walked into the lobby of the courthouse. He stepped into one of the bank of phone booths and dialed *The Rocksburg Gazette.*

"I want to talk to the managing editor," he said to the operator.

"Thank you." There was a click, a pause, and then an abrupt voice saying, "Murray speaking."

"Mr. Murray," Balzic said, "you don't know me, and I'm not about to give my name, but I got some information about the parking authority I think your paper might be interested in. Only thing is, I don't want to be seen near your paper. So I'll tell you what. I know your reporter Dietz on sight, so if you want to know what I know, you tell him to meet me at nine-thirty sharp in the Nixon Grille. I won't talk to anybody else, got it?"

"Yes, I've got it."

"Nine-thirty sharp. I'm not going to wait even two minutes."

"What's this all about?"

"I'll tell him. All I'm going to tell you is it's about a conflict of interest in the placement of parking authority funds in a certain bank." Balzic hung up and walked back to the hall outside the office of the clerk of courts. Dietz had moved back across the hall from the fountain.

"A late development, Chief?" Dietz said.

"You might say that."

Just as Mrs. Florence Wilmoth, the clerk of courts, came through the lobby, the phone on the information desk in the lobby rang. The courthouse guard who picked it up nodded a couple of times, and then called out to Dietz. "It's your boss, Dick."

"Probably some late development," Balzic said as Dietz hurried past him to the phone.

"Well, Mario," Mrs. Wilmoth said, "you look cheerful this morning." She unlocked her office door and flipped on the overhead lights.

"Just got rid of an itch." Balzic said, following her inside.

"An itch, did you say?"

"Something like that," Balzic said. "Florence, I don't have much time, and unless you've moved things, I know where everything is I want to see, so—"

"Say no more. Help yourself."

Balzic thanked her and went to the file of death certificates. He began with Parilla and went on through Perilla. He found nothing on any male Parilla or Perilla in the age range he presumed would be the age of Mrs. Andrasko's first husband. When he'd gone through all the possible spellings of the name, he stopped, with his chin resting on his fist on top of the cabinets. He closed the drawers of the death

43

certificates and went to the birth certificates. Among the Parillas, he found: "Thomas John Parilla, male, Caucasian, born 20 September 1953 to Tami Antonio Parilla and Mary Frances Spano Parilla." He ignored the other information and closed the drawer and went back to the death certificates. He could find no record of the death of any Tami Antonio Parilla. That left him with only one other thing to check, but in the file holding marriage licenses he found that none had been made out to John Andrasko and Mary Frances Spano Parilla.

He waved goodbye to Mrs. Wilmoth and went out to the lobby and dialed St. Malachy's rectory.

When Father Marrazo answered, Balzic said: "Listen, Father, I just came out of the clerk of courts' office, and I can't find any record of the death of Tommy Parilla's father, and not only that, I can't find any marriage license for John Andrasko. If you know anything, you can put my mind at rest about these things, 'cause already I'm starting to get a little nervous."

"That's strange, Mario, but I'm sure there's an explanation. Let me think a minute." There was a long pause and then: "Listen, Mario, let me check my records here, and I'll call you back. How's that?"

"Better for me to call you. I don't know where I'm going to be."

"All right. But give me an hour or so. I have some young people coming here in a few minutes, and I'll be with them for half an hour at least, maybe longer."

"Good enough, Father," Balzic said, hanging up.

He rooted through his pockets for another dime and called his home. Ruth answered.

"Hey, baby, is Ma close by?"

"Sure. She's right here. I just made an appointment for her at Dr. Wilson's. He wasn't too happy about her coming in on a Saturday, but—what's the matter?"

"Put Ma on, will you. I need that computer she got in her head for family connections."

A pause. "Mario? What's matter, kiddo?"

"Ma, what do you remember about Tami Parilla?"

"Tami or Tommy?"

44

"Tami."

"I don't know. Oh, wait. Sure. He's marry to Mary Spano. Then he die."

"You sure?"

"No. Wait. That was Tony."

"Try to get it straight, Ma. This Tami's middle name was Antonio."

"Yeah, sure. But his brother was name Anthony. He's one die. Tami, him, I don't know what happen with. But I know was marry Mary Spano. They have one kid—Tommy."

"You got it. You're sure it was his brother that died?"

"I'm sure. Anthony. Kill in Korea. Tami I don't know what happen for him."

"You know his wife was married to John Andrasko?"

"Yeah, sure, I know. Oh my God, Mario. I forget John," Mrs. Balzic said. "Oh, I feel so bad about that."

"Yeah. I know. But right now I just want you to be sure about them."

"Only thing I sure is they get marry not here. Virginia, Maryland, some place like that."

"You sure?"

"Mario, what's matter—I go round asking people for to see marriage license? How I know they get marry there? That what people say, that's all I tell you."

"Okay, Ma, that's good enough. Hey, how you feeling?"

"Okay, not so okay. Lousy, not so lousy. I go to Dr. Wilson with Ruth today. She make me go. What the heck he's do—give me more pills? I get up and go bathroom all night now. Them pills he give me last time, yoy, God, I can't stop go to bathroom. Who knows?"

"Well, just do what he says, okay?"

"Oh you, Mario, you like all crazy people sometime, think doctors fix them up. Sometimes no can fix, Mario, when the heck you learn? Not everything can fix."

"Okay, Ma, okay. Just do what he says. Promise."

"Okay, okay. I promise. I promise to go all time in bathroom, that's all I promise. Not do in bed."

"You're going to be okay, Ma. Don't worry."

"Who's worry? You and Ruth worry. I no worry. I just old."

"Okay, Ma, I have to go now. I'll see you this afternoon maybe."
Balzic hung up and stood in the booth fretting. "Goddammit," he
whispered, "don't let nothing happen to her."

Balzic drove to the train station, and when he got up to the
platform, he found Lieutenant Moyer looking morose and talking
glumly with six of his men. Balzic waited until Moyer dismissed
them and then followed Moyer to his car.

"Mario," Moyer said, "I hope to hell you came up with more than
we did."

"You get shut out?"

"All around. Nobody heard anything. Nobody saw anything.
Nobody knows anything. For practical purposes, nobody else was
awake or even alive when it happened. I can't figure it. How'd you
do?"

"I'm not sure yet. I tried to run down the family, and all I've got
so far are loose ends. For one thing, there's the kid."

"What about him?"

"All I found was his birth certificate. Couldn't find anything about
his father, and I couldn't find a marriage license for his mother and
Andrasko. My mother tells me they were married out of state.
Maryland or Virginia. She couldn't remember what happened to the
boy's father. I've got a priest checking his records, but something
tells me he's going to come up short, too."

"So what do you figure?"

"I'll tell you what I figure, but you're not going to want to hear
it."

"Give it a shot."

"What is this place—a train station, right?" Balzic said hesitantly.

"Go ahead. I'm listening," Moyer said.

"So why'd you start to smile, the first thing I say?"

"Well, Jesus Christ, Mario, I mean, we are standing right here."

"Okay, okay. My point is, people are always going away—"

"They're also always coming back."

"I told you you weren't going to want to hear it."

"No, no. Go ahead. Give me the rest."

"You saw Andrasko's face last night. Blotted out, right?"

"Yeah. Go on."

"So it could look like anybody or nobody."

"Okay."

"Well, nobody knows what happened to the kid's father, and the fact that he still has his father's name means Andrasko never adopted him."

"So?"

"Well, put it together."

"Mario, put what together?"

"Don't you see any connections? The blotted-out face, the place, the father that ain't around, the stepfather that didn't adopt the kid?"

"Oh, Mario, what the fuck have you been reading lately?"

"Come on, Phil. You ask me what I think, and then you start to jack me off."

"I'm not jacking anybody off. But tell me this: if you're so sure of what you're saying, how come you're not out talking to the missus right now? I mean, let's go. Let's go sit her down and have a talk with her."

"Nothing doing. I mean, I can't stop you from going, but I'm not going."

"And just why not—you're so full of these connections."

"The funeral. I don't get in the middle of any family's funeral. That's enough for anybody to handle. Let us start stomping around asking questions, and it gets shitty, that's all."

"Mario, I've known you for a long time," Moyer said, "and I've always respected your judgment, but sometimes, I swear to Christ, I can't understand the way you operate. You get me thinking about the kid now, and you know whoever did it had to get blood all over his sleeve at least, but you act like you don't even want to go out this guy's farm and look around."

"I don't. But I'll tell you why. Say we get a warrant and we go out there. Hell, man, Andrasko's got about forty acres out there, and from what I hear, he had most of it under cultivation. We could look on that place for a month, and we'd still miss something. And suppose I'm right. Suppose the kid did it. Who's to say he got rid of the clothes out there? There are a helluva lot of roads around here and helluva lot of water—just where the hell are we supposed to start?"

"One thing's sure, Mario. No matter where he got rid of them—if it was the kid, mind you, *if*—he had to go back to that house again for the simple reason that when you saw him coming back he was clean, right?"

"Right."

"So at least we can ask her about his travels last night."

"Well, that takes us right into the middle of the funeral again." Balzic shook his head. "You know, I don't even know for sure if she knows John was murdered. I can't remember whether I told her, and I don't know if the priest did either."

Moyer shook his head and started to laugh. "Mario, you're some cop."

"Ah, it was tough enough just telling her. Christ, she started crying as soon as I said it was John. Who the hell can give details at a time like that?"

"So you didn't tell her?"

"No," Balzic said, looking at the houses on State Street. "I guess I didn't."

"Oh, brother. Well. Just what do you intend to do the rest of the day, I mean, since you don't want to pursue the investigation?" Moyer asked with a slightly mocking grin.

"Fridays I usually go out and shoot, and yesterday I missed. I thought after I checked back with the priest I'd go out to the club range."

"You're full of surprises. All these years I've known you, I never believed you carried a weapon."

"I don't. Not a handgun anyway. If it was up to me, no beat officer would."

"You kidding me or what?"

"No I'm not kidding. Cops kill too many people, if you ask me. Look what happened in Pittsburgh the other day. Two beat officers are checking out a burglary. One goes in the front of a warehouse and the other goes in the back. The burglar comes out a side door, and the officer that went in the front chases him down an alley and starts shooting. He misses the burglar, but he hits a guy painting his porch about three blocks away. That guy's going to be in a wheelchair the rest of his life. Meantime they still haven't caught the burglar, and from where I stand that's bullshit."

"Those things happen, Mario."

"That's just my point. If beat officers don't carry sidearms, they wouldn't happen."

"Then what are we supposed to do when the punks don't give up their guns? Talk them out of it, I guess."

"Hell, man, that's what we've got radios for and tactical squads. You know as well as I do that handguns aren't worth a damn beyond ten, fifteen yards anyway. Good God, I shudder every time I think of some of the men on my force walking around with those thirty-eights. Hell, some of them can't put five shots out of six on a three-foot-high silhouette target at fifteen yards. And that's when they're standing still and all they're shooting at is paper.

"Jesus," Balzic went on, "Weigh's got some people who can't even hit that damn target two shots out of five with those little snub-nose jobs they're so goddamn proud of. You know the worst nightmare I have is the one where my wife and mother and my daughters are walking out of a supermarket and some guy's just held up the place, and he runs out into the parking lot and Weigh's boys just happen to be there with those short-barrelled thirty-eights. Good God, I see people scattered all over the parking lot—ah, what's the use."

"Well, tell me, Mario, just what do you tell your men?"

"About what—about a guy with a gun?"

"Yes."

"I tell them to call me, and I tell them the first officer that returns fire before I get there is suspended without pay indefinitely."

"You're shittin' me."

"What's so hard to believe? You know, I've been chief for eleven years, going on twelve, and nobody in this town has ever been shot by any of my men? Not one, and I'm prouder of that than of anything. The first month I was chief was the closest I ever came. The thing was, the clown who started shooting hadn't fired his weapon in so long he had two misfires out of the first three times he pulled the trigger. Now, at least, my men have got to fire their weapons twice a week, and I've got a man who hand-loads all their ammunition. But it still gives me the creeps thinking of some of the men I've got."

"That sounds like you're contradicting yourself, Mario. First, you say you have them under orders not to shoot, and then, you say you make them shoot twice a week."

"There's no contradiction. I just want to make them aware of that goddamn thing they're carrying around on their hip. I mean if they're going to carry it, they ought to at least find out what the hell it is. But one of these days I'm going to take them away from them. Nobody thinks twice about sending out a meter maid without a gun or a school crossing guard—why the hell do guys doing practically the same job—giving tickets or directing traffic—why the hell does everybody think they need a gun?"

"Not the same thing, Mario."

"The hell it's not. You're just brainwashed, that's all. You just can't picture a man cop without a gun, but you see meter maids without them, and you don't even think about it."

"Okay, so I'm brainwashed. And just what do you shoot?"

"Meet me out the range about two, and I'll show you."

"I'll just do that. Want to make a little bet?"

"Better wait until you get there, Lieutenant, before you go putting up any money. See you later."

Moyer pulled away, and Balzic went to his car and drove to the rectory of St. Malachy's. He found Father Marrazo in the foyer saying goodby to a young couple with marriage in their eyes.

"Mario, I have to apologize. I've been so wrapped up talking with those kids that I haven't had a chance to do what you asked. But come into my office and I'll get on with it."

The priest led Balzic into his small, square office in the rear of the rectory. Father Marrazo pushed some chairs around and directed Balzic to an overstuffed chair covered in cracking black leather.

"Some wine, Mario?"

"No thanks, Father," Balzic said, sitting down and lighting a cigarette.

"Mario, if you don't, then I won't have the excuse," Father Marrazo said, winking broadly. "Besides, it's really exceptional wine. Mr. Ferrara makes it."

"Well, if it's his, Father, then I better have some. I wouldn't want him to hear that I'd turned it down."

"You know him?" Father Marrazo said, pouring the wine, a very clear, light red wine, into two jelly glasses. "It's not Bardolino, you understand, but it is a very good Ferrara."

Balzic took the glass offered him and held it up to the light.

"Sure, I know him. Fact is, I think we're related some way. I been drinking his wine since I was a kid. Fact, one summer when I was about ten or eleven, he paid me two cents for every good bottle I brought him with a screw cap on. I used to go scrounging through garbage cans every morning, and then he paid me another penny for each bottle to wash it and get the labels off. That was a pretty good summer."

"That must have been a lot of money in those days."

"It was. That was thirty-four, thirty-five. On a good day I used to make sixty, seventy cents." Balzic took a sip and rolled it around his mouth and then swallowed it. "Tell you one thing, Father. Mr. Ferrara hasn't lost his touch."

"Agreed. You know, he brings me two bottles every Sunday night. You don't know how many times I've wanted to say to him, 'Mr. Ferrara, what makes you think I drink only two bottles of wine a week?' For a while, I tried to save him three or four other bottles, empties, to give him to take along with his own empties, but that didn't work."

"Didn't you ever ask him about it?"

"No. I couldn't bring myself to ask. Anyway, I got a very clear impression that he didn't approve because he thought I wasn't very subtle or because he thought a priest shouldn't drink more than two

51

bottles a week. So, I went back to giving him only the bottles he'd brought the week before. He seems content now." Father Marrazo lifted his glass. "Salud," he said and drank.

"Salud," Balzic said and drank also.

"So, now to business," Father Marrazo said, carrying his glass over to a row of wooden file cabinets. He set the glass on top and started going through cards and folders. After five minutes he said: "So far, Mario, my friend, all I can find are baptismal and confirmation records for the children. That is, baptismal records for Tommy Parilla and William and Norma Andrasko and confirmation records for Tommy and Norma. There is no record of either of the marriages." He closed the drawers, picked up his glass, and sat on the front of his desk. "Now what will you do?"

"Don't you have any funeral record for Tommy's father?"

Father Marrazo shook his head.

Balzic scratched his chin. "Damn, I forgot to check for a divorce record," he said. "But something tells me I'm not going to find one. What I can't figure is what happened to the kid's father. Not even my mother knows what happened to him."

"Why is that so important to you, Mario? I don't understand."

"Father, I'll tell you straight. I don't know why it is, but it is. The way this thing is going, we're coming up zero every place we look. In other words, as far as a court is concerned, all we've got is a corpse and a weapon. We got no motive, no witnesses, no nothing."

"And you still think because of the way the boy reacted when you told him and what he said—"

"Don't forget the way it was done, Father. We talked about that. Fact, you're the one put me on the idea about the face being wiped out to make it look like nobody or like somebody else."

"If I follow you, Mario, what you're thinking is the boy—if he did it—did it out of some unconscious compulsion."

"Something like that, Father. I mean, my first thought was that it might've been the result of an argument over the kid taking the car, and for all I know that might still be the reason. But again, this is all based on a guess that it was the boy. I mean, we haven't even talked to Mrs. Andrasko yet about where the kid was when it was

52

happening. She might put it all straight about him in two minutes. By the way, Father, did you tell her how it happened?"

"No. I assumed you had."

"Oh, Christ—excuse me, Father."

The priest waved his hand. "Mario, I regard that as a prayer. Not a curse."

"That means she got it from the paper."

"You didn't tell her, Mario?"

"I didn't get a chance. I just started talking, and she took it from there. Then the two younger kids showed up, and what the hell was I supposed to say—ah, Father, sometimes I think I'm the worst guy in the world for this job."

"Mario, have some more wine."

Balzic shook his head.

"Go on. Here, give me your glass."

"I don't want to get a buzz on, Father."

"Nor do I want you to. But there are times, Mario, when Christ offers practical solace for our weaknesses. After all, it was He who turned water into wine. He knew that water may quench our thirst, but wine, Mario—wine helps quench the thirst of our soul." The priest held out the bottle. "Give me your glass."

Balzic held it out, and Father Marrazo filled it. "Drink, Mario. You need it. At times like this, there are no other solutions for our deficiencies."

"You're a damn good talker, Father."

"Not me, Mario. Not me." Father Marrazo made a silent laugh and then grew pensive. "We each made a mistake. Yours was in an omission, and mine was in a presumption. The other, Mrs. Andrasko, now suffers for our blunders. What solace have we left for our blunders but the blood of Christ, eh? Drink up. The newspaper, that epistle of gloom, corrects our mistakes, and where does that leave us. . . ."

"I don't know about you, Father. It just leaves me feeling stupid."

"You're not alone, Mario. I feel stupid ten times a day and twice that on Sundays. Thus . . ." Father Marrazo's voice faded, and he lifted his glass and nodded to it. "Well, what will you do now?"

"Same thing I been doing, Father. Keep checking records to find out if anybody knows what happened to Tami Parilla. Because the way things are going so far, I'm getting closer to the idea that he didn't die. Which reminds me—may I use your phone?"

"Of course."

Balzic put his glass on the priest's desk and dialed the station.

"Rocksburg Police. Sergeant Stramsky speaking."

"Vic? Balzic. Got a pencil?"

"Right here. Go."

"Call the state houses in Maryland and Virginia and see if John Andrasko and Mary Frances Spano or Mary Frances Spano Parilla got married there. Should have been, oh, eight, nine years ago."

"That it?"

"Yeah. Any calls for me?"

"No calls, but your neighborhood district attorney was here about fifteen minutes ago, and was he steaming."

"What did you tell him?"

"What could I tell him? I didn't know anything."

"Good. Let the bastard burn awhile. It'll do him good."

"Where you going to be in case anybody wants to know?"

"Right now I'm in St. Malachy's rectory. In about five minutes I'll be talking to Bill Joyce in the F.B.I. office. After that, I'll call you. Anything else?"

"Not much. Some fenders got bent on Maple, and a missus, lemme see, a Mrs. Scarafolo wants us to do something about some kids cutting through her yard."

"Is that the Mrs. Scarafolo on South Eustice?" Balzic said.

"Yeah."

"Is Ippolito around?"

"Just walked in."

"Well tell him to go down there and listen to her and see if she needs groceries."

"Oh, it's that Mrs. Scarafolo."

"Now you got her. If that's it, I'll check later." Balzic hung up, shaking his head. "Wish that's all I had to think about."

"Mario," Father Marrazo said, "I couldn't help overhearing. This Mrs. Scarafolo, does she belong to my parish?"

"You'd know that better than I would, Father. She lives in the 600 block of South Eustice. I'll tell you something, though. If you're thinking of doing something for her, don't do it yourself. That woman does not like priests."

"Is it a nuisance to you?"

"No, so far it hasn't been. The thing is, up until a couple of years ago she took care of herself pretty good, but then she broke her hip. So what she does is she calls us and makes a complaint, usually about the kids running through her yard, and then when the officer gets there, she sits him down and gives him some wine and maybe a little pasta, and then she asks him if he's going past Brunetti's Market. She's pushing ninety and got about two hundred years' worth of pride, and she thinks she's foxing us. She only does it once a month, when her Social Security comes. I don't mind it, understand, but there may come a time when I can't let a man and a cruiser go."

"What does she have against priests?"

Balzic shrugged. "Father, when somebody pushing ninety tells me she don't like something, I don't ask questions. Don't you have a committee to work on things like this?"

"Yes, we do. What disturbs me is that if she is in my parish she hasn't been receiving the sacraments."

"Well, that's your department, Father. But if you go down there and get your ears fried, don't say I didn't tell you."

"Oh, there's no problem to that, Mario. I just put on a sport shirt and my raincoat and pose as a detective."

"Let's have another glass of the Ferrara, Father, and then I got to go."

"What shall we drink to?"

"I don't know. How about your career as an actor?"

"Wonderful. To all my frustrations. Salud."

"Salud . . ."

After leaving the priest, Balzic drove to the rear parking lot of the courthouse. He hustled up the back stairs to the regional office of the F.B.I.

A receptionist told him to go right in to the office of the agent in charge, William Joyce.

"Mario," Joyce said, coming around his desk to shake hands. "Where the hell have you been?"

"Oh, around. How about you?"

"Same old things. I hear you've got something."

"I got something all right."

"I also hear you're going no place fast."

"'Fraid so."

"What do you need?"

"I'd like you to run down a couple of names. Here, let me write them down." Balzic wrote the names on Joyce's desk calendar.

"You looking for anything special, Mario?"

"Put it this way. I'm just looking right now. For anything anybody has."

"This Andrasko—wasn't he the victim?"

"Yeah, but I'm looking for anything. Credit records, life insurance, service records. I knew him since I was a kid, but I really didn't know him, if you take my meaning."

"Okay. What about the other one?"

"He's the puzzle. Andrasko was married to a woman who was married to this Parilla, and they had a kid. The kid still goes by his father's name, so apparently Andrasko didn't adopt him, and from what I gathered when I told the kid about John, the kid couldn't have cared less. But nobody seems to know anything about what happened to this Parilla, not even my mother. Ordinarily, I'd put her head up against F.B.I. files anytime."

"You want me to see if anyone put a chaser on him through Missing Persons, too?"

"If you would. You'll get a quicker answer from them than I would. I'll be obliged, Bill."

"No trouble, Mario. Just give me a couple of hours, that's all."

"Good enough. I've got somebody checking marriage bureaus in Maryland and Virginia about Andrasko's marriage. But you'll really help a helluva lot."

"Why are you checking the marriage bureaus?"

"I can't say, really. I just have the feeling that old John never married that woman. Don't ask me why, and don't ask me what difference it's going to make, but I'd like to know about it if it's true."

"All right, Mario. I'll see what I can do."

"Thanks. Say, why don't you and Marge stop up the house some night? Play a little penny ante, drink some beer, and tell each other a lot of lies about the time we captured the James boys."

"Last time I did that it cost me three dollars and fourteen cents."

"It went for a good cause. I had a helluva steak from that money," Balzic said soberly. "I can still taste it. Haven't had one that good since."

"Go to hell," Joyce said.

"Okay, Bill. Take care, and give my best to Marge."

Joyce waved, and Balzic stepped into the corridor and went down the back stairs and out to the parking lot. He got in his car, sat for a moment, and then went back into the courthouse.

He hurried to the office of the clerk of courts. Mrs. Wilmoth looked up from her conversation with a lawyer for whom she was going over some files and nodded approval to Balzic after he mouthed the words that he wanted to check something. He went back to the indexes listing divorces filed and divorces granted and checked the Spano-Parilla marriage both ways. He found what he already suspected: if Mary Frances Spano and Tami Antonio Parilla were divorced, they hadn't gone through the proceedings in this country. "That's that," he said to himself and closed the drawers, waving to Mrs. Wilmoth as he left.

He was almost to the rear exit when someone touched his arm.

"That was pretty cute," Dick Dietz said. "I never gave you that much credit, Chief."

Balzic glared at Dietz for a moment, then let his face go soft. "Not that I give a good goddamn, Dietz, but just what am I supposed to be getting credit for?"

"Oh, you know what I'm talking about."

"Dietz," Balzic said, blowing out a sigh, "why the hell is it that every conversation with you turns into riddles? I mean, if you got something to say, why not just come out with it?"

"I don't have to, now. I know what I want to know."

57

"Good. I hope you'll sleep better tonight."

"I don't ever have trouble sleeping, Chief. Do you?"

"I haven't slept right since 1943, Dietz, and you want to know something? You know what some of the kids are saying these days about not trusting anyone over thirty? Well, I don't trust anyone over thirty who sleeps good. See you around."

Balzic bounded through the exit and down the steps and across the alley to his car. He drove home but found the house empty. A note on the kitchen table written in Ruth's hand said: "Mario, Took your mother to Dr. Wilson. Ella gave us a lift. Meat loaf in the refrigerator. Have a good day. One of these days I'm going to brush my teeth."

Balzic smiled and whistled all the while he made himself a plate, filling it with chunks of meat loaf, cheese, and olives. He opened a bottle of beer and was just sitting down to eat when he saw the paper. Page one of *The Rocksburg Gazette* bore this story:

FEW CLUES—

NORTH ROCKSBURG MAN FOUND BEATEN TO DEATH

by Dick Dietz

ROCKSBURG GAZETTE STAFF WRITER

Police are still searching today for the killer of John J. Andrasko, 45, of Route 986 North, Rocksburg RD, who was found savagely beaten to death Friday night on the platform of the Pennsylvania Station, where he was apparently waiting for the 11:38 train to Knox.

State police Lt. Philip Moyer, chief of criminal investigation division of the Rocksburg Barracks, in charge of the investigation, said he has few clues to go on and no witnesses. Moyer said, however, the murder weapon had been found but would not reveal what it was. Moyer also said no motive has been determined but did not rule out robbery as a possible motive. He did not elaborate.

Dist. Atty Milton Weigh said the murder was "the most vicious and savage thing I've ever seen." He said detectives assigned to his office were assisting in the investigation, but he had little to add to what Lt. Moyer said.

Informed sources close to the investigation told The Rocksburg Gazette both police departments were working on the theory the murderer was possibly a drug addict.

Balzic threw the paper across the kitchen and finished eating, furious with Weigh and Dietz, tasting little of what he ate, eating too fast, and knowing he was letting himself in for a bout of indigestion. He washed the dish and set it in the drainer in the sink. He finished his beer and then picked up the paper, restoring it to something like its original shape and putting it back on the table.

He locked the house and drove slowly out to the Rocksburg Police Rod and Gun Club range, keeping the radio open, smoking and looking at the trees turning color, pulling off the road when cars approached from behind to let them pass. He turned into the club grounds and drove in low gear along the half-mile dirt road to the range, stopping on the crest of a low hill, so Moyer could see him from the road. He opened the trunk and then sat on the browning scrub grass and lit another cigarette, looking around at the trees and listening to the squirrels and birds.

Off to his right he saw the tall grass and brush moving and then heard a pheasant calling. He watched the tall grass and guessed there were at least three hens following the cock. Something spooked them, and the parting grass gave the appearance of the wake of a speeding boat.

"Run now, beautiful," Balzic said through clenched teeth, "'cause in a couple more weeks I'm going to be right behind you."

He sat there long enough to finish the cigarette, butting it out carefully on the ground and splitting the paper and letting the tobacco crumble through his fingers, as Moyer's unmarked cruiser came slowly up the road, leaving small clouds of dust that hung for a moment before floating off. Balzic stood and brushed off his seat.

Moyer parked beside him and got out and stretched. "Mario, what's the good news?"

"It's quiet out here, that's the best news I've got."

"Yeah, it is that. God, look at those trees."

"That's all I did, driving out here, was look at the trees. Fantastic, this time of year."

"You know something, though, Mario? I used to think this time of year was the best, because it was so damn pretty, but the older I get the more I think spring is."

"Well, you said it, Phil. It's 'cause you're getting older."

"You think so?"

"Hell, I started thinking spring was better ten years ago."

"Maybe you're right," Moyer said. "Well, what do you say, sport? You ready to make some holes in the paper?"

"I'm ready. Anything new?" Balzic said, leaning into his trunk.

"Not a damn thing. Saw the paper, though. I don't know who's got less between the ears—Weigh or that reporter. You see it?"

"I saw it. Made me forget what I was eating."

"What the hell you got in there, Mario? What's this big secret weapon of yours?"

Balzic unzipped a rifle case that hung from wide leather straps attached to the underside of the trunk back an inch or so from where the lid swung up. He drew out a rifle with a telescopic sight.

"What you got there?"

"This, my friend, is a modified Springfield '03."

"This is what you shoot with? Why, for crying out loud?"

"You grab those profile targets in there and, as we walk along, I'll tell you. Just let me get this box of cartridges."

They set off over the crest of the hill and headed for the hollow of land that lay between it and another ridge more than three hundred yards away. The range extended between the two ridges.

"Hope you brought some way to fix the targets," Moyer said.

"Oh, there're always plenty of tacks on the butts."

"So tell me about the rifle."

"The whole thing is, if I ever do have to shoot somebody—and I hope to hell I don't—then at least I know I can hit where I'm aiming with something that's going to knock him off his feet without killing him or hurting him too bad."

"And just how do you figure that?" Moyer asked.

"Well, I talked to a couple doctors about it, and they said—both of

60

them were hunters, too—they said a two-hundred-grain bullet from a 30.06 would knock any man off his feet no matter how big he was, especially from under a hundred yards. Then they showed me on an anatomy chart where the big veins and arteries were, and they both said that a bullet that size traveling that fast—well, here. Let's put these targets up, and I'll draw it for you."

They fixed four life-sized silhouette targets to the butts, and Balzic took out a pen and drew circles, using a half-dollar piece as a guide, on the shoulders. "There," he said. "That's about a half-inch from the outside of the shoulder and about a quarter-inch from the top of the shoulder. The nearest artery's about two inches away, and the nearest vein's a little less. But that's bone under there. That's right at the socket. I got it from two doctors, as I said. I hit anybody right there, he's going down, he's not going to be able to move that arm, and he's not going to die."

"Well now, Mario, that's just fine if the guy stands up nice and tall and gives you his word he's not going to move."

"Yeah, yeah. I know. That's what everybody says. Okay, I'll show you something." Balzic paced off twenty-five steps. "Would you say this is about the width of a two-way street with room for cars to park and for sidewalks?"

"That's about right," Moyer said.

"Okay," Balzic said. "Let him have it. You got six shots in that thirty-eight or five?"

"This one has six."

"Is that the one you carry?"

"No."

"Where's the one you carry? I'll bet it's one of those snub-nose jobs."

"Yeah, I do."

"Hell, you're as bad as some of my men. Go ahead. Use that one then. All six shots. He's just standing there, and he just promised you he wouldn't move. Go on. Start shooting."

Moyer scowled, then turned, dropped to one knee, held his revolver with two hands and fired six times.

"Damn," Balzic said, "that thing makes more noise than my rifle."

61

"In a pig's ass it does."

"That's your opinion. Well, let's see how many times you killed him."

They walked to the target and Balzic said: "No doubt about it. You're a killer all right. Look there. One got him right in the heart. Those two got him in the lungs, which means he's got maybe twenty minutes before he drowns in his own blood. That one's a real beauty—you got him right in the abdominal aorta and probably through the interior vena cava, which means he's got about ten, fifteen minutes before he bleeds to death, and even if you get him to a hospital in time to stop that, the slug probably hit him in the spine, which leaves him in a wheelchair. That one went through his stomach and a kidney. That's about twenty-to-one against him, and holy hell, Phil. Look at that one. You shot off the guy's pleasure."

"Very funny," Moyer said, frowning more deeply. "All right, doctor, let's see what you do with that piece of equipment you're so goddamn proud of."

They walked off the same distance, and Balzic loaded four rounds into the Springfield. "You got a second hand on your watch?"

"Yeah."

"Okay, time me. I'm going to shoot four times at the right shoulder on each profile. You ready?"

"I'm ready when you are."

Balzic planted his feet and fired, working the bolt, aiming, breathing, and firing in an even rhythm. "How long?" he asked when he'd fired the last round.

"Twenty-seven seconds."

"That's a little slow. But let's have a look."

When they got to the targets Moyer said, "You sonuvabitch, you must come out here every day of the week."

"Only two or three times a week, Phil," Balzic said, grinning broadly. "You want to try it from, oh, say, fifty yards?"

"You got to be kidding."

"Let's just try it. I'm really trying to prove a point here, you know that. Tell you what. You shoot from fifteen yards, and I'll shoot from fifty. How's that? Fair enough?"

62

"How much time do I get?"

"I'll give you a minute." Balzic stepped off fifteen yards. "When you're ready. Just shoot for the left shoulder."

"All four targets?"

"Sure. That's what I'm going to do. That's what I did."

Moyer grumbled something under his breath and then said he was ready. He went into a crouch, held his revolver with two hands, and fired.

"Forty-six seconds, Phil. That's not bad."

"Aw, go screw yourself," Moyer said as they walked toward the targets. He started grumbling again.

"One out of four's not bad, Phil. Not bad at all. I've seen guys come out here with a handgun and shoot one out of thirty. Don't forget, this is only paper, and he's not doing anything while you're taking almost a minute to hit him once out of four shots."

"You really like to lay it on when you make a point, don't you?"

"Yeah, I do. But only when I'm trying to make this point. But I'll skip the sarcasm. Give you my word, okay?"

Moyer nodded and then, to ease the moment, took a pen and circled the shots on or near both shoulders on all four targets. "Go ahead," he said as Balzic paced off fifty yards. "Just let me get clear."

Balzic loaded four more rounds into the rifle, turned and nodded to Moyer, and then began firing in the same steady rhythm he'd used before.

"I'll be damned," Moyer said when they inspected the targets.

"How long did it take me?"

"Thirty-one seconds," Moyer said, shaking his head.

"If you'll notice, Phil, each one of these is just a shade lower than my first ones were, but they're still on the socket, with plenty to spare."

"You do this three times a week?" Moyer said, as they walked back to their cars.

"I try to," Balzic said. "In all kinds of weather, in all kinds of light. I just want to be sure."

They reached the cars, and Balzic slid the Springfield into the case

63

hanging in his trunk. "I just wish I could be halfway sure about this other thing."

"About Andrasko?"

"What else? The only thing I'm sure about is, he's dead and somebody killed him, and now our district attorney is running his mouth about drugs again." Balzic started to laugh. "Though I'll admit, that part of it kind of tickles me."

"What do you have against him, Mario—I mean, has he ever done anything to you personally?"

"To me? Hell no. Unless you call that kind of thing he pulled last night personal. But that's really stretching it. No. I just don't like small men with big ambitions. They always wind up using a red herring to get where they want to go. With Weigh, it's drugs. He's going to talk himself right into Harrisburg on that pitch. Wait and see. I'll give him five, six years. 'Course by that time, he might have to dream up a new fish to say he knows how to catch."

"Well, Mario, you can't deny that drugs are on the increase."

"Aw, come on, Phil. For every drug bust you've made this year, I'll bet you've made twenty drunk drivers. Hell, Weigh's been in office a little more than a year now, and I don't know of one prosecution he's made involving a death connected in any way with heroin, never mind marijuana, and how many deaths have been caused by boozers behind a wheel? Fifteen? Sixteen? Hell, Phil, there've been eighty-four traffic deaths in this county this year, and I know for a fact that at least ten of them have been because somebody was drunk."

"Can't argue that."

"And where do those things wind up? I think three of them made it to the grand jury, and only one made it to trial. Then our hero blew that one."

"I remember that one very well," Moyer said.

"I know you do."

"Yeah. Second offense for that guy. Yeah, boy, that was the day I wanted to choke Weigh."

"So?" Balzic said, throwing up his hands. "What is all this stuff about drugs? Hell, he's too lazy to file a proper information over a surety of the peace—how the hell can I believe anything he says about drug abuse right here in old Rocksburg? He's the goddamn music man, is what he is. Ah, I've seen D.A.'s come and go. 'Least he's a little smoother than the last one."

Moyer started to howl. "Old Froggy. Jesus, somebody ought to write a book about him."

"Nobody'd believe it."

"Hey, you had to be around for this one. I heard about it, but I was on vacation then. Did Froggy really bust that Greek that runs the newspaper store on an obscenity?"

"Yes, he did. And everybody said he couldn't be that stupid. I mean, they knew a couple days before that he was going to do it, and nobody believed him."

"So he actually did it."

"Yeah. Walked right in there himself with the warrant. That was two weeks before the election. About the dirtiest thing the Greek had in there was the *National Enquirer,* and one block away is Janus's joint. Hell, he had to walk right by Janus's to serve the warrant on the Greek."

Moyer was roaring. "He really thought that Greek was backing Spagnos for judge?"

"No. He thought he was Spagnos's cousin."

"You're kidding."

"So help me."

Moyer laughed until tears ran down his cheeks. "I don't believe it," he sputtered.

"You better believe it. You know where old Froggy finished in that election."

"Who doesn't? Last out of five."

"Last out of five," Balzic said, smiling. "He couldn't have won that one with two million dollars."

"Didn't Spagnos finish third?"

"Yeah. But you know where most of Spagnos's money came from, don't you?"

"I heard. I also heard Spagnos didn't know anything about it, but I kind of doubt that."

65

"No. It's true. He didn't know anything about it until after. That's when he found out how much money the others got. All those plain envelopes full of tens and twenties. Jesus, they were practically floating around the county. But Spagnos really didn't know where it was coming from. Take my word for it. I've known Spagnos all my life, and if ever there was a guy who didn't believe in an organized book, it's him."

"Well, he's got to believe now."

"Jesus, they must've sent him over thirty thousand. But knowing him, it still wouldn't surprise me if he thought they all wanted him to win 'cause he had a pure heart and knew the law. They were just fed up with paying Froggy, and then, when Froggy busts the Greek, they knew they'd been paying a clown all those years, and they couldn't stand it. Jesus, he embarrased them."

"You tell that to most people, they'd never believe you," Moyer said, wiping his eyes on his sleeve.

"I'll tell you, I'll be the happiest guy around the day they legalize the book," Balzic said. "Then maybe goddamn judges and D.A.'s will get elected 'cause they know the law. Do you know, my mother to this day thinks I don't know she plays the numbers?"

"Honest to God?"

"Every day she calls Vinnie down at Muscotti's and gets her dime down."

"How old is she?"

"She'll be sixty-nine. But the best part is, she tells Vinnie to put her bill on my beer tab, and then she sneaks two dollars into my pants every time she gets her Social Security. She's been doing that for, hell, I don't know, must be twenty years. Long as I've run a tab down there."

"She ever hit?"

"Oh, yeah. That's when the real fun starts. She turns herself inside out with stories about where she got the extra fifty. One time she said she got it from a cousin with a guilty conscience in Italy. Another time she said it was an income tax refund. That was in July or something."

"Vinnie never lets on?"

"Oh, no. He thinks I think he's cheating me."

66

"You know what you ought to do?"

"What's that?"

"You ought to bring her down there some day, and I'll bust them both on a lottery charge. Be real serious about the whole thing."

"That might be pretty funny just to see their faces. Maybe we'll do it, soon as this thing's over."

"Yeah. There's that, isn't there? Think we ought to be going, don't you?"

"Guess so. Enough fun for today. Maybe I'll see you later on, Lieutenant."

"Okay, Mario," Moyer said, getting into his cruiser.

Balzic watched Moyer drive off, then closed his trunk, and stayed long enough to smoke another cigarette, listening, as he smoked, for the pheasants.

He drove back as slowly as he had come, knowing that sometime today, sooner or later, he would have to run into Weigh, and he wanted to put that off as long as he could.

Balzic parked in the lot in back of city hall instead of in the spot reserved for him on the side. He went in the back door and down the hall leading to the station. At the corner that opened onto the big rooms where the switchboard and teletypes were, Balzic stopped and listened. Sergeant Stramsky was trying to persuade somebody to take his complaint about garbage collection to the sanitation department on the second floor.

Balzic peeked around the corner and was much relieved to see that no one else was in the big room. He walked in and went through the swinging gate, nodding to Stramsky in passing, and continued to the rear of the room, where the coffee pot was. He poured himself a cup and waited for Stramsky to finish with the man, a stoop-shouldered fellow long past retirement, his face flushed with indignation.

"You don't understand me," the man said. "I want those nincompoops arrested."

"Yessir," Stramsky said. "I understand you, but I've told you twice already that you could do a lot better by going upstairs and talking it over with the people who run the department. I know

67

most of them. They're pretty nice people. I'm sure they'll try to get things straightened out for you."

"But those nincompoops spill my garbage all over the place, and last week they didn't even show up. I want them arrested."

"I'm sorry, sir, but your complaint isn't a criminal complaint. It's something that can probably be handled in five minutes if you'd just go upstairs and talk to the right people."

"You're the police, aren't you? You're supposed to arrest criminals, aren't you?"

"Yessir."

"Well, their service is worse than criminal, I tell you."

Balzic took his coffee to a phone and called upstairs.

"Sanitation Department," a woman said.

"This is Chief Balzic. We got a citizen here who wants to have somebody in your department arrested for bad service. How about sending somebody down to hear the gentleman out. I'm sure he wouldn't be here talking to us if he didn't have a legitimate complaint." Balzic turned his back to the elderly man and lowered his voice. "I think the reason he don't want to come up is, he's probably not allowed to walk up steps. Besides, if somebody came down instead of making him come up, that'd be enough right there to satisfy him."

"We'll see what we can do," the woman said and hung up.

Balzic stepped to the counter beside Stramsky. "Somebody'll be down in a few minutes to talk with you about your problem, sir, so why don't you have a seat while you're waiting?"

"I'll stand, thank you."

"Suit yourself. Like a cup of coffee?"

The man shook his head once. "Not allowed to drink coffee."

"I see," Balzic said, nudging Stramsky's elbow and walking back toward the coffee pot.

"Arrest the garbagemen, for crissake," Stramsky said.

"Aw, what the hell," Balzic said. "Got to give the old boy a chance to get in his licks, too, you know. Everybody else is pitching a bitch these days, so why not him? Be glad we ain't in New York or Berkeley."

"Don't think I ain't glad."

68

"So. There you are. Boy, is this coffee lousy. D'you make it?"

"You never complained before, dear," Stramsky said.

"Nothing tastes right today ever since I read the paper. Before we get interrupted, what did you come up with on the marriage thing?"

"Maryland said no record, and Virginia said they'd call back."

"Weigh been in again?"

"No," Stramsky said. "But I spoke too soon." He nodded toward the side door.

Weigh came through the swinging gate in the counter and said, "I'd like to speak with you, Mario. Alone."

"Certainly," Balzic said, setting down his coffee. "Let's go back here." He led Weigh into one of the interrogation cubicles in the rear of the big room and shut the door behind Weigh.

"Have a chair, Milt."

"Let's skip the amenities, Mario. Just tell me what the hell you think you're trying to pull?"

"You don't mind if I sit down, do you, Milt?" Balzic said, sitting in one of the three straight-backed chairs, so that the small table was between them.

"Sitting or standing makes no difference. I want an explanation."

"About last night, I take it, is what you mean."

"You know damn well what I mean. Cut the coy routine."

Balzic lit a cigarette. "You move too fast, Milt."

"That's it? That's all you have to say—I move too fast?"

"You talk too fast. You think too fast."

Weigh thrust his hands in his pockets and glared at the ceiling. He appeared to be counting ten silently. "You listen to this, Chief of Police Balzic, and you listen to it very carefully. You pull a stunt like that one again, and I'll file an information against you for malfeasance in office and violation of the public trust."

"Easy, Milt, easy. That's a two-way street you're on now."

"Of all the goddamn—who the hell do you think you're dealing with, Balzic? Some ridge runner from Fayette County that took a correspondence course in law. Dammit, man, I was Phi Beta Kappa at Cornell, and I studied law at Dickinson."

Balzic smiled in spite of himself. "I know who you are, Milt. But I know something else. Any time you or your boys make a bust and then expect me or my boys to do the pencil work for you, I'm going to do exactly what I did last night. And since we're in a warning match, I may as well tell you that you file an information against me for what you said, I'll file one against you for the same goddamn reason. And then we'll let a judge decide. You want to chance it?"

"Of all the petulant—" Weigh could not go on. The flesh between his brows and under his eyes was starting to go blotchy. "Mario," he said, stepping to the door of the cubicle and jerking it open, "I promise you, I won't forget this." He rushed out of the big room, sending the swinging gate bouncing and slamming the outside door.

When Balzic came out, Stramsky was directing the elderly man and somebody from Sanitation into another cubicle.

"Looks to me like our hero was a touch unhappy when he left," Stramsky said.

Balzic rubbed his chin. "Aw, the sonuvabitch wouldn't give me a chance to let him save some face. He just started threatening and promising. I can't handle that crap. So I threatened him back, and it was a standoff. Hell of a way to do things. But that's what happens when you go against a guy that won't sit down. I sat down. I sat down for him, but the dummy didn't even know what I was doing. Shit," Balzic said, picking up his cup and going for more coffee. He changed his mind and washed out the cup. "Vic, I'm going up the funeral home and pay my respects and have a look around."

"Which one is it?"

"Bruno's, I think. Maybe I ought to check with Father Marrazo. He took care of it."

Balzic paused in the middle of dialing the rectory. "That's one thing I always liked about Father Marrazo, you know that, Vic?"

"What's that?"

"I've known him for eight, nine years now, and he never once told me where he went to college."

Balzic hoped he would get to Bruno's Funeral Home before the family. He wanted a couple of minutes alone to say the things he thought he ought to say to what was left of John Andrasko. But

70

when he walked in and followed the tiny white arrows on the directory, he found the family already there.

The casket was closed. Mary Andrasko and her two younger children were kneeling before it. Another woman Balzic did not recognize was kneeling on the floor slightly behind and to the right of Mrs. Andrasko. Standing behind this woman and to her right, his hands folded behind his back, was Tommy Parilla.

The other woman got up as soon as she heard Balzic step into the room and came to his side. She was younger than Mary Andrasko, but the family resemblance was unmistakable.

"They'd like to be alone for a little while longer," the woman whispered.

"I understand," Balzic whispered. "But I hope it isn't for too long. I have to talk to her." He nodded toward Mary Andrasko.

"You can tell me," the woman said, and led Balzic outside to the parking lot.

"What I have to say, I really have to say to her," Balzic said.

"You can tell me. I'm her sister."

"I don't know why, but I just assumed she didn't have any relatives."

"Just me. I'm Angie. Who're you?"

"Mario Balzic. I'm chief of police here."

Angie took a small step backward. She was very dark-skinned and wore no makeup. Her long hair was pulled back under a black babushka. Dressed as she was, entirely in black except for her stockings, she gave the appearance of being of an earlier generation.

"Are you the one didn't tell her?" she said. "So she had to find out from the paper?"

"Yes. That's why I came so early. Or why I tried to. I wanted to apologize."

"What good do you think that's going to do? The damage is already done, Mr. Chief of Police."

"Look, Mrs.—"

"It's Miss."

"Spano?"

She nodded.

"Well, look, Miss Spano, I can understand why you're mad about this—"

"You think so, huh?"

Balzic squared himself. "Just a minute, Miss Spano. My first name is Mario. My mother's maiden name was Petraglia. So I know about courtesy. But what I'm trying to tell you is I never got a chance to tell her how it happened, and then I thought the priest told her. It turned out he thought I did, so that's how it happened she had to learn it the way she did. And that's why I came now. You can take that or leave it, but it's the truth."

She folded her arms and flushed slightly. "I'm sorry," she said.

"I didn't tell you that to make you say you're sorry."

"I know."

"All right. So then we understand."

She pursed her lips and took off her babushka and shook her hair. "I hate these places," she said.

"Yeah. They try to make you think what happened didn't happen. Well, not with John. I mean, with the casket closed."

"You called him by his first name. Did you know him?"

"Since I was a kid. I didn't know her, though. Your sister. I never saw her until I had to tell her. She's older than you?"

"Eight years. How did you know John?"

"I just knew him, that's all. Not really very well. I was sort of hoping now, maybe you could tell me more about both of them."

"John and Mary? Or John and Tami?"

"You knew Tami?"

"A lot better than I knew John. I moved from here ten years ago. I've only been back three or four times."

"What happened to Tami?"

"He left her."

"Just like that?"

"How else is there? You leave or you stay. When you leave, what can anybody say, except you left? You can put all the pretty words on it you want, it still comes down to the same thing. He left her."

"You know why?"

"What's to know? Tami was a regular bastard. When he was nice,

72

he was nice. When he wasn't, he was one of those rotten wops that
make you sick you're Italian. Then one day he just walked out, and
she never heard from him again."

"How did he leave?"

"How? He left. That's all. How many ways are there?"

"Yes, but this is important. If you could remember."

"My God, man, that was eleven, twelve years ago. I don't know.
One day she called me up and said he left. I didn't ask her how. I
was just glad he was gone. What did I care how?"

"How did she take it?"

"How could she? He stuck her with the kid. No money. After he
was gone for a week, she found out he hadn't paid the rent in six or
seven months. She moved in with me, and I supported them until
she found a job."

"How old was the boy then?"

"Well, he's seventeen now, so he must've been four or five then."

"Did you two—you and Mary—did you talk a lot about Tami? In
front of the boy I mean?"

"Sure. For a long time she wouldn't talk about anything else.
Every time I tried to talk about something else, she'd change the
subject back to him. That's the big reason I left. I got sick of hearing
about it.

"After she got back on her feet," Angie went on, "I mean as far as
the money went, I left. The son of a bitch made a pass at me once,
and then he slapped me when I wouldn't go for it. She doesn't know
about that, but every time she'd start talking about him, that's all I
could think about. She didn't have to tell me how rotten he was, but
after a while I started to feel guilty, you know? Like I had
something to do with him leaving her. Which was crap, because I
didn't. I couldn't stand to be around him before. Before he made the
pass I mean. After, well . . ."

"But the boy heard lots of talk," Balzic said.

"Sure he heard it. Didn't I just say so? I only had two rooms and a
bath. We all slept in the same room. How could he not hear it?
Anyway, that's history. What difference does it make?"

"Little pitchers have big ears, Miss Spano. I got two of my own, and the biggest education I ever got in my life was watching them get acquainted with the world. You never know how things you do or say affect them until you ask them about it. And some of the answers I used to get from my kids about some things I said really used to set me back. Still do. Let me give you an example.

"I know a family lives a couple blocks from here. They have a son who's allergic to all kinds of things, but especially animal fur. Dogs and cats. He's seven years old now, and as long as he can remember, his parents have been telling him to stay away from dogs and cats—they're bad for you and make it tough for you to breathe—stuff like that.

"So last year, we started getting complaints from people in this neighborhood about their pets getting killed. And not just killed. Mangled. Make a long story short, this kid was going around killing all the dogs and cats he could get his hands on. Six years old and a really bright kid. But in his head, all that talk from his parents about cats and dogs make it tough for him to breathe, well, he figures all he had to do is kill them all and his troubles are over. That's the kind of thing I'm talking about."

"Wait just a minute," Angie said. "If I understand you, what you're saying is Tommy—are you trying to tell me you think Tommy killed John?"

Balzic nodded and then shrugged, as though to apologize.

"But that's crazy. Because of what we said about Tami? But that was Tami. That wasn't John we were talking about back then. My God, she hadn't even met John then. She didn't meet him until about a year or so later."

"I know it sounds crazy," Balzic said. "But that's what I'm talking about. Whoever did it wasn't right. John wasn't robbed. But he was beaten so bad I didn't even know who he was. I had to be told. I mean his face—well, never mind. I didn't recognize him, that's enough."

"Oh, my God, I don't believe I'm hearing this. But wait a minute. If you know this or if you think you know this, how come you don't arrest him?"

"In the first place, I don't know. I'm just guessing. In the second place, even if I did know it, I can't prove it, and in the third place, even if I could prove it, I wouldn't arrest him. Not now."

"Why not?"

"Because I made one mistake with your sister. And I'm not about to make another. When I do—if I do—I'm going to make sure there's a doctor, a lawyer, and a priest standing right there beside me. But to tell you the truth, I can't do anything until I get something solid to go on."

"God," Angie said, chewing her lips, "I used to feel guilty because that creep made a pass at me. Now this. You know what you're telling me, don't you?"

Balzic nodded.

"You're telling me that me and Mary—our big mouths—are the cause of all this. And you're telling me that the kid is so screwed up he wasn't killing John at all. Isn't it?"

"That's the idea. That's why I wanted to know if you could remember how Tami left. If you'd told me he left on a train, I'd be willing to bet a hundred to one the kid did it."

"Well you just go to hell, mister," Angie said. "You're not sticking me with this thing. The rest was bad enough. It took me five years to get over that. So you just go straight to hell." She brushed past him and ran into the funeral home.

"Dummy," Balzic said, blowing out a sigh. Then he kicked at a leaf and said it again.

"S'matter, mister? My aunt make you mad?"

Balzic jumped. He had not heard the boy coming.

"Hey," Tommy Parilla said, "aren't you the chief of police, the one that told my mother?"

Balzic nodded. "That's me." He looked directly at the boy. "And I'm the one that didn't tell her how it happened."

"Is that why my aunt was mad?"

"Yes. She had a right to be."

"She makes everybody mad, and she gets mad at everybody," Tommy said, shoving his hands into his pockets and looking at the sky. "Say, you wouldn't have a cigarette on you, would you?"

"Yeah," Balzic said, fishing in his pockets for his pack. "I keep trying to put them in different pockets so I'll have to think whether I want one or not. It's a lousy habit, Tommy. You shouldn't have started."

"That's what John used to say," Tommy said, taking the pack from Balzic, taking a cigarette out, and handing the pack back. He refused Balzic's offer of a light. "I got a lighter. Zippo. Best little lighter made. Got a lifetime guarantee."

Balzic watched the boy light his smoke and then said, "You don't seem to be too upset about all this."

"About John? Why should I? I didn't like him." Tommy took several deep drags on his cigarette and tried to blow a smoke ring.

"Did you get along with him?"

"I didn't see him that much. In the daytime he was always working around the place, and I'd be in school. Then when I'd get home from school, he'd go to sleep. Then he'd get up around ten, ten-thirty, and go to work. The last three summers I worked, so I didn't see him that much."

"Where'd you work?"

"Out the Blue Pine Driving Range. All day and half the night."

"I take it you didn't help around the farm."

Tommy shook his head. "Nah. I didn't like that. Only thing I ever help with is the canning. I always help my mother with that. But that stuff with planting and running the cultivator—you can have it."

"Is that why you didn't like John?"

Tommy shook his head. "What difference would that make? Lotsa people do stuff I don't like, I could care less. I didn't like him 'cause he wouldn't marry my mother."

"He wouldn't do what?"

"I said he wouldn't marry my mother. They were always having arguments about it. I thought that was the least he could do. But I gave up on him a long time ago. I never said nothing to him about it, but it made me mad."

Balzic blew out another sigh. He tried to read the boy's face. It seemed incapable of pretending. Finally Balzic said, "Well, you know, Tommy, they were married."

"What—what are you talking about?"

76

"Just what I said. They were married. Just as married as if a priest or a justice of the peace married them."

"I don't believe you."

"Well, there's a thing called common law marriage. If a man and woman live together for a couple of years in this state, and they call themselves mister and missus, the law says they're married, and the law treats their marriage the same as any other."

"I don't believe you," Tommy repeated, rolling the cigarette between his thumb and forefinger.

"Believe it or don't. All you have to do is call up any lawyer."

"Well, how come my mother didn't know about that? How come she was always fighting and arguing with him about it?"

"I don't know," Balzic said, "but I can guess. Probably for a long time she was embarrassed about it. I mean what the law is and what social custom is are two different things. There are lots of people who don't give a damn about social custom, but apparently, from what you say, your mother wasn't one of them. I guess it could be pretty embarrassing to a woman to live with a man all that time and think that maybe other people are thinking that what she's doing isn't the right thing, if you get what I mean."

"I still don't believe you," Tommy said, dropping the cigarette on the macadam and crushing it out with his heel. "But I'm going to call a lawyer, all right."

"Good idea. Then you can be sure. Just remember where you heard it first."

"Why? You think you did me a big favor or something?"

"No. I just told you the truth, that's all."

"Boy, you sound more and more like John. He was always walking around telling me stuff like that. 'Honesty is the best policy.' 'Don't take any handouts.' 'If you don't take care of yourself, nobody will.' You and him must've had the same teacher or something."

"As a matter of fact, we did."

"What?"

"I said we did. I went all through school with John. We had a lot of subjects together."

"Did *you* like him?"

77

"I didn't have any reason not to. But then, I didn't have to live with him."

"That's for sure." Tommy looked squarely at Balzic and for a second looked as though he was going to say something else, something Balzic hoped would be significant, but he didn't.

Balzic waited a moment longer and then said, "Think we better be getting back inside. I still haven't told your mother what I came to tell her. You going in?"

"Nah," Tommy said. "Think I'll stay out here for a while. I don't like the way it smells in there."

"All right. See you again sometime," Balzic said, walking away.

"Yeah, sure," Tommy said, spitting between his teeth.

Inside the door, Balzic stopped far enough away from the window to be sure he couldn't be seen and watched the boy in the parking lot. But the boy did nothing. He just stood there with his hands jammed in his pockets, spitting every so often, and looking either at the sky or at the cars and trucks going by on Market Street. If Tommy was disturbed by anything Balzic had said, he gave no indication of it.

Balzic stood a minute longer, waiting for some sign, some gesture, with which to feed a conviction that Tommy had killed John Andrasko. He got none. Worse, everything the boy had said and the way he'd looked when he'd said it, made Balzic begin to doubt everything he'd thought about the reasons the boy would have had to kill Andrasko.

On the other hand, everything Angie Spano had said about the boy's early years fitted perfectly. It was all there: the loss of the real father, the sense of rejection, the feeling of abandonment, the constant harping by the mother about the father—everything, in short, to convince Balzic that the boy was not killing John at all when he'd beaten him to death, that he had been killing his blood father who, in all likelihood, he could not consciously remember.

Yet there the boy stood, having just given Balzic every reason for believing that he was aware who John was. How then was it possible for him to confuse John with his real father? More importantly, Balzic thought with a growing sense of frustration, how was the boy able to act as he was now? Especially when he had a perfectly clear reason for hating John just as John was? It made no sense. Balzic knew he couldn't have it both ways: either what Angie Spano said was right and the boy had killed someone who had come in his mind to stand for his blood father, or—or what, Balzic asked himself. Or the boy killed John because he wouldn't marry the boy's mother? No way, Balzic thought. He would never have said the things he'd just said.

As he walked back into the room where the rest of John Andrasko's family waited, Balzic kept trying to interpret something in the boy's words and manner to keep his conviction alive. It was useless. He had the dizzying feeling that unless somebody came up with solid evidence, the chances were doubling by the hour against proving the boy did it.

Balzic approached Mary Andrasko. She sat in the front row of straight-backed chairs with her son on her right and her daugher on her left. Their eyes were raw, and they breathed through their mouths. Two chairs away sat Angie Spano, her face rigid.

Balzic had to stand in front of Mary Andrasko because she wouldn't look at him. He knew that Angie had told her why he'd come. He hoped she had not told her the rest.

"Mrs. Andrasko," Balzic said, "I came here to apologize. I'm not going to make any excuses. I should have told you."

"All right," she said, her eyes fixed on the coffin. "Now you said you're sorry. Just go away now."

"Mrs. Andrasko—"

"Please just go away now," she said, her eyes filling with tears.

Balzic gave a slight nod. "I'm sorry," he said and walked quickly to the back of the room where he turned toward the coffin and, without kneeling, crossed himself and prayed for the soul of John Andrasko. He crossed himself again and left.

Out in the parking lot, he stopped to light a cigarette and was almost to his car before he noticed that Tommy wasn't where he'd been. Balzic looked around but couldn't see the boy anywhere. He sat in the car thinking a dozen contradictory and conflicting thoughts and then drove to St. Malachy's rectory.

Father Marrazo was in his office typing.

"Don't get up, Father," Balzic said. "Just tell me where the wine is. I need a little something."

"It's right here," Father Marrazo said, turning on his swivel chair and reaching into the bottom drawer of his desk. "The glasses are in the bathroom."

"Want some, Father?"

"Not right now. I want to hear what's caused your aggravation, though."

Balzic got a glass and filled it. Capping the bottle and holding the glass aloft to look at the wine in the light coming from a window behind the priest, he said, "Father, I just made an ass of myself all around. I don't know how many more ways I could've done it today. Something tells me there aren't any other ways."

"You're too abstract, Mario. Concrete problems must be solved concretely."

"You must be working on tomorrow's homily, Father."

"Ah, that's how it goes when you have a one-track mind like mine." Father Marrazo smiled. "But it's not a bad idea, don't you agree?"

"Yeah. I guess. Well. To put them in a row, I made a mess with the D.A., I made a mess with Mary Andrasko's sister, I made a mess with Tommy Parilla, and I really did a job with Mary Andrasko."

"By mess, do you mean you've alienated all of them?"

"That's a fancy word, Father, but I guess that's what I did."

"You learned nothing useful?"

"Oh, I learned a lot. I learned that Tami Parilla just took off one day when Tommy was about four or five. I learned he made a pass at his sister-in-law. I learned that Mary and her sister lived together for a year or so after Tami took off and that they talked almost constantly about Tami in front of the boy. And I learned from Tommy that he didn't like John—are you ready, Father?—he didn't like John because John wouldn't marry his mother."

Father Marrazo's eyebrows shot up and his mouth looked as though he had just mistaken a lemon for an orange.

"Yeah, Father. And when you get that much information and then you manage to turn off your sources all in one hour, well . . ."

"Why are you so sure you've turned off the sources?"

"Take my word for it. I managed to say all the wrong things at exactly the right times. I won't get anything out of the sister anymore. I blew that one about as bad as you can blow it. As far as Mrs. Andrasko goes, well, it'll be a miracle if she tells me which way up is. As for Milt Weigh, he's looking for an excuse to make fried ass out of me. And then there's Tommy. That kid is either the best actor I've ever seen, or else he's the sickest. All I managed with him was to plant one little seed. One lousy little seed. To tell you the truth, Father, I handled myself today as though I didn't know anything about people. Nothing."

Balzic drank his wine and then held up the bottle and looked imploringly at the priest. Father Marrazo waved for him to fill his glass, and then went to the bathroom to get a glass for himself.

"Tell me, Mario," Father Marrazo said when he returned, "This seed you planted in Tommy. What was that?"

"I just told him that legally his mother was married to John. And that was the only time I got something besides indifference out of him. But you see what's wrong with that."

"No. I can't say that I do."

"Well, Father, let me put it this way. If he gets guilty about that, it means he's not sick at all. Or not in the way I figured he was. The way I got it figured, he did it, but he didn't know he was doing it. Or even if he knew he was doing it, he wasn't really doing it to John. John getting killed was just incidental—or at least that was the way I had it figured."

"What makes you doubt it now?"

"The way it bothered him when I told him about John and his mother being as married as anybody else. He said two or three times he didn't believe me. It was as though he had to keep believing they were the way they'd always been."

"If I understand you, Mario, what you're saying is that he would have been unconcerned about whether they were married if he had, in fact, killed John in the belief he was killing Tami."

"Something like that, Father."

"I suppose it would be no comfort at all for me to remind you that the rationalizations of psychopaths are often extremely well conceived and at times even brilliant—would that offer no consolation?"

"Yeah. I've thought about that. That's why I said he's either the best actor or the sickest. But that's not what's really bothering me now, Father. What's really eating me now is we don't have anything on him. Nothing. And I don't think we're going to get anything, either. And that leaves me with a very unpleasant thought."

"Which is?"

"I hate to even think about it, Father, but unless somebody else gets killed, it's all over."

"By that, you mean under nearly identical circumstances."

"Not necessarily identical. But they'll have to be similar as hell, Father."

"Yes, I see. But then, the circumstances of hell are always similar, aren't they?" Father Marrazo filled their glasses again and then frowned at the nearly empty bottle. "I hope Mr. Ferrara comes today. Ah, but what a foolish hope that is. He always comes on Sundays."

"Would you like me to get something for you at the state store?"

"No, Mario—oh, what's the use? My mouth says no, and my face gives me away. Of course. If it isn't out of your way. Here, let me get some money."

Balzic was already at the door. "Forget it, Father. I'm buying." He left then, walking quickly because he didn't want the priest to catch up with him to force the money on him.

After Balzic bought a half-gallon of California Mountain Red at the state store, he stopped in the courthouse to see Bill Joyce.

"Mario," Joyce said. "How goes it?"

"The same," Balzic said in Italian. "You come up with anything?"

"Yes. Much sooner than I expected, too."

"Such as?"

"About Andrasko, he had a top rating from the local credit bureau, had insurance policies at Knox Steel for life, major medical, and hospitalization. He also had a five-thousand-dollar policy on himself and on his wife and two-thousand-dollar policies on the three kids, all with Prudential. He had the farm mortgaged with Knox Savings and Loan and insurance that guarantees payment in full. He would've paid it off in six more years, anyway. The truck was his unencumbered, and he had seven payments to make on a Ford sedan, with insurance on that guaranteeing payment as well. The only time he missed payments on anything was during a three-month period back in sixty-two when Knox was on strike."

"Solid citizen, huh?"

"Down the line."

"What about Tami Parilla?"

"Just as easy. He holds an able-bodied-seaman's card issued in San Francisco in 1959, and since sixty-one he's been working regularly out of Seattle on ships leased to the U. S. government, moving matériel to Vietnam. No indication of any activity even slightly questionable."

"Anything about his family life?"

"The only thing of interest to you is that the government insurance issued to him and the policy he carries through the union both list Mary Frances Spano Parilla and Thomas John Parilla as beneficiaries, in that order."

"Any idea where he is now?"

"Yes," Joyce said, picking up another piece of paper. "Right now he is aboard the U.S.S. *Mondeville* in Manila Harbor, and he's been on it since it left Seattle seventeen days ago."

"Well, that takes care of that."

"I couldn't get anything out of Missing Persons about him. If anybody cared about him leaving Rocksburg, they didn't care enough to ask for a search. And as far as Andrasko's marriage went, well, I didn't press that because your man Stramsky called about an hour ago looking for you, and he said that both Virginia and Maryland replied negative."

"Yeah. I know that. Fact is, they weren't married. It was common law."

"Where'd you learn that?"

"From right next to the horse's mouth. The kid told me. Said his mother was always arguing with John about marrying her, but apparently John wouldn't. Well, he didn't, anyway. What his reasons were I don't know yet, but I'm not sure it's all that important. All I know is the kid didn't like it and didn't like John because of it."

"The kid tell you that?"

"Yup. Matter of fact as all hell. Wasn't the least bit shy about it. Shook him up a little bit, though, when I told him that legally they were married. I can't figure just how much it did shake him. But we'll see. One way or another."

"Anything else I can do for you?"

"Nothing I can think of, Bill. You got what I needed a damn sight faster than I could've. Thanks." Balzic stood and headed for the door.

"Does it help?"

"Well, it narrows things down. And it hasn't changed my mind about anything."

"You think it's the boy."

"Yeah. But put it this way. Even if it isn't the kid, it had to be somebody with a grudge, which means it had to be somebody who knew him. I haven't read the coroner's report yet, but I'm betting that any bruises John had on the back of his head came from bouncing off the platform. And nobody heard anything."

"So he was facing whoever it was and there was no shouting beforehand, is that the way you figure it?"

"How else? Which also leads me to believe that if there was a grudge, John wasn't aware of it, and that's what keeps me thinking it was the kid. But hell," Balzic said, "I might be making the whole thing too complicated. My first thought when I went out to tell the wife and then the kid showed with the car—I thought, hell, it's probably nothing more than an argument over the car. I still don't know where the kid was last night. When he took the car, whether he had permission, where he went—I don't know. All I know is what time he came home in it. The rest, well, you know—that's where we wear out the rubber. I'll see you, Bill, and thanks again."

"Anytime," Joyce said, picking up a phone that had started ringing.

Balzic went down the back stairs and to his car, drove to St. Malachy's rectory to drop off the wine for Father Marrazo, and then went on to his home.

He found his daughters in the living room on the floor, eating popcorn and watching *Dick Clark's American Bandstand*.

"Hi, group," Balzic said, loosening his tie and dropping into the recliner. He got no answer. "Hey," he said, leaning forward, "some guy just walked in and said something to you two. I think it was hello."

"Oh, hi, Daddy," Emily said.

"What's with your friend there—she lose her voice cheering for Rocksburg's lost cause last night?"

"No, Daddy, I didn't lose my voice," Marie said.

"Well, then. Do you think you might trouble yourself to speak to me? Frankie Avalon I'm not, but—"

"Oh, Daddy. Frankie Avalon's ancient history."

"Ex-cuse me. Who's this guy?"

"Tony Joe White," Emily said.

"Guitar, mouth organ, jeez," Balzic said. "All he needs is a couple cymbals on his knees and a bass drum and he's a regular one-man band. What's he singing about? What's that he's saying—pork salad? What's that?"

"That's poke salad, Daddy," Emily said.

"It is not. It's polk with an 'l,' " Marie said. "P-o-l-k."

"Poke, polk—what is it?"

"That's something that grows in Louisiana."

"Does he eat it or smoke it?"

"He eats it," Emily said. "It's a small plant that has berries on it, and people make dye from the berries, and they eat the roots, and it's spelled p-o-k-e."

"Just where did you hear anything so dumb?" Marie said.

"I looked it up, that's where. Nyahhhh."

"I still say it's with an l."

"I'll say one thing for him," Balzic said. "He's sure no virtuoso on that mouth organ."

"That's a harmonica, Daddy," Emily said.

"Do you two mind?" Marie said. "I would like to hear *some* of him."

"Yeah, Emily. Keep quiet. Can't you see the girl's intoxicated?"

"Daddy!"

"Speaking of that," Balzic said to himself, "I wonder if we got any beer left." He got up and went into the kitchen. When he came back with the last cold beer a commercial was on.

"See what happened because of you two?" Marie said. "I didn't get to hear half of him."

"Why don't you go buy the record?" Balzic said.

"'Cause she used up practically all her allowance last Tuesday, that's why," Emily said.

"Big mouth."

"All right. That's enough of that. You're both getting a little too salty."

"Well, she didn't have to tell you that," Marie said.

"It's true," Emily said. "Why shouldn't I say it?"

"And I said that's enough, Emily. Marie, you want to buy the record?"

"I did use up my allowance."

Balzic reached in his pocket and fished out two dollar bills. He handed one to Marie and the other to Emily. "Okay. So now you can both buy a record."

"Thanks, Daddy," both said.

"All I ask is you don't buy any headache makers, fair enough?"

They promised they wouldn't.

"By the way, either of you two know Tommy Parilla?"

Marie shook her head no, but Emily said, "You do so know him. You danced with him a couple of weeks ago. At the P.T.A. dance."

"Oh, him. Yuk."

"What's that mean?"

"Yuk, that's all. Just yuk."

"Come on. Use words that mean something," Balzic said.

"Oh, he's got pimples all over, and he thinks he's really cool."

"You should've heard her two weeks ago," Emily said.

"You keep quiet!"

86

"All right, you two. What else do you know about him?"

"Oh-oh," Emily said. "What did he do, Daddy?"

"Never mind. Just tell me what you know about him."

"Like what?" Marie said.

"Like anything. Anything you can think of."

"Well, he has to dance with sophomores, and he's a senior," Emily said.

"So? That's nothing. Your mother was a freshman when I was a senior."

"Did you dance with her?"

"Certainly I danced with her. But never mind about that. I want to know about Tommy."

"He doesn't wash his hair very often, I can tell you that," Marie said.

"Come on. Be serious."

"Well, you're asking me what I know about him, and I'm trying to tell you, Daddy. He puts some kind of goop on his hair, and—"

"What else? Skip the hair business."

"Well, he bragged the whole time I was dancing with him."

"About what?"

"About how fast he drives."

"About anything else?"

"No. But I really wasn't paying much attention to him."

"Ha! Get a load of her," Emily said.

"I'm going to belt you one—"

"Knock it off," Balzic said. "Look, Marie, I'm not trying to spy in your private life. But I'm not asking like your father—you understand?"

"You still haven't told us what he did," Emily said.

"As far as I know, he hasn't done anything. I'm trying to find out if he's capable, and you two aren't helping much. Think a little bit, Marie. What else did he brag about?"

"He said he didn't take any crap from anybody, and—and, well, he said if I'd go for a ride with him, he'd show me a better time than any football player could."

"Were you dancing with a football player earlier that night?"

"With a couple of them," Emily said.

"Emily, I swear—"

"Marie, did you ever talk to him before?"

"Oh, sure. He's always talking to all the girls. But nobody talks back. Nobody can stand him. I danced with him that night because I felt sorry for him. Everybody was turning him down all over the place. But the longer we danced—well, it was funny. I mean, I just kept feeling sorrier and sorrier for him, but at the same time I just wanted to get away from him. I mean, I knew why everybody wouldn't dance with him, but then I wished I hadn't danced with him. And then I thought if he'd just wash his hair and do something about his acne he'd be kind of cute—if he'd just quit bragging about how cool he was. He was really a good dancer."

"Yeah," Emily said. "Better than anybody at that dance. Of course Billy Francis wasn't there. And neither was Bobby Ceretti."

"Have you talked to him since?"

"Uh-huh. Couple of times. But since then I've been trying to avoid him."

"Why? Did he say something?"

"No. Just the same routine about showing me a better time than any football player. He feels so inferior, and it's so obvious, but he really got mad when I told him."

"Told him what?"

"I told him he ought to give himself a chance to be nice once in a while and that he didn't have to be bragging all the time. Wow, did he ever get mad."

"Mad enough to look like he was going to take a swing at you?"

"Yeah, boy, did he ever. I really got scared for a minute, but then he got up and left."

"Where was that?"

"In the cafeteria. About a week ago. Last Monday, I think."

"You talked to him since?"

"Uh-uh."

"You have so," Emily said. "You talked to him last night. When we went to get a hot dog."

"Oh that. I just said hi to him, that's all."

88

"You sure that's all you said?"

"Well, not exactly. He gave me the same routine about a better time and all that, and he said he had his car."

"When was that?"

"That was at half-time."

"And you told him no?"

Marie shook her head yes.

"How did he take it?"

"He—he told me to go to hell. He said he could find lots of girls, and I felt rotten because I know he can't."

"Did you see him after that?"

"When we went back to our seats, he followed us and sat right behind us," Emily said.

"But then he left," Marie said.

"When?"

"I don't know exactly."

"It was the beginning of the fourth quarter. Right after the score was forty to six. Lots of people left then," Emily said.

"You see him leave the stadium?"

"Well, no. But he left and was walking toward the gate with everybody else who was leaving then. But I didn't see him go out, I mean I wasn't watching him. I just saw him go past us."

"How about you, Emily? You see him leave the stadium?"

"Uh-uh. I was just glad he wasn't behind us anymore."

"Beginning of the fourth quarter. That'd be about nine-fifteen or so, wouldn't you say? Had to be, 'cause traffic really started backing up about nine-thirty. Okay, group, thanks."

"What did he do, Daddy? You still haven't told us."

"Wrong. I told you twice he hasn't done anything as far as I know."

"Oh, Daddy," Emily groaned, "you never tell us anything."

"You got it, kid. I wouldn't last very long in my business if I went around telling everything I know to everybody who asked, now would I?"

"We're not just everybody," Marie said.

"I'll buy that, and as soon as I know something, I give you my word you'll be about the tenth or twelfth persons to know. How's that?"

Emily groaned again and buried her face in her arms. Marie rolled on her side and propped her head on her fist as the dance contest started on Dick Clark's show.

Balzic went into the kitchen to finsh his beer and stood by the table, hoping he was wrong about what he was thinking.

Balzic could not sleep. He tried for a time on the bed beside Ruth, and then on the recliner in the living room, and finally on the living room floor. It did not matter where; the moment he closed his eyes he saw Tommy Parilla telling Marie to go to hell and then smashing her face with a Coke bottle. At three o'clock he stopped prowling around the house, dressed, and drove to Muscotti's.

The bar was empty save for Vinnie, who was wiping the coolers behind the bar.

"You closed, Vinnie?"

"Am I closed? What the hell kind of question is that? Crissake, you know the law. I was closed an hour ago. Who's open?"

"I mean are you getting ready to go home, or can I have a beer?"

"Yeah."

"Yeah, what?"

"Yeah, I'm getting ready to go home, and yeah, you can have a beer. How's that suit you?" Vinnie poured a draught. "You paying or you charging?"

"Charging. Anybody in the back?"

"Yeah, they're playing. Nine or ten guys back there. They might even have two games. Before, they had just one. Kokomo they was playing, but now I think they got two games. Go back and see. What do I know about what goes on back there—I'm just a bartender."

"Oh-huh," Balzic said under his breath, "and the Pope's just a Catholic." He picked up his beer and walked down the narrow hall to the door beyond the men's room. He went in and drew up a chair behind one of the two tables and straddled it.

A stud game was in progress at the nearest table; the other table was going with Kokomo. Balzic watched one hand before he noticed Father Marrazo sitting with his back turned, directly in front of him. As many times as Balzic had see the priest in street clothes, the sight always put him off momentarily. He slid his chair closer and said, "How're you doing?"

"Terrible," the priest said barely opening his mouth. Then he threw in his hand and turned. "Oh, Mario. It's you. I wondered who was asking me. What brings you?"

"Couldn't sleep."

"Well, you've come to the right place. This nest of insomniacs beckons us all," Father Marrazo said and then smiled. "Hey, that's pretty good, don't you think? I'll have to think of a way to use that. Can't use it tomorrow, but another time perhaps."

"You really doing lousy?"

"Oh, only fair-lousy. Not lousy-lousy. I'm getting close to my time limit anyway. It's not three-thirty yet, is it?"

Balzic looked at his watch. "You got five minutes."

The priest nodded. "Last hand, men," he said to the other players.

"Last hand," one of the other players said. "Listen to him. Takes all the money, and then it's 'last hand, men.' "

"Frank has a bad habit of exaggerating," Father Marrazo said to Balzic. "Did you ever notice?"

"This is going to be interesting," Frank said, dealing the first two cards. "A priest asking a cop. Go ahead, Balzic, tell him."

"He's too polite," Balzic said. "He calls it exaggerating."

"You'd call it something else, right?" Frank said.

"Right," Balzic said, looking at the up card, a four, in front of Father Marrazo and the corner of the down card as the priest turned it up. It was also a four.

"Ace bets," Frank said.

The player to his left with the ace said, "Check."

Everybody checked with him.

The next round of cards showed no obvious improvement in any of the hands. The player with the ace checked again, and everybody checked along with him.

91

In the next round, the player with the ace got another, Father Marrazo got his third four, and Frank, the dealer, got another three to go with one he had showing.

"Pair of aces bets two-fifty."

"Call and raise five," Father Marrazo said.

The two players between the priest and Frank dropped.

"Your bet, Frank," the player with the aces said.

"I know it's my bet. I learned the rules this afternoon. Read a book on them." Frank studied the pair of fours in front of Father Marrazo and the pair of aces on his left. "I'm out," he said.

"Your five, Father, and ten back at you," the player with the aces said.

"Hum," Father Marrazo said. "I think I'll just call," he said, laying a twenty in the pot and taking a ten out.

"Last card," Frank said and dealt a five to the player with the aces and a queen to the priest.

"Twenty," said the player with the aces.

Father Marrazo sighed. "I am obliged to call, but something tells me . . ."

"Should've saved your money, Father," the player with the aces said. He turned up his hole card.

"Well," Father Marrazo said, looking at the third ace, "that is the way it isn't done." He pushed back his chair, picked up the bills and change in front of him, and put on his raincoat. "Good night, men. I hope I'll see some of you tomorrow morning." He led Balzic out to the bar and took a stool.

"Vinnie must've gone home," Balzic said, "or else he's in the can. Want a beer, Father?"

The priest nodded and Balzic got two bottles from one of the coolers.

"Now why didn't I believe him when he raised me ten?" Father Marazzo said.

"You want an answer, or you just thinking out loud?"

"Just thinking, I suppose, That's the way I played tonight. I'd play very well for a while, and then suddenly I'd have a lapse like that. I should've known immediately from the raise after he'd been checking like that that he had the ace underneath. Why do I do that?"

"You come out ahead?"

"Oh, of course. I can't remember the last time I lost, but it's as though I have some subconscious limit for winning. It must be my conscience."

Balzic laughed. "You serious?"

"I don't know. Am I? I must be. You know, tonight I was ahead at one point, oh I can't say for certain, but I must have been over a hundred dollars ahead. And what do I have now—I started with twenty-five and, let's see, there's forty, forty-one, forty-two, forty-seven-fifty. Twenty-two dollars and fifty cents. Do you know that the most I've ever won here, and I've been playing here now for eight, nine years, longer, almost ten years, and the most I've ever won is thirty-four dollars. And that night at one point I was over two hundred dollars ahead."

"At least you don't lose," Balzic said. "Tell me, Father, just what do you do with these winnings you take out of here—what is it? Twice a week?"

"That, my friend, is none of your business. Drink your beer, and tell me why you couldn't sleep."

"Bad dream," Balzic said, sloshing his beer around in his glass. "You know anything about dreams?"

"Some. Enough to know that only experts and fools dare to interpret them, and I'm more fool than expert."

"Well, it wasn't a dream really. I mean I wasn't asleep. You'd have to be asleep to have something you could call a dream, wouldn't you?"

"That is something only a very clear-talking psychiatrist could say, and I must say I've met very few of them in my life. What about day dreams, so-called? Or any flight of the imagination? When is one a dream, and when is it a hallucination, and so forth? I'm certain that somebody somewhere has troubled himself to try to define these things, but I haven't read them, and something tells me I wouldn't understand them even if I had. All I can do is offer the consolation that nearly everyone I know suffers from unpleasant thoughts

93

whether awake, asleep, or in any degree of consciousness. Was it about someone in your family?"

"For somebody who claims to be no expert, you're pretty good at guessing."

"No," Father Marrazo said. "That's just the usual pattern of these things, that's all. When we have dreams we don't even begin to understand, we generally dismiss them. But when we have the ones about those we are close to, again whether awake or asleep makes no difference, that's when we start worrying about ourselves, or at least that's been my experience in trying to deal with it when some of my parishioners come to me with the problem."

"Nobody ever comes to you about dreams he just plain doesn't understand? They only come when it's about something bad happening to somebody they're close to?"

Father Marrazo nodded. "And you'd have to admit that it would be naive to assume that those were the only kinds of dreams they had, but that's the only kind they tell me about. To narrow the thing down even more, generally the only time this comes up is when there's been a very superficial article about dreams in the slick sections of the Sunday papers. You know the kind of thing—'your dreams and what they reveal'—articles like that. I dread seeing those things, because by Wednesday I'll get a dozen calls from people who just have to talk to somebody. And when they get into my office, these poor people, all they want is to be told they're not crazy.

"In other words, Mario, what I'm trying to say is, forget about your dream. Admit you can't sleep, and do what you have to do about that. Stay awake as you're doing. Drink, if that helps, but don't worry about your dream. You only compound the problem, and not being able to sleep is problem enough for any man."

"Well, I would forget the dream, Father, but this one's a little different."

The priest started to ask how but changed his mind and waited.

Balzic rubbed his forehead for a moment. Then he said, "First, you have to know that Tommy Parilla has been trying to get my daughter to go out with him."

"Marie?"

"Yeah. Then you have to know that the last time he tried was at the football game on Friday night, and when she wouldn't, he told her to go to hell. There's more to it than that, but that's enough."

"That isn't your dream?"

"No, no. That's fact. The dream is Tommy telling Marie to go to hell and then smashing her face with a Coke bottle. That's the thing I saw every time I closed my eyes tonight."

"Well, I said before that only experts and fools dare interpret things like this, but, Mario, this is so obvious I'm wondering why you haven't figured it out yourself."

"May be obvious to you, Father, but not to me. I mean there was something pretty obvious about it to me, but from the look on your face, something tells me what you think is obvious and what I think is obvious are two pretty different things."

"Yes. Well. Tell me what was obvious to you."

"Aw, come on now, Father. I mean what do you think would be obvious to me? What else? I saw my daughter getting hurt."

"What else?"

"Whatta you mean, what else? Isn't that enough?"

"No, my friend. You're talking only as a father now, or rather, as the father you like to think you are. You have a dream such as you describe, and then you forget everything you've been saying about Tommy Parilla."

"Keep going. I'm listening."

"I wonder whether I should," Father Marrazo said.

"Well, don't stop now. I mean, what the hell. You give me this stuff about me being the father I like to think I am, and then you're going to hang it right there?"

"All right, Mario. As the father you like to think you are, you see your daughter in the place of someone else someone who was horribly beaten. Killed.

"But the fact remains that if this were true, if your daughter were in danger, then everything you've said about the reasons for John Andrasko's murder would be completely false."

95

"I don't follow you, Father."

"Yes, you do. What you mean is that right now you don't want to."

"Okay, then you explain it to me. I'll listen."

"You're daring me now, Mario, and I don't like to find myself on the other side of dares."

"Well, what do I have to say?"

"It's not what you say now. It's the way you're looking at me, and the tone of your voice—that's what's making me hesitate now."

"So forget my tone."

Father Marrazo took a swallow of beer and let it go down his throat slowly. "All right, Mario. What you saw in your dream and what you didn't like seeing is Marie having some responsibility for Tommy's act that night. To be sure, it was something completely beyond her control, never mind whether she had any knowledge of what Tommy had in mind. She doesn't know anything at all about this, does she?"

"No. I mean, well, I was going to say that she must know about John Andrasko, but I can't even say she knows that for certain."

"So there is a great possibility that she knows nothing at all of the connection between Tommy and John."

"Probably," Balzic agreed.

"Then any responsibility she may have had in triggering Tommy's act that night is something only you would know about."

"I'm with you so far."

"Something tells me you're not, Mario but . . ." The priest took another swallow of beer. "What I'm trying to say is this: your dream appears to you as a father as a very real danger to your daughter. But to you as a cop, it appears to you that your own daughter is partly responsible for what happened that night, though she is totally unaware of what happened. And please remember your theory about Tommy is that he is also unaware of what he did." The priest paused and searched Balzic's face a moment. Then he said: "Mario, the cop in you is angry at her for that, and she gets hurt in your dream because people who do wrong deserve punishment."

"Now wait a minute, Father—"

96

"No. You wait. I started this, and I want to finish it, otherwise you're going to go away with some misconceptions."

"Okay. Then finish it."

"Your dream, Mario, is a dream of justice—no, retribution would be closer to it. It's a very common dream among parents. Every time a son or a daughter stays out too late and doesn't call home, the parents begin to suspect the worst, a traffic accident usually, but what they're really acting out in their minds is a way to safely punish their child, because, you see, by staying out too late, the child is causing the parent some anxiety. How does the parent get even for this momentary suffering? By fantasizing suffering for the child, and invariably, when the child comes home safely, the parent starts to lecture him about staying out late and about the dangers on the highways and so forth.

"Mario, I tell you I hear this sort of thing five, six times a week, either from the children or from the parents. The children come to complain about the parents, and they go away feeling contrite for making their parents anxious, and the parents come to complain about their dreams and go away feeling contrite for having such terrible thoughts about their children."

"So what you're saying, Father, is that I really blame my daughter for what Tommy Parilla did, is that it?"

"Not so fast, Mario. It's not this or that. You were anxious about your daughter being anywhere near Tommy. You still are, otherwise you would not have had the dream. So that's a large part of it, but another part of it is because of the cop in you, and still a third part of it is that quite possibly you don't like being a cop where your daughter is concerned. In other words, Mario, the reason you can't sleep is, you don't like yourself for having that particular dream."

Balzic shrugged, as though to accept what the priest was saying, but after a moment he started to grind his teeth.

"Mario, at the rist of stepping beyond friendship as well as beyond my abilities, I have to say that such dreams are very common among people who—people like yourself—people who are always striving to be good."

"I don't know whether I like that, Father."

97

"Give me a moment, Mario. I'm trying to think who it was who wrote something about this. It was an Irish writer. I'll think of his name in a second." The priest tapped his lips with his knuckles. "The name escapes me, but he wrote: 'The momentary relief from the necessity for being good is a feeling that I suspect most decent men and women have shared'—that's it. Frank O'Connor. That's who it was."

The priest again searched Balzic's face before continuing. "And that's what I'm talking about, Mario. Somebody else wrote that this was the function of dreams—to allow decent people to have indecent thoughts. Dreams give you the momentary relief from being good that you don't permit yourself while you're awake—"

"Goddammit, Father, I was awake."

"Mario, Mario. How did we begin this whole conversation? Didn't we have some doubts about when a dream was a dream and when a hallucination and so forth? You're taking me too literally now."

"Maybe I am."

"Don't be angry with me, Mario. More important, don't be angry with yourself." The priest paused. "If you'll permit me another observation?"

Balzic shrugged morosely.

"I think that you're seeing Marie in more or less the same position you saw Mrs. Andrasko, or at least seeing the potential for Marie. You didn't tell Mrs. Andrasko—nor did I—and she had to find out about John the worst possible way, and now you see the potential for your daughter to find out that she may have had something to do with what Tommy did that night."

"Ah, this is all getting too complicated."

"Certainly it is, Mario. When is anything like this ever simple?"

"At least I'm starting to see what you're getting at anyway."

"Are you?"

"Yeah. About that last thing anyway. For sure I don't want Marie to get burned in this, and I guess I was thinking she was too close to the kid for anybody's good. And you're right that she doesn't know anything about what I'm thinking about him."

"Well, Mario, all your problem with Marie stems from whether you ever arrest the boy, isn't that it?"

"I suppose."

"It seems then that Marie will have to be among the first to know if you do."

"Yeah, Father, but all this depends on whether anybody every gets enough on the kid to make an arrest, and the way it's going, it doesn't look like that's going to happen, not unless the state boys come up with something in the car."

"Are they investigating that?"

"Hell, yes. They probably did already. I mean I told Moyer to stay away from the kid, and I know he'll respect that, at least until after the funeral, but he won't be sitting on his can about the car. Fact is, I'm a little surprised nobody's called me about it yet."

"And if the boy didn't use the car—I mean, the car will only help if the boy drove it to and from, isn't that it?"

"You got it, Father. If he didn't take the car, or if he changed clothes somewhere—wait a minute. He had to have the car. Marie said so. That's what he told her at the game. Oh, Father, what a dummy I am. Listen, I got to go. You need a lift?"

"No. I have my car."

"Well, how about marking the beer up on my account in the cigar box under the counter, okay? I'll see you, Father," Balzic said, taking the steps to the side door two at a time.

Balzic found Lieutenant Moyer dozing off on a cot in one of the offices. A desk sergeant directed him to the room.

"I was wondering when you were going to show," Moyer said, sitting up and rubbing his eyes.

"I'm a little slow tonight," Balzic said. "Been a little slow the whole damn day and half the night before."

"We got the car. That's what you wanted to know, isn't it? I mean, you told me to lay off the kid, and I laid off, but I couldn't lay off the car."

Balzic lit a cigarette and waited.

"Mario, you never saw such a clean automobile in your life. You know where we pick it up? Coming out of the car wash on 986. Mrs. Andrasko's sister is driving it, and she just had to clean that car. It was absolutely filthy, she says. Jeezus, that woman must've taken lessons from the people who clean operating rooms. The only thing is, she says she didn't clean the trunk, and the trunk is like it came out of the showroom yesterday—no, make that this morning."

"So now we know."

"Sure. Now we know. And where does that get us? We scraped up a couple of envelopes, and ten'll get you a dime all the lab finds is good old pine tar and Lysol. And brother, that woman, is she something. She didn't buy any of it. We tell her it was just a routine inspection, except we have to keep the car until she produces the registration. We send her back with one of our men, and he's trying to stall, but we didn't get nearly the time we needed, and you just knew she wasn't buying any of it."

"I didn't think she would. Fact is, I may've had something to do with that."

"Yeah? How so?"

"It's not important how. What's important is, she won't be any help to us," Balzic said, looking away from Moyer's steady gaze. "Anyway, we got the circumstantial that somebody took a lot of trouble to clean the trunk, even if the lab doesn't come up with anything."

"And what'll any lawyer worth a pint of cold piss do with that? Can't you hear him? 'Your honor, the prosecution expects this court to believe that the fact that people want to keep their automobiles clean is reason to suspect my client. Why, your honor, if that were true, half the adult population in this country would be suspicious.' Then he'd give the jury a nice little grin, and they'd grin back, and there we'd be with our thumb up our ass." Moyer stood and scratched himself. "What did you come up here to tell me? Anything?"

"Oh, just that I'm almost positive the kid had the car most of that night." Balzic nearly apologized for saying it. "Course, you probably had that figured a while ago."

"Nobody up here was so sure of that. How come you're so sure?"

"My daughter told me. The kid tried to take her out during half time in the school game, and he told her he had the car."

"What time was that?"

"Nine. Nine-thirty, the latest."

"So we got him from nine-thirty until you see him coming home about one-thirty, right?"

Balzic nodded.

"Wonderful. We got John Andrasko from eleven-thirty until that train comes. Wasn't it about ten minutes late?"

"If that's all the later it was, it must've been late from an earlier run."

"Probably won't make much difference, but I ought to get a time-check from that fireman. One of my people talked to him yesterday. He better as hell have asked him about that."

"Well," Balzic said, "there's no use my hanging around, so I'm going to take off."

"Yeah, sure, Mario. Anything comes up, I'll let you know."

"Right," Balzic said and walked to his car feeling less and less useful.

At dawn, after having driven around Rocksburg for nearly two hours, Balzic turned into Delmont Street, where he lived. Halfway down the 200 block a car parked under a street light caught his eye. On its rear bumper was the sticker: "Support Your Local Police." Balzic passed the car, then stopped, and backed up. He sat staring at the sticker for a minute, then got out, went over to the bumper, and peeled the sticker off. "Dummy," he said, jamming the sticker in his coat pocket.

He drove on to his house and fell asleep in his clothes on the recliner in the living room. If he dreamed, he did not remember them when Ruth woke him two hours later.

John Andrasko was buried Monday morning at ten in St. Malachy's Cemetery. Balzic assisted the funeral director with the cars, though so few people came that the last three cars in the procession were occupied only by the drivers.

Balzic kept his eyes on Tommy Parilla throughout, but the boy showed nothing except concern for his mother. He stayed at her side, helping her in and out of the car, holding her arm when she knelt or rose during mass, and leading her gently by the elbow over the uneven ground of the cemetery. Mrs. Andrasko never looked at Balzic, or if she did, Balzic was too preoccupied with her son to notice. Angie Spano looked at Balzic once, in the parking lot as the casket was being carried from the funeral home to the hearse, a look so intensely hostile that Balzic had to turn away.

After it was over, and Balzic was driving out of the cemetery, he saw Lieutenant Moyer standing beside an unmarked cruiser across the road from the exit. He pulled in behind Moyer's car and rolled down his window.

"See anything, Mario?" Moyer said, leaning with his forearms on the door of Balzic's car.

"The kid's a stone. A good and proper son looking out for his mother, but a stone. He didn't blink. What did you get?"

"Nothing from the lab except what kind of disinfectant was used, and we found that. There were about three gallons in a drum in the barn and a couple more gallons in another drum in the garage. The same kind we'd find in half the barns in the county."

"You go over the place good?"

"Except for the grounds. Barn, garage, and house. We got them good. They just happened to leave the kitchen door unlocked."

"Nothing?" Balzic said.

"Not a damn thing except for the Coke in the kitchen. You saw that."

"Yeah, I saw it. Who doesn't drink Coke?"

Moyer sighed. "I think it's about time we went to work on the kid. Time we told him his rights and put it to him."

Balzic frowned.

"Come on, Mario. What the hell are we supposed to do—give her a six-month period of mourning? What choice do we have? Christ knows, I don't like this any better than you do, but tell me something else to do and I'll do it."

"If I had something else to tell you, I would. The only thing I can say is—ah, never mind."

"Let's hear it."

"Nothing. You're right. There's nothing else to do, but you're going to catch another zero. That kid's psycho. He won't know anything, and he'll be telling the truth."

"Don't you even want to find out if you're right?"

"Uh-uh. Right now I'd just like to go get a beer—no, wait a minute. On second thought, you pick him up and let me have him."

Moyer screwed up his face.

"Put it this way," Balzic said. "How long do you think you can hold him before his aunt shows up with a lawyer? She'll be on the phone before you get him out of the house. That means you get at most an hour with him before the lawyer walks in and tells the kid to shut up, period. Then where are we? Just let me have him for a half-hour down at the train station."

"You think his aunt's going to sit still for that any longer?"

"No, but at least I'll have a half-hour alone with him. By the time she shows up at your office with the lawyer, we have the kid on his way home."

"And just what do you plan to say to him down there?"

"Tell the truth, I really don't know. But I told him a couple things already, and I'd like to find out if he's been thinking about them."

"Mario, first you say the kid's psycho and he won't remember anything, and now you tell me you told him some things to make him think." Moyer stood away from the car. "You know I respect you, Mario. Of all the local police in the county I got more respect for you than for half the rest put together. But since when are you a psychiatrist, number one, and number two, just what do you think a lawyer's going to do with you on the stand? I mean, suppose you do get something out of the kid. If the kid's really psycho, what the hell's he going to say that'll do us any good in court?"

"I know, I know. The lawyer asks me where I went to college and where I went to medical school, and I wind up looking like fried ass. But that's not what I'm thinking about."

"Well, what then?"

103

"I was thinking about setting myself up."

"Ah, Mario, I didn't know you watched those kind of TV shows."

"Okay. So it sounds like bullshit. So what—if it works?"

"Yeah. So what if you stand on that platform every night for ten years waiting for that kid to show up with a Coke bottle?"

"Then do it your way, Lieutenant."

"You're not going to get pissed off about it, for crissake."

"Why should I? This is your case."

"Mario, cut it out. You sound like a rookie."

"So I sound like a rookie. Just promise me one thing."

"All right. I promise. If we come up short with the kid, you get next crack. But psycho or not, we get him going for a couple of hours, he's going to bend some way."

"Don't forget the aunt, Lieutenant. Don't forget that little lady. You're not going to have time to give him the full go-round."

"Well, I'm going to make a damn good start."

"Okay. You want me, I'll either be at the station or else down at Muscotti's."

"Good enough. I'll let you know."

Balzic drove to city hall and busied himself with routine matters for the better part of an hour. He kept looking at his watch and checking it with the wall clock. He was reading a preliminary report of the salary board of the Fraternal Order of Police when he suddenly tossed it aside and told Sergeant Stramsky that he was going out to the club range to shoot.

"Moyer'll probably be calling in a little while, Vic. Tell him where I am, and if it's important, tell him to get me on the car radio."

"Where will you be after?" Stramsky said.

"At Muscotti's," Balzic said over his shoulder as he started out to his car.

"Ah, for the life of a chief," Stramsky said.

Balzic turned back at the door. "You say something?"

"Me? I didn't say nothing."

"You lying Polock. I heard what you said, and I'm going to tell you right now why you'll never be chief. You eat too much kolbassi, and it's starting to affect your brain."

"How 'bout that ginzo crap you eat—what's 'at doing to yours?"

"Making me smarter and smarter. And better looking, too. Hell, just the other day I looked in the mirror, and I said to myself, Balzic, be grateful you weren't born a Polock. Your face'd be a mess today. Just like Stramsky's."

"Hey, that reminds me," Stramsky said, reaching in his back pocket for a book of raffle tickets. "Next Sunday's the big day. You want a couple chances on a bushel of booze?"

"You talking about that corn roast at the Falcons?"

"Yeah. Corn, kolbassi, holupki, kapusta—all for the benefit of the building fund. Two o'clock until."

"I'll take a couple, but I'm damned if I'm going to that thing. Last year I had the runs for a week."

"Buck a chance," Stramsky said, holding out the book of tickets and a ballpoint pen.

"A buck? Last year it was fifty cents."

"So? That's inflation for you. Blame it on Nixon."

"You fill them out. I'll take three. Leave them on my desk."

"Uh-uh. Where's the dough?"

"Aaaw, Vic. You don't trust me?"

"No way. Last year it took me three months to collect."

"There was a rumor it was fixed last year, Vic. I was making an investigation."

"My ass. Dollar a throw. Come on, you goddamn half-breed, get the lock off your wallet."

"Put them on my desk," Balzic said, going through the door. "I'll catch you payday."

"Payday," Stramsky said. "That's shit." He filled out three chances for Balzic and laid the tickets on Balzic's desk, muttering the while about being a sucker.

At the Police Rod and Gun Club range, Balzic fired his usual twenty rounds with the 30.06 and then leaned against the back fender, smoking and thinking about what he would say to Tommy Parilla if he ever got the chance.

The longer he thought about it, the less certain he was about what to say. Other thoughts crowded in: the possibility that Moyer would get something out of Tommy; the possibility that Angie Spano would raise a large stink; the possibility that Milt Weight would start

105

to use the newspaper to ridicule Balzic's part in the investigation and aggrandize his own office; and the most serious possibility of all—that Tommy Parilla had nothing to do with it. "But if he didn't," Balzic said to himself as he drove back into town, "then who the hell did? Some other nut?"

He shook his head as he parked in front of Muscotti's, as much to restore his conviction that Tommy Parilla was the murderer as to shake loose those other possibilities.

Balzic pulled open the front door and hesitated. Standing at the end of the bar with their heads together were Dom Muscotti and Sam Carraza. Balzic knew he could ignore them if he chose, but Pete Muscotti, Dom's nephew, was tending bar, and that immediately set Balzic on edge.

He had been arresting Pete Muscotti for the better part of ten years, the first time when Pete was fourteen, after Pete had decided, because he'd been thrown out of a typing class in high school, that it would be fair to pour maple syrup over the insides of all the typewriters. Dom had bailed him out of that one and every one since: every stupid scheme from the theft of automobile state inspection stickers to trying to run an independent handbook in territory assigned by somebody in Pittsburgh to somebody else's cousin.

All of Pete's troubles with the law had been costly but easy for Dom to set right; the bookmaking in protected territory had nearly cost Pete Muscotti his life, but, fool that he was, he thought it had been his own guts and moxie that had saved him. Dom indulged Pete because Pete's father had been Dom's favorite brother; Balzic, however sympathetic he tried to be to Dom's indulgence, could barely stomach Pete and sometimes not enough to stand being waited on by him.

Still, Balzic was thirsty, and priming himself to ignore the lip Pete would send his way, he went in and ordered a draught.

"You want this on your bill, Chiefo?" Pete said, pouring the draught. At the word "Chiefo" both Sam Carraza and Dom Muscotti looked up.

"Why don't you get a bullhorn?" Balzic said.

Pete smirked and said, "You paying, or what?"

106

"On the bill," Balzic said, trying not to let his eyes meet Pete's.

"Hey, Mario," Sam Carraza called out. "You seen the paper yet?"

"No. Is there something I should see?"

"Give him the paper, Petey," Carraza said.

Pete reached under the bar and came up with the city edition of *The Rocksburg Gazette*. He glanced at it and then turned it so that when he slid it across the bar in front of Balzic, the story Carraza was talking about was immediately obvious.

Across the bottom of the front page was:

HIPPIE GANG MEMBERS CHARGED IN ANDRASKO MURDER

by Dick Dietz
ROCKSBURG GAZETTE STAFF WRITER

District Attorney Milton Weigh announced this morning the arrest of what he termed "prime suspects" in the murder of John Andrasko, 45, of Rocksburg RD. County Chief of Detectives Samuel Carraza was credited by Weigh for having broken the case.

Arrested were Charles W. Reilley, 24, who gave his address as The Community Store, 616 State St., Rocksburg, and William A. Morrow, 20, of the same address.

The two men were arraigned before Magistrate Thomas Coccoletti Monday morning within minutes after John Andrasko's funeral cortege left St. Malachy's R.C. Church.

Dist. Atty. Weigh said Carraza, acting on a tip from a former member of the hippie-type group which makes its headquarters at the State Street address, arrested the two men early Monday morning as they were in Weigh's words "obviously preparing to leave town." Weigh also said that Carraza and his men confiscated a quantity of marijuana, some pipes, six marijuana cigarettes, and a quantity of pills.

Balzic stopped reading at that point and pushed the paper away.

"What's the matter, Mario," Carraza called out, "you don't like what you read in the paper these days?"

107

"You guys don't ever give up," Balzic said, sipping his beer.

"Maybe you ought to," Carraza said.

"All right, Sam," Dom Muscotti said. "Be nice now."

"I'm being nice. Friend Balzic is the one not being nice."

"So why don't you tell me how you broke the case, Sam," Balzic said. "I'm not too proud to learn something about my business."

Carraza laughed. "This is one trade secret I think I'll just keep to myself."

Balzic restrained himself until he saw Carraza and Pete exchanging grins. He set his glass down and started toward Carraza. "How 'bout if I tell you how you broke the case. How would that be?"

"You're the one doing the talking," Carraza said.

"That's all he can do," Pete said. "Sure as hell can't make anything stick on anybody."

"Pete!" Dom said, and Pete leaned back against a cash register and folded his arms.

Balzic glared at Pete for a second and then continued toward Carraza. "I'll tell you how you broke this case, Carraza, and you can correct me if I'm wrong."

"You're still the only one talking."

"Well, it went something like this. You picked up some punk on a narcotics, and you scared the piss out of him, and when he was ripe, you put a few hints in his head that just maybe if he could remember a few things you wanted to hear, just maybe you could arrange a lesser charge or maybe even drop all charges. And when he started to make the music, you gave him the words—isn't that the trade secret?" Balzic stopped a foot away from Carraza, who remained seated.

"Easy, Mario," Dom Muscotti said. "Go easy now."

"Tell your flunkey to go easy," Balzic snapped.

"Watch what you say now, Mario," Dom said. "You don't want to be sorry tomorrow for what you say today."

"I won't be sorry for anything tomorrow except maybe that I didn't catch this double-breasted ass-kisser where there weren't any witnesses."

"That's enough, Mario," Dom said.

"Who says so? You? Better think some more, *padrone*. It ain't like

108

it used to be, and I know you from before this flunkey was out of grade school."

"I wish there weren't any witnesses," Carraza said.

Balzic's left hand, his fingers stiff, stabbed Carraza in the throat and Carraza went backward off his stool. He lay on the floor holding his throat, gasping and coughing, his eyes filling with tears.

"You make a move, you sonuvabitch," Balzic said, "and I'll kick you."

"Mario!" Dom said, hustling out from behind the bar with his hands outstretched.

"Don't touch me, Dom."

"I'm not touching you. I wasn't going to touch you. I just don't want you to do nothing foolish."

"Then make sure he doesn't do nothing foolish till I get out of here."

"Okay. All right. He won't do nothing. Just go easy, that's all. That's all I'm asking. Just go easy."

Balzic backed toward the steps leading to the side door. "You keep your hands where I can see them, you hear, Carraza?"

"Mario, quit talking like that," Dom said. "Sam wouldn't do nothing like that in a million years. It's over. You won."

Balzic reached the landing to the side door. "It's not over," he said, "but it will be he ever puts it to me again."

Outside, Balzic swallowed and took a couple of deep breaths. He shook his left hand and pulled the fingers one by one. The middle finger was stoved. "Goddamn," he whispered, as he went around the front to his car. "Goddamn."

He drove back to City Hall. Before he went inside to the station, he went across the A&P parking lot and bought a paper from a machine.

When he got inside the station, Stramsky said, "I see you got the paper already. Hey. You feel okay?"

"Why? Don't I look okay?"

"Hell, man, your hands're shaking. Look at them."

"Ah, I just did something I wanted to do for a long time, and I guess I ain't as young as I used to be, that's all."

"What d'you do?"

"Never mind—what the hell. You'll hear it sooner or later. May as well hear it from me."

Stramsky sat on the corner of a desk. "So?"

"So I laid Carraza out. He started to give me some crap about this," Balzic said, thrusting the newspaper out, "and I took the heat. He said something, I said something, then he said something else, and I let him have it. I wanted to do that to him a long time."

"Where was this—Muscotti's?"

"Yeah," Balzic said, reading the rest of the story he'd begun in Muscotti's. "Look at how these bastards operate. They give you this big headline about arresting the murder suspects, and then you get down to the last paragraph and you find out what they really booked them on was possession of narcotics. Jeezus Christ."

"That's our hero for you."

"Weigh, that sonuvabitch. He makes me want to puke. He's so far up in that tree of his, he don't even know how he won that election, do you believe that? And if that ain't bad enough, he actually thinks Carraza and Dillman were his own choices, the jerk."

Stramsky looked puzzled for a moment. "You really think he don't know what Muscotti sent his way?"

"I know he doesn't. He thinks he made it on his pretty teeth and his country club memberships and his old man's money. Some day for laughs I just might tell him."

"Well, what did Carraza say?"

"He didn't say nothing I didn't back him into. But I have never been able to take him. Ever since the first time I saw him flunkeying for Froggy. I don't know. There's just something about a punk like that—he's so stupid he thinks nobody knows how many corners he's working. Weigh at least thinks he's honest. But guys like Carraza, they work three corners out of four, and they think they're slick-assing everybody."

"What did Dom do?"

"Ah, for a while he tried to come on like he used to before all his goombas went to the Bahamas, but the only thing he really did was tell his nephew to shut up."

"Petey boy," Stramsky said, shaking his head.

110

"Another weasel. The worst kind: big ambitions and no brains."

"So Dom didn't do anything?"

"Oh, he got between me and Carraza after I put him off his stool, but he knows better than to do anything else. I did him too many favors."

"Tell me something, Mario, just between us girls—did he used to be as big as everybody says he was?"

"Dom? Hell, no. But his old man was. His old man was number three in the county. After prohibition, the old man got every punch board, pin ball machine, and dice game from here east to the county line, never mind numbers and horses. He had those before. He had it all except from here west which numbers one and two had. Then number one goes to Vegas and number two goes to the Bahamas and the old man had a stroke and that leaves Dom. Then there was that thing in the *Saturday Evening Post* or *Collier's* or one of them magazines, and then Kefauver started up his heat, and up jumps old Froggy, who says he's going to clean up the county.

"So," Balzic went on, "Dom makes a deal with Froggy, and it worked okay until Froggy started thinking about his retirement. That's when Dom gets Carraza on Froggy's staff, and all of a sudden, the raids Froggy's making for the benefit of the papers and the little old ladies start to go wrong, and Froggy starts looking like a clown. And the more he looks like a clown, the madder he gets, and the more stubborn Dom gets and, well, you know the rest. Froggy finishes dead last out of five for judge and here comes Weigh riding in on his white horse. Maybe I should invite Weigh and Froggy to a barbecue in my backyard and let Froggy give it to him straight."

"Boy, I'd like to hear that," Stramsky said.

"Ah, that's just wishful thinking. From what I hear, Froggy's so whacked out now, he has three drinks, he forgets where he lives."

"It'd still be worth the price of admission to hear it."

"Weigh wouldn't believe it anyhow," Balzic said, heading for the door. "I'm going up to see Moyer, if anybody wants me."

"Okay," Stramsky said. "Hey, I put the tickets on your desk. How 'bout the money?"

"See me payday," Balzic said and went out to his car.

He drove to the state police barracks, pulling on his stoved middle finger at every intersection. By the time he parked in front of the barracks, the finger was throbbing.

Lieutenant Moyer was standing by the desk staring off into space when Balzic came in. His eyes focused on Balzic, and he shook his head slowly. "Should've listened to you, Mario," he said.

"How much time did you get?"

"Just time enough for him to say, and I quote, 'You think I killed him, don't you?' end quote, and in walks Miss Spano with one drunken Greek, and that was that."

"She got the Greek, huh?"

"Himself, and in living color. Myron M. Valcanas."

"Well, you got to admit, he's a hell of a lawyer."

"Sure. If you can stand the bastard."

"Got the kid out of here, didn't he?"

Moyer stared off into space again. "Who would've thought she'd get him?"

"Well, you know, it really didn't make much difference who she got," Balzic said.

"I know that, goddammit. I just thought we'd get maybe an hour anyway."

"You didn't. So that's that. Now what I think we ought to do is—"

"I know what we do. We set you up. Like the movies. It's disgusting."

"What if I go talk to Valcanas?"

"What for?"

"Look, whatever else that Greek is, he isn't stupid. If I tell him what I'm thinking, he might go along with a court order to have the kid examined by a psychiatrist."

"No, he wouldn't. Not as long as we're in on it. He's memorized all the times we picked him up for drunk-driving. He bends over backward and inside out to give us trouble."

"That's probably true, Lieutenant, but I never arrested him for that, and neither did any of my people. He doesn't have any grudge with me."

Moyer threw up his hands. "Go ahead. What the hell've we got to lose?"

"Incidentally, you seen the paper?"

"About Weigh? Yeah, I've seen it. What do you want me to say? That he got his feet three feet off the floor? Okay, so I've said it. Go talk to the Greek," Moyer said, disappearing into one of the offices, his head going from side to side. Balzic could hear the sighs of disgust before the door slammed.

Balzic found Myron Valcanas in the back room of the Rocksburg bowling alleys—Rocksburg Bowl, 24 Lanes, AMF Pinsetters, Good Food and Drink. Valcanas was playing captains gin and losing.

As Balzic drew up a chair beside him, Valcanas said to the bartender who followed Balzic in and was picking up the glasses and taking orders, "For crissake, this time put some whiskey in it."

"S'matter, Mo," Balzic said, "somebody trying to cheat you?"

"All a bunch of goddamn thieves," Valcanas said, lighting a cigarette-sized cigar. "Everywhere you go, thieves and liars in public places. And then there's my countryman, our distinguished vice president."

"Your deal, Greek," Valcanas's opponent said.

Valcanas took the cards and shuffled. "I'd give everything I made last year and everything I'm going to make this year to buy fifteen minutes of prime-time television to debate that lying fake."

"Oh, yeah?" Balzic said. "And just what would you say to him?"

"What would I say to him? Why I'd just ask him about four questions, that's all it would take. Mr. Vice President, I'd say, how do you pronounce democracy in Greek? Then I'd ask him how many political prisoners are being held incomunicado in Greek jails. I wouldn't even bother asking him if he knows what Greek jails are like. Then I'd ask him just what the hell is so subversive about Mark Twain's books—among others—that those goddamned colonels banned them. Imagine it. *Tom Sawyer* for crissake. Now there's a really dangerous book. And the last thing I'd ask him is which side he'll sell guns to when the blood starts to run in the streets over there. The colonels have it all their way now, but I give them about three more years."

"You going to play cards, or you going to give a goddamn sermon?" Valcanas's opponent said.

"What's your hurry, for crissake? You're six bucks ahead right now, and we've only been playing for twenty minutes." Valcanas turned to Balzic and said, "Oh, it's you, Mario. I wondered who the hell I was talking to. A man of common sense, I could tell that. A rare individual these days."

"I only got nine cards, Greek."

"Then pick up another one, and you'll have ten. That's simple enough, isn't it?" Valcanas turned back to Balzic. "Nine and one makes ten, doesn't it? I mean I have always been led to believe that, haven't you?"

"No argument," Balzic said. "Listen, Mo, I want to talk to you about a client of yours."

"Is this an honest inquiry, Mario, or are you trying to find out how I intend to defend him—whoever the hell it is."

"Let's just say this is friendly business."

"Impossible. No business with Greeks is friendly."

"Your play, Greek," Valcanas's opponent said.

"I know that, for crissake," Valcanas said. "Nothing I like better than playing cards with someone who keeps reminding me of the sequence of play." Valcanas glanced at Balzic's hands. "You don't even have a drink, for crissake. How are we to talk about anything—business or otherwise—when you're emptyhanded?"

The bartender returned then with a full tray of drinks for the players.

Valcanas took a long swallow of his drink. "That's more like it, for crissake. And bring my friend here a drink. On my tab."

"Beer," Balzic said.

"Knock with six," Valcanas's opponent said.

"Six! Why, you thief. I have four. Did you actually believe you could get away with six? Who dealt these cards anyway?" Valcanas grinned at Balzic, his gold fillings glinting in the light coming from a

114

window opposite them. "This innocent listens to our vice president, listens to him and watches him on the tube, and he still trusts Greeks."

"I don't mind losing the hand, but do I have to put up with the bullshit, too?"

"The lament of losers everywhere," Valcanas said. "If it's not the wind, it's the rain. It wasn't my fault, coach, the ball was muddy. Deal, for crissake. What's my partner doing?"

"I caught him with half the garage," Valcanas's partner said.

"See there, Mario. Justice, that blind and virginal beauty, triumphs again. Good conquers evil, the world spins on, rectified," Valcanas said. "Now who's this client of mine you want to discuss?"

"Here?"

"Where else? I'm behind, for crissake."

"Okay. The one you left about a half-hour, forty-five minutes ago."

"I'm listening."

"He did it."

"Mario, from a policeman's point of view, I've never heard of one who had not done it. Say something else."

"He's sick. I mean I think he's so sick he doesn't even know he did it."

"Oh? And how many hours have you had him on your couch, doctor? And where did you say you went to school?"

"Come on, Mo. This isn't for a jury."

"Then say something intelligent."

"Honest to Christ, Mo—"

"No appeals to saviors. I said say something intelligent."

Balzic squirmed about on his chair. "Give me a chance."

"I knew a whore used to say that," Valcanas said, grinning. " 'Give me a chance, sailor, that's all I ask. Just a chance to make a couple of honest dollars.' And the next morning there'd be a conciliatory note pinned to the pillow explaining about the flat condition of said sailor's wallet. It was very touching."

"Okay," Balzic said. "Put it this way. There's nobody else."

"There's always somebody else."

115

"Not this time. No way, no reason."

"But a moment ago you said my client had a reason. A reason he doesn't understand but which you do, and again I ask, Doctor, where was it you said you interned? Was that the Menninger Clinic or was that with the Mayo brothers?"

"Mo, let's go someplace else. I can't make any sense in here."

"I'll drink to that," Valcanas said, draining his glass in three swallows. "Innkeeper!" he called out. "Another round for my friends and enemies—whoa, that card gives me gin, I believe." He spread his hand on the table. "That is gin, is it not?"

"No shit," his opponent said.

"I'm still listening, Mario. But get to the point. I have nothing doing in court for four or five days, and I intend to let my liver know who's boss."

"Okay. Right to the point. I want you to go along with a court order to have your client examined by a psychiatrist."

"On what grounds?"

"On what—Mo. Not a half-hour ago, you got him out of a session with Moyer and his boys. They were ready to turn him inside out."

"That's all they were—ready."

"Well they'll do it again. If not tomorrow, then the day after."

Valcanas turned on his chair and faced Balzic. "Get some things straight, Mario. Number one, nobody does anything to any client of mine without adhering to the letter of the rules and procedures. The letter. Not the rules and procedures as they would like them to be, but *as they are*. Number two, Moyer picked my client up today and got him into one of his back rooms and had not—I repeat—had not even made a notation in his log about ever having picked him up, never mind making a notation about informing him of his rights. Number three, those two little facts are a direct violation of rules and procedures for proper arrest and interrogation from Washington to Harrisburg to little old Rocksburg. Number four, that such violations occurred and that such improper, not to say crude, methods were tried—tried, I said—indicates a clear attempt at coercion. And there's only one reason for police coercion. The same one there's always been—they have nothing else to go on that would stand up in court for two minutes. And number five, I get almost as

much pleasure from making Moyer and his boy scouts uncomfortable as I do from scratching my hemorrhoids."

Balzic hung his head and sighed. "Mo, do I look like Moyer?"

"No to that. Ask another."

"Do you want to see somebody else get it the way you know who
got it? 'Cause that's what's going to happen."

Valcanas thought for a moment. "You that sure of that?"

"I am."

"Then go talk to a judge. I won't interfere. But do it right. And I
mean everything. If there's one comma out of place, I'll stuff it
down your throat in the hearing."

Balzic blew out a deep breath. "Thanks, Mo. I appreciate it."

"Save your gratitude. Your war's just starting. I read the paper,
you know. Just what do you think little Milty Weigh's going to do
when he hears about what you're up to? That's for openers. For
callers, court's recessed until Thursday, and there's a bar association
meeting tonight honoring that fat fart that got himself appointed to
federal district court. All the judges will be there, which means
they'll all get loaded, which means, furthermore, you'll be lucky to
find one of them willing to listen to anything before Thursday.
Maybe not even then."

"Well, thanks anyway."

"It's your deal, Greek."

"For crissake, don't you think I know that? Why is it that of all
the card players in the world I have to play the ones who can't quit
telling me when to deal. There," he said, shuffling the cards,
"satisfied now?"

"I want to cut."

"Cut then. Shuffle them if that makes you happy."

"See you, Mo," Balzic said, starting for the door.

"Won't you be lucky," Valcanas said without looking up.

Balzic turned back, "Just one more thing, Mo."

"Yeah?"

"Try to keep the sister out of it."

"Sweet little Angie? That shy violet? Why, she's a wonderful
person. I could tell that after five minutes with her."

"Yeah, sure. Just do everybody a favor and keep her quiet."

"Mario, if I didn't know better, I'd say you were afraid of her. Now what gives me that impression?"

"Say whatever you want. This thing's a big enough mess without her stomping around in it."

"All I can guarantee is to tell her the most agreeable lies. If that doesn't work, well . . ." Valcanas shrugged.

"Gin," Valcanas's opponent said.

"Gin! Let me see those cards. Take your hands away, for crissake."

Balzic left while Valcanas was making some sort of oration in Greek.

Balzic covered the judges' offices in the courthouse in twenty minutes. Each of the six secretaries gave him more or less the same response: "The judge is out," or "The judge has left word he will not be in until Thursday."

He went down to the lobby pay phone and dialed their residences, and one by one, either by recorded message or from a member of the family, heard the same story.

Whispering curses in Italian and Serbian, he used his last dime and dialed again."

"State police. Sergeant Stallcup speaking," came the answer.

"This is Balzic. Let me talk to Moyer."

"He's not here, Mario."

"He say where he'd be?"

"Yes, he did. He said he was going out to see Mrs. Andrasko."

"What? What the hell for?"

"That he didn't say."

"How long ago'd he leave?"

"About five minutes."

"Oh Jeezus Christ," Balzic said. He slammed the receiver on the hook and ran through the lobby down the back stairs to his car. He tried for nearly a minute to get Moyer on the radio. Nothing. He squealed rubber out of the alley and left a trail of horns blowing behind him as he bullied into traffic on Forbes Street.

In three minutes he bounced off Route 986 onto the driveway of

118

the Andrasko farm and skidded to a stop behind Moyer's car, just in time to see Angie Spano doing everything short of actually shoving Moyer off the porch. Balzic did not bother to get out of his car.

Moyer came over and said, "You say one word, Mario, and so help me . . ."

"All I'm going to say is, I talked to the Greek."

"And?"

"And he said he wouldn't interfere if I got a court order authorizing a shrink to examine the kid."

"What else?"

"I can't find a judge, that's what else."

"You know what, Mario? We're a couple of geniuses, that's what we are."

Balzic fiddled with his keys.

Moyer looked at the sky and then down at his shoes. "Okay," he said, "I was in the office wearing out the seat of my pants, and I kept getting more steamed by the minute, so I broke my own rule."

"What rule's that?"

"It's one I made about six, seven years ago when I made lieutenant. I told myself then that whenever I didn't know what to do, I'd never make the mistake of doing something."

"That's a damn good rule, Phil."

"Yeah. I always thought so. What do you suppose made me break it today?"

"You got me."

"What say we get the hell out of here? The longer I stand here, the more embarrassed I get. I can feel the woman looking at me."

"You going back to your office?"

"No," Moyer said. "I think I made enough mistakes for one day. Think I'll go home and take a nice, long shower and read some old *National Geographics*. Stimulate my mind. And don't look for me tomorrow either, 'cause I'm taking tomorrow off. Tomorrow I'm not even going to make the mistake of getting out of bed except to take a leak. You want anything, call Stallcup."

"Okay, Phil. I'll do that. See you Wednesday, maybe."

"Don't bet on it. Maybe tomorrow night I'll get lucky and die."

Balzic backed the car and turned around. He could see Moyer

following him as he pulled onto 986, but soon he quit looking back and when he looked back again Moyer had turned off.

At city hall, when Balzic walked into the station, Stramsky gave him a quick nod. Balzic looked in the direction of the nod and saw Milt Weigh, Sam Carraza, and John Dillman with their heads together by the large window fronting Main Street.

"Something I can do for you, Milt?" Balzic said, approaching them.

Weigh turned with a start. He cleared his throat and said, "There is. You can turn over your weapon to Detective Dillman."

"*Detective* Dillman," Balzic said. "It's going to be like that, is it?"

"It is," Weigh said. "I'm placing you under arrest. I have the warrant here. I don't think I have to inform you of your rights."

"Mind if I read the warrant, Milt?"

"First, your weapon."

"I don't have one."

Carraza's eyebrows shot up. "You don't have one?" he said.

"You want to search me?" Balzic said, opening his suit coat and lifting it and turning around slowly. "Maybe you better search me. Maybe I carry it in a holster sewed to my skivvies." He put his arms down and took the warrant Weigh extended to him. Before he started reading, Balzic said, "I can hear your wheels grinding, Sammy boy. You think your boss can hear them, too?"

"What's he talking about, Sam?" Weigh asked.

"Ask him," Carraza said. "What do I know what this crazy man talks about?"

Balzic glanced over the warrant. "Not bad, Milt. Assault, assault and battery, assaulting an officer of the law. The last one's pretty funny, but I guess the other two are okay."

"There is nothing funny about any of them," Weigh said. "Evidently you're forgetting a few things."

"Like which few things?"

"Like your conduct following the arrest of certain persons for surety of the peace last Saturday night. For instance, in the plain view of these two detectives you struck with your hand one of those persons. For another instance, you're forgetting our conversation the day after that incident. And for another instance—"

"That's enough instances, Milt. I get your drift," Balzic said.

"Well. What are we waiting for? Let's go."

"Go where?" Weigh said.

"To the magistrate's—where else? You plan to file the information by proxy or something?"

"Not so fast, Balzic."

"Sergeant Stramsky," Balzic called out, "I think you better come over here. I don't want you to miss any of this. Something tells me the district attorney is about to make some sort of an offer."

"You stay where you are, Stramsky," Dillman said.

"It's okay, Mario," Stramsky called back. "I can hear okay."

"Well, Milt, what's it going to be?"

"I want your resignation, Balzic."

"My what? And just what the hell am I supposed to be resigning for?"

"Your health," Carraza said. "What else?"

"So either I resign because my health's gone bad all of a sudden or else what—you're going to prosecute?"

"That's the idea," Weigh said.

"Milt," Balzic said, "I never realized until this minute what a real amateur you are. And to think that in, oh, say, twelve, sixteen years, you'll be down in Washington, after you do the bit in Harrisburg, of course. What are you thinking about, Milt—you going to hustle for state's attorney general, or you going right after the governor's house? Will it be the House first and then the Senate? Course, it'll all depend, won't it?"

"The joke's over, Balzic. I want an answer."

"Do you now? Okay, I'll give you a couple. Number one, I'm not sick. Number two, you file this information against me, and you won't even get re-elected to the office you're sitting in now, never mind those other places, and I'll tell you why, Milt. 'Cause you don't know your territory. You don't know who is who around this county, and most of all, you don't know who was who in Muscotti's when I allegedly assaulted friend Carraza here. Why don't you ask him what would happen if Dom Muscotti and that little prick nephew of his had to testify against me? Go ahead. Ask him."

"What's he talking about, Sam?" Weigh said.

121

Carraza shrugged nervously. "What do I know what he's talking about?"

"I'll say one thing for you, Sammy boy," Balzic said. "When you told your boss here what happened, I'll bet it never even occurred to you he might try to pull this, and then I'll bet you started thinking it might not be such a bad idea, but right now I can see from your face, dumb as you are, it's starting to sink in that it's a pretty shitty idea."

"Sam, if there's something you haven't told me," Weigh said, "I want to hear it right now."

"Well, while you girls are talking it over," Balzic said, "I think I'll just give my lawyer a call. You know him, Sam. Mo Valcanas."

"Hold it, Mario," Carraza said. "We can work this thing out."

"What's going on here, Carraza?" Weigh said.

John Dillman started walking for the door.

"Where are you going?" Weigh shouted.

"Outside," Dillman said. "I don't want to hear none of this."

"What is this?" Weigh snapped. "He mentions that drunk's name, and you two fold up. What the hell's going on?"

"Tell him, Sammy boy," Balzic said. "Tell him what a good memory that drunk has. Tell him who was Froggy's campaign manager sixteen, seventeen years ago. And then tell him how come Mo Valcanas wasn't Froggy's campaign manager the next time around."

"Listen, Milt," Carraza said, "I think we better forget this. No kidding, Milt. I think we just better forget the whole thing. I'm sorry I said anything. I don't know what I was thinking about. He never hit me. I mean, he hit me, but I called him a name. Dom heard me. So did Pete. It didn't happen the way I said. Honest."

The veins in Weigh's neck started to swell. He stormed past Balzic and out the door. Dillman and Carraza trailed after him, and for a long moment, Carraza's pleas and excuses filtered in from the parking lot.

Stramsky laughed until tears flowed. "Since when is Mo Valcanas your lawyer?" he said after he stopped laughing.

"What the hell's so funny?" Balzic said. "What other bluff you want me to use? That bastard was out to put me on unemployment, and you want me to play nice?"

"Yeah, I know all that," Stramsky said. "But what the hell does Valcanas have to do with anything?"

"Remind me to tell you some other time," Balzic said. "All you need to know right now is, Carraza is scared shitless of Valcanas 'cause one time Carraza got wise with the Greek and started running his mouth about who he was and what he could do. So Valcanas told him he had it all written down about how many times Carraza tipped off Muscotti about state police raids back when Dom was still number three. And in the meantime, Valcanas is still Muscotti's lawyer, so Carraza knows that Valcanas knows a hell of a lot from that side. But what Carraza doesn't know—and neither does anybody else—is whether Valcanas wrote anything down or not, and Carraza may be dumb, but he's not dumb enough to get on the stand with Valcanas asking the questions. Especially not when the only witnesses are Dom and that dumb-ass nephew of his."

"Hell, Vic, if I could handle half my problems as easy as this one, I'd be thinking about running for public office myself."

"What the hell would you run for?"

"What else? Clerk of courts. Pays close to nine thousand a year and you work about as much as the average Polock desk sergeant."

"Well, up yours, too. And where's the money for those tickets?"

"Payday I told you. How many times I have to say it?" Balzic said, starting for the door. "Man, you're getting mercenary in your old age. I remember when you were on a beat, Vic. All you used to think about was God, flag, mother, and kolbassi."

"Hey, where you going to be?"

"Home," Balzic called back. "And if anybody wants me, tell them I went south."

"Hey, baby," Balzic said as he came into the kitchen. "What's for the stomach?" He put his arms around Ruth's waist from behind.

"Lasagna," Ruth said. "But it's going to be sloppy. I had to use cottage cheese. Louis was out of riccotta."

Balzic kissed her on the neck. "So. It won't be all that bad. Where's the girls?"

"They said they were going to Theresa Androtti's house. To do

123

their homework, no less. God knows where they'll wind up."

"Where's Ma?"

"Laying down. She doesn't feel so good."

"Those pills not helping her?"

"Oh, Mar, you know what she says. All they do is make her go to the bathroom. Half the time I don't even think she takes them."

"We got any wine? I feel like some wine."

"That's not all you feel like."

"Oh, yeah? And just what do I feel like?"

"Well, I know you don't carry a gun, and even if you did, you wouldn't be carrying it there."

"Oh. That. Funny thing about that. That always happens when I catch you alone cooking."

"Big deal. When I'm cooking."

"I notice you're not trying very hard to get loose."

"As much as I've seen you in the last week . . ."

"Keep talking. I hear you."

"If it's not football games, it's an accident, and if it's not that, then it's—never mind. Look out, Mar, I have to get the sauce."

Balzic let go and backed up. "Where's the wine? We got any?"

"There's a whole gallon under the sink."

Balzic got the bottle and poured a water glass full. He loosened his tie and sat at the kitchen table. He took a couple of sips and then a long drink. "This is pretty good. How much?"

"I don't remember. Three something. Three-forty, I think."

"Not bad."

"Mar, there's something we have to talk about."

"Go ahead."

"It's Marie."

"S'matter with her?"

"She's been acting funny for the last couple of days."

"Maybe it's her time of the month. You act pretty funny when it's your time."

"No. It's not that. I thought of that, too. She hasn't said beans for, I don't know, since Saturday."

"Yeah. Well then, I know what it is."

"You do? Then tell me—would you mind?"

124

"It's something I told her. I didn't tell her. I asked her, and she must've put two and two together."

Ruth put down her spatula and turned around. "Well, what did you ask her?"

"It was about this Parilla kid."

"And?"

Balzic took another drink of wine. "Look, Ruth. It's nothing to get all worked up about. I mean it is, and it isn't. But I've already talked it over with Father Marrazo, so I know what needs to be said when the time comes."

"Okay. So you know. Now, would you mind telling me?"

Balzic recounted the conversation he had with Marie and Emily about Tommy Parilla and then the one he had with the priest.

"Well, at least now I know," Ruth said. "The way she was acting I thought I'd done something. Or forgot something."

"Nah. No chance. But she's no dummy. She had to add it up. The thing Father Marrazo said was, if I ever do arrest the kid, I have to be sure to tell her what's going on. Otherwise, she might jump to all kinds of wrong conclusions. But don't worry about it."

"Are you going to arrest him?"

"Toss a coin on that one, baby. Right now all we have is a lot of ideas. They all fit, but that's all they do. I mean if we took it to court, it'd get tossed out in five minutes. I'm just waiting on the judges to come back from wherever the hell they are so I can get the kid examined."

"What if you can't?"

"Ruthie baby, you still got a hell of a pair of legs, you know that?"

"Boy, are you ever subtle."

"That's me. Old smoothie. Smoothest guy you ever knew."

"So what are you going to do in the meantime?"

"Well, for one, I plan to spend the hours between ten and twelve down at the station."

"Mar! Not tonight."

"What's tonight?"

"Tonight we're going to the Joyces' house—how could you forget that?"

125

"How could I forget what I didn't know?"

"Oh, Mar, honest to God."

"Okay, we can still go, but from ten till twelve I won't be there, that's all. Ruthie, Jeezus, who better than them would understand?"

"It's just the idea. I mean, it was the first date we've had in weeks."

"We'll have the date, okay? No problem. Now finish with the lasagna and come here."

"Nothing doing. Just when we'll get started, the girls'll come bouncing in or Ma'll wake up."

"Ah, where's your guts? Press your luck a little."

"Press my luck a little. Ha. Keep quiet and drink your wine. Go in the living room and have a daydream—press my luck a little. What do you think I've been doing since I married you? If I'd've married a doctor I would've seen him more."

"Okay for you," Balzic said, filling his glass again. "Think I will go have a daydream. Let me see, today I think I'll have one about Anna Magnani—how's that?"

"Good. Have two. Bet the first thing she says is, 'Where the hell you been for the last two weeks, big boy?' "

Balzic left Ruth at the Joyces' house at nine-fifty. They had played penny ante for about an hour, and when Balzic left, he was sure Ruth believed that when he'd said he was going to the station, she understood that to mean the police station.

That he meant the train station turned out to mean nothing very much at all. He stood on the platform from ten until after midnight, and except for the arrival of the eleven-thirty-eight to Knox, which was ten minutes late, he saw nothing else.

Balzic spoke briefly with the fireman and a porter and a man in the mail car, but he learned nothing from them he didn't already know. When the train pulled away toward Knox the uselessness of what he was doing crowded in on him and left him with a sour stomach and a bad taste. He tried to blame that on the cigarettes he'd smoked, but it didn't work, and he drove back to Bill Joyce's house filled with a rising irritation that he might be wrong

126

about everything and that if he was, then somebody else had to be right.

The only somebody who had an alternative was Milt Weigh, and that thought caused Balzic's stomach to erupt in a volley of flatulence, a series of belches and burps both loud and sour.

He made his apologies to the Joyces and took Ruth home at about a quarter to one.

On Tuesday night and again Wednesday night he was on the train station platform. The result both nights was the same.

On Thursday morning, when he went to President Judge Arnold Friedman's chambers to get the order to have Tommy Parilla examined by a psychiatrist, Balzic had to reconvince himself that he knew what he was doing. He started into the judge's secretary's office twice before he finally summoned the nerve to ask her to let him in to see the judge, and then nearly lost it all in the middle of his request to her when the door to Friedman's office opened and Milt Weigh walked out.

Only the expression on Weigh's face when their eyes met kept Balzic from leaving. Weigh looked as though he had spent long hours talking with people who knew more than he and had come away from the talks racked with mistrust of his own ability to judge anything.

For a moment, Balzic felt obliged to console Weigh, or, if not that, then at least to whisper his sympathy that Weigh had to learn certain things the way he had.

Balzic, for his part, could not remember a time when he did not know that public officials were used in ways they did not recognize until it was too late. Weigh, from his slouch, seemed never to have considered the possibility that he could be used as easily as he used others, and the slackness in his mouth when he spoke confirmed how much the learning had shaken him.

"Morning, Milt," Balzic said.

"Morning," Weigh said. "If you want to see Judge Friedman, you can now."

"Yes, thanks," Balzic said. "Maybe you ought to know, Milt, uh, I'm here to get an order to have the Parilla kid examined."

"I know that," Weigh said.

127

"You do?"

"Yes. I had a long talk with Mo Valcanas yesterday. That was just one of the things he told me."

"You don't—you have no objection?"

"Why should I?"

"I just thought you might."

"I don't," Weigh said. "As a matter of fact, I've already talked to Friedman about it, and you won't have to do much talking. Just tell him what you want. I'll follow it up."

"Okay, Milt. Okay. And thanks."

Judge Friedman appeared in the doorway. "Mario, did you want to see me?"

"Yes, I did," Balzic said and then said so long to Weigh, but Weigh was going through the door of the outer office and didn't hear.

"Come in, Mario, and have a seat," Friedman said. "Before we get to business, tell me who you like in the National League."

"Oh, Cincinnati all the way."

"You don't think the Pirates have a chance?"

"Who doesn't have a chance? But they don't have the pitching or the catching."

"You know, Cincinnati's pitching is wearing a little thin."

"Yeah, but that won't hurt them until the Series."

"You think the Pirates will win their division?"

"I don't really think it'll make too much difference who wins. Cincinnati has too much."

"So if someone offered you, say, five to seven, you'd take the Reds?"

"I'd take them against the Pirates at one to five."

"Really?" Friedman said, leaning back in his chair. "Well, what can I do for you?"

"Well, I want a lot of red tape cut in a hurry. I want to book a kid on a general charge of murder, and then I want him examined by a psychiatrist, but the thing I want to make sure of—well, two things, really. First, I don't want any problems with the charge, and second, I want to make sure the kid gets the works from the doctor just as fast as possible." Balzic looked at his fingernails. "Least that's what I

128

wanted, and that's what I thought I was going to have trouble getting. But Milt Weigh just told me he already said something to you about it."

"He has," Friedman said. "You file your information, Mario, and I guarantee to move this thing for you as fast as possible."

"How soon would you—I mean, how long do you think it'll take?"

"Well, Mario, if I declare no bail, what difference does it make?"

"Can you do that on a general charge?"

"That depends on who his lawyer is, and how much pressure is put on him."

"His lawyer's Valcanas."

"Oh."

"And he has an aunt."

"Why not make it first degree then?"

"That means premeditated, and I don't think this kid had the faintest idea of what he was doing."

"A technicality, Mario. You can't have it both ways. Make it first degree, and he doesn't get bail. It's that simple."

Balzic cleared his throat and rubbed his chin.

"Mario, don't be so cautious. I should say, rather, detach yourself from this. What does it matter if you have your man examined?"

"Nothing, I guess."

"Of course not," Friedman said, standing up. "Give his name to Elaine. She'll take care of the papers. Then you go get him."

"Right. Okay." Balzic stood. "And thanks, your honor."

"Mario, about this other thing?"

"What other thing?"

"You'd give one to five on the Reds?"

"Sure. But nobody'll need to. I would, though."

"You think the odds will come off much lower?"

"No question about it. I'd say they'll go off at six to five or even eleven to ten. It'll be way down."

"So you're suggesting that a fellow should wait?"

"Sure. He'd be foolish not to." Balzic turned for the door and then turned back. "One more thing, your honor."

"What is it?"

"I don't want to put this boy in a lockup. I want to take him right out to Mamont."

"Go ahead."

"Well, what I mean, could you give me a name out there, so I can be sure they'll go to work on him right away."

Judge Friedman walked past Balzic and called out to his secretary: "Elaine, get me Mamont State Hopsital. Dr. Lester."

Elaine looked through her desk directory and started dialing. "Is he the only Lester out there?"

"First name is Lou, Elaine. Louis G., I think." The judge went back to his desk to wait. "Good man Lester," Friedman said. "But they've turned him into an administrator, and I'm afraid he's being wasted."

A button lit up on the judge's phone. He picked it up and said, "Lou? Arnold Friedman here . . . Oh. fine. You? . . . Good, glad to hear it. Listen, Lou, I've got a problem. Trying to cut through channels and so forth . . . Yes, well this one's a little different. The chief of police here . . . Yes, that's the one. Balzic. He has a suspect in a case and he has reason to believe the suspect may not be in control of himself. I don't know all the details, but from what I gather, the suspect has some members of his family who are trying to interfere. . . ." Friedman looked at Balzic questioningly.

"And Chief Balzi wants a complete examination done on the suspect as quickly as possible . . . Well, Lou, I'm not going to say what the case involves. I don't want you looking for things that may not be there . . . Now you've got it. That's the idea. Just make a complete examination . . . Right, but don't wait on the paperwork. It will be along in a couple of days . . . Yes, I'm certain he'll have his man out there today." The judge again looked at Balzic for confirmation. Again Balzic nodded.

"Fine, Lou. And thanks. Bye," Friedman said, hanging up. "There, Mario. Done."

"Can't thank you enough, your honor."

"Thank me for what? A little while ago you gave me some information that's going to help me skin a couple, shall we say, friends of mine? I've been waiting ever since last year's Series when

130

those Mets were my undoing. I hate to tell you how much that cost me."

"Didn't cost me a thing," Balzic said.

"Well, then, I'll save you from some other trouble."

"How so?"

"Keep that damn Greek informed of what you're doing. Better yet, see if you can't get him to go along with you."

"You mean through the whole thing?"

Friedman nodded. "If he's free, it would save everybody a lot of grief. Have him with you when you pick your man up—I keep calling him a man, but he's a juvenile, isn't he?"

"Yeah. I don't think he's seventeen yet. Might be, but he's not eighteen. That I know."

"Well, see if you can't talk Valcanas into going along for the ride. If he's there to see that everything's done properly, he'll—well, he'll be able to deal with the family better."

Balzic doubted the reasoning of that, but he wasn't about to question it. Instead he thanked the judge again and went out to give the facts to his secretary. She filled out a warrant for him, which he shoved in his inside coat pocket. He thanked her and went downstairs into the lobby to inquire about Valcanas. There was no telling where Valcanas might be, and Balzic began to fret that Valcanas had made good his promise of letting his liver know who was boss. The more he fretted over that, the more he thought about Angie Spano, and the better he thought Judge Friedman's idea was to have Valcanas along.

"Try Muscotti's," Jimmy Rullo, Judge Scarpattie's tipstaff told Balzic. "That's where he usually winds up. He's probably over there right now half bagged and making speeches."

Balzic hesitated about going back to Muscotti's so soon after his trouble with Sam Carraza. He knew Dom Muscotti would expect an apology, and he knew just as clearly that he didn't feel like making one. With luck, Dom wouldn't be there.

He went in through Muscotti's back door and could hear Valcanas singing along with the juke box. Balzic came down the steps as Iron City Steve came shuffling in the front door, sawing his hand across

131

his mouth and diving into his pockets for money for a muscatel and beer.

"Stevie boy," Valcanas called out. "Man of the world, raconteur, man about Rocksburg. Tell me, Steve, how did it all begin?"

"It all began in the beginning," Steve called back, "and it was all a mistake." He fished a wadded dollar bill out of his pocket and unfolded it slowly, holding it out at arm's length finally for all to see. "A wine and a beer," he said to Pete Muscotti behind the bar.

"Put the money up," Pete said without moving.

"Put the money up," Steve mimicked him. "What do you think I'm going to do with it? The next time you give anything away'll be the next time I get a hardon."

"When you put the bread on the bar, I put the wine in the glass," Pete said.

"Give him a drink, for crissake," Valcanas said. "Can't you see the man needs respite from the world?" He staggered to the juke box and put another quarter in and punched some more buttons. "Mario! How goes it? What brings you to this quaint and humble septic tank? At this time of day—you must be drunk."

"I'm not, but you are," Balzic said.

"No shit. Am I really? How can you tell?"

Peggy Lee began to sing "Is That All There Is," and Valcanas shouted to Steve, who had emptied the glass of muscatel Pete had finally served him and was waiting for a refill. "Hey, Stevie boy. Iron City Steve! Are you listening, old compadre?"

"I'm listening," Steve said. He turned his head and pointed to his ear. He had half a match pack rolled into a horn stuck in his ear. "See? Got my hearing aid all wired up. I can hear anything. Go ahead. Say something."

"The music, Stevie boy. Miss Peggy Lee right here for your listening pleasure, coming to you live in absentia from high atop the Hotel Septic Tank, formerly the Hotel Muscotti, from downtown Rocksburg, P. A."

"Is that all there is," Steve croaked in a monotone that vanished behind the back of his hand as he wiped his lips and took aim on the full glass of muscatel.

"Mo," Balzic said, "I'd like you to do a favor."

132

"A favor? Hell, yes. Innkeeper, a drink for my friend here. What's your name again? Oh. Mario. Mario—don't tell me. I'll think of it in a second."

"What'll you have, Chiefo?" Pete said.

"Nothing. A big glass of ice water. For him," Balzic said, nodding toward Valcanas and pushing Valcanas's glass of whiskey away.

"Hey. Just what the hell do you think you're doing?" Valcanas snapped.

"You had enough."

"I'll be the judge of that. I don't need any goddamn instruction from you or anybody else in how to run my life. Do I tell you what to drink? Or when? Or how much?"

"I said I needed a favor."

"And I said I'd buy you a drink, for crissake. I know they don't pay you cops enough. Don't you think I know that? What the hell do you think I am? Stupid, like that wise-mouth dago behind the bar?"

"I need you sober to do this favor."

"Sober! Why you can go take a flying trip to the moon. Sober. Shit. What the hell could you possibly want done that I couldn't do practically comatose? Name it. Name one thing I could do for *you* I couldn't do standing on my elbows whistling the Dartmouth alma mater."

"Sober up. I bet you couldn't get sober."

"How much?"

"Five bucks says you can't."

"You're on, you bastard. Innkeeper, a glass of ice water and keep them coming till I tell you otherwise."

"There's one in front of you," Pete said.

"Oh. So there is. Imagine that. A mind reader. Knows what I'm going to order before I do. Have to apologize. You're not as dumb as the ordinary wop."

"Watch it, Greek," Pete said.

"Okay, forget it," Balzic said.

"What are you going to do about it, you overstuffed prosciuttini? Come around from behind that bar, and I'll lay you out."

"Okay, Mo. That's enough."

"I come out from behind this bar, counselor, you'll wish you were back in Greece," Pete said.

"All right, goddammit, that's enough. Both of you. Can it."

"Well, who the fuck's he think he is?" Valcanas shouted. "Primo Carnera? Tony Galento?" He jumped up from his stool and nearly fell as his ankles turned inward.

"That's what started it all," Iron City Steve said. "Abel said to Cain, 'Who the fuck you think you are—Tony Galento?' And Cain said, 'Joe Louis, that's who,' and he knocked him out. Boom. Abel hit his head on the ring post. That's what happened. Ever since people been arguing about who was the best boxer. Some say Abel. Most say Cain. Can't prove it by me. I wasn't there. How the hell would I know?" Steve looked deeply into his muscatel.

"Drink the water, Mo," Balzic said.

"Keep your shirt on, for crissake," Valcanas said. "You still haven't answered me. Who the fuck's he think he is talking to me like that?"

"Forget it. No harm done."

"Take the advice, counselor," Pete said. "For once Chiefo's making sense."

"Quit calling me that, goddammit."

"What's the matter with that? That's what you are, ain't it?"

"I'm a lawyer. A tradesman, that's all. That name you're calling me—that's pretentious horseshit."

"Some say Abel could move better," Steve said. "Had a better left. But there ain't no doubt who could hit harder. Cain all the way. Big right hand. Boom. Course, some say Cain butted him. How the hell would I know? All I know is what I read in the papers. Where's my beer?"

"Give my friend Steve his beer, for crissake, you goddamn chiseler," Valcanas said.

"If you was twenty years younger, Greek . . ." Pete said, going down the bar to pour a draught for Steve.

"If I was twenty years younger, what?"

"Drink your water," Balzic said. "We got a bet, remember?"

"So we have. How much time you giving me?"

"Half hour."

"Fair enough."

"Going to show a rerun on TV," Steve said. "Wide world of sports. Computer fight just like Clay and Marciano. In this corner, weighing one-seventy-three-and-a-quarter, in the purple trunks, from Eden—Cain! In this corner, wearing the white trunks with the black stripes, weighing one-sixty-nine even, also from Eden—Abel! And right here at ringside to bring you the blow-by-blow account—Howard Cosell! Hey, Mo, I'm taking Cain seven to five. Who do you like?"

"I'm a sport,"Valcanas said, wobbling over to the juke box. "Make it nine to five, and I'll take Abel."

"You got twenty-five minutes left, Mo."

"What the hell you worrying about? It's only five bucks, for crissake. Listen to this song. It breaks me up."

Balzic could see he had no choice. But twenty-five minutes later, and after six tumblers of ice water and two trips to the lavatory, Valcanas was walking with only a slight tilt.

"Okay," Valcanas said. "Where's the five?"

"See me next week. That's payday. Right now we got more important things to think about."

"Crissake, payday's always next week with you," Valcanas said. "See ya, Stevie boy. Don't do anything I wouldn't do, but make sure you get a good lawyer anyway."

"In the beginning was the word," Steve chanted, sawing his hand across his mouth, "and on the seventh day, 'long about eleven o'clock, the word was muscatel. God knew he had something there. . . ."

On the sidewalk Valcanas stopped Balzic. "Just where the hell are you taking me anyway?"

"To the high school," Balzic said, hurrying on.

"Hey, what's the big rush?" Valcanas called after him. "At least give me a chance to go to the state store to get a pint."

"No way. Come on, get the lead out."

"To the high school?" Valcanas muttered.

Balzic tried his best to explain to Valcanas in the car on the way, but Valcanas stared glumly out the window and said nothing.

135

"I'm just taking Friedman's advice, that's all. You're along to see that everything gets done right."

"I suppose you think that's a compliment."

Balzic parked the car and got out. "Listen, Greek, I can think of at least two hundred people I'd rather compliment. You want to come in, or you going to sit out here and sulk?"

"I'll sulk, thank you. Unless you think you need assistance apprehending your suspect."

Balzic was back in five minutes. "We got problems," he said.

"Where's the kid?"

"That's the problem. He hasn't been in school since last Friday, which, in case you've forgotten, was the day Andrasko got it."

"Whatta you mean, *we* got problems? And just where the hell are you going now?"

"Out to their house."

"Then you can just drop me at Muscotti's."

"Nothing doing. You're with me all the way on this one."

"And just what am I supposed to do out there—sanctify your little plan, or protect you from little Angie?"

"Little of both," Balzic said. "But something tells me what you're really going to have to do is get little Angie to 'fess up and tell us where he is."

"You're starting to sound like a ridge runner, for crissake," Valcanas said. He blew his nose, and after he pocketed his hanky, he said, "And what makes you think I'm going to get her to tell me where he is—what do I look like? A priest?"

"Nothing makes me think it. I know she sure as hell isn't going to tell me—if she knows. But I think she does know, and I also know the first person she called when the state boys picked the kid up was you. You add it up."

Valcanas snorted. "We'll see how far either one of us gets."

Balzic pulled up to the Andrasko house and said, "Well, let's just go see."

Angie Spano answered the door. "What do you want?" she said to Balzic, but before he could answer, she glared at Valcanas and said, "Which side of the street are you working?"

"Relax," Valcanas said, "and listen to what the man has to say."

"Mind if we come in?"

"Sure, I mind. Do I have a choice?"

"Not really. But it would be more comfortable inside."

Mary Andrasko came up behind her sister. "Who is it?"

"Guess," Angie said, holding the door open for Balzic and Valcanas to come in.

"I have a warrant here for the boy," Balzic said, taking it out of his coat pocket. "He's not in school."

"What? What for?" Mary Andrasko said. "For Tommy? What did he do? My God, don't I have enough . . ." She sank into a chair. "What's going on? The day we buried John, the state police came for him. They didn't say a word. They just took him. Now you. What's going on?"

"Go ahead, big shot," Angie said. "Tell her."

"Mrs. Andrasko—" Balzic started to say and then looked nervously at Valcanas.

"Mrs. Andrasko," Valcanas said, "I've known this police officer for a long time, and I've never known him to do things without good cause. Furthermore, your sister retained me the day of your husband's funeral to act in your son's behalf. Chief Balzic here, in my judgment, has the best interests of your son in mind. That is a warrant he's holding, and it is a murder warrant charging your son, Tommy, with the murder of your late husband."

"Oh, my God," Mary said, her hands flying to her face.

"Mrs. Andrasko," Balzic said, "I don't think Tommy knew what he was doing. I think he's sick—"

"Sick! What do you think I am? You're telling me this—first, he murdered my John. Then he's sick! Do you know what you're telling me? My God, don't I have enough grief?" She was shouting and tears streamed down her face. "You're saying he killed my husband—his own father! My God, my God, I can't stand any-more. . . ."

"You son of a bitch," Angie said.

"You keep quiet," Valcanas snapped. "Mrs. Andrasko, get hold of yourself and listen. Mrs. Andrasko!"

137

Mary Andrasko's wailing turned to short bursts of sobs and then abruptly to coughing, sending violent tremors through her shoulders. She gripped the cushion of the chair and looked up at them.

"Now, listen to me," Valcanas said, going down on one knee in front of her and taking her hand. "This is not what it sounds like."

"Sure. Give it some fancy names," Angie said.

"I told you to keep quiet," Valcanas said, "and if you open your mouth once more I'm going to ask this police officer to restrain you with all necessary force. Do you understand that?"

"I'd like to—"

"You'd like to what?" Valcanas said.

Angie turned and walked to a chair in the corner near the television and dropped into it.

"Mrs. Andrasko," Valcanas said, "listen carefully to me. In the first place John Andrasko was not Tommy's father."

"I know that," she said. "My God, don't you think I know that?"

"A moment ago you said he was. I wanted to make it clear that you knew that. At this moment, I want to make sure you know the things you know, and I want to tell you the things you need to know.

"Chief Balzic here has already got the word of a judge to order a psychiatric examination for your son—is that correct, Chief?"

"That's correct, Mrs. Andrasko."

"And this whole business about the murder warrant is strictly a matter of legal procedure, Mrs. Andrasko," Valcanas went on. "It's a way of making sure that your son is properly arrested, properly charged, and properly remanded—I mean, properly turned over to the psychiatrists who will examine him. That's all this warrant does. That's what the whole procedure is about. Mrs. Andrasko, are you still hearing me?"

She nodded.

"This warrant does not mean that Tommy murdered your husband. This warrant is not a conviction. It isn't anything but what I've said it is. That is, to be more explicit, it isn't anything more than the legal means necessary to have Tommy examined. The fact of the matter is that no one has the least substantial evidence to indicate that Tommy had anything to do with it. Am I right about this,

Chief? Am I leaving anything out or attempting to make something appear to be something else?"

"He's right, Mrs. Andrasko. Everything he's said."

"Believe me, Mrs. Andrasko, it's a way of protecting your son," Valcanas said.

"But why?" she asked. "What in God's name makes you even get such an idea about Tommy. . . ." She buried her face in her hands.

"Take your hands away and listen, Mrs. Andrasko. Mario, tell her."

"Mrs. Andrasko, in anything like this, we have certain things to go on. We look at the way a thing was done, at where and how. We look at all the circumstances and possibilities. Your husband wasn't robbed, and your son didn't come home until one-thirty that night."

"Is that all? On that, on those two things you think my Tommy did it?"

"Not only on those two things, Mrs. Andrasko. There are others. Things Tommy said to me that night. The fact that somebody took a lot of trouble to clean your automobile, not just clean it, but clean it with disinfectant. The same kind of disinfectant that was found in your barn. Then there's the way—the way John was killed. He wasn't just killed. He was beaten beyond recognition. Mrs. Andrasko, I knew John all my life, and I had to be told who he was. All of these things put together don't mean for sure that Tommy did it, but these things give me reason for thinking that he might have, and I'm trying to find out whether I'm wrong as much as I'm trying to find out whether I'm right. You have to understand that."

"So tell her the rest," Angie said. "Tell her what you told me down at the funeral home. Go ahead."

"What's she talking about? Angie, what are you talking about?"

"Don't worry about what she's talking about," Valcanas said.

"Don't I have a right to know if it's something about this?"

"Damn right you do, honey," Angie said, looking defiantly at Balzic. "Well? What's the big problem? You didn't have any trouble telling me. Tell her now. What you said in the parking lot."

"Tell me what, for God's sake?" Mary pleaded.

"The rest of his nice theory," Angie said. "The rest of why he's after Tommy. Go ahead, cop."

"I will," Balzic said. "When the time comes. But if you make me tell her that now, then you're going to have to tell her what you told me. About a certain somebody making a pass at somebody else. How would that be? Fair enough?"

Angie flushed. She jumped up and ducked between them into the kitchen. Cupboard doors started banging, and then the refrigerator, and then came the sound of ice cubes and a bottle scraping against glass.

"Are you going to tell me?" Mary said.

"Mrs. Andrasko," Balzic said, "right now I don't think any good would be done if I told you what your sister wants me to tell you. Later on, if my idea is right—mind you, if—then I give you my word I'll tell you. But if I'm wrong, well, I don't see any good reason for you to know what your sister's referring to. You'll just have to take my word for it."

"Oh God, if John was here, he'd tell me who to believe. He would. John was always so sure. . . ." Mary leaned forward with her elbows on her knees and covered her face. "I don't know what to think."

"For right now, Mrs. Andrasko, just tell us where Tommy is."

Her head snapped up. "He's in school—isn't he?"

"No, he's not. We just came from there. The people there said he hasn't been in school since last Friday."

"That's crazy. Sure he's in school. I pack him a lunch every day. He won't eat the cafeteria food. He makes me pack him a lunch. I know I packed him a lunch on Friday. And since the—well, my God, I know I packed him a lunch today. And he left the house at the same time he always does."

Angie came back from the kitchen and stood in the doorway. The drink she'd made herself was deep amber. "He's gone," she said.

"What does that mean?" Balzic said.

"Just what it sounds like. Gone. Phfttt. Bye-bye."

"And just what did you have to do with that?" Valcanas said, advancing on Angie.

"Who said I had anything to do with anything?"

"Don't get cute with me, dearie. I've been dealing with liars too long," Valcanas said. "Do you know what you're fooling with, withholding material evidence?"

140

"I don't know what you're talking about."

"Then I'll spell it out for you. Let's try obstructing justice for openers. Then how about aiding and abetting the flight of a fugitive from justice? How about accessory after the fact? Those good enough for you? You know what I'm talking about now?"

Angie stiffened. "I gave him some money, and I told him to take off," she whispered.

Mary stood and confronted her sister. "Angie! What are you saying?"

Angie gulped her drink. "I didn't stutter," she said.

She was starting to turn away when Mary slapped her, the blow glancing off the back of her head.

Angie whirled around. "All right. All right, goddammit. Do you want to know what that cop's talking about? He's thinking Tommy killed John all right, but he wasn't really killing John—am I right, cop?" She squinted furiously at Balzic and then turned her rage on her sister. "He was killing Tami, that's who he was killing. And you want to know why? 'Cause we put the idea in his head. You. And me. Us. Do you remember, sister dear, all those bitch sessions we had in my place after Tami took off on you? I remember them. Oh God, do I ever. And we didn't have sense enough to shut up around Tommy. And what we said stuck in his head, and he grew up on that, and he waited and waited, and finally he went after John.

"You think I'm crazy? Ask the cop. I thought he was crazy, too, the son of a bitch. But then I thought about it some more. And I remembered all those nights. Night after night after goddamn night. You and me sitting around bitching about what a bastard Tami was and there was little Tommy, sitting there and crawling around and taking it all in."

"But he was so little," Mary said. "He was only so little."

"Sure. Just a baby. But he heard it all—ain't that right, cop? Am I telling it right?"

Balzic nodded in spite of himself. He wanted to tell her to shut up. He wanted to choke her, but he kept on nodding.

"And it all stayed there in his head," Angie kept on. "And then one day he couldn't handle it anymore, right, cop? One day—last Friday he got everything mixed up. . . ." Angie turned abruptly and darted into the kitchen. First there was the sound of the bottle and the ice cubes. Then there came the sobs.

Mary turned glazed eyes on Balzic. Then she brushed past him into the living room and sat on the edge of a chair. She chewed her little fingers and began to rock on the edge of the chair.

Balzic went into the kitchen. "Where is he?" he said. When he got no reply, he said, "Do you want a hanky?"

Head down, Angie said, "No."

"No, you don't want a hanky, or no, you're not going to tell me where he is?"

"No I don't want your goddamn hanky, and no I'm not going to tell you where he is, because I don't know where. I gave him every cent I could spare. Sixty-two dollars. He took the car this morning, and that was the last I saw him. Satisfied?"

"No," Balzic said, sighing, "are you?"

She told him in Italian to fuck himself.

"That's not going to help. You got any ideas?"

"You're the one with all the ideas," she said. "How many you got?"

Balzic left Angie Spano in the kitchen and went out to his car. He got Stramsky on the radio.

"Vic, get out an A.P.B. on Thomas Parilla, male, Caucasian, age seventeen. Got that so far?"

"Hold it," Stramsky said. "Okay, go."

"Height five-nine, weight approximately one-thirty-five, slender build, hair black, eyes brown, complexion dark with bad acne."

"Okay, go."

"Driving a 1967 Ford Sedan. Maroon. Check with Moyer on the license."

"Anything else?"

"Yeah. Murder warrant on same. Probably psycho. Probably not armed, but approach with caution anyway. Never can tell. I don't know what he's holding."

142

"Roger. You want me to call Moyer first?"

"Yeah. Tell him I'd like everybody he can spare—as a favor to me." Balzic hung the speaker on the hook and sat back to light a cigarette. "Goddamn you, woman," he said. He sat smoking for a minute and then went back into the house.

Mary Andrasko was still sitting on the edge of the chair, her hands still pressed against her face. Her eyes were clouded over. Mo Valcanas was looking anxiously at the kitchen.

"Where's Angie?" Balzic asked him.

"Still in the kitchen."

"Why don't you go bum a drink? That's what you want, isn't it?"

"Best idea I've heard in the last hour," Valcanas said, heading for the kitchen.

"Mrs. Andrasko," Balzic said, "do you have a recent photograph of Tommy?"

"What?"

"I said, do you have a recent picture of Tommy?"

"What for?"

"It would make things a lot easier."

"For you."

"Yes, ma'am."

"What's going to make it easier for me?"

"Nothing," Balzic said. "I'd be lying if I said anything would."

She continued to stare. "Was Angie telling the truth before?"

"It's still just a theory."

"I don't care what you call it. Was she telling me what you told her?"

"More or less, yes."

"So then you think it's my fault. Mine and hers."

"Mrs. Andrasko, I'm not a judge. I—"

"Oh, how easy for you to say that. But you don't mean it. Listen to the way you say it. You *are* a judge. You already decided whose fault it is. But let me tell you something, mister, it wasn't easy when my first husband left me—"

"I'm sure it wasn't."

143

"How would you know what it was like? How would you know? You probably never did nothing wrong in your whole life. Baloney, mister. Ba-loney. All you people that think you never did nothing wrong, you're always the ones making mistakes, only you never see any of them—"

"It may look that way, Mrs. Andrasko, but it isn't that way, believe me."

"Who're you to tell me that? You know what I say to that? I say bullshit. You people, people like you, you make me sick. Always looking down your noses at me 'cause John never . . ." Her eyes, which has focused angrily on Balzic, clouded over again and then disappeared behind her hands. She began to sob.

"Mrs. Andrasko, it may come as a surprise to you, but everybody I know who knows you thinks you and John were married. What's more, as far as the law's concerned in this state, you two were as married as anybody gets."

"No, we weren't!" she cried out.

"Yes, you were, Mrs. Andrasko. And any shame you feel about your marriage with John is shame you brought on yourself. If you don't believe me, ask Mr. Valcanas. He knows the law better than I do. He'll tell you. There can be no shame about your marriage."

"Marriage, marriage. Quit it! We weren't married—how many times do I have to tell you? I was never divorced from Tami."

"Well, the law covers that, too." Balzic turned toward the kitchen. "Hey, Mo, come in here a minute."

"I don't care what any lawyer says. We were living in sin, and now God's punished us for it."

"I heard that, Mrs. Andrasko," Valcanas said, "and I wouldn't presume to tell you how your religion looks at your marriage—"

"Quit calling it that, for God's sake! It wasn't a marriage. It was sin."

"All right, Mrs. Andrasko. But will you answer a couple of questions? Will you tell me how long it's been since you've lived with your first husband?"

"Thirteen years. Tommy was four when he left."

"All right. The law here grants what amounts to a divorce without proceedings after desertion by one of the spouses after seven years.

That's common law. So you were in fact divorced from your first husband."

"No, I wasn't."

"Believe what you will, but tell me this: how long had you lived with John?"

"Eight years."

"Again, common law says you were married. No question about it."

"What about all those years in between? What about them?"

"Mrs. Andrasko, all those years you're worried about become hypothetical in the eyes of the law. The fact that your first husband never returned after deserting you is all that counts. That, plus the fact that you presented yourself to the world as Mr. and Mrs. John Andrasko. That's all that matters."

"Maybe to you. Maybe to some judge. But you don't know how many times I didn't go out of this house because of what people were saying about me."

Valcanas shrugged. "Madam, I can only tell you about the law. Social custom is something I merely witness, like any other citizen. I gave up trying to understand it long ago. Now, if you'll excuse me, I have a drink in the kitchen." Valcanas nodded at Balzic and motioned with his head for Balzic to follow him out to the kitchen.

When they got there Valcanas said, "Let her alone, for crissake. She'll never take your word for anything. What she needs is a priest. She's Catholic, isn't she?"

Balzic nodded.

"Well, for crissake, if you know a priest, then get him the hell out here. She doesn't want a legal explanation. She wants absolution. The best thing you could do is tell her to confess her sins. She'll love you for understanding what an evil woman she is. Hell, anybody can see she's got sins a mile wide, and she's been working them for twelve or thirteen years. If she works it right, they'll be good for another fifty thousand miles."

"How smart you two guys are," Angie said. She was sitting at the table, running her fingers over the condensed vapor on her glass. "You two know all the answers."

"Quit crying in your sauce, for crissake," Valcanas said. "Neither one of us pretends to know all that much, but I know when a man's wasting his breath trying to explain a very simple thing, and I also know when somebody doesn't want to be explained to. That doesn't take any goddamn genius on anybody's part. Where'd you hide the bottle?"

"Go get your own," Angie said. "You lawyers make enough. You don't need to freeload off of me."

"I'll subtract the price of two drinks from your bill, how's that?"

"Come on, Mo. I'll drop you at Muscotti's," Balzic said, tugging at Valcanas's elbow.

"Fine," Valcanas said, bowing to Angie and lifting his hat. "And a good day to you, madam. Your generosity is exceeded only by your looks, which wouldn't be half bad if you knew how to make up your face and bought some decent clothes."

"Come on, Mo, before you get us into more trouble than we can handle."

"You better get him out of here, the two-faced son of a bitch," Angie said.

"Temper, temper," Valcanas said, grinning.

Balzic led him out of the kitchen and into the living room. "Mrs. Andrasko," he said, "if Tommy should come back, it would be better all around if you called me."

Mary Andrasko did not look up.

"You're wasting your time," Valcanas whispered. "Besides, I'm really getting a thirst on."

In the car on the way to Muscotti's, Valcanas asked, "What now?"

"Now? Now I wait and hope I don't do anything dumb like get drunk while I'm waiting."

"An admirable ambition. If you plan to wait in Muscotti's, I hope for my sake you don't succeed."

"Since when do you need company?"

"I don't, but it would bother me to be having a good time knowing I was standing beside someone who was waiting to avenge an injustice."

"No more. You make my side hurt."

"Can't you make this thing go any faster, for crissake?"

"Patience, Myron. Nobody's threatening prohibition."

146

"You call me Myron again, and you're going to have to defend yourself, goddammit."

"All right, counselor," Balzic said, restraining his grin.

"Don't call me that, either—hey, you just passed up two parking places, for crissake."

"There's one ahead, Mister Valcanas. Don't get excited."

Balzic parked, and the two of them went into Muscotti's, Valcanas going at something faster than a walk.

Iron City Steve was at one of the tables, looking impatiently at an empty beer glass and an empty wine glass in front of him. "No drilling, no well," he said, sawing his hand across his mouth. "Let's not scratch the surface, let's pick the surface up and throw it away. . . ."

"Let's have a drink," Valcanas said.

"Best idea anybody had all day," Steve said, rising unsteadily and following Valcanas to the bar.

Vinnie was working behind the bar.

"Since when did you start working daylight?" Balzic asked him.

"Since about an hour ago," Vinnie said. "Since the state cops walked in and grabbed Petey boy."

"Pete Muscotti?" Balzic said. "What for, this time?"

"Give us a drink, for crissake," Valcanas said. "You girls can talk later."

"What happened, Vinnie?"

"What do I know what happened? They walked in and put the grab on him. So what's it going to be?"

"C-C and water for me," Valcanas said. "A muscatel and beer for my compadre Steve. Mario can speak for himself, but I'm buying."

"I, too, can speak for myself," Steve said.

"That'll be the day anybody can get you to shut up. What's for you, Mario?" Vinnie said, pouring the drinks.

"Nothing. I just want to know why Pete got busted?"

"A buck even, Greek," Vinnie said. He rang it up. "What do I know? Last I heard he was trying to hustle furnaces. You know him. He's pulling crap like that all the time. Probably some old lady smelled something and got on the phone. What do I know?"

"Was he alone?"

147

"What—are you kidding? He's too dumb to have a partner," Vinnie said. "Meantime, I got to go on daylight now for who knows how long."

"Dom pissed off?"

"Pissed off! He can't even see. He told Pete the last time was the last time. He ain't about to put him to work no more, blood or no blood. So it's me from now on, pal."

"You never had it so good, for crissake," Valcanas said.

"Then there's the wind," Steve said. "What good is the wind? But there it is. . . ."

"You're the wind," Vinnie said. "You're a goddamn hurricane. Shut up for a minute. Just try and see if you can do it."

"You know," Balzic said, "I never could stand that weasel."

"Pete? He sees too many movies, that's all that's wrong with him," Vinnie said. "He's harmless."

"He is like hell harmless," Balzic said. "He just never had the right opportunity."

"What would he do? Nothing," Vinnie said.

"He just hasn't seen the chance," Balzic said.

"Opportunity knocks several times," Steve said, "but chance never knocks. Doesn't have to—here's to you, Mr. Mo, and a lucky day it was for me when you walked in."

Balzic walked to the end of the bar nearest the front door and motioned for Vinnie to follow him.

"So what's up?" Vinnie said.

"You telling me everything you know?"

"What's to hide?"

"Come on, Vinnie. What was that prick into?"

"Furnaces I'm telling you. You know the bit. He walks in and wants to inspect the furnace, all that shit. Only he picked the wrong old lady. She listens to his hustle, and then she gets on the phone to the better business people, and that was that. Turns out he made about four phony contracts for replacements—after a substantial down payment, understand. Why? What did you think he was into?"

"He's been into so goddamn much, nothing would surprise me,"

Balzic said. "He was no good when times were good. He's been looking for a big score for I don't know how long."

"Come on, Mario, who ain't looking for a big score? Look at me. Last week I got ninety-six bucks on my house number. You going to arrest me for hoping?"

"That's different. Petey boy's been a mean prick since he was a kid."

"Since he was a kid? He's still a kid, for crying out loud. He can't be twenty-three, twenty-four at the most. I'm telling you, he sees too many movies, that's all."

"That's what I mean. He sees those movies, he believes them. He's been trying to get close to Dom now for how long?"

"There again, how many people you know been trying to get close to Dom? What's that mean? Jesus, if I wasn't around to keep all the figures straight, Dom would be dead. He can't remember who he's laying off for. He can't remember from last week. But all the creeps that come in, who do they go for? Me? Or Dom? But without me, Dom's history. But the hot dogs still go for Dom. So?"

"Okay, we both know all that. But think a minute. Of all the people that come in here, all the ones that know Dom, all his relatives, who's been trying longer and harder to get close to him than Petey boy?"

Vinnie scratched his stubble. "You got a point there. He's been hanging tight for a long time now."

"That's what I mean."

"But so what? What the hell are you worrying about him for?"

"I don't know," Balzic said. "I just got a funny feeling. Give me a draught."

"Hey, Vinnie boy," Valcanas called out. "Why don't you have the baseball game on?"

"It's over, that's why."

"Who won?"

"Who do you think? Cincinnati. Who else—the Pirates?"

"Is that the playoffs already?" Balzic said.

"Sure it's the playoffs," Vinnie said. "Where you been?"

"What was the score?"

Vinnie shrugged. "All I know is, the Reds won. I wasn't watching."

"Sometimes the Reds win," Steve said, "sometimes the Blues. Mostly it's the Blues. . . ."

"Did it get a lot of action?" Balzic asked Vinnie.

Vinnie screwed up his face and came to where Balzic was and leaned over the bar. "You wouldn't believe how much. Dom had to call Pittsburgh," he whispered. "All Cincinnati. Nobody was buying the Pirates. Christ, he couldn't cover a third of it."

"Between that and Petey boy, he's going to be rare for a while."

"Everybody takes a bath, brother. It was his turn, that's all. What pisses me is I told him to stay away from it soon as I saw how it was going, but you know him. He says nothing doing, the action got to go the other way. I tell him it ain't, and he tells me to tend the bar and keep the numbers straight, and I tell him, okay, don't say I didn't tell you. But you better believe it didn't go the other way. And he got it for two more days yet, and don't you know Cincinnati's going to kill them. Hey, he's so fuckin' smart, sometimes he makes my head hurt."

"Give us a drink here, for crissake," Valcanas said. "Is this a saloon or a bridge club?"

"Bridges and clubs," Steve said, "clubs for doing business and bridges for the getaway. . . ."

Balzic tried to call Father Marrazo, to get him to talk to Mrs. Andrasko about her marriage or sins or both but couldn't locate him. He called his own station every fifteen minutes and the state police as often. Not only was Tommy Parilla nowhere to be found, but the desk man at the state police barracks couldn't say where Lieutenant Moyer was either.

Balzic called home and told Ruth it was going to be another long night.

"Mar, we have to do something about Marie," Ruth said.

"More of the same?"

150

"She's getting worse. She came home from school and went straight to her room. That's the second day she's done that. Yesterday, she didn't want any supper, and—oh, I'm just getting worried, that's all. You sure you know what you're doing about her?"

"No," Balzic said. "But I don't know what else to do. Anyway, I can't do anything about it tonight. But maybe this will all be over tonight."

"Are you just saying that?"

"I guess I'm just saying that 'cause I want it to be that way."

"Well, will you at least say something to her tomorrow?"

"Uh-uh. I told you before, I'm not going to say anything to her about this until I know for sure that the kid did it. It looks almost a hundred per cent certain he did, but I still won't be satisfied until I hear a psychiatrist say so. But that's all beside the point now. Now we got to find him."

"You mean he ran away?"

"You got it, babe. His goofy aunt gave him fifty, sixty bucks, and he took John's car. Something tells me he isn't going far, but you can't tell. Hell, he might be halfway to Florida by now. I got to go, babe. I'll call you soon as I know something. And quit worrying about Marie. She'll be all right."

"You always say that."

"'Cause it will. See you later," Balzic said, hanging up. He rooted through his pockets for another dime and called the state police again. This time Moyer was in.

"Balzic. Where the hell you been?"

"I had a meeting with some boys from the Washington barracks. What's up?"

"Didn't anybody tell you? The Parilla kid's gone."

"That? Yeah, they told me. What do you want to do about it?"

Balzic felt suddenly foolish. He had no answer for what he wanted to do about it. "I was hoping you might have some ideas," he said.

"Well, look, Mario. You're the one's had a theory about this from the start. Where would you guess that kid's going to be—that is, if your theory is right?"

151

"At the station."

"Don't know why it took you so long to think of it. You sure as hell have been spending enough time down there at night."

"How would you know?"

"How do you think? I've had two men down there right beside you. You didn't see them?"

"No," Balzic said. "They must be pretty good men."

"Well, hell, Mario. You've been out there under the lights. They just been where you would've needed a spotlight to see them, that's all. Anyway, my suggestion to you is just to go on back down there tonight. I think that's where the kid is going to be."

"Yeah," Balzic said. "Hey, one other thing. What about young Muscotti. Pete, Dom's nephew. What did you pick him up for?"

"I don't know anything about it. That's Stallcup's case. He's been working on young Muscotti for a while, but I didn't even know he picked him up. Wait a minute."

Balzic could hear Moyer calling out to someone in his office.

"Mario?"

"Right here."

"Stallcup booked Muscotti on four counts of fraud and one for attempt to defraud."

"Where is he?"

"He's down the Southern Regional. Looks like nobody wants to take a chance on him, not even the professional bondsmen. Why?"

"Just curious. I heard about it from the bartender here."

"You in Muscotti's?"

"Yeah. Shouldn't I be?"

"I'm not telling you where to be. Just don't get a load on, that's all. I like my guinea pigs to be sober enough to help out—in case." Moyer thought that was very funny.

"Well," Balzic said, "that'll be me under the lights tonight. See you afterward if nothing happens by midnight or so. Maybe we can catch a couple beers."

"Good enough," Moyer said and hung up.

"Shit," Balzic whispered, going back to the bar.

"You look like somebody poisoned your dog, for crissake,"

Valcanas said. "Have a drink. A real drink. Not that lousy green beer."

"What I need doesn't come in bottles," Balzic said, walking past Valcanas and Iron City Steve, and staring through the triangular window in Muscotti's front door.

"Who needs to know what they need?" Steve said, his hand going back and forth under his nose.

"Exactly," Valcanas said. "And what we need right now is a little music." He went to the juke box, dropped in a quarter, and punched some buttons.

"Why don't you two form a club?" Vinnie said.

"A form I don't need," Steve said. "A club I don't need either, not unless I meet somebody with a bigger form...."

"Riddles," Vinnie said, emptying the ashtrays and wiping the bar. "More bullshit."

Balzic locked his hands behind his back and started to rock impatiently on his heels and toes. Through the window, he could see the traffic starting to pick up. He didn't have to look at a clock to know it was near four-thirty, and there he was, he thought, wearing out his shoes going nowhere.

It was six minutes past midnight when Balzic, heaving out a sigh, crushed out the last cigarette he had, and, taking one last fruitless look around, stalked off the platform of the Pennsylvania Station. He wanted to call out to the two troopers he knew had been covering him on Moyer's orders—the ones he still hadn't spotted—to forget the whole ridiculous business. It was all stupid. Tommy Parilla was probably asleep somewhere, probably wishing he hadn't let his aunt talk him into running away, probably wishing he was home drinking a nice, cold Coke. Which is where I ought to be, Balzic thought. Home, drinking a nice cold beer and reading the want ads looking for sensible work.

He went down to the lower level. Frank Bennett, the station master, was dozing in his swivel chair, and Balzic continued past to the parking lot and his car. He stopped with his hand on the car door

153

and reached for cigarettes he knew weren't there and debated whether to go back and bother Bennett for a smoke.

"This is really getting to be a drag," someone said, and Balzic's head spun.

The two troopers were not fifteen feet from him, but he hadn't heard them coming. "What the hell you guys got on your shoes—soft boiled eggs?"

"S'matter, Chief? You getting careless?" one of them said.

"Yeah," Balzic said. "Every time I start to think these days."

"Guess that cuts it tonight," the other trooper said.

"Yeah," Balzic said, patting his pockets. "Say, either one of you got a smoke?"

They both reached for their blouse pockets. Balzic turned to face them and saw something move behind them. "Hold it," he said.

"What's up?"

"Behind you. Under that baggage cart. Am I seeing things?"

Both troopers turned and looked. "I'll be damned," one said.

The other sprinted to the cart, drawing his revolver as he ran. Balzic and the other trooper bolted after him. "Easy now," Balzic called out.

"Come out of there," the first trooper said, bending down and motioning with his free hand and pointing his revolver at the squatting figure.

The figure didn't move.

Balzic went down on one knee. "Come on out, Tommy," he said.

Tommy Parilla suddenly started to giggle and stopped as suddenly, the sound catching in his throat. His head dropped and he looked at the tire iron between his feet.

"Oh, Jesus," Balzic said, seeing the slick look of the tire iron. "Tommy, we're not going to hurt you. Come on out, son."

Tommy started to giggle again, and stopped again as quickly.

Balzic held out his hand. "Come on, son. It's okay."

Tommy stared at him. There was a hissing sound and then a dripping.

"What's he doing?" the second trooper said. "Pissin' himself?"

"Yeah, Jesus," Balzic said. "Come on, Tommy. It's all right."

154

"No," Tommy said. "Bad, Bad Tommy."

Some seconds passed. Tommy lurched forward on his hands and came crawling out. "I make pee-pee," he said. "I make pee-pee."

"It's okay, Tommy," Balzic said, helping Tommy to his feet.

Tommy crossed and uncrossed his legs, standing each time with the heel of one shoe on the toe of the other.

"God, look at him," the trooper with his revolver drawn said.

"Looks like we been watching and waiting in the wrong place," the second trooper said.

"Where is he, Tommy?" Balzic said.

"Who?"

"Daddy," Balzic said. "Where's Daddy?"

Tommy stopped crossing his legs and pointed with his right hand to the back edge of the parking lot. The maroon Ford was parked beside a black Chrysler Imperial. Tommy started to chew his left thumb nail, and, as he pointed again, his thumb slipped into his mouth.

"Who'd believe it?" the second trooper said, trotting off toward the cars parked at the extreme edge of the lot. In a moment, he called back: "He's still got a pulse!"

The first trooper broke for his unmarked cruiser and called for an ambulance.

Balzic led Tommy to his own car. "Better pick up that tire iron," he said to the trooper who'd called the ambulance and was now trying to get Lieutenant Moyer.

The second trooper came trotting from between the Ford and the Chrysler and got a blanket from the trunk of his cruiser. He ran back with it, and, after a moment, came back shaking his head.

"Get in the car, Tommy," Balzic said, holding open the back door.

Tommy crawled in and curled up on the seat, his thumb still in his mouth. He glanced back wildly at Balzic, but when Balzic closed the door, the boy put his head down and closed his eyes.

"You think he'll be okay like that?" the second trooper said.

"Right now he's four years old," Balzic said. "He ain't going nowhere. Let's have a look." He started for the cars at the edge of the lot.

155

"I'll wait for the ambulance if it's all the same to you," the second trooper said.

"Suit yourself," Balzic said. He found the man between the cars near the front fender of the Imperial. His breathing had an ominous gurgling sound. Stretched above his head in his left hand was a doctor's bag. Balzic had to pry his fingers off the handle.

Balzic set the bag down and went through the man's pockets, doing that as much to keep from looking at the man's face as to find out who the man was. He found a considerable stack of bills in a billfold and a set of keys in a leather case. Balzic took the small key and hesitated. Something told him he wouldn't find medical equipment or supplies in the bag.

He got out of the way when the ambulance came and was still hesitating about the bag when it pulled away. He didn't unlock the bag until he saw Moyer pulling in, leading two other cars of troopers.

"Look at this," he said when Moyer approached him. "Poor bastard, he thought he was being robbed."

"How much you think is there?"

"Well, Phil, it's a little more than you or me'll make in a couple of paydays."

"I'd say so," Moyer said. "You get a name?"

"No cards in the billfold. Just more paper. Maybe he has some cards in the car. The Imperial."

"Check it," Moyer said to one of the troopers who had come with him. "Well, Mario, how's it feel to be right?"

"Shitty."

"Where is he?"

"Back seat of my car," Balzic said. "Sucking his thumb."

Moyer looked doubtful.

"See for yourself," Balzic said.

Moyer went and looked and came back with the vaguest trace of a smile. "Mario, you're in the wrong business," he said.

"Ain't I though," Balzic said. He looked at the doctor's bag. "I sure as hell don't like this."

"So he hit somebody's bag man. So what? He's a psycho. He's not a robber. What does it matter anyway?"

"It matters that Dom Muscotti was taking a real bath on the

156

National League playoffs for one thing. It matters that this bag is still full for another." Balzic shook his head. "Why the hell did this have to get into it? I don't like this even a little bit."

"Mario, quit acting like we got a gang war on our hands or something. You forgetting who you got in your car?"

"No. I'm also not forgetting that Dom Muscotti was waiting for this money."

"Why are you so sure it was for him?"

"I know, that's all. He got caught in a lot of one-way traffic."

"Well, pity poor Dom. He doesn't know the chances. Hell, for that matter, you want to worry about something, think about whoever sent this guy out here. Seems to me that whoever that is is going to be a little distressed about it, too." Moyer threw up his hands. "Mario, we could go on worrying about things all night. For what? You got your man. What does it matter how the book gets burned?"

"It matters. It also depends how things go."

"What things?"

"Well, I got it set up to get the kid out to Mamont, but I still don't know if the paperwork's taken care of yet."

"So what's the problem? We book him and take him out to Southern Regional. They isolate him and that's that."

"I still don't like it."

"What's not to like? Mario, sometimes I swear I don't get you."

"For things not to like, take a look at who's coming."

Moyer looked over his shoulder. A car pulled in behind his, and Dick Dietz, *The Rocksburg Gazette* reporter, got out and came striding toward them.

"Mario, old friend, he's all yours. I got work to do."

"Your people know what to do."

"At moments like this, they have to be supervised," Moyer said, walking off toward the Chrysler Imperial.

"Bastard," Balzic said under his breath.

"What's up, Chief," Dietz said, trying to look everywhere at once.

"Not much. Case of assault, that's all."

"That'll be the day. I count seven state cops plus you and Moyer. Come on, let's have it."

"You got it. Assault. Victim's on his way to the hospital.

Assailant's in custody and on his way to the magistrate's for arraignment. What else do you want?"

"Some names for a start," Dietz said, taking out his notebook and pen. "And then you can tell me what the money has to do with it."

"What money?"

"The money in the bag you're holding," Dietz said, smiling.

"This, you mean. This is my bingo winnings. Had a hell of a night at the Eagles. Just couldn't keep the corn off the cards tonight."

Dietz let his hands drop to his sides. "Chief, I know you don't like me. I know you never have. Yet everywhere I go in this town, in this county for that matter, I keep hearing what a fair man you are."

"You must talk to some real winners."

"Winners or not, that's what I hear. So what I'd like to know is why you can't be fair with me. What have I ever done to you?"

"To me personally? There's nothing you could do."

Dietz shook his head. "Then, what the hell is it? Hell, man, I have a job to do the same as you."

"I don't like the way you do it."

Dietz looked at the sky in disgust. Then he started to laugh. "Well, just how should I do it—I mean, considering that you've never asked me whether I like the way you do yours?"

"Dietz, don't make me laugh. You got the whole alphabet and a whole lot of space six days a week to tell me and everybody else what you think of the way I'm doing my job. Go back and read the stuff you've written about me and my men ever since you landed in this town.

"You want specifics? Go look at the headline you wrote about those two kids Weigh's boys busted on a narcotics. Go back and read everything you wrote about John Andrasko. And try, while you're reading it, to read it like you was me."

"I was just reporting what Weigh told me, that's all. *You* wouldn't tell me anything. I had to get it from somebody."

"Wrong. Maybe I'm dreaming, but my idea is you get the right stuff. You don't just get any stuff from the first jerk with a loose jaw. Or is that too much to hope for?"

"No."

Balzic searched Dietz's face. "Maybe I'm a real dummy," he said, "but I'll give it to you—on the condition that you tone it down and bury it in the back somewhere. And I mean tone it down so low I can hardly hear it. You read me?"

"Yes."

"Because there's a lot of people mixed up in this. One of them is very close to me. And I've already made a couple of mistakes in this thing. I mean some real beauties. You with me?"

"So far."

"Okay. Here it is." And Balzic told him as much as he thought Dietz could handle, which was most of it. He told him about Marie with Tommy at the football game and about his blunders with Mrs. Andrasko and with her sister, and he even explained Dom Muscotti's bath on the Cincinnati-Pittsburgh playoffs.

"So that's where the money comes in," Balzic said. "And that makes things different. Now come here. I want you to see something."

He lead Dietz over to his car and pointed at the back seat. "Take a look."

Dietz peered in and saw Tommy Parilla still curled up on the seat, his knees drawn up to his abdomen, his thumb still in his mouth, his eyes wide and unblinking.

"That him?"

"That's him. So when you start typing, just remember him. And his mother. And my daughter. I'm not trying to tell you your job, Dietz. I'm just trying to tell you to do it with sense, 'cause if you fuck this one up, you'll never get another word out of me—not even about the weather. Understand?"

Dietz stepped back from the car and nodded slowly. "What can I say, Chief? I'm sorry, I guess."

"Stick the sorries up your ass. Just use a little sense, okay?"

Dietz nodded.

"Now if you wanted to finish doing your job," Balzic said, "you'd go ask Moyer if he found who the guy was. And then you'd check with the hospital. I don't think the poor bastard will last an hour. He was as bad as Andrasko. Worse. He got it with a tire iron."

"Where you going?" Dietz asked.

"Take the kid down and get him booked and put away someplace safe until I can get him out to Mamont. See you around, Dietz."

Balzic got in his car and started it.

Tommy lurched upright, sucking furiously on his thumb.

"It's okay, Tommy. We're just going for a ride. It's all right. You can lay back down. Go to sleep if you want. I'll wake you when we get there, okay?"

" 'Kay," Tommy said around his thumb, dropping back on the seat.

"Atta boy," Balzic said, backing out of the lot. He stopped after he got the car fronting the right way and rolled down his window. "Hey, Phil," he called out to Moyer, "you want to come along?"

Moyer left the troopers he was talking with and came trotting past Dietz. He got in.

"Get a name?"

Moyer held up two cards, a driver's license, and a vehicle registration. "Vitale Joseph Ducci. 2627 Washington Boulevard, Pittsburgh."

"East Liberty," Balzic said. "It gets worse."

"Yeah. They're not going to think it's Christmas. Ah well, their loss is the commonwealth's gain—isn't that the way it goes?"

"Something like that," Balzic said dourly. "Ready?"

"Hell, yes. Let's get out of here before Dietz comes up with another question. What did you say to him anyway? He looked pretty subdued."

"I gave him the story, and I told him to play dead. He must've got the message for once in his life. I hope so, 'cause the extra attraction here really turns things."

"I still don't know why that's got you so worried."

"Phil, you got to understand. I've lived in this town all my life, and—never mind. You want to know what would really ease my mind?"

Moyer looked at him and waited.

"You're going to think I'm nuts, but it would really ease my mind if Dom Muscotti got this money."

"Are you shittin' me?"

160

"No."

Moyer shifted about on the seat. "Mario, this is your territory, like you say. I'm due for a transfer. You want to give it to him, I won't remember anything."

Balzic grunted and turned up the street toward Muscotti's.

"Was that supposed to be an expression of gratitude?"

"What?" Balzic said, parking across the street from Muscotti's.

"That noise you made."

"Yeah. Be back in a minute. I'm going to get the priest if he's in here, so it might take a couple minutes. Maybe you can talk to the kid."

"Thanks a lot. What am I supposed to talk to him about?"

"Well, you might verify his present condition and state of mind for one thing. Then—I don't know. You're the lieutenant. Tell him about the benefits of civil service."

Balzic grabbed the doctor's bag and hurried across the street into Muscotti's. Dom Muscotti was behind the bar, looking sour. One man was asleep at one of the tables and two community college students were arguing about something at the front of the bar. Balzic walked quickly back to where Dom Muscotti was standing and said, "Got something that belongs to you." He set the bag on the bar.

"What's this?"

"You know. But there's one thing. The messenger's in the hospital."

"What?"

"He got beat up pretty bad. I don't think he's going to make it."

"Acey?"

"I don't follow you."

"Was it Ducci?"

Balzic nodded.

"Oh, my God."

Balzic waited for Muscotti to say something else, but Dom just picked up the bag and stared at it. He made the slightest move as though he was about to throw it against a wall.

"My God," he said. "Acey . . ."

"Father Marrazo in the back, Dom?"

161

"What? Oh yeah. He's back there. You sure it was Acey?"

"Vitale Ducci was on the license and owner's card. I forget the middle name. Washington Boulevard. That him?"

Dom nodded slowly, his face going slack. "What hospital? On the hill?"

"Yeah. Better call somebody quick if he has anybody, Dom. He—I'll tell you what, Dom. It'll be better if he don't make it."

"Go on back and get the Father," Dom said. "I'll make the calls. And take the Father up there, okay, Mario? Acey was a real religious guy, know what I mean? A real religious guy."

Balzic said he would and went on to the back room. He found only one game going on. Father Marrazo, dressed in his poker clothes, was frowning a loser's frown.

Mo Valcanas was sprawled in a chair by the other table, his head rolling and his mouth agape. His lips trembled with the silent words of a dream.

"Sorry, Father," Balzic said, "but I need you for a while."

"Mario," the priest said. His frown turned to a look of reprieve. To the other players, he said, "Cashing in, gentlemen. You understand how it is."

"Do what you got to do, Father," Balzic said. "I'm going to try and get this Greek on his feet." He shook Valcanas's shoulder.

"I told you I don't need a haircut goddammit," Valcanas bellowed, his face pinching into a rage, his eyes fiercely shut. He tried to jerk away from Balzic's hand and fell off the chair, coming awake when his hip and elbow hit the floor. "Hey, Jesus Christ . . ."

"Come on, Greek. Time to go."

Valcanas focused bleerily up at Balzic. "For crissake, don't you have anything better to do? Why don't you go solve a felony? Earn your pay, for crissake."

"Let me help you up."

"I can get up." He put his hand out and tried to push up, but his hand slipped, and he bumped down on his seat. "If you laugh, you would-be J. Edgar Hoover, I'll show you how Greeks take care of their traitors."

"I'm not laughing. You want some help or not?"

"What the hell for?"

"I got a client of yours outside."

"Screw him, whoever the hell he is. Let him get his own goddamn lawyer. Well don't just stand there—give me a hand, for crissake."

Balzic and Father Marrazo got Valcanas up, put his hat on him, and steered him out to the bar. Valcanas wanted to have a drink. "Just one, for crissake. What's one going to hurt?"

Balzic ignored him and said to Dom: "You call the people?"

Dom nodded. He put his head down and pinched the bridge of his nose. His shoulders began to quiver and he turned away.

"What's the matter with him, for crissake?"

"Never mind. Let's go. You got a good hold, Father?"

"As good as I can manage. I'm not used to this sort of thing, you know."

"No shit, Father," Valcanas said. "Aren't you really? How do you think I feel? Me, poor little me, between a priest and a cop . . . all I need now is a crown of thorns. . . ."

"Aw, shut up," Balzic said.

"Hey, Dom, how about a couple of draughts here?" one of the two college students called out.

"Go home," Dom said. "I'm closed."

The students looked at each other and then at the clock above the cash register. "Hey, Dom, it's not even one o'clock."

"I'm closed," Dom said. "Go on. Hit the bricks. Go study something." He picked up their glasses.

They were still protesting when Balzic and Father Marrazo got Valcanas through the door and across the street. Moyer got out to lend a hand. They wedged Valcanas into the middle of the front seat and then Balzic took the priest aside.

"In case you're wondering, Father, that's Tommy Parilla in the back. The worst happened."

"There's no doubt?"

"Not this time, Father. But you better go get what you need and get on up the hospital. The victim's name is Vitale Ducci and Dom says he was a religious guy. Better hustle, Father. He ain't going to last too long."

"I have my things in my car," Father Marrazo said. "Will you need me later on?"

"Yeah. Soon as we take care of the kid. I'd like you to be with me when I tell his mother. I don't want to screw it up this time. Meet you back here in about an hour, how's that?"

"All right," Father Marrazo said, turning toward his car parked around the corner.

Balzic got in behind the wheel. "Come on, counselor, give me a little room. We're going to book your client. Try to sober up, too, will you. So you can make sure we do it right. You hear me?"

"I'm just drunk, Marshal. I'm not deaf. Drive on."

After Magistrate Angelo Molanari got over the sight of Tommy Parilla, splashed with blood, smelling of urine, and sucking his thumb, the arraignment went off smoothly enough to suit Balzic. Valcanas, drunk as he was, functioned sufficiently to correct two procedural mistakes Molanari made, and, to Balzic's surprise, did so with a measure of tact.

Tommy Parilla played with a plastic apple throughout, tossing it up and catching it with his left hand while his right thumb stayed firmly in his mouth, coming out only to wipe his nose. When they were getting ready to leave he asked if he could keep the apple. Angelo Molanari shook his head, and Tommy started to cry.

"Keep it then, kid," Molanari said. "You want to take something else too? An orange, maybe. How about a banana?" Molanari held them up from the basket of false fruit on his desk.

"Apple," Tommy said, wiping his eyes on his sleeve. The drying blood from the sleeve left an ocher smear across his brow.

On the way to Southern Regional Detention and Correctional Center, Balzic started to relax. Nobody said anything, and Balzic was thinking that the first thing he would do tomorrow would be to arrange for Tommy's transfer to Mamont State Hospital. The only hitch he saw in that was that maybe some pencil pusher would want to ship the boy back to Southern Regional as soon as the tests were completed, and Balzic planned to see Judge Friedman about that. After that, he would take Marie for a drive and tell her how things were and how she ought to take them. With a little luck, she'd believe him.

As he pulled up to the gate, Balzic said, "Well, I hope he's only here until tomorrow morning."

"Mario," Moyer said, "you worry too much. I thought you said you had a court order to get him out to Mamont."

"No, I didn't say that. What I said was, I'd talked to Friedman about it and he called somebody out there, but I don't have any court order transferring the kid."

"You didn't get any paper?" Valcanas said.

"No. He told me to give the information to his secretary. Which I did. But the only paper I got then was the warrant. Then the kid got lost, and all I was thinking about was finding him. I guess I should've made sure about the paper."

"Don't worry about it," Valcanas said. "Friedman's all right. He's one of the few judges we've got with any guts. And if he said he'll do something, he'll do it. Not like those other shits."

"What's to worry about anyway, Mario?" Moyer said. "Nothing's going to happen to the kid here. Besides, it seems to me you got things a little twisted. I mean who killed who?"

"That's right," Valcanas said, "restore my faith in the state police. Retribution is what we want. Fuck justice."

"Ah, you're just sore 'cause you don't have the sense to stay out of your car when you're loaded," Moyer said.

"Yeah? And you're still sore 'cause you dummies couldn't even prove that. This man's interested in the welfare of another human being, a sick, bent kid—schizophrenic I'd say from the looks of him and the things he's done—and all you give a good goddamn about is getting rid of him. Putting him away, that's all. Forget him, what the hell? That's your attitude. They must make you guys memorize that down at that imitation of a school you call the state police academy."

Moyer coughed and said, "I'll call the gate man."

"Thanks," Balzic said. After Moyer got out, Balzic said, "Lay off, Mo. He's been backing me on this thing all the way with only one exception."

"Which only proves that even idiots are capable of clear thought once in a while. So give me another reason I should lay off him."

"As a favor to me."

165

"Bribery again, for crissake. Is that all you cops understand?"

"Aw, go piss up a rope."

Moyer got back in, the automatic gate opened, and they passed through. It closed behind them, and they made their way up the half-mile-long drive to the inner compound, waiting briefly for that gate to open, and then going on to the administration building. Valcanas began to sing, "Miss Otis Regrets."

"Very funny," Moyer said.

"A cheerful song for a cheerful place," Valcanas said. "You try to put them in, Lieutenant, I try to keep them out. We're both in the same game. But the best-looking cheerleaders are on my side."

Balzic stopped the car in the gravel by the front door. "Tommy? Come along, son."

Tommy sat up and rubbed his eyes. He looked at the building, and his lips began to tremble. Balzic had to call him again before he slid out of the car and walked beside Balzic into the building. Moyer followed, but Valcanas stayed in the car singing the rest of "Miss Otis Regrets."

Inside, a bony man with long arms and a lower lip puffed full of snuff came out from behind a partition. His uniform was crumpled, as though he'd been sleeping, but his face gave no evidence of it.

"Where's Hartley?" Balzic said.

"Transferred," the bony man said. "Who're you, and what you got?"

"I'm Balzic. Chief in Rocksburg. This is Lieutenant Moyer, Troop A, state police."

"You got ID's?"

Balzic and Moyer produced their cards.

"Who's the mess?" the bony man said, looking at Tommy Parilla.

"Name's Parilla. Booked on a general charge of murder."

"Sure looks fucked up," the bony man said, walking to the side of a desk to spit in a coffee can on the floor.

"He's got problems," Balzic said.

"Don't we all," the bony man said, spitting again. He picked his teeth and wiped his fingers on his hip. "Well, all you got to do is sign him over, and I'll take care of him."

"I want him isolated," Balzic said.

166

"Do you now?"

Balzic shot a glance at Moyer.

"You're new here," Moyer said.

"You catch on quick," the bony man said. He went to a drawer and took out a pad of forms and a ball point pen. He laid them in front of Balzic. "Write him up, cowboy."

Moyer reached in his coat pocket and brought out a pen and a small black notebook. He stepped close to the bony man and peered at the badge on the man's shirt pocket.

"Hey. What're you doing?"

"What's it look like?" Moyer said, writing the badge number in his book.

"I can see what you're doing. What the hell for, is what I want to know."

"Do you now?" Moyer said.

"Damn right I do. Anytime somebody starts taking my number, I want to know what for."

"For not knowing your job," Moyer snapped. "You don't know who's supposed to fill out the forms?"

"I–I am."

"Then do it. And make a note on there, and print it big, the prisoner is to be isolated."

"Yessir."

The man slid the pad of forms and pen around and sat behind the desk.

"Just a minute," Balzic said.

"Huh?"

"What's your name?"

"Derr. R. C. Derr."

"You don't sound right, Derr. Where'd you come from?"

"North Carolina."

"What did you do down there?"

"Same as I'm doing here."

"What did you do before that?"

"Same thing. I always done it. Always been in correctional work."

"Where?"

"Before that I was in South Carolina."

"And before that?" Balzic said. "I'll just bet you were someplace else."

"Matter of fact, I was. I was in North Carolina."

"And I'll just bet you like to travel."

"What's that s'posed to mean?"

"You know goddamn well what it means," Balzic said, leaning with his knuckles on the desk. "I've known a few of you guys who've 'always been in correctional work,' and I know why you keep moving.

"I don't know who hired you, and I don't know what they were thinking about when they did, but you can bet your ass I'm going to find out. And I'll tell you something else. This prisoner is being put here for a very short time, and then he's being transferred to a hospital. It's all a matter of paperwork. But while he's here, you better make it a personal thing to see nobody bothers him. You understand that?"

"Yessir."

Balzic straightened up and directed Tommy to a chair by the wall. Then he gave R. C. Derr the information needed to complete the admission form.

They had just finished when a back door opened and into the office, carrying a can of beer in each hand, walked Pete Muscotti. At first he walked straight, and it was hard to see that he was drunk, but the nearer he came to the group clustered around Derr's desk, the more obvious it was that he was drunk.

"What the hell's going on here?" Balzic said.

"Hey, Chiefo," Pete Muscotti sang out. "My old buddy, Chiefo Mario."

Derr sprang out of his chair and tried to turn Pete Muscotti around and head him toward the door he'd come in.

"Wait a minute, Derr. I asked you, what the hell was going on here."

Derr mumbled something about a trustee.

"Hold it right there," Balzic said. "I want to know what that man's doing here in that condition."

"What's it look like, Chiefo? You're so fuckin' smart. You tell us."

"Shut up," Derr said and tried to push Pete toward the back door

168

again. "Goddamn you, shut up and get back where you belong." He was trying to whisper, but the irritation carried his words.

"Just drinking a little beer, Chiefo. A couple beers and a couple Miltowns, put them both together they spell high, Chiefo. . . ."

"Move out, goddammit," Derr said and put his shoulder into Muscotti's chest and heaved him toward the back door.

Pete Muscotti hit the door with a thump that forced him to drop the cans of beer. One was open, and the suds erupted in a tiny geyser when it hit the floor. "Now look what you made me do, ya fuckin' rebel," Pete shouted. He bent down to pick up the cans, but Derr jerked him up by the shirt.

"Leave it," Derr said.

"Hey, ya fucker, I paid you good bread for that beer."

Derr cracked Muscotti across the face with an open hand. "One more word," he said.

Pete Muscotti opened his mouth but nothing came out. His eyes said, wait till later. He took his time turning around and opening the door, his defiance turning to a smirk, and then slammed the door behind him.

Balzic and Moyer exchanged a look that both took to mean: so this is how it is. Moyer shrugged and started for the door, leaving without a word, but Balzic was filling with a rage that came up from between his legs. He could have taken Derr's throat in his hands and crushed it like a cardboard tube, and because he knew that, he started to back away from Derr.

Derr mistook the retreat. "I think it's about time you all got out of here," he said, "and let me get on with my work."

"Your work?" Balzic said. "Your work! Why you grubbing, grafting, thieving piece of shit." He stopped backing away. He wasn't moving forward, but the way he'd stopped made it plain to Derr that he had mistaken Balzic's retreat.

"You got two things to do here, Derr. You got this boy to put in isolation, and then you got your resignation to write. And God won't help you if you don't do them both right."

Balzic waited a moment longer to see how what he'd said had registered.

Derr didn't move and he didn't speak. He looked frozen for what seemed a long time but was no more than a second or two, and then his adam's apple went up and down.

Balzic went over to Tommy and touched him on the shoulder. He told him to go with this man, that everything would be all right, and that he would see him soon. Tommy looked frantic, then bewildered, but finally he nodded.

Balzic walked out to his car without looking back at Derr.

Valcanas had fallen asleep, his mouth ajar, and Balzic drove back into town with the silence in the cruiser broken only occasionally by the calls and static coming over the radio.

Balzic started to feel the exhaustion when he dropped Moyer off at the train station. It struck him that he had been walking for a long time during a wet snowfall and that only when he'd paused was he aware how heavy the snow was. He amused himself with that idea as he drove back to Muscotti's. He roused Valcanas and got him inside and propped on a stool.

No one was in the bar except Big Henry, the bent-back janitor, and Sal Muscotti, a cousin of Dom's who long ago had indebted himself to Dom for reasons no one knew and was obliged to work the bar when Dom wanted to be other places.

"The priest here?" Balzic asked Sal.

"In the back." Sal started to get off his stool. "You want something to drink?"

"For him," Balzic said, pointing to Valcanas, who was staring quizzically at himself in a mirror beside the cash register. "Put it on my tab."

Balzic went to the back room. His legs were heavy, his feet were aching, and he wanted to sit down, but he wanted more to settle the whole business tonight. He didn't think he had enough left in him to face Mrs. Andrasko again, not even with the priest along, but he knew there was no way out of it.

He found Father Marrazo watching the card players with his hands folded behind his back and shifting impatiently from foot to foot.

"You still want to tell Mrs. Andrasko?" the priest asked.

"No. I don't want to. What I want to do is fall down someplace. Obliterated, if possible."

"If your sense of duty permits," Father Marrazo said, "I'll help you get obliterated."

"Will you see to it that I get home?"

"I'll help you get obliterated. How you get home is your business. I want to get obliterated myself."

"Fair enough," Balzic said. But when they sat at the bar, he said, "I really shouldn't be doing this. I ought to be out there telling that woman I got her son locked up."

"Then let me do my best to talk you out of it," Father Marrazo said, "I've dealt with enough grief for one night, and I know that if you go to see her, you're going to drag me along."

"Pretty rough in the hospital?"

The priest shook his head and sagged. "The family was bad enough, but Dom—Dom was unbelievable. I never knew he had it in him."

"Yeah. I thought he was going to break down here when I told him about it."

"I don't know why anybody let him into the room."

"Was he still alive when you left?"

The priest shook his head. "If ever God was merciful, He was merciful to take that man. Some would say God was too slow. I don't know. I don't think he heard me, but he was conscious for a time. He was making this terrible sound in his throat. That's when Dom came in. In time to hear that, and then it was over. Then Dom went wild."

"Wild? How do you mean? I mean, did he get calmed down?"

"No. The head nurse ordered him out, and when he wouldn't go, she called an orderly. Dom knocked him down and kicked him in the stomach. I tried to talk to him, but he told me to keep away or he'd hurt me. Then two of your men came. I had to leave. I couldn't stand to watch it. Dom is really a very powerful man. I didn't know that. It surprised me."

Balzic covered his face with his hands. "Oh, Jesus Christ, why didn't you tell me this before?" He went behind the bar and got the phone and dialed his station.

"I don't know," Father Marrazo said. "It just surprised me so much. . . ."

171

"Joe? Balzic. What's the story with Dom Muscotti?" Balzic listened and began to curse. "Well, where is he now?" He listened a minute longer and then slammed the receiver down. "Hey, Sal, did Dom have a bag with him when he left? A doctor's bag?"

"No. He left it here. Told me to watch it."

"Thank somebody for that," Balzic said, running for the front door. "Keep on watching it, you hear?"

"Hey, where you going for crissake?" Valcanas said as Balzic ran by.

"Where we came from," Balzic said and then he was through the door.

"Where we came from," Valcanas said to his reflection in the mirror. "Where the hell was that. . . ."

Balzic used the siren to get around the few cars on the road to Southern Regional. The exhaustion was still with him, but the fury he felt for his own men for taking Dom Muscotti to this lockup instead of to his own was greater than any exhaustion he would ever feel.

"Stupid, stupid, stupid," he kept repeating, his head racing with the idea of Tommy Parilla being so close to Pete Muscotti and Dom Muscotti and R. C. Derr. Who knew how close they were to one another? Who knew what had been said? Worse, who knew what had been guessed at, wished for, hinted at, offered, accepted? And Pete Muscotti was floating on beer and tranquilizers, and Dom Muscotti was wild with grief, wild enough to beat hell out of a hospital orderly and give two cops half his age a battle.

Balzic tried to guess when Dom had been locked up. It had to have been sometime after they'd brought Tommy Parilla, which meant Pete Muscotti would know about Tommy. And if Pete had been able to buy Derr within hours, then Dom, with his money, would be able to buy him in minutes, and Pete would be sure to get next to Dom. Who would be happier for the opportunity? What had Pete been working for, flunkeying for, sweet-talking for all these years?

It can't happen, Balzic tried to convince himself. But he knew it could, and he knew that if he didn't get Dom Muscotti out of there, it would.

172

He had hopes: Pete might be too fogged to know what Dom was talking about; Derr might be too scared not to do his job about isolating Tommy; Dom might not make the connection between Vitale Ducci and Tommy; Pete might not even say anything about the bloodied, thumb-sucking kid who had just been brought in. No, Balzic thought. That kind always talks, especially about the tricks the world played on them, the bad breaks, the rotten luck, the crummy abuses they didn't deserve. Oh, they'll talk, all right, Balzic thought. They'll find one another after they buy Derr, and they'll talk until their tongues hurt.

Some hopes he had. Hope. What is hope? Hope is a whore, his mother used to say. Hope goes to bed with anybody. And when you had heads like those working—Pete, Dom, and R. C. Derr, Jesus . . .

He nearly didn't get the brakes on in time at the gate. He lurched out of the car and called the administration building. The phone kept ringing. "Come on, you piece of shit, pick it up."

After more rings than Balzic thought to count, the phone was answered and a voice said: "Administration Building, Officer Derr speaking."

"Open up, Derr. This is Balzic. I'm coming in to move one of the people."

"Who?"

"Balzic. Chief in Rocksburg. I was just here twenty, thirty minutes ago."

There was a pause and Balzic could hear the receiver muffled against cloth.

"Come on, goddammit," Balzic shouted.

"Get in your car, Chief," Derr said and then hung up.

Balzic slammed down the receiver and hustled for his car. He got in, put it in gear, and sat there. The gate didn't open. Thirty seconds passed. A minute. Balzic scrambled back out and to the phone again. This time he counted the rings. Twenty-three.

"You better press a button before I get back in my car, Derr," Balzic said, "or you're going to have real problems, you hear me?"

"I hear ya, Chiefo, only this ain't Derr. He's taking a leak. How do you like them apples, Chiefo? Huh? How do you like them?"

"Where's Derr, Pete?"

"I never heard of either one of them two, Chiefo. You know anybody else up here you might wanna talk to—anybody that'd wanna talk to you?"

"Pete, you'll regret this. As God is my witness, you'll regret this."

"Come on, Chiefo. Get yourself together. This Pete, whoever he is, he ain't here right now. And you know God ain't here. Now is there anybody else?"

"Pete, so help me—"

"What, Chiefo? What you gonna do? You on the outside, Chiefo, you forget that? When you people put them fences up you was only thinking how nobody could get out. You didn't think how you couldn't get in neither if nobody didn't wanna let you. Specially when you want to, like now, huh, Chiefo? What you got to say about that? Ain't that a real bitch now?"

Balzic slammed the phone on the hook and began to pace in front of the gate.

"All right, you fuckers," he said, getting into his car, "if this is the way it's going to be, then this is the way it's going to be."

He called the state police on the car phone.

"State Police. Sergeant Rudawski speaking."

"This is Mario Balzic, Rudy. I'm at the gate of Southern Regional, and the clown on the desk in the admin building is playing games. I want you to call the warden and tell him he's got a disturbance in that building, and if he doesn't answer after twenty rings, I want every unit you got up there out here. Read me?"

"I read you. Give a minute."

Balzic sat back and lit a cigarette.

"Mario?" the voice crackled over the receiver.

"Right here. Go."

"Warden Wolman acknowledges and says he's sending people to investigate. Meantime, he's standing by the master board in his office. In the event he gets no word in five, repeat, five minutes from zero-two-seventeen hours, he will close alternate circuits to gate and alarm systems. Meantime, we are dispatching two nearest units to you and alerting other availables. Time now zero-two-eighteen."

"You're my man, Rudy. Standing by."

Balzic adjusted his watch and waited, tapping on the steering while. At two-twenty-one, the gate slid open, and Balzic called Sergeant Rudawski back.

"No alarm sounded with the gate, so Wolman must've triggered it from the master board."

"You still want the units we dispatched?"

"I can see one coming now. I'll tell him to stand by here at the gate after I go on in. How's that?"

"Roger, Mario. Out."

The younger of the two troopers in the state cruiser looked disappointed when Balzic told him that in all probability whatever had been going on was now under control. The older trooper, the driver, said, "That suits me just fine," and stretched out across the front seat.

Balzic saw the inner compound gate opening as he approached, so that he didn't have to slow to go through. He hoped the worst he'd find was a simple case of drunkenness and dereliction. What he and Moyer had seen earlier was enough for Derr's dismissal; the business with the gate was more than enough. With luck, that was all there was going to be to it, and none of the possibilities that had brought him out here had happened. But no matter what had gone on, he did not intend to leave without seeing Pete Muscotti in a cell, Dom Muscotti in a state police cruiser going to another lockup, and Tommy Parilla in his own car going to his own lockup. He was furious with himself for bringing the boy here in the first place.

When he got inside the office, he found Warden Wolman and three guards with riot guns standing around R. C. Derr, who was sitting with his head in his hands in the chair Tommy Parilla had been sitting in earlier. Wolman was wearing a raincoat over his pajamas, his face creased from sleep, and he was shaking his head in pained disbelief.

"Four years," Wolman kept saying. "Four years, and it never happened before . . ."

"What happened?" Balzic asked one of the guards.

The guard turned his back to Wolman and whispered, "He just hired this guy two days ago, and the first night he's on duty, this happens."

"What happened, man?"

175

"Weren't you the one trying to get in the gate?"

"Yes, but what happened?"

"Everything. Beer cans all over the place, one of the people assaulted, the gate—everything."

"Which one assaulted?"

"I don't know his name. Never saw him before. Must've been brought in today."

"No names at all?"

"Not so far. This damn guy won't open his mouth."

Balzic brushed past the guard and approached Warden Wolman.

"Warden, who's been assaulted?"

Wolman threw up his hands. "I don't know. This man won't say anything. I don't know who was here, who was answering the phones, who was fooling with the gate, never mind who got assaulted. We just got the man over to the infirmary, and the only thing I can say for certain is that he wasn't wearing our issue."

Balzic felt something cold spread over his chest.

"Derr," Wolman said, "I'm going to ask you once more to tell me what went on here tonight, and I'll tell you that no matter what you say eventually, the fact that you remained silent for this long is going to go against you. That, plus the fact that you've made a fool of me. . . ."

"You bastards wouldn't believe me even if I did tell you."

"Well, say something, man, for God's sake," Wolman said, his face blotchy.

"I'll say something," Derr said. "The only thing I'm going to say. I want a lawyer."

"Bullshit!" Wolman bellowed, storming away from Derr. To the guards he said, "Put him in a cell. I don't want to look at him again." To Balzic he said, "I've been hiring people here for four years, but never, never, have I made such a mistake. I ought to have my head examined."

"Warden, will you allow me into the infirmary?" Balzic asked.

Wolman looked at Balzic and seemed for the first time to recognize him. "Were you the one trying to get in the gate?"

"Yes."

176

"Well, will you tell me what you know about this?"

"I'd be glad to if you'd just let me in the infirmary to see who got worked over."

"Better yet, I'll take you, and you can tell me on the way." Wolman called over his shoulder to one of the guards, "Have you called that ambulance?"

"Yessir. Should be here in a few minutes."

Wolman grunted and led Balzic through the back door of the office and across the compound to an adjacent building. Balzic told him everything he could in the time it took to cover the distance, some seventy-five yards.

"Well, I'm afraid this is your man," Wolman said. "I'm not a doctor, but even I could see he's lost an awful lot of blood."

"Most of that blood isn't his," Balzic said as they entered the infirmary. "At least I hope it isn't."

"You say he murdered two men?"

"There was some doubt about the first one, but there's none about the second. But he was psycho. He didn't know he was doing it."

They went into the treatment room, and there lying motionless on a table was Tommy Parilla. The attendant standing beside the boy had his fingers on Tommy's wrist. When he heard Wolman and Balzic come in, he looked up and shook his head.

Balzic thought his legs were going to buckle.

"How bad is it?"

"I'm not a doctor," the attendant said. "All I can tell you is he's still alive—if having a pulse this weak means somebody's still alive. I just took his blood pressure, and it's dropping fast. If that ambulance don't get here pretty soon, no doctor's going to be able to do anything."

"How'd it happen?"

"He's got a puncture wound in his chest. Very little blood coming from that, so it must be going inside."

"Isn't there anything you can do?" Balzic said.

"I told you. I'm not a doc. I'm not even a nurse. And with the stuff we got here, even if I was, there isn't a hell of a lot I could do." The attendant's face was rough cut and badly pockmarked. He

177

walked with a pronounced limp, but his voice was soft and his manner that of a man long resigned to the sort of thing he was party to now. "Pulse is just fluttering now. Barely feel it."

"You know," Balzic said, looking at the floor, "I knew this was going to happen. I knew a half-hour, forty-five minutes ago—hell, what difference does it make how long ago. But I knew it, and it was the very goddamn thing I was trying to prevent—where the fuck's that ambulance?"

"I think I see a red light coming up the drive now," the attendant said. "'Less it's a bull wagon."

"I'm going to get dressed," Wolman said. "It's going to be a long time until tomorrow." He went over and glanced down at Tommy. He said something under his breath about being just a kid, and then left the infirmary.

Balzic waited until the ambulance came—its light had been the one the attendant had seen—and the men strapped Tommy into the stretcher. He took another look at the boy as the stretcher was being wheeled out the door, and that cold spread across his chest again. He forced himself to find out who knew where Dom and Pete Muscotti were.

Halfway across the compound between the infirmary and the administration building, he went down. He sat in the grass, running his hands through the dewy grass, trying to figure whether he had fainted or whether it had just been his legs telling him they had to stop awhile or whether it was the weight he felt on the top of his head and which spread downward through his neck and outward across his shoulders that had just pushed him down. He couldn't figure it, but it took him nearly five minutes to find the will and the strength to push himself up and go on.

After much confusion in the office, trying to find the log, with Balzic trying to explain to the two guards still in the office who he was looking for, one of them found the log, and all three tried to read it at the same time. All they learned was that R. C. Derr, among his other abberations, was a terrible writer. His script was incoherent.

178

"No sober man writes like this," was all Warden Wolman said when he came back into the office and looked at the log. "First, this Muscotti was brought in by the state boys after arraignment, is this it, Mario?"

"Yeah. That's Pete. Sometime early yesterday."

"So we're looking in the wrong place for him. That would have been entered earlier." He thumbed back a page in the loose-leaf book and found it. "Here it is. Muscotti, Peter L. He's supposed to be in C Building. Go get him."

One of the two guards went out.

"And you say your people brought this other one—with the same last name?"

"That's right. But Derr would have made that entry, and I can't make sense of his scribbling."

"I don't know whether this is it or not, but it looks like it," Wolman said, "but it's as near as I can come to it. Try C Building," he said to the other guard. "God knows where either of them are."

The other guard left, and Wolman turned back to Balzic. "I've been in this kind of work since I was twenty-three years old, Mario, and I've seen a lot of stupid things happen. Some of them I don't repeat. Not to anybody. I swore that if I ever got to be warden, I'd do everything in my power not to let things like that happen in any institution of mine. And now look. My God, how could I have been fooled so badly by that man? Everything about him should've told me, and yet, because we needed people, I looked right past all of it. My God."

Balzic knew exactly how Wolman felt, but he was too tired to say it. He was trying to save what was left of his energy for questioning the two Muscottis.

"You plan for these things—against them," Wolman went on, talking more to himself now than to Balzic, "you plan and plan. You make contingency plans. You go over them and over them, and you think you haven't left anything out, and then one day you make a mistake, and the whole damn thing comes down. In an hour's time, everything goes to hell. . . ."

Pete Muscotti was pushed into the office then, interrupting Wolman. The expression on his face told Balzic they were in for a time of it. Pete had always been a gloater, playing his gloating out by allowing the police to know that he'd done what he'd done and then daring them with a continuous smirk to prove it.

Until now, his greatest achievements had been petty larceny and low-score frauds, all carried out with what Balzic knew to be a ridiculous belief that he was proving himself to his Uncle Dom Muscotti. For Pete Muscotti believed in the Black Hand and the Mafia and the Cosa Nostra. No matter that his belief had come mostly from watching Edward G. Robinson movies on late-night television. The belief was religious, and Balzic knew that if Dom Muscotti sat his nephew down in a sound-proof room and explained the truth about himself, Pete would refuse to give up his belief and would go out of the room thinking that the truth Dom told was only meant to goad him into trying still another scheme in the hope of making himself worthy to be accepted by his uncle and men like him.

When Dom was brought in a minute or two later, Pete's face gave him away and convinced Balzic: Pete's eyes danced with the glow of ultimate success. Dom didn't even look at him, coming instead immediately to Balzic.

"Mario," Dom said, his voice filled with injury, "what the hell's going on here? Okay, so I went a little goofy in the hospital, but listen, you know me. You know I'll take care of that kid I kicked. I mean, Jesus, Acey was my paisan. Since we were little kids. I was just mad. Goofy mad, you know how it is. You get like that yourself once in a while. Like you done with Sam Carraza. You know how you can get, but I mean, Jesus, can't a guy show a little grief without getting locked up for it? And your guys, they were pretty rough on an old man—whatta ya say? Get me out of here. I ain't used to this. Jail, Jesus . . ."

Balzic looked past Dom at Pete and knew that Pete believed it was all an act, that Dom didn't mean a word he was saying and was pretending the tone of his voice.

180

Balzic knew otherwise. Dom wasn't acting. Dom believed a man was entitled to display his grief in a rage and that if all the damages were taken care of, were promised to be paid, well, then, that was all there was to it. A man went goofy with grief, he saw to it that the victims were covered, and everybody went home to a hot shower and a cold glass of wine. What else did you do when somebody you loved got killed?

Warden Wolman started to say something, but Balzic gave him a look that meant, let me have first shot. Wolman consented with a shrug. He went to a desk, took out a notepad, and started writing. Though he'd dressed, he hadn't bothered with socks, and his ankles showed very white above his black shoes.

Balzic sat down and invited Dom to do the same.

"Dom, it's not as simple as you think it is."

"What ain't?"

"The whole thing, everything that happened in the last couple hours."

"So tell me what ain't simple. I'll listen. When did you know me not to listen?"

"In the first place, Dom, we had the kid that killed your paisan. Did you know that?"

"No. All you told me was Acey got hurt. Beat up. I didn't know nothing else."

Balzic glanced again at Pete who was slouched against a wall.

"We did. We caught him practically in the act. I'm just sorry for everybody we didn't use our heads a little better, maybe we could have grabbed him before. But we didn't. You know who it was?"

Dom shook his head. "How would I know?"

"It was John Andrasko's stepson."

"You mean the Parilla kid?" Dom's brow arched. "He was—"

"He was what?"

"Well, he was—he was here," Dom said. "I seen him. A little while ago. He was a mess, and I asked him what was wrong—you know, Jesus, I know the kid from . . . you mean he killed John too?" Dom's face was incredulous.

181

"You got it," Balzic said.

"But what was wrong with him? I mean, did he go goofy? He musta been goofy, Mario. Am I right?"

Balzic nodded. "I brought him out here just for safekeeping for a day or so. Then I was going to take him out to Mamont. All I had to do was get some papers from a judge. Believe me, Dom, the kid didn't know what he was doing."

Dom shook his head. "Mario, Jesus, that woman, she must be going nuts. That poor woman . . ."

"That's right, Dom. First she marries a bum, then after she had the kid, the bum takes off and sticks her with the kid. Then she meets John, and everything starts to look up, only the thing is, John won't marry her."

"John A. never married her?" Dom's face opened again in disbelief. "But he was straight arrow."

"He wasn't straight that way," Balzic said, glancing from Dom to Pete and back as he talked. "But when young Tommy killed him, he wasn't really killing him."

"I don't follow," Dom said.

"What I mean is, he was really killing Tami Parilla, his blood father. It's a long story, Dom, so you'll just have to take my word for it, but it was the same way tonight, believe me. He wasn't killing your paisan tonight. He was killing his father, his real father, all over again."

"Jesus, who'd believe it?" Dom said.

"But that doesn't mean you wouldn't take the heat about him," Balzic said. "I mean, if you didn't know anything about this, or even if you did, for a while, you'd really have the heat for whoever did it to your paisan."

"Oh, sure. You kidding? I would've killed him myself if I could've." Dom thought for a moment. "Well, you know what I'm saying now, Mario. I maybe wouldn't 've killed him, but I would've did a job on him. Ah, what am I saying? If it was the kid, how could I 've done that? I mean, I know the kid's story—not this part you're telling me now, this sickness, but even without that, I couldn't 've done nothing to him. Jesus, he's just a kid."

Balzic shot another look at Pete. He was no longer slouching. He had stiffened against the wall, and his mouth was working with his lips together as though he was trying to keep from crying out.

"How long did you see the kid tonight, Dom?"

"Oh, I don't know. Couple minutes. That guard was taking him out. Me and Petey come up here—"

"How were you able to come up here?" Wolman interrupted.

"What?"

"I said, how were you able to come to this office? You just said you came up here as though you were taking a walk on Sunday. How was that possible? How did you get out of your cell? You were in a cell?"

"Well, yeah. Sure I was in a cell. Then Petey came up to see me, and he said I could come out."

"And you just walked out? Just like that? I mean, there was a door on that cell, wasn't there?"

"Well, sure."

"Well how did it get open, man? Did it just open itself?"

"No. Petey had a key. I asked him where he got it, but I don't remember what he said. When he opened up, I just came out, that's all. How was I supposed to know—I never been locked up in my life. I just figured Petey knew somebody. What did I care? I just wanted out. It smelled in there. Like vomit."

Wolman shook his head and started writing things on the pad again.

"Was that the first time you saw Petey tonight, Dom?"

"Huh? No. I seen him earlier. When your guys brought me up."

"Where did you see him?"

"Right here. In here. I knew he got himself arrested, but to tell you the truth, I wasn't thinking about him. I see him around so much, when I seen him here, I really didn't think nothing about it. I was too busy thinking about me, and what the hell was I doing winding up in jail. The first time in my life, Mario. Jesus, I'm fifty-eight years old. And I was a little bit scared, too."

"You thinking about anything else?"

"Sure. Whatta you think? I was thinking about Acey. About his wife."

"You still mad then? You still have the heat?"

183

"Sure I had the heat. Whatta you think? You have the heat for five minutes over something like that and it goes away? Sure I still had the heat."

"You tell Petey about it?"

"I don't know. Maybe I did. Sure, I must've told him—hey, Mario, what is this anyway? All of a sudden, I get the feeling you're not talking to me like a friend...." Dom's expression was sincere enough even for Pete.

"Shut up!" Pete shouted, lurching away from the wall. The two guards stopped him, finally getting a pair of handcuffs on him and then locking that pair of cuffs to another pair which they locked to a heavy chair.

"What's wrong with him?" Dom said, looking first at Balzic and then at his nephew. "What's wrong with you? You nuts or something? Since when do you tell me shut up, huh? Since when?"

"Since he stuck something in Tommy Parilla tonight, Dom."

"What?"

"Shut your face, you goddamn wop. You dried-up goddamn wop!" Pete shouted.

"Get him out of here," Wolman said to the guards.

"Wait a minute," Dom said. He stood and went over to Pete. "Did you do that—what Mario said? Did you hurt that kid? 'Cause of what I said to you?"

"Come on, Uncle Dom. Just a little bit closer, so I can kick you where your balls used to be."

"Mario," Dom said, his eyes wide, "tell me this ain't my nephew." He shuffled toward Balzic. "Tell me this ain't Petey. Tell me I ain't hearing what I'm hearing. Mario, for crissake, tell me something...."

"I can't tell you anything, Dom. You heard it."

"Get him out of here," Wolman said. This time he said it so there could be no delay, and the two guards unlocked the cuffs which held Pete to the chair and started to take him out.

As he was going, Pete shouted, "Stones you got, you fuckin' old wop! Your eggs turned to stones!"

Dom sank into a chair and hid his face behind his hands.

Balzic went over to Wolman, who was making still another notation, and said, "I want to take this man out of here."

184

Wolman glared up at him. "Why?"

"Because he doesn't belong here."

"Who belongs here?" Wolman said. "I don't belong here—ah, take him. Just sign a transfer, that's all I ask. At least we can have that much order." He reached into a drawer and brought out another pad of forms. "Sign it," he said. "I'll have somebody fill in the details later. Now I have to call the state boys. They can have the rest of this." He picked up a phone, shaking his head.

Balzic signed the transfer form and took Dom by the elbow and led him out of the office. Dom didn't refuse Balzic's hand nor ask where he was being taken. Fifteen minutes later, when Balzic pulled into Dom's driveway, Dom looked as though he wanted to explain something, but when he tried, he couldn't clear his throat. He sat looking at his gray stone house for a long moment and then got out of the car and walked up the drive without saying a word to Balzic.

Balzic spun the wheels pulling away and used his siren to get through intersections on his way to the hospital.

At the emergency room admitting desk, he identified himself and said to the nurse, "That boy that was brought in. The one that was stabbed—any word on him?"

"He's still in surgery," the nurse said. "Do you want me to call up there?"

"Please."

The nurse did, and after she hung up, she said, "I'm afraid he didn't make it."

Balzic looked blankly at her for a moment. Then he asked, "Where's the lavatory?"

"Down that hall," she said, pointing. "Third door on the right."

Balzic found it and locked himself in a stall. Then he broke down. He stopped after about five minutes and went out of the stall and blew his nose in a paper towel and washed his face in cold water. He dried his face on the paper towels and started out. At the door, he hesitated. He thought he was going to be sick, but the nausea passed and he went out and back down the hall to the admitting desk.

"Anybody notify the family?" he asked the nurse.

"He didn't have any identification," she said. "We didn't know who to notify."

Balzic pinched the bridge of his nose. "Jesus," he whispered.

"I'm sorry," the nurse said. "I didn't hear you."

"Just talking to myself," he said. "Can you tell me if he ever said anything?"

"I couldn't say about that. I was busy with a little girl, so I don't know. You'd have to ask the resident or the intern."

"Wasn't anybody else here when they brought him?"

"Yes. But we had such a time of it tonight. Six or seven all in a rush. And before that, right after I came on, this man—oh, just beaten up. Terrible. And then there was the traffic accident—"

"Yeah. Okay. Thanks." Balzic started to walk away but then turned back. "All right if I use the phone?"

"Help yourself."

Balzic dialed Muscotti's and asked for Father Marrazo, and when the priest answered, he said, "Tommy didn't make it, Father."

Silence on the other end. "Mario, you've got to fill me in. The last time I saw you, you were running out the door—"

"That's right, you don't know. Well, Father, I hope you're close to some coffee, 'cause it's going to be more of the same." Balzic went on to tell him what had happened.

"I don't believe it," Father Marrazo said. "I just don't believe it."

"Better believe it, Father, 'cause it's true. How 'bout coming up here?"

"Of course. One thing, Mario. Has—does Mrs. Andrasko know?"

"What do you think I'm asking you to come up for?"

"I see. Well, give me ten minutes."

"Right," Balzic said and hung up. He paced the corridor for some minutes and then heard somebody getting off an elevator. Two doctors, followed by two nurses, all in surgical clothes, came around a bend in the hall. The nurses disappeared into a lounge, and the doctors went behind the admitting desk and poured themselves coffee.

The older of the two dropped into a chair, and the other, boyish-looking with almost pink skin, sank onto the desk. His white shoes were spotted with blood. They both sipped their black coffee,

186

not saying anything. Balzic coughed and held out his ID case. They both looked at it and nodded.

"What can we do for you?" the younger of the two asked.

"The boy, the one that just died."

"Yes?"

"Did he say anything?"

"If he did, I didn't hear him," the older doctor said.

"The only thing I heard him say was something about his father," the younger one said. "But he wasn't conscious. I really can't say for certain what it was. Sounded like, 'Daddy did me,' but I wouldn't swear to that. Did his father do it?"

Balzic didn't answer. He asked, "There was nothing you could do?"

"We tried, but no. He was dead when he came in. What fooled me was all the blood on his clothes. Don't know why I thought it was his, but I did, didn't you, Tom?"

The older doctor nodded. "Then we got him upstairs, and it was obvious. Shouldn't even have taken him up."

"What a night," the younger one said. "For a while there I thought I was back in Korea."

"Well," the older doctor said, sighing, "you want to call the coroner, or shall I?"

"I think he's still here. He's had a night of it, too."

"I guess so. What did we have—four fatals tonight?"

Balzic said good night and went out to the parking lot to wait for Father Marrazo.

The heavy dew was everywhere, giving the macadam parking lot the look of an old blackboard that had just been washed. Balzic paced in the lot and smoked and thought about what remained to be done. There was Mrs. Andrasko to be told, and Balzic wished he could take along a doctor as well as the priest.

And then there was Marie. He would have to tell her, and he knew she wouldn't ask questions. She would just look at him, and her look would ask everything there was to ask. And Balzic knew he had none of the answers. Somehow, if he was lucky, he would be able to

187

convince her that what happened to Tommy, what Tommy had done, would have happened whether she had refused to leave that football game or not. It was easy to think he could do that, but he knew that when Marie turned her eyes on him and asked nothing, he would have the worst possible moments.

He saw a car turn into the lot and knew it was Father Marrazo. He looked again at the macadam and was again reminded of an old blackboard recently washed. He could not shake the feeling that it was the kind of blackboard that seemed to invite people to hold the chalk at the wrong angle so that if it were possible for someone to write on it now, the chalk would squeak endlessly, and his ears would hurt and his flesh would crawl.

As the priest came toward him, Balzic wondered why he would associate the dewy macadam with an old blackboard recently washed. And then it came to him: when he was in grade school, John Andrasko's one and only prank to irritate teachers was to purposely hold the chalk at the wrong angle to make it squeak, and everybody would laugh. Everybody except the teachers and Balzic.

The Blank Page

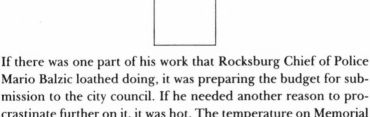

If there was one part of his work that Rocksburg Chief of Police
Mario Balzic loathed doing, it was preparing the budget for sub-
mission to the city council. If he needed another reason to pro-
crastinate further on it, it was hot. The temperature on Memorial
Day had tied a record set in 1910. In the five days since, the
forecasts were notable only for their sameness: the temperature
was far above the average. There was nothing in the upper air
flow, nothing in the ground level patterns out of Canada, no
highs to collide with lows coming out of the Gulf of Mexico or
South Atlantic to bring rain.

Balzic's mind reeled from the heat and the numbers. He
forced himself to check all his calculations twice over, morosely
certain that he was making mistakes correcting earlier mistakes.
All he could hope was that the council would listen to him for
once and allow him to hire an accountant for a couple of weeks
the next time a budget was due.

1

Balzic heard an odd humming about the same time he smelled something burning. He glanced around his tiny office twice before he saw that the oscillating fan atop his file cabinets had quit and was giving off a lazy rope of smoke.

"That caps it," he grumbled, jumping up to shut off the fan. He stood glowering at the fan for nearly a minute, lamenting silently that on this of all nights, when the temperature was locked in the eighties, his fan had to break. He leaned back across his desk and made a note of it, adding that one to a pile of other notes jumbled in a basket on the corner of his desk marked "Essential." He straightened up with a sigh, took one last glance at the heap of papers on his desk, and went out into the squad room where he saw Desk Sergeant Vic Stramsky nodding off at the radio console.

The hair above Stramsky's ears was slick with perspiration, and Balzic observed with some small malice that the fan near Stramsky's head was still working, though all it seemed to do when its breeze passed over Stramsky was cause his collar points to flutter.

"Vic. Hey Vic!"

Stramsky roused himself. "What's up?"

"I'm going to Muscotti's to get a couple beers. You want me to bring you back one?"

"Nah. It'd just make me sleepier than I am."

The dull chatter of the switchboard sounded, and Stramsky rolled his chair over to plug in the line. He listened for a long moment and then motioned for Balzic to pick up an extension phone.

Balzic heard Stramsky saying, "Yes, ma'am. Would you mind repeating that so I can write it down?"

"All right," the voice said, a voice full of years. "My name is Miss Cynthia Summer. I live at 226 North Hagen Avenue."

"And what's the trouble again, Miss Summer?"

"Well, I hope there isn't any, but something's very odd. You see, I rent rooms to students, ones who attend the community college, don't you see."

2

"Yes, ma'am."

"And there is one I haven't seen for about two days."

"Maybe he went home for the summer."

"No. That couldn't be. In the first place, it's a she. Janet—oh my, I have to look it up. I have to write everything down. I had a stroke, don't you see, and I just can't remember things the way I used to." There was a pause. "Here it is. Janet Pisula. And she didn't go home for the summer because her classes weren't over until Friday, the twenty-eighth of May. That's today. And then she has final examinations to take, don't you see. All next week."

"Uh, Miss Summer," Stramsky said, "today is the fourth of June."

"It is? Oh my."

"That would mean her classes were over a week ago today, ma'am."

"Well, that makes it even worse, don't you see."

"No, ma'am, I don't."

"Well, young man, if her classes were over last Friday, then she would have had her examinations by now and she would be preparing to move out for the summer, don't you see."

"Uh, Miss Summer, are you sure she didn't leave already?"

"Young man, I do not want to seem impertinent, but I know when my students come and when they go. She didn't leave her key. If she had moved out and I'd forgotten it or didn't notice it, her key would still be here, don't you see. I keep all the keys on a board, right here by the telephone."

"How many students do you have there, Miss Summer?"

"Seven. But I only let six rooms. Two boys are sharing."

"And how many keys do you have there?"

"I have all the keys here."

"What I mean, ma'am, is are we talking about duplicate keys or are we talking about the keys the students themselves had?"

"Why, I have only duplicate keys here, don't you see."

"Then that would mean that none of your students left for the summer."

"Oh my, I'm afraid I don't understand that. But—but that

3

couldn't be, don't you see? Because I have seen all the others."

"Well, ma'am, if you have only the duplicate keys there on your board—"

Balzic interrupted. "Miss Summer, this is Mario Balzic. I'm chief of police here. I've been listening on another phone. Let's just forget about the keys for a minute. Why do you think something's wrong?"

"How do you do," she said. "I've heard a good deal about you."

"Yes, ma'am. Now about this student of yours?"

"Oh. Yes. Well, I haven't seen that girl for, oh my, I thought it was just two days, but if this is the fourth of June, then I haven't seen her for more than a week. And that's just not like her. What I mean to say is that I used to see her every day. We used to chat often. She was a very nice young person. Very lonely, don't you see. But she made a point to stop and chat every day."

"Miss Summer, is it possible you could have seen her and, uh, not remembered? I mean, you said yourself you were having a little trouble remembering things."

The old woman took a moment to reply. When she did, her voice was quivering. "Young man, I did indeed have a stroke, and I do indeed have difficulty remembering things, but I'm not a complete fool."

"Yes, ma'am. I didn't mean for a second you were. But I just thought—never mind. I'll be up to your place in a couple minutes and we'll get this thing straightened out, how's that?"

"Do you think it's necessary for you to come?"

"Well, Miss Summer, we won't know whether it's necessary until we check, now will we?"

"All right. I'll leave the porch light on for you. Oh, what am I saying—I always leave the porch light on. You'll have to excuse me."

Balzic said good-bye and hung up, looking questioningly at Stramsky.

"Why don't you send somebody else up there?" Stramsky said. "What are you going for?"

"If you think a minute, you'll remember who that old lady is."

"Oh yeah. From the coal family. Summer coal. Yeah, how could I forget that? She gave all that land for the community college."

"That's her. I think she rates a chief. Besides, if I don't go there, I go to Muscotti's, get half drunked up, and then I come back here and make like a bookkeeper—and I can't do that sober."

Balzic headed for the door and went out, letting the screen door bounce against its spring.

Lightning flashed vaguely on the horizon as Balzic got into his cruiser. The lightning was a long way off, and he doubted that a storm would reach Rocksburg—if it ever did—before morning. He turned the cruiser around in the lot and then headed north on Main, thinking it was going to be another miserable night for sleeping.

At the last intersection on Main Street serviced by traffic lights, Balzic turned onto North Hagen Avenue, recollecting the gossip and local lore about the Summer family.

As Rocksburg went, the Summers were as near to aristocracy as the town had ever known. Anybody else who had made money in town, either from the mills or from coal or natural gas, had moved out at the first opportunity. The Summers, for reasons no one bothered to speculate about anymore, had chosen to live where they'd made their fortune.

Clarence Summer had risen from timekeeper through college and law school at night to become attorney for a half-dozen small mines working north of town. Sometime during the three decades from 1890 to 1920, when the steel and coal strikes were at their bloodiest, the mines Summer represented went out of production and into receivership, and when they reopened, by some paper shuffling perhaps only Summer himself understood, they were owned by Clarence Summer.

Sometime in that same period, Summer married. The rumors had been various: he married a Jewess, a Welsh chargirl, a

5

Canadian prostitute. Whatever she had been, she became an alcoholic hermit. Her tastes were odd—gin and beer—and her consumption legendary. The empty bottles that were carted away by garbage collectors were the subject of bets. No one in Rocksburg could say with certainty he had ever heard her first name.

Summer and his wife produced four daughters, and the general opinion was that if Summer was trying to build a dynasty he couldn't have made a worse start. The daughters couldn't wait to escape. Whether they fled from him or from their alcoholic mother or from Rocksburg itself, no one knew. The only one who stayed was the one everyone—including herself—called Miss Cynthia, the first born, the only one who never married.

For years, well into the late 1950s, Miss Cynthia sustained her wealth and her remoteness. Then, bit by piece, things began to slip away. The mines veined out. Where once there had been four main shafts, each bearing the name of a daughter and the number of the order of her birth—Cynthia Number One, Edna Number Two, Elaine Number Three, and Roseann Number Four —each employing nearly a hundred miners, by 1960 all four shafts had been sealed on orders of the state bureau of mines to prevent the possibility of surface air feeding a fire that had begun in a shaft owned by another company but which came very near Elaine Number Three.

Clarence's wife died in the last great diphtheria epidemic in the thirties. Clarence himself lost to cancer in the early forties. The other daughters, Edna, Elaine, and Roseann, appeared only as names and faces on the society pages of the Pittsburgh newspapers and then, one by one, on the obituary pages. Miss Cynthia clung to the house and life.

The chauffeur went first. Then the gardener, the maids, and the cook. The Lincoln Continental went soon after the chauffeur. The rock gardens, the rose gardens, the hedge gardens with the fountains and the sundials began to look like parodies of themselves.

Miss Cynthia shopped for herself; she could not even command a taxi to wait until she finished. When she entered the supermarkets, she clutched a sheaf of coupons cut from *The Rocksburg Gazette* offering discounts on certain products, and when she left and waited for another taxi to pick her up, she tried not to lean on a shopping cart in which a solitary bag was filled mostly with frozen dinners.

Sometime in the mid-sixties, she made an arrangement with the Conemaugh County commissioners for the land behind the house. The commissioners had been planning for some time to begin a community college, but were stymied by the price of land at a time when they'd been advised the bond market was unfavorable. Miss Cynthia, it was said around city hall and in the county court house, offered the forty acres behind her house in return for an exemption from real estate and school taxes on the house in which she insisted she was going to live until she died. It was also said that the house would at her death automatically become county property with the provision that it become part of the community college and be named Clarence Summer Hall.

In 1968, when the first college building was completed on her land—a combination of classrooms, library, and student union—Miss Cynthia's financial desperation became clear: she placed an ad in *The Rocksburg Gazette* welcoming students to lease rooms from her at the incredible rate of twelve dollars a month; this, when a single room with bath in Rocksburg was going for a minimum of fifty dollars a month.

Balzic approached the house now, once an imposing and impeccable two-story red brick structure said to have six bathrooms, over a pitted asphalt drive leading to the front portico. Two faded white columns supported a weather roof over the drive. As Miss Cynthia had said, the portico light was on, but only one light of the two still burned. When Balzic knocked, he saw that the other lamp no longer had a bulb in it.

Miss Cynthia answered the door herself. Her left eye was half closed and her left cheek sagged, drawing down the corner of her

7

mouth. She was disconcertingly thin, and her left arm dangled lifelessly.

"Miss Summer," Balzic said, holding out his ID case. "I'm Mario Balzic."

"Please come in, Chief Balzic." She tried to smile. "I can't tell you how sorry I am to have to meet you like this." It was an effort for her to close the door. "You'll want the key, won't you?"

"Yes, ma'am," Balzic said, following her across the foyer, noticing with a vague remorse the difficulty with which she walked, her left shoe never leaving the floor but sliding along. She led him to a telephone under a stairway. Balzic was not surprised to see that it was a pay phone.

Miss Cynthia took a key off a square board by the phone and handed it to Balzic. "Her room is the last one on the right upstairs. I'm sorry I can't take you up. Those stairs are just impossible for me these days. I really hope . . ."

"We'll see, Miss Summer. But first we have to look."

He took the stairs slowly, observing the house as he went. It was more generally deteriorated than he'd expected, and he had the feeling of being in a house just a signature away from a sheriff's sale.

At the top of the stairs he oriented himself. There were two halls: one led straight ahead of the stairs, the other began about ten feet back from the stairs and led to the left. Balzic went straight ahead to the last door on the right.

He could hear voices in the room opposite, young male voices involved in what sounded like a mild argument over a problem in mathematics.

Balzic had trouble with the lock. It seemed a fairly new lock and the edges of the key were still sharp. It took Balzic a moment to realize that rather than opening the door he had done the opposite. He repeated his motions with the key and was certain when he finally pushed open the door that it had been unlocked when he first inserted the key.

Inside the room, a gooseneck lamp was burning on a tiny desk against the far wall. Balzic noticed that first. Then the smell hit him and he saw the rest and nearly gagged.

She was on her back on the floor beside the bed and naked except for her panties. Twisted around her neck was another undergarment, a slip or a brassiere perhaps, but Balzic did not want to get close enough to look. Her features were horribly distorted from the swelling, and her flesh from her neck to her hairline was the color of a week-old bruise. On her stomach was a plain white sheet of paper. As far as Balzic could tell there was nothing written on it, but he couldn't bring himself to reach down and pick it up.

Something kept wanting to come up in Balzic's throat. He had to force himself to look at her. Her body was slender, boyish almost, with small breasts, and she did not appear to Balzic to be much taller than his eldest daughter. He swept his gaze around the room long enough to notice that there was no particular disarray, then he backed out, locked the door, and hurried down the stairs to the phone.

As he was dialing, he heard Miss Cynthia ask him if everything was all right.

"No, ma'am, it isn't."

"Oh my," she said.

"Rocksburg Police, Sergeant Stramsky speaking."

"Vic. Mario. Get the D.A., the coroner, and the state boys. We got a homocide at 226 North Hagen Avenue. I'll be waiting out front for them."

"Got it," Stramsky replied, and the phone went dead. Balzic hung up and saw Miss Cynthia. He reached out and touched her on the shoulder.

"Oh my," she said. "Oh my . . ."

The state police Criminal Investigation Division squad, under the temporary command of Lt. Walker Johnson, arrived first. Much to Balzic's spiteful pleasure Johnson had been transferred from Erie to replace Lt. Harry Minyon while Minyon rode out a bout with his ulcers in Conemaugh General Hospital. Any replacement for Minyon would have pleased Balzic, but Johnson was especially welcome to him as their friendship went back to days when Balzic had first made chief and Johnson was a sergeant on the narcotics squad. Two nights ago, on Johnson's first night back in Rocksburg, the two of them had gotten pleasantly drunk on Balzic's back porch, regaling each other with decade-old anecdotes. . . .

Johnson came downstairs after he'd put his squad to work and waited for Balzic to introduce Miss Cynthia. A moment after the introduction, Johnson nodded to Balzic and led the way out to the foyer near the front door.

"This is a hell of a way to start," Johnson said.

"Well, at least it won't be dull."

"Yeah. It won't be that. So, old buddy, what do you have?"

"Next to nothing. The lady had a stroke—which you noticed —and I don't know what we're going to get out of her. She thought today was the twenty-eighth of May."

"How about the two kids in the room across the hall—you talk to them yet?"

"I'll tell you what, Walk. I damn near got sick up there. That girl's not much bigger than my Marie. Older, I'm sure, but not any bigger. It just got to me, so I just locked up and came down and called you."

"Say nothing. I couldn't stand it myself. By now every one of those poor bastards up there'll have a handky in his mouth." Johnson thought for a moment. "Is Grimes still coroner here?"

"Yeah. He should've been here by now. The D.A., too."

Johnson shrugged. "You want to stay with the lady? Or you want the two kids upstairs?"

"I better stick with her. She's supposed to have four or five more roomers in here, you know."

"Wonder where they are. They live here, they can't be locals. This is a hell of a time. School year's damn near over. They're all students, aren't they?"

Balzic nodded.

"I hope to hell they haven't left for home," Johnson said. "If they have, we'll be chasing all over hell." He shrugged again and went back upstairs.

Balzic went back into what had once been the living room where he found Miss Cynthia sitting listlessly on the corner of a worn and faded maroon velvet couch.

He sat beside her. "Miss Summer, I'm going to have to ask you some questions, so is there anything I can get you before we get started?"

"No, thank you. You're kind to think of it, but no. I'm just worried that I won't be able to help, and . . ."

"And what?"

"Well, all these police. Is it really, I mean—"

"I'm afraid so, Miss Summer. The girl—well, didn't you hear me when I was talking on the phone?"

"Yes," Miss Cynthia said slowly. "Yes, I heard you. I suppose I didn't want to believe it." Her mottled hand went to her papery lips. "She was such a lovely person. But so lonely."

"How so?"

"She was an orphan. She was raised by an aunt and uncle. That much I remember, but for the life of me, I can't think where. I have it written down. I can get the address for you."

"Not right now. Later on you'll have to give me the names and addresses of all your roomers. But for now, let's just talk about what you remember about her."

"What I remember—oh my. I don't even remember very clearly when I last talked to her. I thought it was three days ago. Now, I'm just not sure."

"Well tell me what you are sure of."

"I'm sure that she had no parents or brothers or sisters. I'm sure she was kind. Practically the first thing she said after she said hello was to ask if there was anything she could get me. Why, that first week I was home from the hospital after my stroke, she stayed down here with me all night, don't you see. I never asked her to, but when I'd wake during the night, she'd be asleep in a chair near my bed. We had even discussed the possibility of her living down here with me next year as a sort of, oh you know, a sort of companion to me."

"She must have had friends," Balzic said.

"I really can't say. I don't know how she got along with my other students. She never discussed them with me—or if she did I just don't remember."

"Do you remember anyone visiting her?"

"No. I can't say for certain. She may have. The students are always coming and going. I can't say if anyone was coming to see her. I just have this impression that no one did. I can't say why."

"Did she have dates?"

"I don't think so. We talked about that occasionally. I used to tell her that youth was not to be squandered, things like that. Things old people try to tell young people. But it struck me that she really wasn't aware that she was a woman. She could have been very attractive, but she seemed not to know how to make herself attractive. She had a rather plain face, and it seemed she didn't know anything about cosmetics. She had a lovely, slim figure, but she didn't think about clothes at all."

Balzic nodded. "Do you remember hearing anything unusual?"

"No. I'm sorry. I just missed seeing her. That's why I called you. But I don't recall any noises, anything out of the ordinary. But you must understand, chief, this stroke has also left me deaf in my left ear. You have a very powerful voice. Very resonant. It's easy enough to hear you. But much goes on that I don't hear. I suppose for that reason I make a very accommodating landlady for my students. Their music—well, all I hear is a rhythmic thumping. I would dearly like to hear it, but . . ."

"Did she ever speak to you about any trouble?"

"No. She wasn't rich, heaven knows. But she had been cared for, some sort of trust fund. She told me about it once, but I don't remember any details. I don't think she was having any difficulty with the relatives who raised her. At least I don't recall her speaking about anything like that."

12

"Didn't she ever talk about anything that was bothering her? There must have been something."

"The only thing I remember like that was something about a course she was having problems with. A composition course I believe it was. For a time she was bewildered by it all. I recall her saying once that she didn't know what that man wants, something like that. But that was some time ago. In the winter. December or January, I think. Of course, you must consider my sense of time these days."

"That was the only thing?"

"I'm sorry, chief. You must understand. That's all I can remember."

Balzic stood. "Miss Summer, I'll have to see your records now. The students' names, home addresses, how they stood with the rent."

"I'll get that for you. I keep it all locked in my desk in the kitchen. I can tell you now that all of my students were very prompt about the rent."

Balzic helped her up and then followed her into the kitchen. He had just finished copying the names and addresses from her ledger when Dr. Wallace Grimes, the county coroner, appeared in the foyer. He was still wearing his suit coat and his tie was knotted tightly. He wiped his forehead with a folded handky and replaced it carefully in his breast pocket, nodding to Balzic and saying, "Mario," by way of greeting and asking at the same time where he was to find his work.

"Upstairs, doc," Balzic said.

Grimes went up without a word, and a moment or two later Johnson came down. Balzic met him at the foot of the stairs.

"What did you get, Mario?"

"Not much. Names and addresses of the other students. Nobody owed. The lady's hearing is bad and her memory's about the same. The only thing she could say for sure was that the girl was an orphan. No brothers, no sisters. Raised by an aunt and uncle. The only thing she thought might have been bothering the girl was some trouble in her classwork. A composition course. But she thought that was around last December or January. She couldn't remember hearing anything more about it since. What did you get?"

"The two kids are a blank," Johnson said. "All they remember is seeing her once in a while. They didn't even miss her. One of them thought he heard something funny about a week ago, but he didn't think anything more about it. The other one thought he saw a guy standing in front of her door a couple of weeks ago, but then when he thought about it he couldn't say whether the guy was standing in front of her door or was just standing in the hall. He says he never saw the guy before or since. Couldn't give me the vaguest make. Had no idea whether the guy was old or young, tall, short, nothing. All he said for sure was the guy was white. And then he started to think about that."

"Your people come up with anything?"

"Well, who knows what was there? But there's plenty of money still around. For a college kid, I mean. Twenty-five-something in bills and change in her desk drawer, another couple bucks in bills and change in her wallet. Nothing was knocked over. The rest of her clothes were on the foot of the bed, laid out neat, like she was just undressing and hadn't thought to hang anything on hangers.

"Just as a first guess," Johnson went on, "I'd say somebody either talked her into getting undressed and when she got that far he just slipped the brassiere around her neck and strangled her with it. Either that or else he walked in on her when she had got down to just those two pieces of clothing. Either she knew him or else he caught her completely by surprise because the two across the hall definitely did not hear anything resembling a scream or a yell for help. And they also claim they've both been in their room every day and night for the past two weeks except to go to classes and to eat. They both say they're too broke to do anything else."

"You don't think them?"

"Who knows? But right now, they just look too goddamn goggle-eyed. You know the look. Couple of squares. They got all this information to volunteer, they want to say all this stuff to help, but it all comes out a lot of words."

"What do you make of the paper?"

Johnson gave a barely audible snort. "That's the goddamndest thing I've ever seen. The guy that did it had to put it there, but why?"

"Nothing on it?"

"Not a damn thing. Unless you count the smudge of a print. Just a piece of white typing paper."

"More like it in the room?" Balzic said.

"Yeah. About half a ream by the typewriter on the desk. Same stuff."

"Anything else?"

"I looked at her fingernails. I got a man scraping them, but I have the feeling he's not going to find a thing. I couldn't see anything myself. Not even a crack in one of them. Like she didn't put up any resistance at all."

"Maybe she was surprised."

"Sure, there's that possibility. But you'd think she'd have made some attempt to save her life. I mean, what the hell, Mario? Even if she was grabbed from behind, caught completely unaware, you'd think she would've dug her nails into something. Her own throat, something, just trying to get that thing off her neck. Nobody loses consciousness that fast. But nothing—unless it's something that has to go under a scope. But that paper. Wow . . ."

Dr. Grimes came down the steps then, buttoning his collar and running up his tie.

"What's the word, doc?" Balzic said.

"That should have been obvious," Grimes said evenly. "Suffocation caused by strangulation. Six, seven, maybe eight days ago. Give me some time and I'll get it down to the day.

What's keeping the ambulance people—or did somebody not think to call?"

"They should have been here long ago," Balzic said. "I'll get on them."

"Tell them to go right to the hospital morgue," Grimes said, going for the door. "I'll be waiting for them. Good night."

Balzic called Stramsky to hurry the ambulance and learned that every available one was on a call. "Couple heart attacks and a four-car pile-up coming out of Conemaugh Shopping Center. Nothing serious, but every car had a family in it," Stramsky said. Balzic grunted and then hung up. He went back to tell Johnson and saw him talking to a plump, barefoot girl who kept peeking around Johnson's shoulders, darting glances at the officers coming and going on the stairs.

Johnson introduced the girl—Evelyn Embry—to Balzic. She had a pleasant enough face, softened by its roundness, but her reticence in answering Johnson's questions had an edge of arrogance about it that Balzic found immediately disagreeable. In spite of himself, Balzic kept glancing at the girl's feet and the dirt caked between her toes.

". . . so you didn't know her very well," Johnson was saying.

"Yeah, uh, I mean I talked to her, you know, but that's all."

"Do you recall the last time you saw her?"

"Uh-uh. Couple days ago, I guess."

"She's been dead longer than that."

"Oh. Well—I don't know. Maybe a week ago."

"Did you ever see anybody with her?"

"No. But like I said, I really didn't know. I mean, I didn't see her that much. I only talked to her a couple times." She thought for a moment. "Does this, uh, mean I have to stay around? I mean, I am getting ready to leave. I'm all packed and everything."

"Stay around for what?" Johnson asked.

"Oh, you know—I don't know," she said, giggling nervously. "Don't you guys always make the witnesses stay around or something?"

16

Johnson shot a wearied glance at Balzic who, again in spite of himself, was looking at the girl's filthy feet. "No, Miss Embry. We have your home address if you want to leave. If we need to talk to you again, we'll get in touch with your parents."

"Oh, I'm not going home."

"Well, your family will know where you'll be, won't they?"

"I hope not."

"Uh, Miss Embry, it's not likely that we'll need to talk to you again, but just in case, you better let your family know where you're going to be. You can go now. Just please stay out of the way upstairs, okay?"

Johnson shook his head at Balzic as the girl went up the steps.

"You know," Balzic said, "I was talking to a chemist a couple weeks ago. If these barefoot kids only knew how much crap they walked through in a day. . . ."

The ambulance came and left, the attendants soaked with perspiration by the time they got the stretcher to the bottom of the stairs.

District Attorney Milt Weigh stopped on his way home from a county Democrat meeting, staying only long enough to make general inquiries and to offer the services of his squad of detectives.

"He looked like the Democrats are serving better booze than they used to," Johnson said after Weigh had gone.

Balzic smiled weakly, feeling too hot to make a rejoinder. "Think your boys came up with anything yet?"

"About time I checked," Johnson said, going slowly up the steps.

Balzic walked through the foyer to the front door, catching sight of Miss Summer sitting on the worn velvet couch, fanning herself with an envelope. He stepped out onto the portico and scanned the horizon looking for lightning. When it flashed, it seemed even duller and more distant than it had earlier.

He smoked and thought about that single sheet of paper on the girl's stomach and then about the girl and then about his own daughter, Marie. His thoughts were a jumble. Nothing made sense. He felt the way he felt when he read a newspaper account of some seemingly isolated act of violence, when the reporter called the act "senseless." The word annoyed and angered him because he believed that no violence was truly senseless. It always made sense if you took the time to analyze it. He believed that was as true about the violence done upstairs as about any other violence he had known, except that everything about this violence did indeed appear senseless. There had been no robbery, no sound, no struggle, and he was willing to bet that there had been no sex. He would have to wait for the coroner's report to be certain of that, but, without being able to explain or justify his feeling to himself, he was sure sex had had no part in what had happened to this orphan, this Janet Pisula. He was as sure of that as he was unsure what the piece of paper on her stomach meant. There was a message there, but one without words and one that therefore said everything at the same time it said nothing.

Balzic flipped his cigarette butt into the night and went back inside just as Johnson was coming down the stairs.

"Anything?" Balzic said.

"About a thousand prints up there. Naturally, the ones we'd like to have—off that paper—we're not going to get. Whoever it was probably licked his index finger and just got enough of his index finger and thumb to lift it and put it on her. We'll have to send it to the FBI lab anyway to make sure. They're the only ones with the equipment to get a print off paper, but my man says they're not going to be able to do anything with what's there." Johnson scratched his chin. "Mario, tell me again how the room was when you went in."

"The door was unlocked, I'm certain of that. The desk lamp was on, nothing was knocked around. That's about all I really noticed. The smell got to me and I had to get the hell out."

"How do you figure that?" Johnson said. "In this heat—God. You'd've thought somebody would've smelled it before this. They all had to come down these steps. Her door's not fifteen feet away from the top."

18

"I didn't get it until I opened the door, if that's any help. Do you remember when it first hit you?"

"Now that you mention it, no," Johnson said. "But it doesn't make sense. It goes against all the laws of the nose." He looked thoughtfully at the floor. "Where the hell are the rest of them? How many are there again, total?"

"Seven. We've seen four. That leaves three."

"Male or female?"

"Two females, one male."

"And they're all still here? None left for the summer?"

"According to Miss Summer and to the keys on her board, they should all be here."

"Did you try to get the next of kin?"

"Not yet. But I hate like hell to tell anybody that over the phone. And that's a long drive down there. Thirty-five, forty miles. Why don't you see if you've got some people in the vicinity?"

"I suppose I better," Johnson said.

Balzic handed him the address of Mr. and Mrs. Michael Pisula, and Johnson went outside to his cruiser to make the call to the barracks to have the detail assigned. He returned in a few minutes and said, "We got some people in the area. They'll handle it."

"A piece of paper," Balzic said, shaking his head. "One piece of blank typing paper . . ."

They were standing there, smiling absurdly at one another when the front door opened and two girls came timidly into the foyer. The first was very tall, very slim, dressed in faded jeans, a sleeveless cotton jersey, and sandals. The other, shorter but equally slim, also wore jeans and sandals with a man's tee-shirt which had been dyed a myriad of pastel colors. Both carried books and notebooks and had similar shoulder bags made of fringed suede.

Johnson introduced himself and Balzic to the girls.

"Which one of you is Kimberly Marsinsky?" Balzic asked.

"I am," the taller one said, flushing.

"And you're Patricia Kein?" Balzic said to the other.

"Keim," she corrected him.

"What's the matter?" Kimberly asked. "What happened—I mean, what's going on?"

"One of your fellow tenants is dead," Johnson said. "Janet Pisula."

"Janet who?" Patricia asked.

"I never heard of her," Kimberly said. The girls looked at each other quizzically.

"She lived in the room at the top of the stairs. On the right."

"Oh. Her," Patricia said.

"Why do you say it like that?" Johnson said.

"Well, I didn't mean it to sound like it sounded—I guess. It's just, well, I don't know. But if you're here, then . . ."

"I'll save the speculation," Johnson said. "She was murdered."

Both girls sucked in their breath. "Oh my God," Kimberly said. "When—how—you mean right here?"

"Right here. In her room. We know how, but we don't know when exactly. We were hoping you could help us with that."

"I didn't even know her," Kimberly said. "I never even talked to her. I didn't—I'll bet I didn't see her four or five times. And every time I saw her, she was in there talking with the old lady."

"You knew her, Patricia," Johnson said.

"I didn't *know* her. I talked to her twice. Once for about fifteen minutes over in the Union. She wanted to know about an assignment we had in comp. The other time was outside the library about, oh, three or four weeks ago. We talked for about a half-hour or so."

"Why did you say, 'Oh, her,' the way you said it? Before, I mean, when we told you who it was."

"I don't know. I guess because she impressed me as being a very unaware person."

"Unaware in what way?"

"I don't know. It's hard to say why you think somebody is

aware and why somebody else isn't. Awareness is a difficult thing to define."

"Well try," Balzic said. "We have to have some idea what you're talking about."

"She was just out of it, that's all."

Johnson scratched his neck and glared at the wall beyond Balzic's shoulder. Balzic let out a heavy sigh and said, "Look, Patricia—"

"Please don't call me that. Just Pat, okay? I hate Patricia."

"Okay, Pat. But look. I've got two daughters, and I know what it is to try and understand them when they start using their slang, and I'm aware—huh?—aware that slang changes pretty fast. The point I'm trying to make is you got to put your impressions and feelings about this girl into something specific, something solid that a couple foggy bottoms like the lieutenant here and me can understand. Saying she was a 'very unaware person' or 'out of it'—that tells us nothing. Because I'll tell you something she was and is for a plain fact. She was a victim. She is now a corpse. And whoever victimized her and turned her into a corpse—no matter how out of it you thought she was—that somebody did it right here. Where *you* live. And there is nothing we know now to guarantee us or you that he doesn't have it in his head to turn some other young girl into a corpse. Is that plain enough for you?"

"Oh wow," Kimberly said.

"That's plain enough," Pat said. "I'm sorry. I'll try."

"Good," Balzic said. "Now let's start with the first time you talked to her. What was that about?"

"Well, that's funny—I mean, obviously it isn't funny. It's ironic though, because the first time I talked to her was last semester. About the second week. We were in the same comp class, and the assignment was to define an abstraction as concretely as we could. And I remember telling her almost exactly what you just told me, I mean, I told her she had to be as specific as she could. I tried to tell her to take as simple an abstraction as she could think of, something very elemental like a season of the year and just make a list of all the things she could think of when that word came into her head. But she didn't even have the awareness that a season of the year was an abstraction."

"And that's all you talked about? Nothing else?"

The Keim girl nodded.

"What about the second time, by the library I think you said."

She nodded. "Well, that time she stopped me and said she had to talk to somebody about something very important but she didn't know who to talk to. And then she said something—I couldn't help it—when she said it, I just started laughing at her. Oh, wow, what a bummer for her."

"What did she say?"

"Oh wow, she said she'd always admired me. It was the way she said admired. So worshippy, God, it was like she should have been lighting a candle or something."

"Go on," Johnson said.

"Well, she got so embarrassed, she just turned crimson. I've never seen anybody blush like that in my life. And then she started talking real fast and it was all about comp again, but I could see right away that wasn't what she really wanted to talk about and that she was just making that up as she went because she didn't know how to get out of talking to me."

"So," Balzic said, running his tongue over a molar, "you got the impression—well, let me ask you. Did she talk about anything else?"

"No. And after a couple more minutes, she started blushing again and said she had to go someplace, and then she practically ran away from me."

"Let me get something else straight," Balzic said. "You were both in the same composition class the first semester. Were you still in the same class this semester?"

"No. She couldn't get along with Keenan at all. She used to catch a lot of flak from him. So did everybody, really. But everybody gave it back to him. Except her. And I really gave it back to him. I guess maybe that's why she said she admired me. I

22

couldn't think of any other reason. I never saw her anyplace else. Just class and here. But I never talked to her here. Just to say hello."

"Keenan was the teacher?"

"He's also chairman of the department. And the only one with a doctorate. The others, Winoski and Farrell, they just have their master's."

"Don't forget Snavely," Kimberly said.

"That toad," Pat said.

"I don't think he even has a bachelor's," Kimberly said.

"Who did Janet have for composition this semester?" Balzic asked.

"Farrell, I think," Pat said. "I'm not sure. She told me that time outside the library, but I forgot."

"Do you know, Kimberly?"

"No, I don't."

"Okay, let's forget about teachers for a while. What about the last couple weeks? When was the last time either of you saw this girl? And please think carefully."

"The last time I saw her was a couple weeks ago," Kimberly said. "She was in there talking to the old lady."

"Pat?"

"A week, maybe ten days ago. She was just going into her room and I was coming up the steps. I didn't talk to her though."

"Ever see anybody going into her room or standing outside her door or knocking on her door or coming out of her room?"

Both girls shook their heads.

"Did you hear anything or see anything out of the ordinary in the last week or so—anything at all?"

Again, the same negative response.

"What the hell," Balzic said under his breath, half turning away from the girls and speaking softly to Johnson. "A girl lives here since when—last September? Six other people pass fifteen feet from her door every time they go out or come in and nobody knows a goddamn thing about her. You tell me, Walk."

Johnson shrugged and scratched his neck. "Listen, girls,

23

thank you very much for your cooperation. There's just one more thing. Let whoever you live with know where you're going to be. If we want to ask you anything else, we'll get in touch with you. We have your home addresses. You can go now. And thanks again."

The girls apologized for not being able to help much, then went up the stairs to their rooms, leaving Balzic and Johnson once again to stare at each other and shake their heads foolishly.

"Who's left?" Johnson asked.

"Uh, one Nicholas Cerovich," Balzic said, reading from the list he had copied from Miss Summer's ledger.

"What do you bet he knows as much as the rest of them?"

"No bet," Balzic said, going into the living room to ask Miss Summer if she knew anything about him.

"Cerovich," she said slowly. "Oh, yes. Nicholas. He's working. He won't be here until after midnight."

"Do you know where he works?"

"You'll have to give me a moment, chief. It's here in Rocksburg, that much I know. I'll think of the place." She frowned and closed her eyes as though trying to visualize the name of the place.

"Is it one of the mills?"

"It's a mill, but give me another word for a mill and I might be able to think of it."

"Uh, factory, fabricating plant, foundry, forge—."

"That's it. Forge. He works at a forge."

"Fort Pitt Chain and Forge?"

"Yes. That's it."

"Thank you, Miss Summer," Balzic said, going to the phone and rooting through his pockets for a dime. "I located him," he said to Johnson. "You got any dimes?" he said, flipping through the pages of the directory. Johnson handed him some dimes just as Balzic found the number. He dialed, identifying himself when he got an answer, and asked for someone familiar with the names of employees. "Just a routine verification that a man is employed there, that's all."

"I'm only a security guard, chief," the voice replied. "There's nobody here in any of the offices."

"What's working now?"

"Just the forge crew. Plus some guys on the loading dock."

"The name Cerovich mean anything to you—Nicholas Cerovich?"

"Oh yeah, sure. The college kid. Yeah, he's here. He's down with the labor gang in the forge. You want to talk to him?"

"No. I'll tell you what. Let me talk to his boss."

"Sure, sure. Hold on." There was a click, a buzz, then a ringing.

"Forge. Sokolosky," a voice shouted over the roar of the furnaces and the thunderous slamming of forge hammers.

"This is Chief of Police Balzic," he said, holding the phone away from his ear. "I'm just trying to verify that you have a Nicholas Cerovich working for you. Is he there now?"

"Yeah. You wanna talk to him?"

"No. Just tell me what shift he works and whether he misses work."

"He works steady second trick. He don't miss any work. Hasn't missed a day since he started. He's a good kid. Helluva worker."

"When did he start?"

"Four o'clock like everybody else."

"No, no. I mean, when'd he start working there?"

"Oh. Last summer. June I think. Been about a year now."

"Have you been his boss all this time?"

"I been everybody's boss on second trick for eleven years."

"And he hasn't missed any work at all? Especially in the last couple weeks?"

"Hey, look. Maybe you ought to talk to him. I don't like this talking about somebody that works for me with a cop. If he did something wrong, you come talk to him."

"I don't need to talk to him. All I want from you is your word that he hasn't missed work, that's all."

"Well you got it, brother. Not only don't he miss work, the

25

sonuvabrick is always yapping can he get some overtime. Is 'at what you wanna hear?"

"That's good enough," Balzic said. "And thanks for your help."

"Yeah, sure. Anytime. Just remember me the next time my old lady gets a ticket. Joe Sokolosky. See you around, chief." The phone clicked, and Balzic was laughing as he hung up.

"So?" Johnson said.

"So, Nicholas Cerovich works steady second trick at Fort Pitt Chain and Forge, he's been working for almost a year, and he hasn't missed a day. Which means he probably knows as little as the rest."

"Oh boy," Johnson said. "You know what that means."

"Yeah," Balzic said. "I wonder how many people there are tied up with this damn college."

"Well, how about you finding out, okay? I'll hang in here until we run everything down or pick everything up. I also want to talk to those two across the hall from her room again. They might've remembered something; I might've forgot to ask them something. See how many names you can get, and then we'll see how we divide the labor. We'll probably have to use the D.A.'s people . . . you got somebody you can call?"

"I can start with the president of the college," Balzic said. "I met him last year at some banquet or other."

"Well, he's all yours," Johnson said, starting up the stairs again and muttering something about the heat while Balzic thumbed through the phone directory looking for the home address of Dr. J. Hale Beverley, president of Conemaugh County Community College.

Dr. J. Hale Beverley lived in the Crestmont Plan, a post-Korean War development known among Rocksburg's blue collars as Pill Hill. As a hill it didn't seem much, a gentle rise of ground on the northeastern edge of Rocksburg, but from its crest on clear days when there was no suggestion of a temperature inversion, all of Rocksburg was visible beneath it. As for the pills, most of the staff of Conemaugh General Hospital lived there, plus the majority of specialists, generalists, and dentists who kept at least one office in Rocksburg or its environs. Lately, some lawyers had moved to its fringes, and here and there an engineer had crept in, but among the thirty-five or forty houses clustered on the slopes there was not one chiropractor, mortician, minister, insurance agent, or automobile dealer. How Dr. J. Hale Beverley had managed to find entrance piqued Balzic's curiosity. Either realtors were becoming more democratic or else they didn't know one doctor from another.

Balzic counted fifteen cars either in or near the driveway to the Beverley's two-car garage, and he knew he was going to have to interrupt a party, most likely the year-end bash a college president was expected to throw for his faculty and staff.

As Balzic pushed the button and listened to the two-toned chimes, he caught the sound of a stereo, and when the door opened, a tall, stiffly erect man with a wispy reddish mustache and beard stood in the door frame. He had a nearly empty tumbler in his hand and a tipsily foolish grin on his face.

"Welcome," he said. "Come and join us. Don't tell the host, of course. I was just on my way to the ice and thought I'd stop and invite you."

"Uh-huh," Balzic said, taking out his ID and holding it up. "I'm here to see Dr. Beverley. I called about five minutes ago and talked to Mrs. Beverley, I think. She said she'd tell her husband I was on the way, but maybe you could tell him I'm here—on your way back from the ice."

"Of course. I'll be more than happy to tell him. But why don't you step in and have a drink while you're waiting?"

"No, thanks. Just give him the message."

"Who is it, Mal?" asked a woman, coming up behind the man.

"The fuzzzzzz," Mal said, holding his finger up to his lips in a hokey gesture to be cautious, spilling in the process the last drops from his glass on the lapel of his corduroy jacket. "Whoopsey," he said. Then he abruptly shifted the glass to his left hand

27

and thrust out his right at Balzic. "Forgot my manners," he said. "Malcolm Keenan here. I'm a poet who teaches as a public service."

Balzic took the hand and felt the shaking up to his shoulder.

"Your name again, sir?" Keenan said.

"Balzic."

"Ballsy did you say? I remember a limerick which goes, let me see now—ah, yessss. 'There was a man from Boston, who had a little red Austin; there was room for his ass, and a gallon of gas, but his—' "

"Mal, for god's sake, you're not going to start with those awful things again, are you?" the woman said. She put her hands on Keenan's shoulders and gently began to turn him around and away from the door. "To the kitchen with you," she said.

" '—but his balls hung out and he lost 'em,' " Keenan said, grinning over his shoulder as he submitted to her pushing.

"Don't mind him," the woman said. "Now. What can I do for you?"

Balzic held up his ID again and said, "I called a few minutes ago—"

"Oh yes," she said, studying the ID while Balzic studied her. She was young, thirty at most, with a rather ordinary face that was meticulously made up, and her black dress had what struck Balzic as an improbable combination of propriety and allure about it which he imagined she must have spent some time trying to find. It was unadorned, buttoned to the neck, sleeveless, but made of a material which clung to her more than ample figure.

"Well, I must apologize," she said. "I'm the person to whom you spoke on the phone. I'm Mrs. Beverley, but I'm afraid I haven't had a chance to tell him that you want to see him. Why don't you come in while I do that?"

"Fine."

"I imagine you'll want to be alone," Mrs. Beverley said, "so why don't you just go into the den? Right through that door." She pointed to a door down a short hall. "Right next to the john," she said, turning back into the large living room on the right.

Balzic paused in the opening to the living room on his way to the den. He saw at least twenty-five people, the men dressed for the most part informally, the women wearing a variety of styles. One rather blocky woman wore short denim culottes, flat-heeled sandals, and a blue tee-shirt upon which were painted the words "POT POWER" above a crude outline of a toilet. Another wore a long-sleeved white blouse buttoned to the neck and a red satiny skirt that nearly touched the floor but was split halfway up her thighs. Still another wore silver backless pumps, an extremely short silver lamé dress to show off her very good, very long legs, and clutched a silver bag like a shield to her chest.

They all turned to look at Balzic as Mrs. Beverley approached someone just out of Balzic's view and announced, "The chief of police is here, Jay Hale, and he wants to see you."

Balzic waited a moment longer to see their reaction. It was mostly curiosity he observed, except for the blocky woman in the tee-shirt who went immediately to the stereo and turned up the volume on a rock song and began a provocative dance which belied her construction. After she was sure Balzic was watching her, she danced her way to a squatting, bullishly built young man who looked familiar to Balzic, pulled him to his feet, and continued her dance with him, looking then straight into Balzic's eyes.

Balzic couldn't resist. Before he stepped out of the doorway, he blew the blocky dancer a kiss. It stopped her cold, and then she threw back her head and shook with laughter.

Balzic found the john and was about to open the next door when Keenan reappeared, his glass a deep amber color with only one ice cube in it. "Say," Keenan said, "have you heard the one that goes, 'There was a young lady named Alice, who peed in a Catholic chalice; 'twas done out of need, the bishop agreed, and not out of Protestant malice'—have you heard that one?"

"I just did," Balzic said, smiling.

"Oh," Keenan said. "Too bad. It's one of my favorites." He weaved around Balzic and headed back toward the living room, stumbling once on a deep-pile throw rug.

"Oh boy," Balzic said, going into the den and switching on a desk lamp. "So that's Keenan."

He recalled what Patricia Keim had said about Keenan: chairman of the English department and the only Ph.D. And how had he described himself? "A poet who teaches as a public service"—was that what he'd said? Of course, he was in the bag, Balzic thought. Then again, *in vino veritas*. In boozo, trutho. . . .

He looked around the den, stepping over to the shelves of books behind the walnut and stainless steel desk. He ran his fingers over the shelves and then over the tops of three or four books. The Beverleys had an efficient and dedicated cleaning woman.

He took note of the desk. Everything was in order, making Balzic wonder whether Beverley did any work here. The room seemed more a refuge than a shop. The few pencils in the leather-covered oval container had been recently sharpened, or perhaps they had been sharpened some time ago and never used.

Balzic lit a cigarette, not because he wanted to smoke, but because he wanted to throw a match and the ashes in the ashtray on the desk. He had just flicked off the first ash when the door opened and a short, compactly built man in his mid-thirties came in, closing the door quietly but firmly behind him. He stepped briskly toward Balzic with his hand extended, saying, "I'm Dr. Beverley. And you're?"

"Balzic. I'm chief of police here," he said, shaking hands and watching Beverley's eyes to see if he glanced at the ashtray.

Beverley didn't look at the ashtray but said, "There's an ashtray on the desk."

It amounted to the same thing, Balzic thought, suppressing a smile.

"Sorry to keep you waiting," Beverley said. "My wife neglected to tell me that you'd called earlier. I, uh, assume it's important."

"It is. One of your students is dead."

Beverley's face drained of color and for a second it appeared he was going to lose his balance. He recovered quickly and said, "I presume from the way you said that, uh, that it was not—that it was unnatural."

"You presume right. She was murdered—"

Beverley wavered and had to support himself on the desk. "Oh, good Lord."

"We don't know when exactly, but our first guess is that it happened at least a week ago. We won't know for sure until we get the coroner's report."

"My God, that's awful. Terrible."

"In more ways than one," Balzic said. "The semester's over, right?"

"Huh? Oh yes. The last exams were given today. Who was it?"

"Name was Janet Pisula. She lived with Miss Summer. Rented there, I mean. We've talked to all the people there except one and we'll get to him as soon as he gets off work, but we're going to need all the help we can get from you."

"Certainly. Of course. Anything I can do, just say it . . . my God, this is awful."

"Yeah, well, I get the drift of what you're thinking, Dr. Beverley, but it, uh, was a hell of a lot worse for her than it's going to be for you or the school."

Beverley flushed. "I'm sorry. I—"

Balzic held up his hand. "Say nothing. What I want to know right now is if there is any way you can notify the students here to stay around. They get away from us now, we're going to be chasing all over the county trying to run down whatever information they might have, and it would make things a lot simpler if you keep as many of them around as you could."

"I don't see how," Beverley said. "Most of them have left already. Some finished with their exams yesterday. There were a number who finished Wednesday. There would be no reason for them to remain here unless they were planning to attend the

31

summer sessions. Even so, they would more than likely have left because the summer session, the first one, the six-week session, doesn't begin for three weeks."

"Well how about the ones who took exams today and tonight? Is there any way you could get word out to them to stay put?"

"That's going to be rather difficult."

"Uh, Dr. Beverley, there isn't any of this going to be easy, I'll tell you straight. We don't have diddly-damn to go on so far, and the people we've talked to already haven't given us a damn thing except that the girl kept pretty much to herself. We also know she wasn't robbed, and we've got pretty fair odds she wasn't raped, and that's about it. Which means, in short, that we've got a lot of talking to do to a hell of a lot of people. Which means, furthermore, that all the people you can keep close for a while is going to make it just a little bit easier. Not much, but a little. So if you can get the word out, I'd appreciate it."

"Yes, of course, I understand what you're saying, chief, but I don't even know where to begin. We don't have dormitories. All our students live wherever they can. A great number of them commute."

"Well you must have a list of students. Somebody has to have a roster with addresses, right?"

"Right. Of course."

"Well would you mind picking up that phone and calling whoever that might be and asking him to get over here with that roster?"

Beverley flushed again. "Certainly." He reached for the phone and then rubbed his temples. "What am I thinking about?" he said to himself more than to Balzic. "He's here now. In the living room."

"Oh sweet Jesus," Balzic said to himself, turning his back as Beverley wheeled about and went out. A minute later he returned with two men, both in their mid-to-late thirties, both dressed casually, and both looking as concerned as the amount they'd obviously had to drink would allow.

32

"Chief Balzic," Beverley said, "this is Roy Weintraub, our treasurer, and this is Dr. Larry Ellis, our academic dean."

"Gentlemen," Balzic said, shaking hands.

"I haven't told them what this is about, chief," Beverley said. "I just told them that it was extremely important."

Balzic nodded. "I'll keep it brief, gentlemen. A student of yours, one Janet Pisula, was murdered approximately a week ago and—"

Weintraub's hand shot to his mouth. Ellis's lips parted and he sucked in a breath with an audible hiss.

"—as I was saying, so far we have practically nothing to go on. All the people we've talked to either didn't know the girl or, if they did, they hardly spoke to her. The only person who did speak with her often was her landlady, Miss Cynthia Summer, and if you know Miss Cynthia, you probably also know she had a stroke not too long ago, which means she can't remember very much about the girl except that she was kind and pretty lonely.

"I've already learned from Dr. Beverley," Balzic went on, "that most of the students have gone home for the summer and that a lot of others are commuters. What I want from you gentlemen is a roster of students—with addresses."

"Are you assuming it was another student?" Ellis asked.

"We're not assuming much of anything right now. What we want the roster for is to try and find somebody who knew this girl, knew something about her, knew who she was with, maybe knew somebody who wanted to be with her. And when I say I want a roster with addresses, naturally I mean both addresses. Home addresses and addresses of the places where they lived in town."

"Well, home addresses are easy to obtain," Weintraub said. "They'll be on permanent record cards. But residences here are another matter."

"Why's that?"

"Because we just don't have one. We don't keep track of who rents rooms to students," Weintraub said. "Our experience has been that students move around a lot anyway. They're always looking for ways to save money—moving in and out with one another. And that's perfectly understandable."

"Then how do you go about finding a student in an emergency? What do you do—wait until they show up in class or what?"

Weintraub, Ellis, and Beverley looked sheepishly at one another.

Balzic cleared his throat and waited. When he got no response he said, "Well, gentlemen, I'm not about to start telling you how to run your college. That's out of my line. But right now, I've got a problem, and I'd like to hear some suggestions."

"About what?" Weintraub asked.

"Hey, goddammit," Balzic snapped, "maybe you didn't hear me right. One of your students is dead. Murdered. That was five, six, maybe eight days ago. We won't know for sure until we get the coroner's report tomorrow. In the meantime, whoever killed her is still walking around, and nobody gave us any guarantee he won't get it in his head to do it again. So you people better get organized. I want some names and addresses. Everybody connected with this college—faculty, students, custodial people—everybody. And I want them now. What do I have to do—drive you all over to Conemaugh General so you can watch the autopsy?"

"Uh, Chief Balzic," Beverley said, "if you'll give us a moment to discuss this, I'm sure we can provide you with what you need, and I give you my word, you'll have our full cooperation on this."

"All right," Balzic said, going to the door. "I need to use your bathroom anyway." He shut the door to the den and knocked on the door to the bathroom. When he heard nothing, he opened it.

Inside, the short blocky woman with the blue tee-shirt and the bullish man who had looked familiar to Balzic reluctantly broke apart from what had obviously been a strenuous kiss. Rather, the bullish man tried to break away. He dropped his arms and backed up, but the woman clung to him and only the sink

34

against his backside prevented him from losing his balance entirely.

"Excuse me," Balzic said, looking away. "I didn't hear anybody say anything when I knocked."

"That's all right," the woman said. "We don't mind."

"Uh, I'm sure you don't, but I'd like to use the facility."

"The what?"

"The toilet. You know. You got one painted on your shirt."

"Oh well. You can't use this one. I mean, it's already in use."

"I can see that. But I really do have to use the one on the floor. The one behind you?"

"Be our guest," the woman said.

"You're not going to leave?"

"Leave? Whatever for?" she said. "I mean, my God, man, it's just a simple biological function. You don't have to have a doctorate or anything."

Balzic nodded several times, muttering, "Yeah," each time. "Well," he said, slipping past the woman and unzipping his fly, "when in Rome and all that . . . teachers, huh." He shook his head and caught a glimpse of the woman grinning at him.

"What's so funny?"

"Oh, I was just making a bet with myself. I bet you were the kind who got down on one knee so you wouldn't sound like a shower. I guess I lost."

"You made a study of that, huh?"

"I know Rocco does it that way, and you two look like you've got other things in common."

The bullish man groaned and rolled his eyes.

Balzic zipped his fly and pushed the toilet lever. "Rocco," he said, "your last name wouldn't be Cimoli, would it? The reason I'm asking is when I saw you two dancing out in the living room, I had the feeling I knew you from someplace. Am I right?"

"Yeah. Yeah, you're right," Rocco said, putting his thick hands on the sink to support himself as the woman continued to lean into him. He looked suddenly apprehensive.

"Uh, young lady," Balzic said, "if you don't mind, I'd—"

"I do mind. I am not a lady. I am a woman."

"Okay. Uh, woman, would you mind very much excusing us? I got something I want to talk to Rocco about."

"I most certainly do mind. I have things I want to *do* with Rocco, and I'm not about to go sit with the ladies while you boys talk about football."

"Have it your way, woman," Balzic said, facing Rocco. "Rocco, you correct me if I'm wrong, but the last time I saw you, you were crawling in the back of the sheriff's wagon on your way to Southern Regional. That was about, oh, four, maybe five years ago—am I right?"

"Six years ago," Rocco said, closing his eyes and pursing his lips.

"Rocco!" the woman nearly shouted. "You were in prison?"

He opened his eyes and nodded slowly.

"That's great!" she said, throwing her arms around his neck and trying to kiss him on the mouth, but missing because he turned his face away and began to pull her arms from around his neck.

"Come on, willya. I mean, Jesus . . ."

"Rocco, what's wrong? That's terrific that you were in prison. You never told me. Why didn't you tell me? Oh, we have lots of things to talk about now. And do. And doooo. Do we ever!"

Rocco took the woman by one arm and moved her toward the door. For a second she looked as though she was going to resist, but Rocco's strength surprised her. She even began to look a little frightened.

"Rocco, you're hurting me."

"That's right, I am. 'Cause I want you to leave and I don't want to hear anything about the National Organization for Women or anything like it. I have some things I got to say to the chief, and they're not about football. And one more thing," he said, pushing the door shut again after he'd started to open it, "you get out there in that living room, you just forget what you

36

heard in here, you hear me? I mean, I know you like to tell the people what you think the people ought to know and all that jazz, but you just put a lock on your mouth, honey, 'cause if you don't, I *will* hurt you."

"Rocco . . ."

"Go, baby. Now." Rocco pushed her out the door, shut it, and locked it.

"Okay, Rocco, let's have it."

"Okay. Straight. And I know you'll check the papers."

Balzic nodded. "I will."

"I got eleven and a half to twenty-three. I did thirteen months and out. I finished high school in there, and when I got out I went to West Chester State. I got a bachelor of science in physical education, and I did it in three years. I worked my ass off. I pumped gas, washed dishes, swept locker rooms, worked in a laundry. I never cheated on a test, and I came out of there with better than a B average. And believe it or not, twelve more credit hours and I get my master's degree. And what you just saw is the first time I put my hands on anybody outside of a gym since you know when—for any reason. I even got into karate to learn how to control myself, and if I keep going the way I'm going, I'm going to have a black belt in about two years. In other words, man, I'm straight. I'm so straight that broad was right. I do go down on one knee so I won't make noise when I piss."

Balzic nodded. "Who knows?"

"One person too goddamn many right now."

"Rocco, you kidding yourself, or what? That even made the Pittsburgh papers."

"Hey, man. That was six years ago. Do you know there's not one person from this town on this faculty? They're all from out of town. Hell, most of them aren't even from Pennsylvania. And this place has only been in operation for three years."

"What about students? There have to be a lot of them who remember, right?"

"Well, all I can tell you is they never let on if they know. In fact, sometimes I get the impression the ones who do know, sort

37

of, I don't know, look up to me, like I'm some sort of a guy who got trapped into something and then got himself untrapped—on his own. I don't know. Maybe that's just what I like to think." Rocco paused. "What about you? What are you going to do?"

"Me? I'm not going to do a damn thing. Why should I? Be happy for you. Ask how your mother is, that's all."

"She's okay. I'm making enough now so that she doesn't have to do that shit anymore."

"You see her often?"

"Once a week, maybe twice. I make sure she's all right."

"Well, next time you see her, tell her I said hello."

"I'll do that," Rocco said, sighing and looking at his shoes.

"Let's forget about it, okay? Tell me about something else. You ever hear of a student here named Janet Pisula?"

"I don't know anything about the female students. You should ask Toni."

"She the one just in here?"

"Yeah. She's the girls' phys-ed teacher. She talks a lot of garbage, but she's all right. At least I hope she's all right. I don't know whether I wanted her to hear that."

"You think it would do some good for me to talk to her?"

"I doubt it. As far as she's concerned, you're an oink-oink. I'm surprised she let you off as easy as she did. Man, she can really put some bad mouth on people. Wow. Course, you broke her up when you blew her that kiss. I never saw her laugh that hard at anything any man ever did. I mean, except when she's laughing at them. But when she was laughing at you, that was real. She really enjoyed that."

There was a knock, and then Dr. Beverley's voice asked for Balzic. "Are you in there?"

"Maybe I'll talk to you later, Rocco," Balzic said, opening the door and confronting Beverley.

"I think we can get you what you want," Beverley said.

Balzic nodded and followed Beverley back into the den. He found Ellis and Weintraub staring blankly at one another, caught in that limbo between where the alcohol they'd drunk was start-

38

ing to wear off and the reality of the situation was beginning to crowd in.

"You can get the rosters?" Balzic asked.

Ellis nodded. "Yes, but I wonder if it would be possible for someone to drive me to my office. I'm afraid I've had more than my share of party."

"No problem," Balzic said, going to the phone. He called his station and asked Stramsky to send a mobile unit. After he hung up, he told Ellis to take the rosters to the Summer house and turn them over to Johnson.

Ellis nodded and said, "I think I better have some coffee while I'm waiting."

"Wouldn't be a bad idea," Balzic said. Turning to Beverley, he asked, "How many people from your English department are here?"

"All of them, I think."

"How about getting them in here, will you please?"

Beverley followed Ellis and Weintraub to the door, but stopped. "You mean one at a time or—"

"No, no. All of them."

Beverley left and returned a minute later leading Malcolm Keenan and three other men. All had had too much party and were trying, with the exception of Keenan, to look properly somber. Beverley excused himself without making introductions, saying that he had to explain to his wife what was going on, and Keenan took command, or tried to, at once. He made the introductions, mispronouncing Balzic's name each time as he presented Joseph Winoski, James Farrell, and Edward Snavely.

Snavely gave the appearance of a man who worked at trying to disgust others. He had one button missing from his shirt, another missing from the front of his suit coat, and still another missing from his sleeve. He seemed unable or unwilling to open his mouth fully when speaking so that saliva bubbled at the corners of his mouth, and he kept inhaling the mucous in his nose with a sound that must have set his students' skin crawling. He weighed easily two hundred seventy pounds and was adding to

39

his girth with a beer and a salami and cheese sandwich plastered with yellow mustard. When he shook Balzic's hand, mustard dripped on the rug. A man, Balzic thought, who did everything he could to make certain no one got close to him, probably bemoaning the fact all the while.

Joseph Winoski was as neat as Snavely was sloppy: his ankle-high boots seemed spit-polished, his double-knit suit, though a conservative blue-gray check, was up to the minute in cut, and his build was of a man who spent his lunch hours in the YMCA gym. Balzic could smell Winoski's after-shave lotion as they shook hands, a brand advertised on television by seamen and adventurers, and could feel the hours at the gym in the handshake. He couldn't help wondering how Winoski would react if he were told that he was just a step away from Snavely in motive, that his neatness probably had the same fear behind it as Snavely's sloppiness. Somebody who told Winoski that would more than likely have to learn what sort of physical shape he was in, Balzic thought, resisting his urge to smile.

James Farrell was the only one of the four who seemed at ease with himself. He dressed, moved, and spoke like a thousand other men who would have been lost in crowds. His only distinction seemed to be that he had no distinction, except for his name, which, when Balzic said the same sounded familiar, he said was the result of his father's love of author James T. Farrell. "He used to call me Studs when I was a kid."

"I don't get the connection," Balzic said.

"My namesake wrote a book, well, three books actually, called *Studs Lonigan,* and my father loved them so much, he took it out on me." He smiled when he said it, without the slightest trace of resentment.

"You never heard of *Studs Lonigan?*" Snavely asked, his mouth full of sandwich.

"Sorry," Balzic said. "I just thought the name sounded familiar."

"Well, chief," Keenan said, "don't you think you ought to tell us what this is about?"

"Sure. But first I'd like you to get my name straight. It's not Ballsy. It's Balzic."

"Sorry about that," Keenan said, laughing much too hard and then putting his hand on Balzic's shoulder and saying, "No offense intended—or no intense offended, whichever the case may be."

Balzic nodded. "Yeah, sure. Okay, gentlemen, here's the problem. One of your students was murdered. Her name was Janet Pisula." He watched their faces as he spoke. Their reaction seemed genuine enough: Snavely and Winoski looked astonished at first and then baffled; Keenan and Farrell looked plainly shocked.

"Did you say Janet Pisula?" Keenan asked.

"Yes. And I understand she was in your composition class last semester. What I want to know, among other things, is whose class she was in this semester?"

"She was in my section," Farrell said, shaking his head. "Little Miss Nobody."

"All right," Balzic said. "Mr. Snavely, Mr. Winoski, unless you know something about this girl, you can leave."

"I never heard of her," Winoski said.

"Neither did I," Snavely said, chewing his sandwich as though he had forgotten how to swallow.

"You know nothing about her—never heard anything about her?"

Snavely and Winoski both shrugged and shook their heads, waiting a moment longer until Balzic nodded toward the door, and then left.

"All right, Mr. Keenan, Mr. Farrell, whatever you know."

"I think I should begin," Keenan said, "but since, uh, I mean, I had no idea—I think I better get some coffee. I've really had a lot—no more than my usual, understand, but . . ."

"Go ahead," Balzic said. "Why don't you see if you can bring back the pot? If it won't be too much trouble for the host."

"Of course. I'll do that," Keenan said, leaving the room.

"Mr. Farrell," Balzic said, "a minute ago when you said the

girl was in your section, I think I heard you say something about 'little Miss Nobody,' am I right?"

Farrell nodded. "Yes, I did. That's the way she struck me."

"How did she strike you? What did she do? What didn't she do?"

"That's just it. She didn't do much of anything. I can't recall ever hearing her say anything at all in class. She just sat there, looking pretty much bewildered. Sometimes when I'd call on her, ask her opinion about something we were discussing, she wouldn't answer. She'd start to say something, and then she'd— she'd just go mute. Literally dumb. As though some circuitry between her brain and her voice box had been shorted. She looked as though she would have given anything to be able to say something, not necessarily something intelligent or brilliant or even charming—but she apparently couldn't say anything."

"Did you ever talk to her privately about it?"

"Yes, I tried to. Twice, as a matter of fact. Privately, it was even worse. She was petrified. She couldn't speak at all. All she could do was nod her head and blush. I never had a student like her before—of course, this is only my third year of teaching. The second time, I tried to suggest to her that she might do well to get some kind of counseling. I must've approached it completely wrong because she practically ran out of my office. It was embarrassing."

"Embarrassing?"

"Well, the fact is, I like to think of myself as knowing something about communication. After all, that is supposed to be my profession, and there she was, a person with whom I couldn't communicate at all. She brought me face to face with my limits. That's what I meant by embarrassing."

"How did you suggest it to her, about getting counseling?"

"I don't recall what I said exactly. I think I told her that she had to have some kind of blockage, that it didn't seem logical or even sensible that she should be able to write the way she did and then on the other hand, have so much trouble talking."

"Was she a very good writer?"

42

"Oh yes. One of the best. She had a very good eye for detail. Her papers were always filled with solid examples of the abstractions she used. That's something you generally have trouble with in freshman comp. Freshmen are generally in love with abstractions. I keep trying to tell them that the further removed one is from fact the more difficult it is for one person to understand another."

"I take your meaning," Balzic said, "but that's damn strange. Because I'll tell you, the one person who seemed to know anything about her—I mean the one person I've talked to so far—another student, a girl named Patricia Keim—do you know her?"

Farrell shook his head.

"Well, the Keim girl said just the opposite of what you said. She said that was the one thing the Pisula girl couldn't do. She said one of their assignments the first semester was to take an abstraction and break it down, and the Keim girl said she tried to explain to the Pisula girl how to go about it. I think she said she told her to take a season of the year and write everything solid she could think of when she thought of that season. But the Keim girl said that the Pisula girl wasn't even aware that a season of the year was an abstraction. Now how do you figure that?"

Farrell shrugged. "I can't figure it. I don't understand it at all. Unless . . ."

"Unless what?"

"Well, unless she took a great jump in understanding. Sometimes a student may not be able to comprehend what you're saying for a long time, and then suddenly, for no reason that anyone can explain, the insight comes to them. It's not uncommon. In fact, it's the thing you hope for, the thing you hope will happen in a classroom, or at least that's what I hope for. That's what bothered me so much about her. She wrote so well, yet she wasn't able to talk. Usually, it's just the reverse. They all talk well enough to be understood, given, of course, that they know what they're talking about, but when they sit down in front of that blank page, they just come unhinged."

"What did you say?"

43

"I said they come unhinged. Lose their confidence—"

"No, no. Before that. You said something about a blank page."

"Yeah. I said that some people talk well enough, but when they sit down in front of that blank page, they—"

"That's it."

"What's it?" Farrell said.

"Blank page."

"I don't understand. What's that have to do with this?"

Before Balzic could answer, though he was not saved from answering as much as he was saved from making up some reason for being concerned about a specific blank page, he saw the door being pushed open. Keenan came in with a large silver tray, balancing a pot of coffee, some mugs, and a creamer and sugar bowl.

Keenan poured, acting a perfect host, giving Balzic the impression that much of what Keenan did was an act. Balzic couldn't put his finger on why exactly, except that Keenan's smile and gestures while pouring were laced with an exhuberance that seemed contrived, an exhuberance Keenan immediately turned off the moment Balzic asked him what he knew about Janet Pisula. Then Keenan switched faces at once, going from perfect host to concerned head of department, from smiling waiter to frowning, fretful witness to tragedy.

"I can't tell you very much about her at all," Keenan said. "I can only, in all candor, give you some impressions. I found her to be as inarticulate as any student I've ever had—and I don't mean to say for a moment that I had her."

Balzic had to turn his back to Keenan to keep from telling him to shut off the nonsense.

"That was not meant as a pun, I assure you," Keenan said quickly when Balzic turned back to him. "I wanted that to be clear. The reason I want that clear is that, well, I have somewhat of a reputation as a, well, uh, a seeker of pleasure."

"You fuck around with your students," Balzic said evenly.

"Yes. You could put it that way. Well, not exactly that way—"

"And you don't want me to get the idea that there might be some connection between you and Janet Pisula in that way."

"Yes. Right. Absolutely. Because there wasn't. She was, in a word, incommunicado. And I cannot make it with females who are incommunicado."

"Well, Mr. Keenan, now that we've eliminated that possibility, would you mind giving me some impressions that I could use?"

"Of course. Though I don't know what you mean when you say you need impressions you can use."

"Oh Jesus Christ, man, tell me what you know about her."

Keenan flushed. "Yes. Uh, well, as I said, she was incommunicado."

"Which means exactly what?"

"Which means she wouldn't respond verbally. Anywhere. In class or out."

"I see. What was your reaction to her?"

"Well, to be perfectly candid, I thought she was rather doltish. Not someone on whom I should waste my energy. She was one of the thousands too many young people who don't belong in any college classroom taking up the space. In my opinion she would have been much better off touring the country on a bicycle or waiting tables at some resort near the ocean."

"Uh-huh," Balzic said, "and what did you think of her writing?"

"Incredibly bad. Worse. Atrocious." Keenan reflected for a moment. "Except for near the end of the semester. Then, as I recall, she turned in a couple of papers that were very good. So good, in fact, they made me suspicious. And then when she took the final, I was sure of my suspicions. I had to get drunk to give her a D."

Farrell, who had been listening calmly, suddenly couldn't keep his hands still. "You had to do what?"

45

"Get flat out stoned," Keenan said. "Sober, I couldn't have given her a Z."

"I don't believe that," Farrell said. "She was one of the best writers in my section."

Keenan shook his head. "Jim, just as a friend and absolutely not as department chairman, I'd have to say she may have *known* the best writer in your section, but there's no way she could have *been* the best writer in anybody's section. I'm making no judgments about her as a person, you understand, but, well, no one with her limited ability should be in college. I'm sorry."

"I can't believe you said that," Farrell said, jamming his hands into his pockets and hunching his shoulders.

"Well," Keenan said, "there it is."

"Uh, let's get off this," Balzic said. "Let's get on to something solid. Mr. Keenan, who was she with, who did you see her with, who did you see trying to be with her?"

"Nobody. I can't recall ever seeing her with anybody. I don't recall ever seeing her talking to anyone. She'd come into class, sit in the seat nearest the door, keep her head buried in her notebook most of the class, and she'd leave as soon as I dismissed the class."

"Mr. Farrell, how about you?"

"She did exactly the same thing in my class. Even to the point of sitting in the seat closest to the door."

"You never saw her talking to anyone?"

Farrell shook his head. "And I've already told you about the times I tried to talk to her out of class."

"Hmm," Balzic said. "Anything else? Anything at all?"

"Nothing," Keenan said. Farrell just shook his head and jammed his hands deeper into his pockets.

"Then I guess that's all, gentlemen," Balzic said. "Just do me a favor. When you go back out there, tell anybody who had her in class to come in here, will you?"

"Certainly," Keenan said. "Would you, uh, like more coffee, or would you like me to take the tray out?"

"Suit yourself. I don't want any more coffee. You can take

46

the tray." Balzic watched them go, fuming to himself about what he'd just heard. It made no sense. A girl who never talked to anyone. That was impossible. There had to be someone. Someone who knew her well enough to know she lived alone, someone who knew her well enough to know she probably wouldn't make a sound if she got in trouble. Then again, whoever killed her didn't have to know any such thing. Whoever killed her didn't have to know a damned thing about her—except that he wanted her dead.

Moments after Keenan and Farrell left, Balzic went to the phone and dialed the Summer house.

"Summer residence, Lieutenant Johnson speaking."

"Walk? Mario. My man get there with the dean?"

"About two minutes ago. He's still here."

"Well, I busted into a party at the president's house. Most of the faculty is here. There might be a couple missing, I don't know. But right now, from the ones I've talked to so far, I'm getting nothing. The only thing anybody's agreed on is that the girl wasn't one for talking. What d'you come up with?"

"About the same," Johnson said. "Our print man won't know for sure until tomorrow, but as of right now, his best guess is that all the prints in the room belonged to the girl. Except for a couple on the door which probably belong to you."

"Yeah. Did you talk to those two across the hall again?"

"Yep. They say the same things. Didn't hear anything, didn't see anything—except for that guy one of them thinks he saw, but he still can't say anything definite about that guy. Now he thinks the guy was young and white, but he shakes his head everytime I ask him if he thinks he could identify the guy. And they swear they weren't out of their room except to go to class, take tests, and eat."

"How about the Cerovich kid—he come back from work yet?"

"Yeah. He's a zero, too. He never even saw her. Her name didn't mean a thing. And we know where he's been every night

47

for the last year. Course, what we don't know is time of death. So he's still a remote possibility. But from talking to him, I'd say no. He's too goddamn solid. He wasn't here five minutes and he had two phone calls from broads. Good-looking kid. Probably getting more ass than a toilet seat. Guys like that just don't kill broads. You didn't get anything at all from her teachers?"

"I haven't talked to all of them yet. I just talked to her compositon teachers so far. One of them thinks she was the best writer in his section. The other one, the chairman of the department, thinks she was the worst. He suspected her of cheating, still thinks she was, and told the other one, the one who thinks she was the best—he told him he'd been suckered. But both of them agree, the girl talked not at all. Big fucking deal."

"Yeah."

"Hey. Did her guardians, her aunt and uncle, did they show yet?"

"No, but I got a confirmation they were notified, so they should be pulling in soon. If they don't need a doctor."

"Oh boy. Well, I'm going to hang in here a while. There are a couple more teachers I want to talk to. You going to stay there?"

"I'll have to until the relatives show. Christ, that's going to be fun. How 'bout you taking them up to identify the body?"

"Up yours, buddy. That's one party I don't need." Balzic was going to hang up, but then said quickly, "Hey, Walk, when the dean showed with the rosters, did he have one for local addresses for the students?"

"No. He apologized all over the place for that. But what could I say? He didn't have it, he didn't have it."

"If that isn't bad enough, when I asked the president if there was any way he could keep the students here, he just shook his head. That's when I found out they didn't have local addresses. Christ almighty . . ."

"How much longer you think you'll be there?"

Balzic looked over his shoulder as the door opened and a man and a woman walked in. "Not long," he said to Johnson. "I think the last of her teachers are coming in right now. Soon as I finish with them I'll be down." He hung up and introduced himself to the two who had come in.

The woman, short, roundish, in her late thirties, with no make-up and her hair cut severely short, introduced herself as Miss Ulishney. "Janet was in my advanced shorthand course," she said somberly.

The man, shorter than the woman, a collar of jet black hair flowing downward around his ears but shiny bald on top, shook Balzic's hand and introduced himself as Phil Castro. "The girl was in my American history course, but I'll tell you right now and save us both a lot of time. I know practically nothing about her except that she never missed class and that she was just an average student. A low C student, and her grades were more a matter of my generosity than her effort."

"Mr. Castro, did you ever see her talking to anybody? Ever see anybody talking to her?"

"I never paid attention to that sort of thing."

"Uh-huh. Where did she sit in your class?"

"Sit? What does that have to do with anything?"

"Just tell me, if you can remember."

"I remember that clearly. Last seat, last row. Right next to the door."

Balzic nodded. "Well, unless you can tell me something more than that, you can go."

"All I can tell you is that the last time I saw her was last Wednesday, the next to the last class, and the only class she missed was the last class."

"That next to last class, that would've been, uh, the twenty-sixth of May, right?"

"That's right. Last class was the twenty-eighth of May. Last Friday."

"Well, thanks for your help. But if you think of anything, call me at City Hall or call Lieutenant Johnson at Troop A, Rocksburg Barracks."

"I'm sorry I can't be of more help," Castro said. "I'm sorry

49

that it happened. How did it happen, by the way? Nobody out there seems to know."

"Let's just say she was murdered and let it go at that, okay?" Castro shrugged and left.

"Miss Ulishney, I hope you can tell me more than that."

"I wish I could," she said. "I just feel very bad for her. But I really don't know much about her."

"She was quiet, she didn't talk to anybody, she didn't say much in class—are those your impressions of her? I'm asking, not to put words in your mouth, but because those are the impressions everyone else seems to have."

"I'm afraid I have to go along with the rest. I really can't recall saying anything to the girl."

"Your class was probably all girls, right?"

"Yes. All my classes are. I also teach business math and office machines."

"How was she in your class, as a student, I mean."

"Not very good, I'm afraid. Oh, she mastered the shorthand characters well enough, but she wasn't nearly as fast as she should have been. I think her top speed was no more than eighty-five words a minute. Not nearly fast enough for an advanced class. She should have been able to take at least a hundred words a minute."

"Good but slow."

"Well, not really good either, because when I played my practice tapes at a hundred words a minute, she would naturally miss a lot. She was really competent only when I played the slower tapes."

"I see. Uh, one more thing. Well, two more. When did you see her last, one, and two, where did she sit in your class?"

"I saw her last Wednesday. Yes, I'm sure of that because I remember that she didn't come to last Friday's class and I remembered thinking how unusual that was. She hadn't missed a class for two semesters."

"And where did she sit?"

"Like Phil—Mr. Castro, I mean—I don't understand that

question, but I'll answer it. She sat in the middle of the front row. Right in front of my desk. Why do you ask that?"

"I'm not sure. It's just that her two English teachers, Keenan and Farrell, happened to mention it as though it was important, and then when I asked Mr. Castro—well, you heard what he said. Seems the only thing you people are sure of about this girl was where she sat. That, plus she wasn't a very good student, plus the other thing everybody's agreed on, which is, she didn't say anything, or as little as she could and still get by." Balzic scratched his chin. "Is there anybody else out there who had her in class? So far, I count three courses she was taking. Yours, Mr. Castro's, and Mr. Farrell's. Would that be a full schedule?"

"No. A full schedule is generally twelve to fourteen hours, but I doubt that half our students take a full schedule. Most can't afford it. A great many of them work part-time, and most are from lower-middle-income families."

Balzic thanked her for her help and then went to the door and opened it for her. "Just one more thing, Miss Ulishney. Take a quick survey for me out there, will you please? Ask if there's anybody else who knew her."

"Certainly," she said, going past him.

Balzic left the door open and stood rocking on his heels and toes. It was only then that he noticed he'd stopped perspiring and that he knew the reason: J. Hale Beverley's house was more than adequately air-conditioned. He was thinking about the broken fan back in his office when the blocky woman, the one Rocco Cimoli called Toni, came striding through the doorway and had to stop short to keep from bumping into him.

He backed up and pursed his lips. Apparently she'd responded affirmatively to Miss Ulishney's survey, but Balzic wasn't sure he wanted to ask this Toni, whatever her information, much of anything. He had the feeling that whatever she was going to say about Janet Pisula was going to be starched with feminist propaganda.

"Uh, we didn't meet before, in the bathroom, I mean. Rocco told me your first name was Toni. Your last name?"

51

"Rosario."

"Uh, Miss Rosario—"

"Pronounce that miz, if you don't mind."

Balzic shook his head and started to laugh.

"What's so funny?"

"Oh, I was just wondering what you say to guys with speech problems. You know, the guys who talk like thith? Or hasn't that come up in your meetings yet?"

For the briefest moment, Toni Rosario looked almost ready to laugh at herself, but she instantly put her fences back up and said, "Well, so we haven't got around to that, but I'll tell you what. If that girl had listened to me, she might've grown up to be a woman."

"She was a student of yours then. In your gym class?"

"She was. And I told her just like I told all the others, just like I *tried* to tell all the others, that they would have to learn how to protect themselves."

"The beasties are all around, right?"

"That's right, they are."

"And if she'd just listened to you and learned karate or judo or something, she'd still be alive today, right?"

"Exactly right. No man would've been able to rape her, never mind kill her."

"Well, Miz Rosario, I hate to spoil all your fun, but as far as we know—though we won't know for sure until we hear from the coroner—but right now we're pretty sure she wasn't raped, and, uh, there's nothing really to tell us that it was a man who killed her."

"Well out there," she said, pointing testily in the direction of the living room, "everybody's saying she was raped."

"I have no idea what they're saying out there. A couple minutes ago a guy walked in, Castro his name was, and he gave me the impression nobody knew what happened. Now you come in saying everybody's got the information."

"Well? How did it happen?"

"All I'm going to tell you is what I told the others. The girl was murdered, and she's been dead at least a week, maybe longer. And whoever did it did it very quietly 'cause she didn't make a sound—or else everybody where she lived is deaf."

"Well, that sounds like her, not making a peep. A regular house-mouse. She couldn't do this, she couldn't do that—"

"You mean in gym class?"

"Well of course. Where else would I come in contact with her?"

"I don't know. You tell me."

"Well I didn't. She was in my gym class for two semesters and half the time she'd just stand around looking like something out of a Victorian novel. Like if somebody touched her, she'd just crumble into a heap of sugar and spice and everything nice. Gawd."

"What did she say about standing around? I mean, what reason did she give? Did she have a doctor's excuse for not doing anything?"

"Well, if she'd had a doctor's excuse, she wouldn't have even been there. There wasn't anything wrong with her. Nothing but a stupid, simpering idea that a woman was supposed to be delicate and fragile and weak."

"Did she say that or is that your conclusion?"

"It's my conclusion."

"Ever think you might've been wrong?"

"I'm not wrong about her. One day, gawd, I had them playing field hockey and one of the girls got a bloody nose. It was an accident. She got hit in the nose with the ball and it bled a little. It was nothing. I got it stopped in about two seconds, but the next thing I knew somebody was tapping me on the shoulder and telling me we had other problems. And there she was. Janet Pisula. Stretched out on the ground. Fainted. It was disgusting."

"Didn't you ask her about it? Didn't you check around about her? I mean, there might have been some reason why she was like that. I don't know what happened to her parents, but I do know

53

she doesn't have any. She was raised by an aunt and uncle."

"So? Lots of people don't have parents. That's why there are orphanages."

"So you're telling me that because a lot of people are able to accept being orphans, uh, everybody should, is that it?"

"Everybody has things happen to them. You adapt. What's the big production?"

"And those people who can't adapt?"

"Oh bullshit," she said.

Balzic chewed the inside of his cheek. "Well, let's get back to Janet Pisula."

"I thought that's who we were talking about."

"More or less. But mostly what you've told me is what you thought of her. You haven't really told me what you know about her."

"Well then, I guess I don't know anything about her."

"Boy, I'll tell you something. I never met a bunch of people who know as little about a person as you people do. The girl was one of your students. Do you all know that little about all your students?"

"Do you have any idea how many students I come in contact with each semester?"

"Don't give me that, Miz Rosario. Do you know how many people there are in this town?"

"Are you going to tell me you know them all? Gawd."

"No. But I know the ones in trouble, and if I don't know them myself, then I go find somebody who does."

"Still—"

"Still nothing," Balzic said. "There are a lot more people with some kind of trouble in this town than there are students in this college—ah, forget it. That's all. You can go—oh, one more thing." Balzic stepped around her and closed the door. "What you heard in the bathroom, you didn't hear."

"About Rocco?"

"That's right. Do him and yourself a big favor, and forget you heard it. And don't get your head full of those goofy ideas

54

I see wheeling around in your eyes. Because I'm going to tell you what he did—for one reason and one reason only. I don't like people walking around with bad information. And I'm really going out on a limb telling you this. You better not make me think I made a mistake."

She shifted her weight to one foot and crossed her arms. "It can't be all that bad."

"With some of the ideas you have, it could be dynamite."

"I'm not a complete ass."

"I hope not. Because what he did was kill a guy. He beat him to death with a baseball bat. And he did it because the guy called his mother a whore. The thing was, she was a whore, and Rocco knew it, and the reason he knew it was because she told him she was.

"I didn't know the family at that time," Balzic went on, "and the only reason I found out about it was because she'd gone to a priest and asked him whether she should tell Rocco or not. This was a couple years before this thing happened, and the priest advised her to tell him. I didn't agree with the priest's reasons for telling her to tell him, but it was over by the time I found out about it. I didn't find out until the priest came to me, which was after Rocco killed the guy.

"I was out of town when it happened. Rocco went into a bar to pick up a pizza, and while he was waiting for it, he overheard two guys talking, and one of them was really putting his mother down for doing what she was doing. He took the pizza home and went back with the bat. The owner of the bar was a friend of mine and he knew I was out of town, so he called the state police. I didn't have a chance to do anything about it until right before the trial when the priest came to me and gave me the background. I'm not trying to make myself out a big man, but if it wasn't for me going to the judge Rocco would've got life. He would've done thirteen years instead of thirteen months. And tonight's the second time in my life I've seen him. The other time was when I said, when I saw him crawling in the back of the sheriff's wagon."

"Oh wow."

"Oh wow is right, sister. Rocco's mother is still alive, and she loves her son more than she loves life itself. When she heard from the priest that I'd talked to the judge, she came to me, and if you think a minute, you'll know what she wanted to give me."

Toni canted her head. "Oh, now wait. Are you going to try and tell me that you didn't take it?"

"No. I took it," Balzic said. "Because if I hadn't, I would've shamed her. Also," Balzic said, breaking into a wide smile, "she was a fine-looking woman."

"If that isn't the most typical male bullshit I ever heard—"

"Listen. You think what you want, but that—what I just told you about Rocco's mother and me—that is exactly why you aren't going to say anything to him or about him. 'Cause like I said, I don't like people going around with bad information, and I just gave you good information. All there is. So take it in and then forget it." Balzic studied her face. "Think about it this way. Rocco didn't kill that guy because his mother was a whore. He knew that. He killed the guy because the guy put her down for being what she was. And I did what I did for him and I took what I took from her because that's the way it should have been. I told you because I didn't want you saying, in a party or someplace, something stupid like, 'Tell us what prison was like, Rocco,' or 'Hey, everybody, you want to hear from a real victim of a sexist society?' "

"And what would happen if I did?"

"You just might get to be questioned about who did what to your face, if you know what I mean. Rocco's not the kind of guy you fool around with. Now, unless there's something else you can tell me about Janet Pisula?"

She shook her head and then stood a moment, shifting her weight from one foot to the other, looking confused, then aggressive, then regretful. She started to say something, but then shook her head and stepped past Balzic and opened the door and went out, leaving Balzic hoping weakly that he had not made a mistake in telling her. He knew he had to hope that he'd done right, otherwise he had left himself wide open for a problem. What he'd said about Rocco Cimoli not being the kind of guy you fool with was as true for him as it was for Toni Rosario. "Be right, you big man," he said to himself as he left the den and went into the kitchen.

He found Dr. and Mrs. Beverley facing each other but both staring at the floor, sharing a tense silence.

"Uh, Dr. Beverley," he said, "I think I've learned all I can here. For now anyway. If anybody thinks of anything, tell them to call me down at City Hall or Lieutenant Walker Johnson at Troop A Barracks, okay?"

"Yes. Of course." Beverley moved as though to show Balzic out.

"Don't bother," Balzic said. "I can find my way. Goodnight, and, uh, I'm sorry I had to spoil your party."

Mrs. Beverley did not look up, and Dr. Beverley said nothing, leaning backward to put his rump against the sink. He'd moved farther away from it than he'd thought and hit it with a thump that caused him to throw out his hands to catch his balance, looking as though much more than his balance was at stake.

Johnson was leaning on a pillar on the portico with his thumbs hooked in his pockets when Balzic drove up to the Summer house.

"Whatta you know, Walk?"

"I know it's hot."

"You ought to try walking out of an air-conditioned house into this."

"I'd like to try walking into one."

"All your people gone?"

"There's one guy up there putting a lock on the door. I sent all the rest back with all the girl's notebooks, letters, anything she'd written in. I got three men going through that. Shouldn't take them too long. There wasn't too much."

"Grimes call?"

"Oh yeah. Small surprise there. Not only was she not raped, her hymen was still intact. A very inactive virgin." Johnson stretched and yawned. "You know, I didn't think a girl could get through eighteen years and still have one. You'd think she'd have broken it doing something. Riding a bike, running around in a gym class, something."

"Well, from what her gym teacher told me, she wasn't much for running around."

"What else did you get up there?"

"Not a hell of a lot. I told you most of it when I called you."

"You didn't get any more than that?"

"Just a couple of goofy little things. One—which isn't all that goofy—she passed out when another girl in her gym class got a bloody nose. Two, she was taking four courses: English, history, shorthand, and gym. Except for English, she had the same teachers this semester as she did last, so that makes three men and two women. Never mind the gym class, in the other classes where the men taught, she always sat in the seat next to the door. In the shorthand class with the woman, she sat right up front. First row, right in front of the teacher's desk. Three, the English teacher she had this semester, guy named Farrell, said something about certain people just coming unhinged when they sit down in front of a blank page. I looked at the guy real good when he said it, but it looked to me like something he was just used to saying."

"What was he talking about?"

"He was talking about how some people can talk pretty good, but when they have to write they just can't do it. From the way he said it, I gathered it's a pretty common thing. And Christ knows, whenever I have to write something I go through a shit fit—"

"Yeah. Me too."

"—it was just that he happened to use those words. 'Blank page,' or 'Blank paper'—no, it was page, and they jumped at me."

"Was he talking about her specifically?"

"Yes and no. Yes, if you believe the other teacher she had, this Keenan guy, the department chairman, 'cause he thought the girl couldn't write worth a damn. I told you that on the phone."

Johnson nodded.

"And no, if you believe this Farrell, 'cause he thought the girl was the best writer in his class. Those two had a real difference of opinion over that. I mean, if I hadn't been there, I got the feeling those two would've had a pretty fair go-round over it. But that Keenan—what a ballbuster he is. He lets me in and he introduces himself, you know, with the handshake that dislocates your shoulder, and he says, 'Malcolm Keenan here. I'm a poet who teaches as a public service.' Then he started telling me these raunchy limericks, oh boy . . ."

"What do you make of her sitting close to the door with the men teachers—scared of men?"

"That's what it sounds like to me, but all I know is, that was the one thing all those men were certain of. Hey, you hear anything from her aunt and uncle?"

"Yeah. The woman collapsed. Had to get her to a hospital. And the uncle was shaking too bad to drive, so he's coming down in one of our units. He didn't want to come at all. Which is normal enough."

"How long ago you hear that?"

"Twenty minutes. Should be here in fifteen, twenty minutes."

"You got the rosters, right?"

"Hey, pal. You know how many people there are connected with this college? Close to seven hundred, that's all. Six hundred and twenty-one students. A hundred and four of them full-time. The rest taking two or one course. Then there's the faculty, the deans, assorted other bureaucrats, buildings and grounds people, janitors, charwomen, manager of the student union—oh, shit, from all over the county."

"Well, we start with the ones from in her classes. That cuts it down. That should get us under a hundred."

Johnson yawned again. "You know, Mario, we're starting close to home, but what do we do if it's a goddamn transient?"

"The first thing we do, Walk, is we don't even think like that."

59

"I always like to think the worst. Just to make myself comfortable. Like those two little girls, remember? In that town just north of Edinboro?"

"I remember reading about it."

"Yeah. Well, you know how many people we talked to with that? Over five hundred. More than a hundred grade school kids. And you know what we come up with? Nothing . . . that's what bothers me about this one. Those two little girls were strangled with their own clothes." Johnson stared off into the night. "Sure wish the hell it would rain."

The front door opened and a state trooper came out carrying a small tool chest. "Here's the keys, lieutenant," he said, handing Johnson two padlock keys.

Johnson thanked him and told him he could leave.

"So now we wait for the uncle," Johnson said, stepping off the porch and walking slowly toward his cruiser. "You coming?" he called over his shoulder.

"Yeah. I'll see you up at the barracks."

Michael Pisula came into Troop A's duty room on the arm of the state trooper who'd driven him. He was a short man, slender, with a slight paunch below his belt. His white shirt was sweat-stained and his trousers rumpled. He had a handky wadded in his right hand and kept putting it to his mouth as he was directed to a chair. His eyes were raw and he had difficulty clearing his throat.

Balzic brought him a paper cup of water, but Pisula waved it away. Then he broke down, weeping uncontrollably for what seemed to Balzic an hour, though it was not more than a minute.

"Who would do this to her?" he said after he'd got control. He had not asked Balzic or Johnson; he seemed to be asking as though praying.

"Mr. Pisula," Johnson said, "I know how difficult this is—"

"Difficult! My God, man, you don't have any idea what this girl's been through in her life. And then to, to—like this . . ."

Johnson and Balzic looked at each other, loathing to begin

to ask the questions they knew had to be asked.

"Do you know," Pisula said suddenly, "she was just eighteen two weeks ago? The Sunday before last. She came home and we had a party for her. Ann made a beautiful cake. We had turkey. It was like Christmas. We were so happy for her she was finally getting out, getting to meet people. And she said she was doing so well and having such a good time. She kept saying how much she liked the people in her rooming house, how nice they were to her . . . now, my God—is there a God? Tell me. I'd like to know if there's a God. Would he do this to her, would he allow what's happened to her to happen to anyone? I hope I'm forgiven if there is a God because—because for the first time in my life I don't believe there is."

"Did she tell you which people were nice to her, Mr. Pisula?" Balzic asked.

"Yes. There was a girl, a Pat something. Patricia—"

"Keim?"

"Yes. She said she was very nice to her. Very friendly."

Balzic and Johnson exchanged frowns, remembering too clearly Patricia Keim's indifference to Janet Pisula.

"Mr. Pisula," Johnson said, "were you told what happened?"

Pisula nodded and then started to cry again. In a moment he stopped and blew his nose. "Do you know, she was so beautiful when she was a child. She was my brother's. So beautiful . . ."

"What happened?"

"To my brother?"

Balzic nodded.

"An accident. She was seven. She was in the back seat. They were out for a drive. He'd just bought a new Ford. My God, was he proud. Their first time in that car. The next thing I know, a state police standing at the door. Just like tonight . . . she was brilliant, you know that? They had her tested when she was four. When she was four, she could add three-figure numbers in her head. She could read—and nobody taught her! They put her in kindergarten when she was four, and when she was five, they put her in second grade. The nuns did that. My brother and his wife, they were against it. They wanted her to stay with her own age, but the nuns insisted. And the nuns were right to do that. She was brilliant . . . and then they went for a drive. Some son of a—that idiot, passing a truck on a hill . . . my brother hit a utility pole. They were both dead. My sister-in-law instantly, they said. My brother, that night. . . ."

"Janet?"

"My wife and I, we—we couldn't have children . . . you're not supposed to want what your brother has, I know, but we wanted that little girl. The only envy I had for my brother . . . and then we got her. But how we got her, my God. In a coma for two months, brain surgery, and then, never again the same. How could it? But wasn't that enough? How much torture does God allow in one life?"

Johnson went for a cup of water. Balzic lit a cigarette and looked at the floor.

"And then he came to see her. The day after she regained consciousness. He'd been calling every day. The nurses told us. And then he walked in, just like that, and you know what he said to her? He looked at her for a long time, just looked at her, and then he said, 'You should've died.' Just like that. And then he turned around and walked out . . . it was eight months before Janet said a word, two more months in the hospital, six months at home, and we were sitting down to eat, and she said—the first words in ten months—she said, 'Why did he say that to me?' Then she just played with her food. And what could we say to her, why that—that idiot, why he would even want to say anything at all?"

"Who was he, Mr. Pisula?"

"The driver of the other car, the one that passed that truck. A punk! The only time in my life I ever felt as though I could actually kill somebody myself. All wasted thoughts . . ."

"Why wasted?"

"Because he did it for me. Drove his car off a bridge—that same night. I didn't know until the next day even who he was. The police told us. I guess they thought they were doing us a favor."

"When you say that same night, you mean the night he came to the hospital?"

"Yes, yes."

"And Janet never got over that?"

"Never. It wasn't only the brain damage, it was that, you see? What possessed him to say that? Couldn't he realize what that would do to her? . . . I guess not."

"Did Janet know about the other driver?" Balzic asked. "I mean, did she know he'd killed himself?"

Pisula shook his head. "She never heard it from Ann or me. If she heard it from somebody else, I can't say. I know she never talked about any of it again—not with us anyway."

"Uh, Mr. Pisula, didn't she ever talk to anybody about it?" Balzic asked. "I mean, didn't you think it was a good idea for her to talk to somebody about it?"

"A psychiatrist you mean? Sure. A couple of them. Oh, I don't know what they talked about with her. Not very much, I know that. Because they all said the same thing. All they wanted to do was talk about the brain damage. They talked about percentages. They said we'd have to learn to accept things as they were, that she would never be any better. I thought I would go crazy talking to them when they talked like that. I didn't understand—I still don't—how knowing a figure could make a difference. They talked like her mind was an adding machine, like a couple keys were broke and everybody would just have to go on adding, but without those keys. It didn't make sense to me . . . she was scared to death of them anyway . . . but I never thought the injury was as bad as what that punk said to her. She didn't have trouble taking care of herself. It was only in school that it showed up. She became average, a little below. From brilliant to average, from skipping grades to just keeping up. And she worked very hard. We never pressured her—Ann or me. We just wanted her to have some happiness—wasn't she entitled?"

"But she had trouble getting along with people?"

"With people? My God, yes. She was terrified of strangers. For a long time she wouldn't even go shopping with us. Only to school and then home. Then, little by little, she'd go out at night with us, but she wouldn't sit in the back seat. She'd sit right between us, and we could feel how tense she was all the while the car was moving. Then, when we were in the stores, she'd stay so close to Ann and me that sometimes we'd trip over each other's feet. She was in high school before she'd go anywhere without us. Even then it was only with Francey—my God, what'll this do to her?"

"Who's Francey?"

"Her friend. Oh my God, I can't tell her . . . I have to."

"Who is she, Mr. Pisula?"

"Francey—Frances Milocky. Our neighbor's daughter. She goes to Penn State. More than anyone, she's responsible for Janet coming out of herself. My God!"

"What's the matter?"

Pisula's body quivered as a chill racked him. "She's the one, she persuaded Janet to come here. Janet wouldn't have done it if Francey hadn't convinced her she could do it. Oh, God, what will this do to her . . ."

"She's in school now? At Penn State you said?" Balzic took out his notebook and wrote the name and address as Pisula gave it to him.

"Are you going to tell her?" Pisula asked.

"If you'd rather we did."

"Please. I don't think . . ."

"Did they keep in touch with one another?"

"Oh yes. They wrote all the time. They were very close."

"Did Janet say anything to you or your wife about anybody bothering her? Did she say anything about any trouble she was having? With anybody, about anything."

"No. Only with the work in class."

"Anything in particular? Or was it just generally hard for her?"

"No. The thing I'm talking about happened last semester. In her English."

"Was her teacher's name Keenan?"

"Yes. Dr. Keenan. She didn't like him at all. She was very afraid of him. He talked loud. And she said he was very rude."

"She had trouble doing work for him, didn't she?" Balzic said. "I mean, I know that she barely got a passing grade from him."

"Yes. She got a D. She didn't know what he expected. She didn't know what she was supposed to do."

"Did she talk to you about that? I mean, did you suggest anything to her?"

"I told her to take the course from another teacher. But that wasn't my idea. I didn't know you could do that. I never went to college. Francey told me to tell her that. And Francey told her too. And so she did. This semester she was in a Mr., a Mr., my God, I can't even think of his name."

"Farrell?"

"That's him. She liked him. She said she got along very well with him. She said he was very understanding. Nothing like the other one, that Keenan."

"And she never talked about having problems like that again?"

"No. Oh well, she had problems. But we knew what those were. Like her shorthand course. She used to worry that she couldn't keep up with the others, but I told her, my God, don't worry about that. Do the best you can. We have girls in our office making four hundred dollars a month, and they can't take shorthand at all. And their typing is terrible. And she could type very well. I said that's all you need. Don't worry. But she worried . . ."

"You said you knew what her other problems were," Johnson said. "What were they, aside from the one you just mentioned."

"Well, mostly the big problem. Coming out of herself, getting over that mess with the accident. . . . I remember she called us one night, and she said she was sick. And when I asked her how, she said it was because another girl got hit in the nose in her gym class, and the girl's nose started to bleed, and Janet said she passed out. And I said there was nothing wrong with that if she felt okay then. She said she did, so I wanted to know what was wrong, and all she could say was, 'Mommy, mommy.' She sounded awful. Just like a little girl. And it took me a couple minutes to figure it out, that she must've seen her mother like that in the car. . . . I asked her if she wanted me to come to be with her, but she said she was all right. She just had to tell somebody. And that was the only time she ever said anything about the accident . . ."

Balzic blew out a heavy sigh and wished that Toni Rosario was there to hear this.

"See," Pisula said, suddenly very animated, "I was convinced then that she had never been as badly injured as those doctors had said. Because if she had been hurt that bad, that would've meant to me that the coma she was in began in the car, that she had been knocked unconscious in the collision. But if she has a memory of seeing her mother's face with blood on it, maybe coming out of her nose, then . . ." His voice faded and he became still.

"Are the doctors who worked on her still around?" Balzic said.

"No. The one who did the surgery, Henderson, he's dead. He died years ago. The others, I'd have to look up their names in my records. But they were all old men then."

"Anything else, Mr. Pisula? Anything at all, anything she said about anybody?"

Pisula shook his head and closed his eyes. "My God," he cried out, "if there was anything, don't you think I'd tell you!"

"Easy, Mr. Pisula, easy," Johnson said. "That's enough questions. There's just one more thing, and God knows I hate to do it to you, but it has to be done." Johnson turned to Balzic, but Balzic shook his head and stepped quickly to the water cooler, still shaking his head as he filled a paper cup and drank. Nothing in the world could have made him go along with that man to watch as he identified the body. The sound of hell was the voices of the next of kin in a morgue—Balzic knew that in his bones. And he did not need to be reminded of it again tonight. . . .

Balzic hunched himself into a corner of Johnson's office, the letters of Frances Milocky to Janet Pisula in his lap, smoking and sipping coffee, trying to piece together the picture he was getting of Janet Pisula. All the pieces said "victim," but Balzic was uncomfortable with the pieces. Yet the more he read Frances Milocky's letters—there were thirty-one of them—the more sure he was that the pieces would form the pattern of a victim than that they would not.

What contributed most to the pattern of a victim he was getting about Janet Pisula was that of the first ten letters to her from the Milocky girl every one closed with the same words: "A lively understandable spirit once entertained you. It will come again. Be still. Wait." The words were always the same, always in quotation marks, and always the last words above Frances Milocky's signature.

Balzic went through those ten letters again before he got any clear thought why those words should not only add to the pieces making a picture of a victim but should actually become the frame for it. It was the advice of a doctor to a patient. "Be still. Wait." Be patient. A patient, Balzic had heard from a doctor once while he waited to visit someone in a hospital, was called a patient because he was waiting for someone else to heal him. "That's why doctors make such lousy patients," the doctor had said. "They have no patience—not that kind anyway." The doctor had not smiled when he said it. Balzic tried to think of that doctor's name, but knew that he had never known it. His recollection was part of a conversation between strangers. . . .

In the eleventh letter, the same words in quotation appeared, but were followed by more, these set down in the form of poetry:

The world is for the living. Who are they?
We dared the dark to reach the white and warm.

She was the wind when wind was in my way;
Alive at noon, I perished in her form.
Who rise from flesh to spirit know the fall;
The word outleaps the world, and light is all.

"Jesus Christ," Balzic said, and the three men from John-son's squad who were going through the rest of Janet Pisula's papers and notebooks looked up expectantly.

"Find something?" one of them asked.

"Nah," Balzic replied. "Just some stuff my daughters would call real heavy."

Of the letters Balzic had read, most contained the usual exchange of information he expected to find: descriptions of Frances Milocky's room, her roommates, complaints about her roommates' bathroom habits, harangues about studying to be done, books to be read, assignments to do, grades anticipated and received—everything except even the most casual reference to a boy. Frances Milocky seemed scrupulous about avoiding it.

It wasn't until the twelfth letter that a man was even men-tioned, and that was a brief paragraph about how considerate Janet's uncle ". . . had been to think of it." Whatever "it" is, Balzic thought.

In the thirteenth letter, dated December 1, near the end Frances Milocky wrote: "I hope you'll take my advice. Just don't even think about the worm. Any man who has to use that tactic to motivate anybody has got to be warped. Do what we talked about over Thanksgiving. Do it please, Janet. For your sake. I give you my word, he'll never know the difference." Then came the line about the "lively understandable spirit," followed by some of the poetry from the earlier letter.

In the fourteenth letter, dated December 9: "Quit feeling guilty about doing that, Jan. There's no need to. Really. People do that here all the time. They pay lots more than you're paying, believe me. There are people here who make a living from it. It's as much a part of this place as pot. Nobody even wonders about whether it's done; all they wonder about is whether they should

68

do it, though of course they also wonder if they can afford it. But for God's sake, quit feeling guilty about it. Next semester you'll be all right, as soon as you're out of Keenan's class. Just be sure to get to registration early enough so you won't have to take him again. Registration here is pure chaos. It can't possibly be as bad where you are."

In the fifteenth, dated December 14: "See, dummy, what did I tell you? I told you he wouldn't know the difference. What counts is you still got the grade. And what do you care anyway? Besides, if he had suspected something, don't you think he would've called you in and said something about it? He probably thinks he made some kind of giant progress. From the way you talked about him Thanksgiving, I'd say he has to have the biggest ego in the western world. He's probably telling all his colleagues (don't you just hate it when they call each other that?) that he's really Super Teacher. Can't you just see him? He goes into the faculty-lounge john, rips off his corduroy jacket, and comes flying out in a cap and gown with a big red S on his chest—Super Prof! I'll bet he wears bikini shorts."

I wouldn't take twenty to one against that, Balzic thought.

The sixteenth, dated December 18: "Just a note, Jan. I have to hurry. Going to Scranton with Diane. See you on the 20th." It was the first letter in which the line about the "lively understandable spirit" and the poetry did not appear.

In the seventeenth, dated January 8: "Jan, why do you do that to yourself? I mean, really, there's no point. It's such a waste. If you hadn't done it, you would've flunked for certain. And what difference does it make to Uncle Mike? How can he be hurt by something he doesn't know? And who's going to tell him? You? Do you think I would? Jan, only three people know, and two of us don't want to hurt anyone, especially not Uncle Mike, and why would the third person have any reason? Everything he does depends on maintaining your confidence, otherwise he's out of business. Sometimes you make me so crazy I could scream. Just please put those dumb ideas out of your head because, Jan, please believe me, they are dumb. You've been paranoid long enough. We both know that, and we both know you had every right to feel paranoid. But not about this. There just isn't any reason. How many times have we talked about how your paranoia slips over? We've talked about it too many times to count, and I really thought you were getting over that part of it. Maybe you'll never get over all of it, but at least tell yourself that the original reason for it was valid but that all the others aren't. I know. It sounds so easy for me to say, but I can't help it. It is easy for me to say because for me it is easy. Please don't take this wrong, okay? Remember? 'Who rise from flesh to spirit know the fall'? Think about it some more, okay?"

The eighteenth through the twenty-fifth letters contained nothing out of the ordinary. Everything in them was usual, cordial gossip. In the twenty-sixth, dated April 11, Balzic found this postscript: "As for what we talked about last week, all I can do is repeat what I said. Just keep thinking that you only have to put up with him a couple more weeks."

In the twenty-seventh, dated April 17, again in a postscript: "As for you know who, you have to learn to deal with people like that, Jan, that's all there is to it. I know it can get icky, and I'm not half as hung up about this sort of thing as you are. But you have to get tough. Otherwise, people will be stepping on your mind forever. You've been stepped on enough. Come on, Jan, toughen up!"

The twenty-eighth through the thirtieth letters were gossipy, girlish, drifting occasionally into something about schoolwork that was bothering one or the other but with no sense of urgency. All ended with some poetry. The thirty-first, and last, letter wasn't that much different. There was just one short passage referring to ". . . you know who." Frances Milocky wrote: "Some people give you things and if you aren't careful you'll give everything you have to them. But you owe him nothing!!!! Don't forget that, okay?"

Balzic put aside the stack of letters, took out his notebook, and copied from one of them all of the poetry. Then he put the letters in a manila envelope, marked them, and handed the envelope to one of the three troopers still going through the rest of the papers. He stretched, stifled a yawn, and looked at his watch. Two A.M. He felt suddenly very tired, and he thought the best thing he could do was go home and go to bed. He started out of the office but heard footsteps coming down the hall and waited, leaning against the doorframe.

Johnson came in, looking drained, shaking his head.

"How'd it go, Walk?"

"Shit, Grimes lifted the sheet and that poor bastard went down like somebody hit him in the head with a brick."

"Is he okay?"

"Hell, I thought he had a heart attack, but they got him into intensive care and wired him up to one of those EKGs. The head nurse said it looked normal, but they're still going to keep him until tomorrow anyway . . . man, those nurses in that outfit are really something. You know how old the head nurse was? Twenty-six, and she looked like seventeen."

"Yeah, I know. That's some group they got there. All of them are young. Did, uh, Grimes say anything else?"

"He pegged it down to last Wednesday night. That's as close as he can get."

"You get anything else out of Pisula?"

"Enough. 'Course I didn't want to pressure him. He did tell me how much money he gave the girl. Twenty-five a week, which I thought was a hell of a lot until he said she had to eat out every meal. He also said she went home every weekend—"

"Couldn't have been."

"What do you mean?"

"She couldn't have gone home every weekend, otherwise why didn't they say something last weekend—when she didn't show?"

"You didn't let me finish," Johnson said.

"Oh. So go ahead."

"The reason she didn't go home last weekend was because she told him she wanted to study for her finals. As a matter of fact, she called home last Wednesday afternoon and told him she'd

71

decided to stay the weekend, which would have been her first, and he said he was happy about it. He said he had it measured how well she was getting along by how often she called home. The first month he said she called every day, sometimes twice. Then, he said, little by little, she got to the point where she was only calling once a week. He also said he and his wife made it a point never to call her. And that's about all I got out of him."

"Well," Balzic said, "there's some letters in that envelope on your desk you ought to read. From that Milocky girl who's supposed to be her best friend. There's a guy in it, that's for sure. But no names. Just Keenan's a couple times, and unless I read them all wrong, he's not the guy." That said, he started for the door. He suddenly had to get out of the room. He couldn't say why, and he didn't want to stand around explaining.

"Where you going?" Johnson said.

"I think I'll hit Muscotti's for a couple cold ones, and then I'm going home. My ass is draggin'."

"Don't you want to go through the rest of her stuff?"

"What for? Christ, you got three guys doing that. What do you want me around for?"

"I just thought you might want to stick around. What's the matter? You look edgy as hell."

"I don't know. Maybe all this efficiency scares me. It's hot. I'm tired. You don't do any good when you're beat. I'll call you in the morning." He left before Johnson could say anything else.

He wasn't sure at first what had driven him out of Johnson's office. All he knew was that he had to get out. He sat in his cruiser for a couple of minutes before turning the ignition, telling himself that he probably shouldn't look too carefully at the cause of his leaving the way he did, but he knew that something drove him out and that that something ought to be looked at.

He was halfway to Muscotti's when he got down to it, and he had to laugh out loud at himself. He knew he'd have to be careful who he told about it, otherwise he might have to turn in his shield and resign from the Fraternal Order of Police. There was only one way for him to say it honestly: he really could not stand being around Pennsylvania State Police.

He knew it didn't have anything to do with any one of them or with anything that any one of them had ever done to him. He took them as they came. It had to do with the gray color of their uniforms and the words that came to mind when he tried to describe that color. Anybody else might simply have said their shirts were light gray and their trousers dark gray. But Balzic thought of their shirts as being the color of shale and their trousers the color of slate. Shale and slate—the words a coal miner would use to describe them. No wonder he could not be around them for long. . . .

Inside Muscotti's, Albert Margiotti, Dom Muscotti's son-in-law, was tending the bar and drawing a beer for Father Marrazo who sat in his poker clothes massaging his temples.

"S'matter, Father," Balzic said, "little early for you to be out of the game. It's not even quarter after two."

"I have a headache, Mario. I think it's my sinus. How are you?"

"Okay, I guess. That beer's not going to help your head."

"Naturally not," the priest said.

"Then you—"

The priest swiveled around on his stool and held up his hands. "Mario, please. A homily from you—as much as I like you and you know I do—but please, no homiletics. I'm drinking this beer out of spite for my head. Every man is entitled to spite himself once in a while, ridiculous as it may seem, if for no other reason than just to remind himself at times that he is ridiculous."

"Wow," Balzic said, shaking his hand limply from the wrist with the fingers together. "Give me a beer, Albert. And I got the Father's."

Albert put his hands on the bar and looked at his shoes. "Hey, Mario, uh, Dom asked me to ask you about your tab."

"Ask me about my what?"

"Uh, your tab, Mario—and hey, Mario, please don't come down on me, okay? You know I don't even like this job. I'm just helping the old man out, and if he tells me to ask somebody something, I ask, that's all. I don't want no grief over it. I got enough just being here."

"Hey," Balzic said, leaning on the bar, "you tell that old friggin' Tuscan to ask that skin-head Calabrez who works daylight what he did with the thirty-seven-fifty I handed him Memorial Day morning? You got it?"

"I got it, Mario. Okay? Just remember, I'm just asking, that's all."

"And you remember I'm just telling."

"Mario, not so loud," Father Marrazo said. "My head, remember?"

"Hey, Father, I don't mean to be loud, but goddammit I been drinking in this saloon since 1946, and since 1946 I been running a tab and I never walked him yet. I don't mind Vinnie ragging me about it. That's a standing joke between him and me, but this ain't the first time Vinnie took my tab and played it six bucks around on a number. And Dom knows that. You get what I mean, Father? And I don't like Dom asking Albert to ask me. Dom wants to know, he knows who to ask. This go-through-your-relatives is strictly bullshit, Father."

"Mario. Please," the priest said, rubbing his nose with his index fingers.

"Okay, Father, okay. I'm done." He looked at Albert. "So what're you gonna do, Albert? Do I get a beer or not?"

Albert drew the beer and set it in front of Balzic and then went to a cigar box under the cash register and wrote some figures on a piece of paper taken from the box.

"Thank you, Albert. How's your wife?"

"She's okay. Feeling a lot better."

"Good. Glad to hear that. Tell her I said hello."

Albert nodded. "Mario, you know—"

Balzic held up his hand. "Say no more. You're out of it."

74

Albert backed away and busied himself filling the beer coolers.

Balzic drank his beer without pause and motioned to Albert to draw another. He sipped the second and said, "I guess I should apologize, Father, for being loud, but to say it straight, I don't feel like it. I'm in a pretty foul mood—"

"I'll drink to that," the priest said.

"—from being around those state cops. Driving over here I was thinking about why I can't stay around them for very long. Yeah. Me. Who'd believe it? I have to work with them all the time. But I can only put up with being around them so long. And I know why, too. Which makes it even goofier."

"You are in a foul mood."

"The thing is, I'm not really. Most of the time I don't show anybody, that's all. I manage to keep it covered—usually. But sometimes things haunt you, and you can't keep them covered anymore. I mean, you can still cover them from other people, but you can't cover them from yourself. Like tonight, I was around all these state guys and I was looking at their uniforms, the color, and the words that kept coming into my head were shale and slate. Coal miners' words. And—ah, this is a load. You don't want to hear this."

"Go ahead and say it. Get it out."

"It's not important. Doesn't matter a damn to anybody."

"All right," the priest said. "I won't coax you."

Balzic stared at his beer, running his finger up and down the side of the glass. "We found a girl tonight, Father. Up in the Summer house. Been dead since last Wednesday. Strangled. And I'm really involved with that since maybe ten, ten-thirty, and all of a sudden, I can't stand to be in the same room with state guys. And one of them is a very good friend of mine. And you know why?"

The priest shook his head.

"My father is buried in Edna Number Two. Summer's mine."

"Your father?" the priest said. "You never said anything about that before. I don't know why that surprises me, but it does."

"I was three years old. I have no memory of him at all. None. I mean, except what my mother told me. And tonight, just being there, it's funny how I managed to put that out of my head until three or four hours later when I find myself in a room with four state guys . . . you know, my mother had a real fit when I told her I was going to be a cop. She wouldn't talk to me for two or three days. And I couldn't understand it. I kept asking her what was so bad about being a cop, and she wouldn't say a word. And when she finally did decide to talk to me again, the first thing she said —I'll never forget it—she said, 'If your father was here, he'd spit in your face and throw you out.' The look on her face, God . . ."

"Did he hate cops that much?"

"He was a miner, Father, and all he knew when he was in the mines was the Iron and Coal Police, the Pinkertons, and the Pennsylvania Constabulary. The Pennsylvania Constabulary became the state police. You know what the miners used to call them? The Black Cossacks. I thought my mother was exaggerating, but I did a lot of reading about it in the big Carnegie Library in Pittsburgh. There's another joke for you. I had to read about it in a library set up by one of the most heartless bastards who ever lived. But I found it, pictures and all. You ought to read about that time in this part of the state, Father. It's unbelievable."

"But anyway," Balzic went on, "it all came back to me tonight, and I thought I was going to choke in that room with those state guys. How's that? I felt like I was going to choke. That's what happened to the girl. What do the psychologists call that?"

"Identification? Is that what you mean?"

"Yeah. Something like that. The mind's a hell of a thing. Always surprises me the way it jumps around on you—course, I just might not be too bright."

"Oh, Mario, I doubt whether most people would have the

76

honesty to question themselves about the way they were feeling. Now I understand."

"Understand what?"

"Why you reacted the way you did over your tab, over being asked to do something you'd already done."

"I'm not sure I want to know," Balzic said, motioning to Albert to draw two more beers. "Let's forget me for a while, Father. You read a lot, right?"

"That depends what you mean by a lot."

"Skip the modesty, Father. We both know you read a lot of books, especially psychology. Most of what I know about it, I got it first from you."

The priest shrugged.

"That girl we found tonight—another thing just came to me."

"What's that?"

"Why I made that identification with her."

"Why?"

"The more people I asked about her—except for her uncle —the less anybody could say about her. It's almost the same way with my old man and me. Lots of people knew him, but damn few can tell me anything that gives me a real feel of him, you know what I mean? It's the same with the girl . . . anyway, the thing I wanted to ask you about is this: she had a blank sheet of paper on her stomach. She's naked except for her panties, she's strangled with her brassiere, and according to the coroner, she was still a virgin. But what about that piece of paper, Father? What do you make of that?"

"I don't know. There's nothing on it? It's blank?"

"Nothing at all. And it was her paper. She also wasn't robbed. I'll tell you, it is the goddamndest thing I've ever come across."

"What do you make of it?"

Balzic shook his head. "I don't have the first idea. Neither does Johnson."

"Who? I don't know him."

"He's an old buddy of mine. He's a lieutenant in charge of CID until that asshole Minyon gets out of the hospital."

"What's wrong with him?"

"Ulcers or something. I wouldn't cry if he died."

The back door opened slowly, and, hat and tie askew, eyelids drooping, the left sleeve of his blue blazer ripped at the shoulder, Mo Valcanas shuffled in, singing in a way that only every third or fourth word could be heard.

"Holy hell," Balzic said. "What war'd you lose?"

"None of your goddamn business," Valcanas said. "Just direct me to the head. I have to speak to the ship's captain. Ship's company needs liberty."

"The head's the same place it's always been," Balzic said. "If you don't know where it is now, as many times as you've been in it."

"I'll be a sonuvabitch," Valcanas said. "Muscotti's. Didn't recognize the place. Now hell the how'd—how the hell'd I get here?"

"I hope you didn't drive."

"Who are you? Lou Harris? What do you care how I got here? Oh, it's you, Mario. Should've known. Well, pardon me while I relieve myself. In the meantime, before you arrest me for drunken walking, be advised to go pound sand. . . ."

Valcanas tottered toward the steps leading to the downstairs lavatory. The seat of his trousers and down to his knees was stained with blood.

"Hey, Mo," Balzic called out, "you got blood all over you."

"Wrong," Valcanas called up. "Usual for a cop. The blood is not *all* over me. It's restricted to the area immediate to and directly below my anus. My hemorrhoids cut loose. . . ."

Balzic looked at the priest and they shook their heads.

"What do you suppose happened to him?" Father Marrazo asked.

"Six'll get you five, Father, he smarted off at somebody a lot younger and a lot bigger. That's his style."

78

"With his intelligence—why?"

"My mother says some people have too much brains for their own good. That's Valcanas. He sees too good, hears too good, and he doesn't like what he sees or hears. That's about as near as I can figure him. Course, I don't try to figure him too much. I just take him the way he is and hope he stays out of trouble."

"It strikes me as a terrible waste."

"Oh, I don't know if I'd say that. I think he just doesn't like being sober—hell, what do I know? You want to know, ask him when he comes up. If he feels like it, he'll tell you. But if he doesn't, don't be offended if he tells you to take a flying trip to the moon."

"I won't be offended. I'll just feel sorry."

"Ouu, you better mean you'll be sorry for you. That's one thing I know he'll take your head off for, you give him a reason to think you feel sorry for him."

". . . oh say can you see, the Coast Guard at sea, through the fog, through the smog," Valcanas sang to the melody of the National Anthem as he weaved up the stairs and to a stool beside the priest.

"Don't stop now," Balzic said. "Let's hear the rest of it."

"I would," Valcanas said, grinning, "only I can't remember it. Innkeeper! A large whiskey and water. Canadian Club, if you please."

"Think you had enough, Mo," Albert said.

"I never met a bartender yet who could think. All they can do is add fast and everybody knows that doesn't take anything approaching thought. Pour the goddamn drink. I'll tell you when I've had enough."

Albert looked questioningly at Balzic.

"Go ahead," Balzic said. "Give it to him. He'll just go to sleep."

"Sleep, sleep. Valcanas hath murdered sleep . . . Valcanas doth murder sleep. Fuck you, sleep. You're dead. Bang. . . ."

"You, uh, read Shakespeare?" Father Marrazo said.

"Past tense. Read. I'm possibly the only person alive who

ever finished *Timon of Athens* to the last hideous line. I thought I
was going to learn something about Greeks. What a crock. And
if that isn't masochism for you, give me a better example." Valcanas took out his billfold and, licking his thumb, stripped out a
five. "That's the purest form of masochism I know—reading *Timon of Athens* to the last goddamn line. Hey, aren't you Father
Marrazo?"

The priest said he was.

"Well, good, 'cause I have a question for you. And be honest. Don't quote me some goddamn papal bull."

The priest smiled and shook his head.

"What's so funny about that?"

"Nothing."

"Then what the hell are you laughing for?"

"I was thinking of something."

"There, Mario. See? An honest priest. He admits to thinking. Better be careful, Father. You'll get drummed out of the
corps for doing that. Oh, you can do it. You just gotta be careful
who you tell."

"So what is your question?"

"Oh. And remember. An honest answer. Did Jesus ever fool
around with Mary Magdalene?"

"Aw come on, Mo," Balzic said.

"Stay out of it. You'd've been there, you'd've busted her for
assignation, solicitation, and you'd've probably tried to trump up
an attempt to commit sodomy. Shut up a minute. I want to hear
what the priest has to say."

"You really expect me to answer you?" Father Marrazo said.

"I don't ask questions unless I expect an answer. Did he or
didn't he?"

"Well, going on the evidence of the scripture, I would say
no."

"Okay, then tell me this: do you think he wanted to?"

"That I can't say," the priest said, smiling.

"Well in that holy trinity he was supposed to be, one-third
of him was man, right?"

"Yes."

"And men have desires, don't they?"

"Yes. I suppose most men do."

"All men, Father. All men. You guys are just experts in conning yourselves that you don't."

"Okay, okay," the priest said, laughing.

"Then answer me. Did he desire ol' Mary Mag or not?"

"I can't say."

"Well shit, man, what do you think? I mean, I just got the hell kicked out of me by some wop football player who didn't like my saying that Jesus had to have some eyes for Mary Mag, otherwise he wouldn't have been so damn quick to forgive her. Now, did I get the hell beat out of me for nothing?"

"I'm afraid you did."

"Why?"

"Because any answer would be conjectural. There's nothing written about it one way or the other."

"Then the only other explanation for his forgiving her was nothing but goddamn arrogance. Who the hell was he to forgive any woman for trying to earn her living?"

"Boy, you really are cranked up," Balzic said.

"A hell of a lot of satisfaction I'm getting out of you two," Valcanas said.

"Let's change the subject, okay?" Balzic said. "I got something I want to ask you, Mo. You read a lot—"

"I haven't read four books since Christmas."

"You read enough. I know that. So tell me. Why does somebody kill somebody and leave a blank piece of paper on her stomach? What's the message?"

"Do what?"

"Why would somebody strangle a girl, not rape her, not rob her, and then leave a blank piece of paper on her stomach?"

"Where the hell did you hear that? Did this actually happen or is this supposed to be hypothetical?"

"I wish it was hypothetical. We found her tonight. She's been

81

dead at least nine days. Two people right across the hall from her and they didn't hear a peep."

"A piece of paper. With nothing on it?"

"Plain, ordinary typing paper. It belonged to the victim. And nothing on it."

Valcanas drained his glass and motioned to Albert to bring another drink. "That's the goddamndest thing I ever heard—oh, wait. Wait a minute. Right before Hemingway killed himself—the poor sonuvabitch—one of the last things he said to anybody, he was talking to his doctor. And he said something like, 'Doc, I can't make a sentence any more.' Something like that."

"So go ahead and make the connection," Balzic said.

"Well, he couldn't make a sentence. He couldn't write. He couldn't get it out of him. He couldn't get it on the page. And everytime you start, the page is always blank, right?"

"Right," Balzic said. "But he killed himself."

"Aw, come on, Mario. What the hell's suicide? It's self-murder. And murder's murder. It all depends which way the gun's pointed."

"Okay. So what you're saying is, it was a writer who couldn't write."

"Well, hell, that's just a guess. I mean, there were lots of other reasons Hemingway killed himself. He was sick, his liver was shot. He'd just had a couple trips to the Mayo brothers' hotel. Shock treatments, that bit. But I'm just telling you the last thing he said to anybody before he did it. The connection to that and what you're talking about seems pretty obvious, that's all I'm saying."

"Uh-huh," Balzic said, taking out his notebook. "Well, here. Listen to this. I want to hear what you two think of this. 'The world is for the living. Who are they? We dared the dark to reach the white and warm. She was the wind when wind was in my way; alive at noon, I perished in her form. Who rise from flesh to spirit know the fall; the word outleaps the world, and light is all.' "

"What the hell is this," Valcanas grumbled. "I feel like I'm on some goddamn quiz show for crissake."

"Just tell me what you think of it," Balzic said.

"Are you asking me what I think of it, or you asking me what I think it means?"

"Both, I guess."

"Well I'll tell you what I think of it. I think it was written by somebody who's a bigger goddamn manic-depressive than I am —and that's going some," Valcanas said.

"Doesn't mean anything else to you?"

"What the fuck you want? I come in here all chopped up and you start reading things at me. Christ, I didn't even know I was here when I got here. Still don't."

"What about you, Father? What do you think?"

"I'd have to agree with Mo, at least partly. It certainly sounds like somebody had a very bad time of it and then pulled himself together a little too euphorically."

"I'll drink to that," Valcanas said. "What was that one part again—who rise from what to what?"

" 'Who rise from flesh to spirit know the fall,' " Balzic read.

"Christ, that's a roller-coaster ride if I ever heard one. Even got the rhythm for it. Down up, down up, down up, Jesus. Where the hell'd you get that anyway?"

"I found it in a bunch of letters to the dead girl."

"Well, if somebody was trying to cheer her up, they sure picked some heavy artillery to do it with. Christ, I hear any more of that I'll have a relapse right here—what the hell are you doing making me think about crap like that anyway? All I wanted to do was stay fogged in. I didn't want to think about anything."

"You drink to avoid thinking?" Father Marrazo asked.

"Now you got it, padre. If you think, don't drink. If you drink, don't think. Christ, I should've been an ad man . . . have a Canadian Club adventure, go everywhere and never move off a bar stool. Walter Mitty was really a lush . . ."

"That reminds me of something," the priest said. "I remember reading about a study done by some psychiatrist that of all America's Nobel prize winners in literature, only one, Pearl Buck, wasn't a heavy drinker or an alcoholic. O'Neill, Sinclair Lewis,

Hemingway, Steinbeck, and, oh, who was the other one?"

"Faulkner," Valcanas said. "Champion of them all. He made his own when he couldn't afford it. And that, padre, is true dedication to the pursuit of oblivion. Life, liberty, and the pursuit of oblivion. Liberty, equality, oblivion . . . up everybody's." That said, Valcanas drained his glass and tottered toward the door.

"Hey, Mo, " Balzic called after him, "you're not going to drive, are you?"

"Hell, no. I'm going to my office. I have a cot in the cellar. Maybe there'll be an earthquake."

"Well throw your keys here then."

"Then how do I get into my office? Break a window? Then one of your clowns busts me for breaking and entering."

"Just your car keys."

"Oh, will you quit acting like somebody's goddamn mother. I told you I'm not driving for crissake. It's only two blocks from here. Since when do I have to listen to this horseshit—concern for my safety, Jesus . . ."

"I'm not concerned about your goddamn safety," Balzic said, but before he could say more, Valcanas had bounced off both door and frame and shuffled out.

Father Marrazo shook his head. "I still say it's a waste."

"If it's a waste, Father, I don't know what it's a waste of. I've seen him in court just slightly less juiced, making jerks out of assistant D.A.'s. Why don't you talk to one of them about it?"

Balzic left the priest sometime between three thirty and four, he didn't know exactly when. At home, he prowled back and forth between the living room and the kitchen, drinking cans of beer and eating a sandwich he'd made from crusty provolone, eating the sandwich to satisfy his hunger though it tasted flat as old provolone always does. He threw the last bit away, telling himself that it was a sin to waste food but a bigger sin to insult the stomach. By five thirty he was standing in the kitchen, looking out the window at the birds and squirrels waking, the birds bursting by his window like black darts and the squirrels rushing up and

84

down the maples and diving from the sturdy, stiffer branches of the maples to the whippy, pencil-thin branches of the Chinese elm hedges Balzic used to plan to trim but never did. The hedges and the lilacs he'd planted in front of them formed a nearly opaque wall for most of the year, and what pleased Balzic most about that was that now the neighbors could only guess at how much he loafed. It had taken years for the hedges to grow as thick as they had, but it had only been in the last few years that Balzic felt he could loaf in peace without hearing later on from God knew who about how he stood around with his hands in his pockets when he should have been out rounding up the beasties and nasties and things that went bump.

The neighbors, Balzic snorted thoughtfully. He had to ask himself what their names were. He couldn't think of it. Yurkowski, Yurhoska, something like that. Good solid squares, scared shitless of niggers, dope heads, commies, rabid dogs, girls who went without brassieres, and people who made love with the lights on. His mother told him that about them. They were always complaining to his mother, and every once in a while, when she couldn't think up something new to put them off, she came to him and complained about them. The last time, a couple of months ago, he'd told his mother, "Ma, if I lock up everybody they're scared of, who's left? I'd have to lock up the world." To which his mother had replied impishly, "You big man, you no can do that?"

He turned away from the window and was startled to see his mother standing in the doorway of the kitchen. She was in her flannel gown, barefoot, her swollen ankles showing under the hem, her fingers over her mouth. She looked like she'd been standing there for some moments.

"Hey, kiddo, you still up. You sick?" Her voice was husky with sleep.

"I'm okay," he said. "What're you doing up?"

"I ask you first."

"I said I'm okay. Just didn't feel like sleeping. What about you?"

"Ahh, same thing. Ankles hurt like crazy. Back, too. I think I sleep on floor from now on. You want light?"

"Yeah. Go ahead, turn it on."

She flipped the switch by her shoulder and the overhead fluorescent hummed and then slowly filled the room with its bluish light. His mother sat at the kitchen table and rubbed one ankle with the other. "Hey, Mario," she said, squinting up at him, "what you decide?"

"About what?"

"Oh boy, you forget already?"

Balzic frowned. "I guess I did. What was I supposed to remember?"

"The cottage. You and Ruth and the girls and me. Next week. Tony's cottage. You forget to decide?"

"Oh that." Balzic sighed and rubbed his eyes. "Ma, I was thinking about it. I really was. But something came up and I quit thinking about it. It doesn't look like I'll be able to go anyway even if I wanted to."

"But you don't want. You still no like Tony. What for? What's he do for you? How come? Ruth very disappoint. Her only brother, Mario. All she got left. And you don't like."

"I know, Ma, I know. I can't help it. I just don't like the guy. I never did. I'm sorry he's all she got left out of her family. I wish she didn't have . . ." He let it hang there, wishing he hadn't said even the start of it.

"Oh, Mario. Not nice. Not nice what you was thinking."

Balzic looked away from her and yawned and rubbed his cheeks briskly. "I know it's not nice to think like that, Ma, but I can't help it."

"Mario, no kid around. What's he really do for you, you no like?"

"Ma, don't ask me, okay? It's embarrassing to talk about."

"So he really do something for you. Why you no tell Ruth? Why you never tell me before? Save lotsa trouble, kiddo."

"Ma, believe me, it would cause more trouble than it saves. I know what I'm talking about. Besides, I think it would probably

86

be better if just you and Ruth and the kids went. The river doesn't really do all that much for me anyway."

"Oh, Mario, think how much cooler goin' to be there."

"All right, listen. I'll think about it some more, okay?"

"Hokay, I don't say nothing no more, but you got to say something to Ruth. She wants to know you goin' or not. Kids too. They looking forward, Mario. You know they goin' be swim all summer with that team. They no have more chance after next week." She stood, then winced and felt her lower back and had to hold the edge of the table to steady herself.

Balzic reached out to help her, but she shook her head.

"It's hokay," she said. "Just stiff. I think I go sleep on floor in living room. Don't step on me, hokay, kiddo? Good night."

He said good night and watched her go, still tilted forward from the waist, her feet flat on each step. He scratched his shoulders and wondered why he could not bring himself to tell her why he didn't want to spend a weekend at his brother-in-law's cottage on the Allegheny River. If she kept pressing him about it, he was going to have to tell her and Ruth something. They deserved some explanation, but he knew that when he finally got the nerve to give them one he was going to have to make it good. He arched his back and stared up at the ceiling. Shit, he thought. They'll see through anything I come up with. I'm going to have to lay it out, and is Ruth going to love that. Is she ever . . .

He tip-toed into the bedroom and started to undress. He was down to his socks and underwear when he thought to set the alarm. He set it for nine, hoping he'd hear it but knowing that he wouldn't, and then hoping that Ruth would know he'd set it for a reason and get him up.

He edged into bed beside her and stretched out. The last thing he remembered seeing on the insides of his eyelids was a blank piece of paper on the middle seat of an empty rowboat floating in slow circles past his brother-in-law's cottage. His mother and Ruth and Emily were standing in front of the cottage. Their faces were all confusion, the beginnings of panic. His brother-in-law was on the opposite shore, laughing obscenely and pointing at the skiff with his middle finger. Nobody seemed to know where Marie was; worse, nobody seemed to be doing anything about finding out where she was. Then he saw himself, standing on a sandbar in his underwear and socks. He had a pencil in his hand and he looked like he was trying to find something to write on. . . .

Balzic never heard the alarm. What he thought was the alarm was the phone ringing, and when he rolled over to shut the alarm and saw that it was a quarter after one, he bolted out of bed and hustled out to the kitchen phone, rubbing his eyes, scratching his belly, and swearing.

He picked up the phone and saw the note on the kitchen table in the same instant. He said, "Wait a minute," into the phone and picked up the note and read it. "Mario, I've taken Ma and the girls shopping. Didn't wake you when the alarm went off because you were really snoring and looked like you needed the sleep. Hope I didn't mess you up. Be back around three. Love, Ruth."

"I didn't get you up, did I?" Lieutenant Johnson said. "I mean, the last thing I want to do is fuck up your rest."

"Okay, okay. I'm up. So now what?"

"Well, listen, if you can tear yourself away from that bed, I'd appreciate your help. I'm getting a blister from dialing the phone."

"What, you don't have people there?"

"Hell yes, I have people. Four of my people and three county guys. But they're all getting blisters too. We've only made about a hundred and three phone calls."

"About a hundred and three, huh," Balzic said. He sighed, coughed, brought up some phlegm, and leaned over and spit it into the kitchen sink, turning on the water in the same motion. "Listen. Give me twenty minutes. Just let me get cleaned up and get some coffee."

"Don't get too pretty. It's not your face I need. It's your finger. And we have all the coffee you want right here."

"You got my finger, friend," he said. "The middle one." He hung up before Johnson could retort, and twenty minutes later, with a patch of toilet paper congealed to a cut on his chin, he walked into the duty room of Troop A Barracks.

The air was heavy with cigar and cigarette smoke and the smell of both hot and cold coffee. Balzic nodded to the state men he knew by sight and to the three county detectives, Frank Rusa, John Dillman, and Tony Funari. Johnson appeared out of another office with both hands full of papers and started passing them around.

"Well," he said, "let's see if we can get the other twenty-seven." Seeing Balzic, he said, "Morning, sunshine. I thought you said you were going to get cleaned up."

"Save the smart mouth till somebody makes a movie about you," Balzic said. "Just tell me where's the coffee."

Johnson nodded to a table in the corner, and Balzic went to it and poured himself a cup from the large urn. "Well," he said, "what do you got?"

"I don't know whether you're ready for this," Johnson said. "The thing is, I don't know if I'm ready for it. But here it is. There are one hundred and three people who were in one of four classes with the girl. So far, we've called all of them but we contacted, uh, seventy-six. Of the seventy-six—you hear this?—only fifteen remember ever even hearing her name. And of those fifteen, six were fairly sure they could put a name with a face. And of those six, only two ever remember talking to her, and those were the two who sat on either side of her in her shorthand class."

"And naturally," Balzic said, "all they remember talking about is what they had to do for the next class."

"Oh, one of them had a hell of a conversation with her one day. She asked her if she had an extra pen, and the Pisula girl said, and I quote, 'Yes.' "

"How the hell's that possible?" Balzic said, sipping his coffee.

"Well don't forget what her uncle said about her being scared stiff of strangers."

"Well shit, somebody had to say something to her. I mean, goddamn . . ."

"The newspaper still only come out six days here?" Johnson asked.

"Yeah. No Sundays. What'd you give them?"

"Everything I had, plus a plea for cooperation from anybody who might've seen anything. That was about ten this morning."

"That means it won't be in until Monday. Shit." Balzic sloshed his coffee around. "I been meaning to ask you. What's the word on the Milocky girl?"

"I got her mother around nine this morning. She expects her home sometime today, but she doesn't know when 'cause she's riding with somebody. The mother wasn't even sure when the girl's supposed to leave."

"You tell her mother?"

"I couldn't very well not tell her. People hear from a cop, they want to know something."

"Shit."

"What's the matter? Why the 'shit'?"

"Well, you read those letters. You heard what Pisula said. Those two were close. More than close. I hope she doesn't get the scrupulosities when she hears what happened and do something dumb."

"The what?"

"The scrupulosities. The guilties. That's what the priests call them when they get the people who run to confession after they crossed against a traffic light or got a parking ticket. Some people run to a priest, some run to a friend, some run to a psychiatrist, some of them just run."

"I thought you were the one who said not to think about all the things that could go wrong."

"Hey, Walk, she's it as far as I can see. If she can't tell us, nobody can. And when you get a situation like that, when you get two people and one of them doesn't have any trouble making it and the other one does, and the one who does breaks away from

90

the one who doesn't—especially in this situation. The Milocky girl tells the other one to enroll here and then enrolls someplace else and then this happens—Christ, that's a dynamite situation. It might be that for the first time in their lives the situations are reversed."

"I'm not sure I follow," Johnson said.

"Well, all along, it's the Milocky girl who's the prop. She's holding up the Pisula girl. Now the Milocky girl needs a prop, and maybe the real jolt is going to be for her to find out she needs one. And then, what if there's nobody around? I mean, just for the simple reason she never thought she might need one, so she never looked for one—how about that?"

"Yeah, I see what you're getting at, but I don't necessarily think she's it for us. We still have a lot of lab reports to come in. We really don't know what we have."

"Which means you also don't know what you don't have either." Balzic chewed the inside of his lower lip and reached for a phone book.

"Who you looking up?"

"That Keenan. The one who's chairman of the English department."

"Why? I thought you said he was a real ballbuster."

"I'm not sure. I'd like to talk to him when he isn't half-juiced. Besides, I'm not cut out to sit around dialing phones. I hate fuckin' telephones. All you get is the voice. I want to see the face." Balzic found Malcolm Keenan's home address and made a note of it. He started for the door with a wave to Johnson.

"Well. Let me know," Johnson said.

"Yeah, sure," Balzic said, and went out to his cruiser and headed east to the Rocksburg city line and the beginning of Westfield Township.

Keenan's house, two-storied, covered with white aluminum, was situated on a sloping lot at the corner of Route 286 and Westfield Avenue. Though the township had recently annexed the land, the house and lot still had the complexion of the city, with sidewalks on two sides, an alley in the rear, a mailbox on a utility pole at the corner, and a fire hydrant in the middle of the block.

The house was old and boxy. Fifty years earlier it might have been built by one of Rocksburg's more prosperous businessmen; now, the white aluminum siding made it appear prim at the same time the taped window in the storm door made it appear as though the owners were indifferent to property. Balzic was reminded immediately of Keenan spilling the last drops of a drink on his corduroy jacket.

Balzic knocked on the storm door and was greeted by a large, collie-like mongrel which had been sleeping on the other side of the door and could not make up its mind whether to bark an alarm or wag its tail. It did both.

The door let into the kitchen, and from around a corner appeared a woman Balzic recalled seeing at the party at Dr. Beverley's house, the woman in the very short silver lamé dress.

She spoke through the screened upper third of the door. "Yes?" Before Balzic could reply she said, "Oh, it's you."

"Yes, it's me. Your husband here? I'd like to talk to him."

She hesitated, then said, "Won't you come in." The voice was Southern, possibly from North or South Carolina. She held the door open for Balzic and reached for the dog's collar to pull it back. "She'll jump all over you," she said, smiling nervously first at the dog and then at Balzic.

"As long as she jumps friendly, I don't mind."

"Oh my Lord, yes. She's spoiled rotten and thinks everybody who comes, comes just to see her. Won't you sit down? May I get you something cool to drink before I tell Mal you're here?"

Balzic sat and let the dog sniff at his shoes and legs. "A glass of water would be fine."

Balzic watched Mrs. Keenan moving from cupboard to refrigerator to sink. She was taller than Balzic had remembered, and like many tall women she tended to slouch. She seemed to be moving quickly, but for some reason Balzic couldn't figure she also seemed to be taking a long time to get him the glass of water.

When Malcolm Keenan appeared around the corner, Balzic thought he understood. Keenan was nearly as drunk as he'd been when Balzic met him at the door of the Beverley's house, and Mrs. Keenan was doing her best to avoid looking at him. When she set the glass of water in front of Balzic, she didn't look at Balzic either.

"Yesss?" Keenan said, scowling as though he'd been interrupted in the middle of something extremely important.

"Sorry to bother you," Balzic said and was cut short.

"You have already bothered me," Keenan said.

"Mal!" Mrs. Keenan said.

"Is he a friend of yours, or am I not permitted to know that?" Keenan said, breathing deeply twice and trying not to weave.

"It's the chief of police, Mal. You talked to him last night. At some length. About a very serious thing—or don't you remember that either?"

Keenan focused on Balzic and seemed to make the association and then broke into a loud, staccato laugh, throwing back his head. "Surely," he said. "I was just rehearsing."

"Rehearsing?" Balzic said, watching their faces. Mrs. Keenan looked on the edge of tears, though whether it was from anger or humiliation Balzic couldn't guess. Probably both. Keenan tried to look sincere but could not bring it off. He excused himself, disappeared around the corner, and returned, rattling ice cubes in a tumbler. He opened a cabinet under the sink, took out a bottle of Scotch, and poured himself a couple of inches. Mrs. Keenan winced at the amount and then said quickly, "I think I'll leave you two alone."

"It isn't necessary," Balzic said.

"Oh but it is," she said. She patted her thigh twice and said, "Come on, Keenie." The mongrel lurched away from Balzic's feet and trotted after her. Before she went around the corner, she fired a look of reproach at her husband which seemed to amuse him.

"Women," Keenan said, drawing up another stool and settling uneasily onto it. He shrugged and said, "You are aware of course of what Freud said near the end of his life."

"No. Afraid not."

"He said that after forty years of working with women, he still had no idea what they wanted."

"I didn't know that."

"Neither did he," Keenan said, bursting into that staccato laugh.

Balzic let that go and said, "Uh, a little while ago you said you were rehearsing, and I asked you about it but you didn't answer."

"That's a very bad joke my wife doesn't appreciate. I use it whenever I think she is about to reprove me. I tell her that I am rehearsing for my life which is going to begin its run next week." Keenan smiled wistfully. "It infuriates her."

Balzic had to laugh in spite of himself.

"What is it that brings you here, sir?"

"The same thing we talked about last night."

"Well, sir, I have told you all I know about that girl. It was little enough, but I know no more."

"I didn't come here thinking you knew any more. I just came to have some things cleared up."

"Such as?"

"For one thing, last night you seemed pretty sure she wasn't doing her own work, and I'd like to know the reason you're so sure of that."

"Sir, I have been teaching for eleven years. Four at the University of Pittsburgh as a teaching assistant while I did my graduate work, four at Slippery Rock, and the last three here. One just gets a feel for such things."

"Yeah, well, I can understand that, but, uh, exactly how does one get this feel?"

"Aha! A man in search of cement."

"Cement?"

"Surely. Concrete, cement, the hard. As opposed to the abstract, the nebulous, the soft. You want water, not merely rain. You want the it, as in it is raining."

"Okay," Balzic said. "As long as it's about the Pisula girl, you can call it whatever you want."

Keenan made a humming sound and closed his eyes. "Let me think how to put this," he said, opening his eyes. "In a sentence, sir, the girl's prose took a quantum jump that was simply extraordinary."

"You lost me with that jump, what was it?"

"Quantum. A mathematical premise. The promise of arithmetic. Her words took the leap of a dwarf who suddenly realized his dream of becoming the Jolly Green Giant. It was impossible for me not to notice."

"So did you ask her about it?"

"No. As a matter of form, I complimented her on her jump."

"Even though you were pretty sure it was faked?"

"Even though. Surely. I mean, something must be said for the initiative to cheat, if for no other reason than for the imagination it requires. No. Demands."

Balzic shook his head. "Somehow I get the feeling you could, uh, make cancer sound like a good deal."

"Ah, well, words are the call, and mind outleaps pen, all in all."

"What was that?"

Keenan gulped more Scotch. "What was what?"

"You said something about mind outleaps the pen."

"What I said was, 'Words are the call, and mind outleaps pen, all in all.' "

"Did somebody write that by any chance?"

"I did. But purely as an exercise in form. Purely exercise."

"Sounds familiar."

"It does?"

Balzic took out his notebook and thumbed through it until he found the poetry he'd copied from Frances Milocky's letters to Janet Pisula. "Yeah, here it is. 'The word outleaps the world, and light is all.' "

"Theodore Roethke."

"Who?"

95

"Theodore Roethke. The sanest lunatic of the last forty years."

"What you're telling me is he's the guy who wrote that."

"Indeed, sir, he did. Between vacations to the mind sanctuaries. Or maybe during. But tell me, sir, what is a chief of police doing with the words of a poet in his notebook? Does that mean I can still hope for the age of the philosopher king to come upon us?"

"I don't know about that. I just know that what you said sounded familiar, that's all."

"Aaaaah, we're to cat and mouse, dog and cat, man and woman—is that it? You're to get me to confess that I'm familiar with Roethke. I'm dismayed, sir."

Balzic waited for Keenan to continue, but Keenan stood and poured himself another dose of Scotch. He returned to his stool, eased himself onto it, and took another long drink. Three full swallows.

"If it be treason, sir, to love poets," Keenan said, "then I am a traitor. Do with it what you will."

"Well, treason's a little out of my line. I'm just a cop here in Rocksburg. I don't work for the FBI."

"Your point, sir—" Keenan laughed uproariously. "Forgive me. What is your point?"

"I'm not really sure right now. Just tell me something. Is this, uh, this—"

"It's pronounced Ret-Key."

"Yeah, well, is he popular among college kids?"

"Popular? No, not popular. But his voice reaches those with certain ears."

"Uh-huh. Do you talk about him much in your classes?"

"I do. But that's because I have a singular affection for him. He has got me through more than one long night." Keenan closed his eyes and said, chanting in a voice like an aging priest's: " 'This shaking keeps me steady. I should know. What falls away is always. And is near. I wake to sleep, and take my waking slow.

96

I learn by going where I have to go.' That quatrain, sir, has got me through more than once."

Balzic studied Keenan's face for a moment. Keenan's eyes were still closed and his face was lifted slightly. Balzic turned to another page in his notebook and read, " 'A lively understandable spirit once entertained you. It will come again. Be still. Wait.' Did the same guy write that, what I just read?"

Keenan nodded ponderously and opened his eyes slowly. "He did. It's from 'The Lost Son.' " Keenan closed one eye and opened the other very wide. "Again I must say, sir, I find this extraordinary. A chief of police with poetry in his notebook. Extraordinary."

"Not as extraordinary as you think," Balzic said. "But that's neither here nor there. Last night you said the Pisula girl shouldn't have even been in college, right?"

Keenan nodded slowly.

"You didn't think she was smart enough. She would've been better off waitin' tables someplace."

"Everybody would have been better off."

"Well a little while ago you said this Roethke wasn't popular, and I think you said something about him reaching those with certain ears—I think that's the way you put it."

"I did."

"So, uh, it sort of sounds like you think the people who hear him, the ones with those certain ears, it sounds like you think those people are pretty smart."

"Let me say this. I would not generally equate those with ears sufficient unto Roethke with undue intelligence, but I would say that they have made a wondrous beginning toward an awareness of the limits of their intelligence—yes, I would say that much."

"Okay, then tell me. How can you say what you just said on the one hand and then say on the other that the Pisula girl was dumb, how can you make that add up when I found all this poetry in her room?"

"You found those lines of Roethke's in her room?"

"That's right." Balzic was not about to say exactly where in her room he had found them.

"I'm truly perplexed," Keenan said. "Truly . . ." His chest came forward, his shoulders squared, he took several deep breaths, and he squinted unpleasantly. He started to speak, but before he could say anything, his wife appeared at the corner and said, "Mal, I would like to speak with you." Her teeth were clenched.

Keenan excused himself and followed his wife around the corner. For a minute their words were a jumble of harsh sounds, but then her voice rose and her words came clear.

". . . the third time this week, and I'll be damned if I am going to clean it up this time!"

"Patience, woman, patience—"

"Patience my behind! If the boy is sick he should be under a doctor's care. This is not a hospital. This is my home!"

"Control yourself. I will clean it up."

"I not only want it cleaned up. I want him out of here."

"I will ask him to leave."

"Ask him! Who does he think we are? Who do *you* think we are? Answer me, Mal. It is very important to me to know that at this moment."

"Lower your voice, woman, before you start to sound like a flaming hysteric."

"Do not tell me to lower my voice. And stop calling me woman. I do have a name. Or have you forgotten?"

"No, I have not."

"What is it, Mal? Tell me my name. Say it. I'd just like to hear you say it."

There was a long pause. Then Keenan said, "If you'll be good enough to get the mop and a bucket and some rags, I will go and clean the bathroom."

Mrs. Keenan strode heavily into the kitchen, her eyes brimming with tears, and she went from cabinet to broom closet to sink, gathering rags and sponge mop and filling a bucket with soapy water, taking everything around the corner. In a moment she was back, trying hard to compose herself.

"You'll have to excuse me," she said, taking a paper towel off a roll above the sink and wiping her eyes. "Last night he called me Keenie." A sob caught in her throat. "That's our dog," she said and bolted out of the kitchen.

Balzic chewed his lower lip, then stood and got more water. He was going to drink it and leave, but something told him to stay. He had an impulse to see who it was the Keenans were quarreling about.

He didn't have long to wait. He still had a third of a glass of water left when around the corner slouched a young man—he could have been anywhere from seventeen to twenty-five—wooly-haired, slender but unusually muscular, who was trying with hands and arms that would have fit a body forty or fifty pounds heavier and several inches taller to get a sleeveless denim jacket over a wrinkled and soiled tee-shirt.

His skin was pale, his eyes rheumy, and his nostrils wet. He looked as though he either suffered some allergy or had a cold or had recently been crying or vomiting. Because of the argument the Keenans had had, Balzic surmised the last.

"Afternoon," Balzic said.

"Is that a greeting, a declamation, or a policy position?" the boy-man said, staring, open-mouthed, at Balzic.

"Greeting."

"Then consider yourself greeted." The boy-man turned away from Balzic and looked thoughtfully at the cabinets. "Where the fuck're the glasses?" he asked, going from one cabinet to another.

"I think they're in this one," Balzic said, moving aside and pointing to the cabinet where he'd seen Mrs. Keenan get his.

"Hope you don't expect gratitude for that information," the boy-man said flatly, getting a glass and filling it.

"No."

"Good. Terrific. 'Cause I am philosophically opposed to that. I don't want anybody to get anything they don't expect." He drank the water, emptying the glass without pause, then filled it again.

Balzic couldn't avoid wondering about the disproportionate size of the boy-man's hands and arms. They were so large and obviously powerful that, taken with the boy-man's narrow body, they were grotesque.

The boy-man leaned against the sink and sipped more water. "So you're wondering about my hands, right?"

Balzic thought he had been more subtle. He nodded.

"To save your brain the sweat, my old man almost made the '36 Olympic gymnastics team. Almost, but not quite. So I was supposed to make the '60 or the '64 or the '68 or the '72 Olympic gymnastics team. That's what my old lady kept telling me my old man would've wanted. The thing was, I was never sure what my old man wanted 'cause he got himself killed saving the world from the Communist hordes in Korea. But that didn't matter to the old lady. She had me on the rings and parallel bars before I could walk." The boy-man finished his water and set the glass in the sink. "Satisfied?"

Balzic shrugged. "Are you?"

"Sat-is-fied. I like the first two syllables. Sat is. That's me. I's sat."

"I take it you don't do it anymore."

"You take that right, dad. You take it rickety-rackety right."

"What do you do?"

"You ask a lot of questions, man. You know that?"

"Yeah. I guess I do."

"Don't tell me. You're a cop."

"That's right."

"How about that. First test I've passed in a year."

"You a student?"

"No more I'm not." The boy-man canted his head. "And I'll tell you why, since I see you're gonna ask me. For the same reason I ain't going to the '72 Olympics. I got tired. I got tired doing giant swings, tired practicing dismounts, most of all I got tired trying to keep those fucking rings still."

"You'll have to explain that. I don't know very much about gymnastics."

"You never saw rings?"

"On television a couple of times I think."

"Well, they're just what they sound like. Two metal rings on the ends of a couple of straps. Somebody lifts you up to them and you start out with the rings as still as you can get them. Then you do your routine, man, whatever you do, but the important thing is you have to keep those rings still. Which ain't easy, man. I mean, they're on straps, you know? The more they move, the more points the judges knock off. And that's the way I felt about being little Stevie Student. Every time I took a test, every time I gave a paper in a seminar, I felt like I was just trying to keep those fucking rings still. And I just got tired, man. Sick and fucking tired. I got an ulcer as big as a silver dollar, man. That's how sick I got. And that's how sick I get."

"That why you throw up?"

"That's exactly why I throw up."

"And you don't bother to clean it up."

"You must've heard that little go-round between Keenan and his old lady."

"I couldn't help but hear it."

"So now you want to know why I don't clean it up, right? I mean, you throw up in somebody's house and make a mess, you're supposed to save the people the trouble and clean up after yourself, right?"

Balzic nodded.

"Man, nobody is going to save them their troubles. He wants to be a fucking bohemian and a college professor, chairman of the goddamn department no less—and he don't know how. And her, she wants to be married to the chairman of the department and a bohemian, in that order, plus she wants to be a liberated woman, and she don't know how to be that either. Meantime, they're both something straight out of a Romantic novel—no, Romantic Gothic. No. Romantic American Gothic. Percy and Mary Shelley moved to Rocksburg. . . . I figure I'm doing them a favor throwing up in their bathroom. They both need to look at a little puke with blood in it every once in a while. Just to let them know."

"Let them know what?"

"That it's there, man. That it smells. That it looks like nothing else. I go to my old lady's house every once in a while, and I barf in her bathroom, too."

"Just to let her know what it looks like?"

"Nah. She knows what it looks like. Just to remind her. She gave me the fucking ulcer. And him," the boy-man pointed at the ceiling, "the one mopping up up there, he just made it bigger. He took it from a quarter and turned it into a dollar."

"So you miss the toilet on purpose."

"Oh no, man. I make sure I hit part of the seat. To make it look like I tried. I mean, Christ, I could hit the toilet. I know when I got to heave, man. But every time I bend over, it looks like one of those goddamn rings, and I figure fuck it. I know it's not going to move, but I know I'm not going to stay fucking still."

"What's your name by the way?"

"Segalovich. Anthony George Segalovich, the third. How do you like that—the third, no less. You can bet your hat, ass, and elbow there ain't goin' to be a fourth."

"Why not?"

"Are you kidding me? This line ends with me, dad. The old lady couldn't even come up with an original name for me. Who the fuck ever heard of a hunky with 'the third' after his name. Jesus . . ."

"How'd you meet Keenan?"

"I met him at Slippery Rock State College. Old Slimey Pebble. Yeah. And when I met him, I actually still thought I was happy. Shit, phys-ed major, two-time all-around gymnastics champ of Pennsylvania state colleges, third place NCAA College Division my freshman year, second place my sophomore year. Man, I was getting ready for the university division, the AAU, for those guys from Penn State and Southern Illinois . . . then I had to take an elective course. So I shut my eyes and put my finger in the catalogue and the next thing I know I'm in his poetry class. And the next thing I know, I'm not a phys-ed major anymore. Nah. I'm an English major. All because of Doc-tor Keenan."

"Now you come and throw up in his house and miss the can on purpose," Balzic said. "That's some switch."

"Right, man, right. And his old lady goes crazy, and he walks around, juiced out of his skull and making pronouncements which he thinks are going to move the world right off its axis, you know, except the trees just keep right on growing."

"A lot must've happened."

"I wised up is what happened. He wants me to keep the rings as still as my old lady did. He walks around saying, 'Thisss shaking keepssss me steady,' and all that shit, but he don't have the first idea how much you can shake trying to keep those rings steady, man. He's never been on those rings. Not once in his life. That's why I miss his toilet, man. And that's why I don't even think about cleaning it up. Fuck him. And fuck his old lady, too."

"Doesn't it ever get a little boring?" Balzic said after a moment.

"What?"

"Getting even."

Segalovich snorted and turned toward the door. "Doesn't it ever get a little boring for you, always playing question man? Doesn't that ever bore you?"

"Not as long as the answers are interesting," Balzic said, smiling.

"Then, question man, all you have to do is find answer man, and your life will be endlessly interesting. Stimulating even. See you around." Segalovich stepped out onto the porch and let the storm door bounce against its spring.

Okay, smart guy, Balzic said to himself, figure that monkey out. Figure Keenan out. Figure his wife out. Hell, Balzic thought with a grunt, how can you figure them when their dog doesn't even know what it's supposed to be.

He put his glass in the sink, ran hot water in it, and was starting for the door when Mrs. Keenan came into the kitchen.

"I'm sorry," she said.

"For what?"

"For losing control. I don't usually lose control like that. Usually I am very much in control."

"Well, we all slip once in a while."

She sat on the stool farthest away from Balzic and rested her forehead on her hand. "I presume you met the source of our— my irritation."

"Segalovich you mean. Yeah. Met him and listened to his story."

"Oh, he will do that. He will tell you his story."

"Listen, uh, I'd like to ask you something that isn't very pretty."

"If it's about him, not much is."

"Yeah. Well, uh, does your husband know Segalovich can't stand him?"

"Oh Lordy. My husband—" Mrs. Keenan laughed bitterly. "My husband not only knows. My husband actually thinks it's healthy. There is something affirmative, something positive, even in loathing, that is what my husband says. After all, if you cannot loathe properly, then you cannot admire properly either. And poets must know the depths of their loathing, else they will never know the heights of their admiring—that's what my husband says. Do you want to hear more?"

"That's enough. I get the drift. But what about you?"

"I thought that was fairly obvious."

"Well, your feelings are pretty obvious, but I'd like to know more than that."

"What can I tell you then? We met him—"

"He told me that."

"What do you want to know then?"

"A minute ago you said something about your husband thinking that a poet ought to know his depths, and so forth. Am I right in thinking that because your husband puts up with Segalovich, that he, Segalovich, is also a poet?"

"Absolutely. Mal wouldn't have it any other way."

"Okay. So then how does he make his bread—his living?"

"That would take some telling."

"Well, you know, just briefly."

"I can't be brief about him. I know this isn't going to make any sense, but the reason I can't be brief is because I don't really know. I only have intimations of what he does. He used to go to school. He was working on his master's at Pitt, the main campus in Oakland. Then, he was doing all sorts of things: stealing, shoplifting, selling marijuana, selling practically anything anybody wanted to buy, writing papers for other students. Ostensibly, he had a job as a stock boy in one of the department stores in downtown Pittsburgh."

"What was that one thing you said—writing papers for other students? What's that mean?"

"Oh, that's a flourishing racket these days."

"Well I figured it was some kind of hustle, but exactly what kind of hustle is it?"

"Well, not having participated in such things when I was a student, I can only surmise."

"Go ahead."

"I imagine it's quite simple. A student's workload piles up, or he lets it pile up either because he can't or won't keep up, term papers come due, and when there is demand there is generally supply. I'm told it's a sellers' market."

"You mean one student pays another student to write his paper for him? Do his work for him, is that it?"

"That's what it comes down to. And from what I hear, it's gotten so far out of hand that it has even come up in the state legislature. Some university teachers are demanding that a law be passed making it some kind of crime."

"Yeah," Balzic said, "I remember hearing something about that, but since I didn't have anything to do with it, I didn't pay any attention to it. Well, let's get back to Segalovich. You know for a fact he did these things, or are you sure he wasn't maybe just bragging a little bit?"

"No, I don't know anything for a fact. And he most certainly does have a tendency to distort the truth in his favor—and that is being as polite as I can be."

"So you heard him talking about shoplifting and so on, but you're not sure he actually did these things."

"Well, I would have no way of being sure. All I know is that he hints at lots of things. And he always makes gross statements about himself. I've heard him say things like, oh, 'I have a bottom-less well of evil,' or, 'I have an endless capacity for the corrupt.' They weren't about particular things he had done—or claims to have done. They were just general comments like that, which, I suppose because he disgusts me so much, I chose to believe that he is as capable of those things as he tries to make himself out to be."

"But you really don't think he's just bragging."

"He may be. It may be his way of playing the poet. On the other hand . . ."

"On the other hand what?"

"Well, he certainly has no qualms about freeloading here. He'll take anything he can get from Mal. Money, food, anything. And things that are not Mal's to give."

"You?"

"Yes. He tried that once. Mal went out somewhere, probably to get another bottle of Scotch. And he even tried to take that."

"Without the details—was he clumsy?"

She canted her head, looking half-surprised, half-pleased. "You were very sure of that, weren't you?"

"Just a guess," Balzic said.

"Well, boorish is a better word than clumsy. He disgusted me."

"Did he get a little rough?"

"For a moment I thought he was going to, but then Mal drove up. We both could hear the car. He just backed away and sat down."

"How long ago was this?"

"That was when we were at Slippery Rock. Five years ago at least. Now, he never comes near me."

"How long's he been here? I take it he's been living here, am I right?"

"This time he's been here only a little more than a week. I try not to think how long. Maybe it hasn't been quite that long. Maybe I just think it has. It seems a month."

"Where's he from?"

"Someplace near Pittsburgh. I really don't know. He claims he stays on the road—that's how he puts it."

"Do you know where he was before he came here?"

"Oh, he's back and forth. I don't really care to know so I never ask. I just sit and hope he's not planning to stay when he shows up."

"Okay, Mrs. Keenan, thank you very much. I might be talking to you again. Hope you don't mind."

"Mind? Lordy, nobody's—what I mean to say is, I'll be glad to assist in any way I can." She smiled and then blushed. "I presume all this has to do with last night."

"More or less. Anyway, I might have to talk to you or your husband again. Thanks again. And thanks for the water."

Balzic stepped off the porch into the brilliant sunlight. Coming from the subdued light of the Keenans' kitchen, he felt for a second as though someone had thrown sand in his eyes.

His cruiser was scorching—handles, seat, steering wheel—and opening the vents wide relieved little. He stopped at the first gas station he came to as much to get out of the car as to get gas. As an afterthought, he asked the attendant if there was a phone. The attendant motioned toward the inside, and Balzic went in, mopping his face and neck, and called his station.

"Rocksburg Police, Sergeant Stramsky speaking."

"Vic? Balzic. Where's Clemente? It's not four o'clock yet, is it?"

"It's five till three. Angelo's sick. His old lady called me this morning to take his shift for him."

"What's wrong with him?"

"She didn't say. All she said was they were getting ready to go to the doctor's. Said he didn't sleep last night."

"What, that's the second time this month. You know what I think? I think Angelo's starting to wonder whether he ought to retire."

"Hell, that ain't for six months yet."

"Ah, Angelo worries. He wonders and he worries. So. What's happening?"

"You really want to know?"

"On second thought, unless the Japs bombed the Rocksburg Boat Club I don't want to know nothing. Did my wife call?"

"No. Johnson did though. He said for you to go on up to Troop A."

"Okay, Vic. And listen, don't spend all that overtime on kolbassi. Buy a little cabbage too, you know."

"Funny man."

"Vic, don't hang up. There's about six or seven mobile homes coming through. Should be around quarter to four. See if Angelo set up escorts for them, and if he didn't, you take care of it."

"Front and rear?"

"You got it," Balzic said and hung up. He went back to his cruiser, paid the attendant, and drove to Troop A Barracks.

The county detectives had gone, and the duty room was empty except for the radio operator and a typist. The typist told Balzic that Johnson was in his office, and Balzic found him leaning back in his chair, toying thoughtfully with a pencil.

"So what's the good news?" Balzic said, straddling a chair.

"You're going to love this," Johnson said, closing his eyes and rolling his head from side to side to loosen a kink in his neck.

Balzic lit a cigarette and waited.

"The Milocky girl got the word and took off."

"Took off? For where?"

"Who knows. She came home about an hour ago, her mother told her what happened, she stewed around for a while, and then, according to her mother, she picked up a couple bags and just walked out. The old man was visiting Mrs. Pisula in the hospital and it took Mrs. Milocky a while to reach him."

"And?"

"They drove around looking for her and finally got around to the bus station. The nearest thing anybody could figure was that she caught a bus to Pittsburgh. Christ only knows where she'll go after that."

"You called the Pittsburgh police."

"Yeah, sure. Right before I called your station. About forty minutes ago. I don't know what the fuck they're doing. How long's it take to check the bus stations?"

"Beautiful," Balzic said. "I take it you decided she's it. The lab came up zilch, right?"

"Double zilch. Nothing from her fingernails, nothing from the floor, all the prints in the room were hers—except for the ones on the door which are yours—plus that one lousy smudge on the paper. Man, I read through all those letters and I have to agree with you. If anybody's going to tell us anything, it's going to be Miss Milocky."

"How about the rest of the people who were in her classes?"

"Nothing. I'll tell you, Mario, I never saw anybody as cut off from people as this girl was. She may as well have been in solitary for the last nine months. Nobody knows anything about her." Johnson shook his head wearily. "I got two men nosing around at the campus, but they just keep reporting back goose eggs. They've talked to the manager of the student union, the manager of the bookstore, librarians, janitors, everybody. Nobody can remember talking to her. It's fucking unbelievable. I was just sitting here thinking about it. Never mind that she got murdered. Imagine what her life was like, being that separated, that isolated. I'm really starting to feel for her uncle."

"Yeah, and the poor bastard thought she was coming out of it. Well, goddammit, Walk, she talked to somebody."

"Sure. But who? How about you, you get anything from that Keenan?"

"I got more out of his wife than I did out of him. All he wants to do is make jokes and drink."

"What did the wife say?"

"First of all, Keenan is certain the girl wasn't writing her own papers, then the wife tells me that's a pretty big hustle these days. She told me something I forgot, which was that it's getting so bad some professors are lobbying in Harrisburg to make it illegal."

"What is? What's the hustle?"

"Just what I said. There are people who are making money writing papers for other students."

"Oh, yeah, yeah. I remember hearing that in Harrisburg the last time I was there. But, shit, I always thought that was a hustle."

"It may have been, but apparently it's never been this widespread before. Anyway, you put that with the information in those letters and it's twenty to one that's what we're dealing with. What the hell else would she've been talking about? She kept on urging her to do it—where are those letters?"

Johnson nodded to the corner of his desk, and Balzic leaned over and picked up the manila envelope. He rooted through the letters until he found what he was looking for. "Here, listen to this one: 'Do what we talked about over Thanksgiving. Do it, please, Jan.' And this one. 'Quit feeling guilty about doing that, Jan. They pay lots more than you're paying for it, believe me. There are people here who make a living from it. It's as much a part of the place as pot. Nobody even wonders about whether it's done; all they wonder about is whether they should do it, though, of course, they also wonder if they can afford it.' See what I mean? I mean, what—"

"Hey, Mario, friend, buddy, compadre, I've read it," Johnson said, standing and stretching. "I've read them twice. The fact is, the only name mentioned in any of them is Keenan's, and nobody's going to tell me that the guy teaches a class and then writes papers for his students for money. Christ, that doesn't make any sense at all. Why do the work? If he wants money, why not a straight bribe for a good grade?"

"Agreed."

"Okay, so then where does that leave us?"

110

"Maybe they advertise."

"I'm ahead of you. One of the things I told my people down on the campus was to check all the bulletin boards, see if there was anything that looked even remotely like a pitch."

"And?"

"Everything posted on the boards was ordered off on a memo from the president's office. The boards had to be cleared by the time the last exam was given yesterday. Seems they don't have too much space and they needed all they could get for information for the summer school."

"So it's in the garbage, right?"

"Right. And I already talked to the sanitation department—"

"Oh shit," Balzic said.

"Right. City ordinance number-who-knows says that all garbage must be buried in a landfill the same day it's collected. All of a sudden the whole fucking world gets efficient."

"Christ," Balzic said, "I'll lay a hundred against one if I wanted to go to summer school, if I wanted to do that today, I'd have to go to some dean's house to get the information. It wouldn't be on any goddamn bulletin board if I was looking to find out how to go about it. And if I don't put my garbage cans in exactly the right place, I can start a rat farm waiting for somebody to tell me why they didn't pick it up."

"Well, what the hell, suppose the guy we're looking for is in the business of writing papers. He couldn't make a living off a school as small as this one. He'd have to be working everywhere he can, right? I mean, there are a hell of a lot of colleges around here."

"Three big ones in Pittsburgh," Balzic said, "plus all the small ones. There gotta be twenty, twenty-five within fifty miles."

"So? We run them down. We don't have any choice. I'll—"

The phone rang then and Johnson picked it up.

"Speaking," he said and then said to Balzic, "It's Pittsburgh. Yeah, go ahead . . . Greyhound eastbound . . . Ocean City . . .

yeah, certainly we'll get a mugshot . . . yeah, I'll put it out on our wire . . . hey, man, thank you. I'll take it from here." Johnson hung up. "That guy was something else. He tells me to make sure I get a mugshot and put it out. He must've just got promoted."

"They got her?"

"Yeppie. Ticket seller remembered her because she was very nervous and he asked her if she was all right, and she said no, because a very good friend of hers just died. She's on her way to Ocean City—well, you heard that. So, all I do is get the route and have her picked up. Christ, what could be easier?" Johnson smiled. "How's that for luck?"

"The last time I thought about it, I figured there were at least two kinds of luck."

"Hey, pessimist, look at it this way. If we miss her all the way to Philly, we just wake up the Jersey state people."

"As long as she goes where the ticket says."

"Why wouldn't she? You called her right before. You said it would be a dynamite situation if she found out she needed a prop as much as she thought the Pisula girl did. So? She just found out she needed one. And it looks like there's none around. So she's running where there is one. If she's half that predictable, she's going where the ticket says. I don't think there's any sweat."

"Your confidence in my ideas, lieutenant," Balzic said, "is enough to make a man think he still has a right to go to swimming pools."

"Do what?"

"You know, when you hit a certain age, the legs get a little whiter and the gut hangs and you get a little nervous being around all the young snappers. The ones with the flat bellies and the tight asses. You wonder how they see you."

"Mario, I didn't think you thought about those things anymore."

"Hey, are you kidding? The only time I go to the pool is to watch my daughters swim for the rec board team."

□

There was nothing to do now but wait. If Frances Milocky was on a Greyhound going to Ocean City, New Jersey, it was simple. A state cruiser would be waiting at one of the stops, if not one, then the next. Balzic knew Johnson knew how to coordinate things like this. It was what Johnson did best.

Still, Balzic fretted about it. Frances Milocky went to the largest university in the state. Unlike Janet Pisula, she had to have made many acquaintances. Balzic remembered the letter in which she wrote about going to Scranton with somebody for a weekend. Scranton was east. Suppose she changed her mind about going to Ocean City. Suppose she—ah, suppose, suppose, suppose, Balzic groused. I could sit here supposing until my ass turns to plaster and winds up on somebody's ceiling. Best thing for me to do is relieve Stramsky so he can eat. . . .

He drove to his own station, told Stramsky to take an hour off, and settled himself at the radio console. He found a deck of cards and started to lay out a game of solitaire, then snapped his fingers and went to a phone and dialed his home.

His wife answered. "Mario, where the hell are you?"

"Some hello I get. Where you think I am? At the station."

"Well, I wish you'd come home. I want to talk to you."

"You can't talk to me now? I could swear you were talking to me."

"Mario, don't get smart. This is important and I can't tell what you look like over the phone. I want to see you when I talk to you."

"Awww, you just want to look at my face. I like you, too."

"Mario—will you stop. This is serious. Your mother told me something, and I want to know what it's about. You been holding out on me."

"Holding out on you? About what?"

"About my brother, that's what. And don't play dumb. I know you."

"Listen, Ruth, I don't know what Ma told you," Balzic lied, knowing too well that she knew him. She didn't need to see his

113

face to know when he was trying to con her.

"Listen, you," she said, "ever since I started talking about going to Tony's cottage, I can see something's wrong. And don't try to tell me you didn't say anything to your mother. 'Cause she told me something and I want to know the rest of it. If you have something against Tony I want to hear it. 'Cause I'm not going to spend a weekend with the two of you in that little place and not know there's a war going on behind my back."

"Ruth, listen. Maybe you're right. Maybe we ought to talk about this when we're looking at each other. You started out okay, but your tone's getting a little sharp, and if I told you over the phone, I think you're going to get madder than you should."

"Mario, is it that bad? Is he doing something illegal?"

"No, nothing like that. Look. Give me some time to think how I want to say it, okay? And I promise, I won't hold out. I'll give you the whole story, okay?"

"Promise?"

"I promise. It may take me a couple days to figure how I want to say it, but you'll hear it."

"Okay," she said, her tone softer now. "But don't take too long, okay? If we're going, I'd like to have a couple days to get ready."

"You'll have time," he said. "So how's everybody?"

"The girls are all right. Ma's having one of her bad days. Her back's bothering her. But she doesn't want me fussing over her so it can't be too bad. Listen, when are you coming home?"

"I don't know. Something happened. I'll probably be here for a while. Maybe most of the night. Tomorrow, too."

"So when are we going to have this talk?"

"Will you quit worrying? I told you I'll tell you and I will. I just can't do it right now, okay?"

"Okay, Mario. I'll see you when you get here."

She hung up and Balzic let out a long sigh and cleared his throat. Whatever he told her would have to be said softly, with the right words. This was touchy. He was trying to think of his first words to Ruth when he finally got around to explaining to her what was really bothering him about her brother, talking to himself at first, and then whispering to hear how the words sounded. He thought for a moment he had the perfect way to approach it but lost the thought when he swiveled around and saw A. J. Scumaci standing on the other side of the counter. Balzic had not heard him come in.

Angelo Joseph Scumaci—A.J. to those who indulged him, Johnny Scum to those who didn't—his eyes wildly confessional, swayed from foot to foot, his battered black fedora going in eccentric circles in his arthritic hands.

"A.J., what the hell do you want? If you want to borrow some bread, say so, but save the stories. I don't want to hear anything."

"Mario Chief, I didn't mean to do it, honest to God, I didn't. I don't know what makes me do these things. I'm not right. Everybody knows that. I'm dangerous—"

"A.J., the only time you were ever dangerous was when you used to cook in Romeo's place." Balzic hung his head and laced his fingers and stretched his hands in front of him.

"I mean it," A.J. said. "I should be put away. I shouldn't be allowed to walk the streets. I murdered a girl and I should be put away for the rest of my natural life."

Balzic went through the lifting door in the counter and took A.J. by the arm and led him toward the door. "A.J., you never had a natural life and you're never going to have a natural life. Now get outta here. You want a free ride on the state, do what I told you a hundred times already. Go sign up for welfare. Now go. Out."

"Mario Chief, on my mother's soul I murdered a girl—"

"If you murdered all the girls you said you did, A.J., there wouldn't be a woman alive in Pennsylvania. Now please get outta here. Don't make me lose patience with you."

A.J. shuffled out, but turned around on the porch and stared glumly through the screen. "Mario Chief, could you please—"

"How much?"

"Two—a dollar would be plenty."

Balzic reached in his pocket, brought out some bills, and

held up two dollars. A.J. opened the door far enough to get his arm through. He snatched the bills, jammed them into his hat, and pulled it down to his ears. "God bless you, Mario Chief. I won't forget this. You know me. A.J. never forgets nothing. A.J. remembers all the details."

"Yeah, sure. Go on now. Go someplace." Balzic went back to the radio console, shaking his head, sighing, swearing, asking himself what he'd done to deserve A.J. for a penance. Why A.J., he asked himself. Why not go to Rome and go across St. Peter's Square on my elbows and toes? . . .

He picked up the cards and dealt out another game of solitaire, then another, and another, losing thirty-some times before he quit counting. A few hands later, he stacked the deck, put it back in its box, and tried to tell himself he had been concentrating, which he knew was a ridiculous lie.

All the while he'd been playing, he had been worried by the idea that Frances Milocky wouldn't be able to tell them any more than they already knew. He was sure Keenan was right: Janet Pisula had not been doing her own work. He was just as sure that she had made a deal with somebody to do her work at Frances Milocky's insistence. He was equally sure that, unless they were dealing with a transient as Johnson had first worried about, unless Frances Milocky had a name for them, they'd be no further ahead than they were now. They'd have to run down every piddling, puzzling little note on every college bulletin board in three counties, all on the long chance that those notes were still available, all on the guess that the somebody who had written Janet Pisula's papers was the person who'd killed her, and all that on the even longer chance that that somebody advertised that way. Then there was the reason . . .

Suppose it had been that someone who had written her papers. Why would he kill her? Surely not because she owed him money. If it had been that, then why was there all that money in her desk and in her wallet?

And rape? Forget it. The girl still had her hymen. Sodomy? Nothing doing there either. Grimes's report made a point of noting the absence of sperm or semen anywhere in or on the body.

Which left the blank sheet of paper. And left Balzic with the idea he'd heard from Mo Valcanas: Hemingway blowing his head off because he couldn't make a sentence anymore. Was it that simple? Was that why a man killed himself? If that was so, would a man kill someone else because he couldn't make a sentence anymore? Balzic chewed his teeth. The whole idea, as simple as it had seemed when Valcanas explained it, now seemed as porous and fragile and mysterious as cobwebs.

Yet there had to be a parallel, something Balzic could understand, something he could reconcile himself to, and he fumed about the duty room, telling himself that if only he thought about it enough, he would find it. A half-hour later, he still had not got anywhere closer to the substance of the idea than he'd been when he put the cards away. He'd never felt more inadequate in his life.

The screen door jerked open, and Stramsky, swearing and scowling, came in and stood on the other side of the counter. He put his head in his hands and nearly shouted at Balzic. "Sometimes, Mario, my old lady makes me so fucking mad. She is so goddamn dumb sometimes. Most of the time she's okay, understand, but there are times, Jesus H. Kee-rist . . ."

Balzic started to smile and then to laugh.

"Hey, it's not funny, Mario."

"Vic, you're beautiful."

"What the hell are you talking about? Beautiful, Christ. My old lady just went out and made a deal to sell toys. So she can have Christmas money, she says. The only thing is she don't read the fine print in the contract she signs, and now she gives me the good news she got to come up with five hundred for her inventory. I say where the hell we gonna get five bills, and she says she already borrowed it from a finance company. I say how can you do that without my signing, and she tells me she forged my name. She does all this last week and just now she tells me about it, and you, you goddamn half-breed, you stand there laughing and telling me I'm beautiful. Jesus fuck!"

117

Balzic went through the lifting door and put his arm around Stramsky's shoulders. "Vic, Vic, I don't mean to laugh, honest to God I don't. And I can appreciate your situation—"

"You can, huh? You know what that fucking loan is going to cost us? That five bills is going to cost seven hundred and thirty-something by the time we get through paying it off. And you can *appreciate* my situation! I said, Jesus Christ, woman, there went all the profits you think you're going to make from those toys—that's if you sell them—and she says, oh no, I'll make a terrific profit. She thinks she's going to make so much money she's going to pay off that loan in twelve months. That's what she actually says to me. And you, you bastard, you *appreciate* my situation."

"I do, Vic, honest to Christ I do. It's just that I was sitting in here breaking my head trying to figure something out, and I couldn't, and you just walked in and laid it out for me. Believe me, I'm not laughing at you. I'm grateful. No shit, I am. And I'll tell you what. I'll call Mo Valcanas for you and ask him to get you out of it, how's that?"

"She signed, Mario! How's anybody going to get me out of it? She signed. The toy contract may be a hustle, but that don't cut nothing with the finance company. They don't care how you spent the money. You signed, you pay."

"Yes, but fraudulently, Vic. Fraudulently. She forged your name, right? Listen, if anybody knows how to get you out of this, it's Valcanas—that is, if you want out."

Stramsky hung his head. "Oh, Mario. You should've seen her face. She wants to do it so bad. How can I make her get out of it? She was so excited she was going to make some money by herself. This is the first time since we been married, you know? She never worked, you know that. And she really wants to do it. I almost got to admire her guts."

"Well, you do what you want, then let me know. You want out, I'll get Valcanas for you. If not, just say so, okay? Just believe me, I wasn't laughing at you."

"I believe you," Stramsky said. "I just hope it works out. You want to play some gin?"

"Not now. I'm going up to Troop A. I want to talk to Johnson and wait it out with him. They're picking up a girl I want to talk to. I'll give you a call later unless something comes up. Take it easy, Vic. It'll be all right," Balzic said, going out to his cruiser.

"We got her," Johnson said as Balzic walked into Troop A's duty room. "Picked her up in Blairsville. She should be here in thirty, thirty-five minutes."

"That's the second best news I heard today," Balzic said.

"Second best? Christ, what do you want? What was first?"

"Ah, I'll tell you after we hear what she has to say."

"Okay with me. You eat yet?"

Balzic shook his head.

"Let's go get one of those good antipastos Funari makes. He's still in business, isn't he?"

"Oh yeah."

"Still making those antipastos? It's too hot for anything else."

"They deliver now. We don't have to go."

"Nah, I want a couple beers too. Besides, I got to get out of this place for a while."

"Let's go then."

In Johnson's cruiser on the way, Johnson asked, "So what's this first best news you heard today?"

"One of my people's old lady got sucked into a toy-selling thing."

"That's good?"

"Good, bad, who knows. It really doesn't matter. What mattered was the way he looked and the way he was talking when he told me about it."

"He couldn't have looked too good."

"As a matter of fact, he looked mad enough to strangle her."

"You serious?"

"Yeah I'm serious. He wouldn't do it, but he looked like he wanted to. And that was the thing that's been bothering me about this Pisula girl. Why'd the guy do it, you know? That was really

119

bugging me. He didn't rape her, he didn't rob her, so what's with him?"

"I figure he's a psycho, especially because of that paper."

"Yeah, but, Walk, nobody's just psycho. They're psycho for a reason. Lots of reasons. So he left a message, the paper. But why? I mean, I'm not saying I know, but at least now I think I got a start."

"Which is?"

"She was dumb."

Johnson mulled that over as he pulled into the parking lot of Funari's Bar and Restaurant. He looked at Balzic a few times but didn't say anything until they were inside at a table and taking sips of their first beers. Then, after the waitress had taken their food order, Johnson leaned over and said incredulously, "She was dumb?"

"Yeah, yeah, I know. It sounds ridiculous, but that's it. I mean, she was. Remember what her uncle told us? She went from skipping grades to barely keeping up. I got more or less the same story from all her teachers. Dumb—literally. Practically a mute. Which wasn't her fault, but that's the way she was. You can't get around that."

"And a guy kills her because she's dumb?"

"Yeah. He loses patience with her. He gets frustrated about something. I don't know what. But I'll bet it was something she wouldn't tell him. Wouldn't or couldn't, I don't know which."

"Then, just for the sake of argument, Mario, then what the hell was she doing with just her pants on? Why don't you think he killed her 'cause she wouldn't come across?"

"I don't know why I'm not thinking that way, but I'm not. Maybe it's because of the paper."

"You're thinking if he killed her because she wouldn't screw him, he would've just left, is that it?"

"I'm not sure," Balzic said. "But I think that's the way I'm thinking. I mean, that piece of paper took some thought. It isn't something a guy in a panic does. If he's panicked, all he wants to do is get the hell out of there."

"Okay, then tie it up with her being dumb," Johnson said, screwing up his face.

"I don't know. Maybe he's telling the world she couldn't write. Maybe he thought that was something really terrible. If he's in the kind of business we think he's in, maybe he thought all his customers were extra stupid. Maybe they pissed him off. Christ, I've known more than one bartender who couldn't stand drunks. I even met a doctor once who really couldn't stand sick people. He said they were sick because they were all stupid and didn't take care of themselves. I'm not sure where I'm going with all this. All I'm saying is this is a start for a motive. Christ knows we got the body. But without a motive?" Balzic spread his arms wide.

"I don't know, Mario. You always were one for the psychology bit. Me, I just get them off the streets. Let the head-benders figure them out."

"Well, listen, Walk, look at it this way. How many times have you wanted to cream somebody for doing something stupid? One of your own people—how many times? How many times have I? How many times has anybody? Why do teachers paddle kids? Why do parents? What the hell business are we in, you and me?"

"Oh, come on, Mario. There's a hell of a difference between what's dumb and what's illegal."

The waitress brought the antipastos then and asked if they wanted more beer.

Johnson nodded to her, but Balzic just handed over his glass to her and demanded of Johnson: "Well? What's the difference?"

"To answer the thing about teachers and parents paddling kids, most teachers and parents I know don't really paddle kids for not being able to learn. They do it because the kids misbehave."

Balzic nodded vigorously. "Sure. That's what they say. But most misbehavior is nothing but kids doing what grownups think are dumb things."

"Not only dumb, Mario. Sometimes dangerous. To themselves as well as to other people."

"Yeah, but dangerous things are usually dumb things. Things that aren't good or sensible or reasonable or prudent. How many court decisions go with that one, that prudent?"

"A lot. No argument there."

"Well what's prudent mean? When a judge says a guy did not act in a prudent manner, what's he talking about? I mean, hey, when you get right down to it, if the guy was really prudent, how'd he get grabbed in the first place? What the hell, man, prisons are for screwups. People too dumb to not get caught."

"I think you're oversimplifying it."

"Tell me how."

"Right now I just want to eat. But don't let me stop you. Keep talking," Johnson said, biting into a ripe olive and chewing around the pit.

"Look," Balzic said, gesturing with a piece of Genoa salami, "right now there's a second-story guy I know, and I know he is. Christ, I've had him in so many line-ups in front of people who just caught a glimpse of him that he gives me the rag that I ought to put him on the force. His whole story is burglary, beginning to end. You know how many convictions? One. When he was eighteen. That's like ten years ago. He did six months in the workhouse in Allegheny County. Since then, nothing. The bastard's a pro. He works alone, he never looks the same way twice any two times I've had him picked up, he lives quiet—that fuckin' guy must've knocked over three hundred houses in the last ten years and nobody can come up with even circumstantial on him. You know what he says? He says three things whenever I pick him up. He says, 'Hi, Chief,' 'When's the line-up?' and 'Can I go now?' The last time was the first time he ever said anything else. He said, 'Geez, I been in here so much, maybe you oughta give me a job.'

"Right now," Balzic went on, "there's a lot of noise in Harrisburg about no-fault car insurance, no-fault divorce, and what's the word they're kicking around about drugs? Decriminalizing, that's it. There's a lot of noise. Maybe these things will happen, maybe not. But as it stands now, practically everything is the adversary system. Somebody's at fault, and somebody got hurt, and whoever's at fault has got to give up some time or some money. At least in the civil system, whoever gets burned has a shot at compensation. In the criminal system, whoever gets hurt is supposed to be satisfied his taxes are keeping the criminal off the streets, which is supposed to deter others." Balzic snorted. "Deterring others, Christ. Some satisfaction that must be. I can see me running a gas station or a grocery and some junkie comes in, cleans out my register, and then blows it all on three fixes before he gets grabbed. Then I go give my testimony against him and watch him get one to three and five years pro. I keep on paying taxes to support the whole goddamn system, meantime I don't get my money back, the money the junkie copped in the first place. There's no provison for it."

"What's all this have to do with killing a girl because she was dumb?" Johnson said, smiling ironically at Balzic.

"Not a goddamn thing. You just said to keep talking. You wanted to eat."

"Well, it was a hell of a speech while it lasted. You sounded for a while there like you wanted to be a lawyer for the Chicago Seven."

"Oh boy," Balzic said, laughing, "you should've heard me last winter when I talked to the Lions Club. Three or four guys walked out. You could've heard a flower hit the floor when I sat down, and the president of the club, Christ, he looked like he wished he'd shown a travelogue or something."

"What did you talk about?"

"More of the same I just gave you. You'd be surprised how little the squares want to hear how the criminal justice system really works. What they really want to know is what a good job I'm doing keeping the dopers and long-hairs out of their neighborhood."

"What kind of job are you doing?"

"Aw, shut up and eat, willya? Jesus."

Frances Milocky, disheveled from hours of riding, was waiting in the duty room when they got back to Troop A Barracks. She sat on the front edge of the chair, her face vacant, her left leg crossed over her right, her foot swinging, her fingers turning a pack of cigarettes end over end on her knee.

Johnson introduced himself and Balzic and then asked, "Do your parents know where you are?"

She nodded, her long, straight hair falling over her cheek. "I just called them," she said.

"Would you like some coffee? A Coke maybe?"

"Nothing, thank you."

"I think it would be better if we talked back in my office," Johnson said, leading the way back to it. "We won't have to put up with the radio."

The girl lifted herself out of the chair with great effort and followed Johnson with labored steps, her sandals sliding along the floor. Once inside Johnson's office, she slumped into the chair Balzic held for her.

"Miss Milocky," Johnson began, "I'm sure this isn't going to be pleasant for you, so if there's anything we can do to make it easier, just say the word, okay?"

She chewed her lower lip and nodded, turning the cigarette pack end over end against her knee as she'd been doing in the duty room.

"You ought to know, Miss Milocky," Johnson said, "that we've read the letters you wrote to Janet Pisula."

"I guessed that you did, otherwise you wouldn't want to talk to me. Of course, you could've heard about me from Uncle Mike. Janet's uncle I mean. He's not mine. I've just called him that for so long I sort of think of him as my uncle. Anyway, he would've told you about me."

"He did. But what we're really interested in is some of the things you wrote to Janet. You mention what seems to us—the chief here and myself—at least two men. One of them you named, and we know he was Janet's English teacher last year. Keenan."

"Yes," Frances said, nodding slowly. "Janet was terrified of him."

"Was there any particular reason?"

"You have to understand, lieutenant. Janet was afraid of all men. It didn't have anything to do with sex. Don't get that idea. It was because of the accident."

"Her uncle told us about that."

"Well, then you know. Then he must've told you about the man who caused the accident, the one who came to see her in the hospital."

"Yes, we know about him. The one who told her she should've died."

Frances nodded and pressed her fingers against her forehead. "Well, you must have figured out what that did to her."

"We have a pretty rough idea, yes. But we'd like to hear anything you can tell us."

She shook her head impatiently. "What can I tell you? It was traumatic, that's all. Not the kind of dopey little things people are always calling traumatic. That was a real trauma. It was a real wound. And it never healed. Someday maybe it might have. I mean, coming here to school, getting out of her house and on her own. Nobody will ever know what kind of courage that took. She went into a kind of frenzy whenever we'd be someplace and some young guys would want to talk to us. I could feel her shaking beside me. It was real hell for her to meet strangers. And if they were young guys, it was all she could do to keep from passing out, and I mean literally passing out."

"We gathered as much, but what in particular was there about Keenan? Or was there anything about him?"

"No. I don't think there was anything special about him except that he used to harp about the open admission policy the college had, and if there was anything particular, it had to be that. I mean, Janet had enough reason for feeling that she didn't belong. Anywhere. Not just in college."

"What's an open admission policy?" Balzic said.

"Anybody gets in who wants to. There aren't any prerequisites. As long as you have the tuition, you have to be admitted."

"And you advised her to transfer out of Keenan's class, is that it?" Johnson asked.

"Yes. She didn't have to listen to him. She'd been told once that she didn't belong. That once was enough for anybody, more than enough."

"You also advised her about something else," Balzic said.

"I was always advising Janet. I may be the world's greatest non-stop adviser. I know everything. Except it turns out I didn't know very much at all." Tears started to roll down her cheeks. She blinked a few times but didn't wipe them away.

"What didn't you know?" Balzic said.

"Oh God, what didn't I know! Everything. I didn't know how really terrible it must have been for her. And it was so easy for me to do cartwheels on the sidelines. A regular pom-pom girl of the mind, that's what I was. Bouncing up and down and yelling Janet locomotives."

"I'm sorry," Johnson said. "You just lost me."

"Oh, you must've seen football games. The cheerleaders spell out the name of their team. They yell a letter, the crowd yells the letter back."

"That's what you were for Janet?"

"That's what it turns out I was. Without intending it, but I must've really thought I knew what I was doing, I must've actually believed that all I had to do was cheer long enough and loud enough and Janet would just go out and beat her problem, as though it was a game or something. The really stupid thing is that I didn't realize it until I was on the bus."

"Where were you going?"

"I don't know. I really don't. All I could think of was I had to go somewhere. I just couldn't stay around and face Uncle Mike, even though I knew he wouldn't think I was responsible. But I felt I was. And I felt so stupid. The worst was that my major is psychology. And I went to Penn State actually thinking I was already a clinical psychologist because of the miracle I'd performed on Janet. All I had to do was get the degrees. What did anybody really have to teach me? My God, I'd guided a practically autistic girl into emotional stability just by cheering . . ." She broke down completely then, sobbing into her hands and swaying on the edge of the chair.

Minutes passed before she got control of herself and when she did, she said, "I never thought how cruel and mean good intentions can be. The best intentions. I've heard that platitude about history being bloody with good intentions, or however it goes. I can't even think of it now. But I never thought for a minute I could ever be stupid enough to be one of those people, those super sentimental creeps who think they have all the answers and really believe they know what's best for other people. But, well, here I am." She tried to smile but had to bite her lower lip to keep it from trembling.

"Uh, Frances," Balzic said, "did you advise Janet to get somebody to do her work for her, to write her papers—"

"Yes," she interrupted him. "You have to understand. All Janet wanted to be was a secretary. She didn't want to be a reporter or a novelist or a poet or any other kind of writer. Janet wasn't stupid. She was slow—what other people would call slow —because she had a hard time articulating her thoughts because for a long time everything she thought was so terrible, she just refused to talk about what she was thinking. Then, when she finally did start to talk, she went through a period when she questioned everything, when unless she had a completely satisfactory answer for why she was doing something, she just wouldn't do it. Then, when she started to talk with me pretty easily about what she was thinking I persuaded her to write everything down so we could talk about it—oh, God, she was my project. I had all these methods, these asinine therapeutic methods. . . ."

"I know this is tough for you, Frances," Balzic said, "but you're thinking about yourself now and, uh, you're feeling a little too sorry for you now and you're not doing us much good."

"I know, but I have to give you some background, otherwise

you won't understand why I told Janet to pay somebody to write her papers for her."

"Okay," Balzic said, "tell it the way you want."

She took a deep breath. "Okay. Well, Janet started to write everything down and then we'd talk about it. Her dreams, her questions, her reactions to things that happened to her. They were really amazing things. She had a really terrific insight into herself. That's why I never believed she was badly injured in the accident, or if she was injured, brain damaged, then all it did was bring her down to my level. Not in school. In school she just barely got passing grades, but that wasn't because she couldn't do the work. She'd get sidetracked. She was always questioning why she was doing something. She never took anything for granted. Not the simplest things.

"Like once," she went on, "she was supposed to write a term paper, a research paper with at least ten references in the bibliography, an outline, footnotes, the whole bit. But she never did any research at all—not in the library. She wrote the whole paper on the act of writing. The whole paper was a description of her hand and a pen and the movements and thought which directed the movements. Her teacher didn't know how to react to it—or to Janet. She gave Janet a D because she said Janet just didn't do the assignment. And that's why she had trouble in school. She did exceptional work, only it was never what she'd been assigned to do, and then when the teachers called her in to talk about it, Janet wouldn't say anything to defend what she'd done."

"Is that what happened in Keenan's class?" Balzic said.

"That's exactly what happened."

"So you told her to get somebody to do the papers for her."

"I had to. Because if she went on the way she was, she was going to flunk and I knew she'd just get the guilties over spending her uncle's money and disappointing him—which he wouldn't have been—but that didn't matter to her. It was a choice I really forced on her. I mean, I knew if she paid somebody to do the papers, she'd pass, and then she could get on with what she really wanted to be good at: typing, shorthand, bookkeeping. That was really all she wanted to be. A secretary. And it isn't any great mystery why. She understood it very well."

"Not that there's anything wrong with that, but why did she?" Johnson asked.

"She wanted to get a strange man's approval. She was absolutely honest about it. She used to say that just once in her life she wanted to have the confidence in a few skills so she could ask a strange man for a job and he would give it to her and then he would have to give her raises because of her competence. She never wanted anything to be given to her that she didn't deserve, but she desperately wanted approval from a man she didn't know."

"I don't get that," Balzic said. "Didn't she see Keenan as a strange man? I mean, why wouldn't she try to get his approval? Why didn't she try to write papers that would suit him?"

"In Janet's mind, getting a grade from a teacher wasn't approval. That was just a grade. Approval to her meant getting money to live on. Earning her way was the same in her mind as life itself, especially if the money came from a stranger. Do you see what I mean? I mean, being a good secretary, getting a job from a stranger, being competent, gaining the stranger's approval, all that would have wiped out what that other man said. The one who killed her mother and father and told her she should've died. It may not sound logical to you, but it is psychologically sound, and it was how Janet interpreted her life."

"She had this all figured out?" Balzic asked.

"Oh, yes. She was completely honest about it."

"Then why did you put her in a position where she'd have to be dishonest?" Johnson asked. "I mean, that's what it looks like you did to me."

Frances hung her head. "I know it sounds like that, but what else could I tell her to do? If she kept up the way she was going, she'd get hung up on something that was very important to her but didn't have anything to do with the assignment. And then she wouldn't have been able to become what she wanted. That's why she had the most trouble in English classes. All through school.

As long as it was grammar, she was fine. But when she had to write something, when she saw that blank sheet of paper in front of her, she was just overwhelmed by the possibilities of what she could put on it."

Balzic and Johnson exchanged surprised frowns.

"Would you say that again?" Johnson said.

"What?"

"What you said about the blank sheet of paper and the possibilities."

"Well, I don't know how to say it any differently. She'd look at the paper and she'd say something like, 'I can put anything here I want.' And then she'd say, 'Now what do I want here? There are thousands of words I could use. Which ones do I really want here?' That's the way she used to talk about it."

"So you told her to get somebody who was all business, is that it? Somebody who'd get the assignment from her and wouldn't get hung up. He'd just get right to it," Balzic said.

"Yes. Otherwise, she'd spend hours picking the first word."

"Well," Johnson said, "that leaves only one thing. Do you know who that person was?"

"I don't know him, no. I arranged it through a girl Janet and I knew who went to Pitt in Oakland. I'll have to think a minute to remember his name. It was unusual. I mean I thought it was unusual because his first name was Italian but his last name was Slavic. Serbian or Croatian probably."

"You could be talking about the chief here," Johnson said, smiling vaguely at Balzic. "He's got an Italian first name. Mario. What was your father, Mario? Serbian?"

"Yeah," Balzic said, rubbing his mouth and chin. Then he canted his head and said to Frances, "Wait a minute. That guy's name wasn't Anthony, was it?"

"Yes, that's it. Anthony—oh, it starts with an S."

"Segalovich?"

"Yes, that's it. How did you know?"

"How did I know, huh? How did I know." Balzic was snorting and fumbling for his notebook. "I had him, right in my lap

I had him and was too dumb not to put two with two." He found the Keenans' phone number and address and dialed the phone on Johnson's desk.

"Mario, what're you talking about?"

"I had him. This afternoon at Keenan's house. He was who they were arguing about. Didn't I tell you about him?"

"No," Johnson said.

"I had to tell you. That's how I found out about the paper-writing hustle."

"You told me Keenan's wife told you."

"Yeah, but she told me 'cause I was curious about him. I wanted to know how he made his living. How do you like those potatoes, huh? Right in my mitts I had him. And boy, do things start to fall into place now—hello, Mrs. Keenan? This is Mario Balzic, the chief of—"

"I remember, chief. Can I help you?"

"I hope so, Mrs. Keenan. You remember that guy who was at your house this afternoon?"

"I can't very well not remember him."

"Yeah, well I know you said you weren't sure where he lived, but maybe your husband can, and I'd—"

"That person—for want of a better word—is here right now. Do you wish to speak with him?"

"He's there now?"

"I'm sorry to say he is."

"Terrific. You just keep him there. I'll be right down to take him off your hands."

"Chief, you, uh, sound a little ominous. I might even say a little frightening."

"It's nothing for you to worry about, Mrs. Keenan. I'll be there in a couple minutes." Balzic hung up and headed for the door, tearing the page with the Keenans' address out of his notebook and giving it to Johnson. "Come on, Walk. I'll go sit on him and you go get a warrant. And oh, Frances, you do us a favor and see if you can locate your friend, the one who arranged for Segalovich to write Janet's papers, okay? And when you get her, you tell her to sit tight. We're going to need her, okay?"

Frances nodded slowly, her face slack with remorse, bewilderment, betrayal. . . .

Mrs. Keenan was pacing in the kitchen when Balzic knocked on the screen door. She was startled by the sound and stood very still in the middle of the room. "Is that you, chief?"

"Yeah, it's me. All right if I let myself in?"

"Please do. I'm shaking so much I don't think I could open the door."

Balzic let himself in quietly and said, "Is he still here?"

She nodded once. "Chief, I'm scared to death. I really am."

"You got no problems. There won't be no hassle, believe me."

"You don't understand. I know why you're here, but something happened while I was talking to you on the phone—I mean, I think I can guess why you're here. To arrest Segalovich?" She was talking just above a whisper.

"Yeah, but nothing's going to happen to you—"

"That's not what I mean. While I was talking to you, Mal came out to the kitchen and he—he got some grass, some marijuana. They smoked it in Mal's study and I . . ."

"They're stoned? Both of them?"

"They were having a giggling fit when I last saw them. But I haven't heard anything for a while."

"Well, that'll make things easy."

"Easy?" Mrs. Keenan looked unbelieving.

"Sure. Potheads are the easiest collar—arrest, I mean. They just get nervous in the car. They always complain I'm driving too fast. They see a red light, they start hollering for me to stop a block away from it. I get a kick out of them, to tell the truth. They really make me laugh."

"Yes, but my husband, I mean, isn't possession a felony?"

"Mrs. Keenan, I could care less what your husband's holding. I want Segalovich. If you're worried about your husband, forget it. I should thank him for putting Segalovich in the shape he's in. Hell, now I can sit down and wait until the warrant gets here. If you don't mind."

"Please do."

Balzic settled onto a stool and lit a cigarette. "Mrs. Keenan, when I talked to you this afternoon, I asked you how long Segalovich had been here, and you weren't too sure. Try to think now, will you please? And put your feelings about him aside. I know that part's tough, but try to remember exactly when he showed up."

Before she could answer the sound of heavy, unsteady footsteps came to them, and then Malcolm Keenan appeared from around the corner. His eyes were red and wet, and he was having trouble trying not to giggle.

"Did I hear someone say when was the last time they showed off?"

"No, Mal, you did not. You most certainly did not hear that."

Keenan ignored his wife and tried to focus on Balzic. "You look similar, sir. Are you an original or are you a copy? Have you been . . . where was I?" Keenan started to rumble with giggles. "I remember not, I mean I remember now. Similar, Similac. Baby food. You're a diaper salesman."

Balzic laughed and said to Mrs. Keenan, "See what I mean? They're really funny."

"I am not amused," she said.

"No, no," Keenan said. "It's *we* are not amused. We. Not us. Not I. We are not . . . what aren't we?" He shook with giggles again.

"Amused," his wife said, "and if you could get yourself together you wouldn't be either."

"Wouldn't be what?"

"Oh Mal, for God's sake!"

"God," Keenan said. "Theism, I-ism, you-ism, we-ism, they-ism."

"Will you stop your word games just once! Just this once," Mrs. Keenan said, dropping her head and covering her ears with her hands.

133

"Women," Keenan said, grinning lopsidedly at Balzic. "Woman is a contraction of woe and man. And you can spell it either way; you can spell it *w, o, e,* or *w, h, o, a.* Sorrow and stop. That's women, or whatever . . ."

"Mal, your fellow free spirit, your poet in my residence, the one you always told to test the depths of his loathing, the one you encouraged to despise you, that same person may very well have found the depths of his loathing—do you understand me? Mal? Answer me."

"I would if I could but I can't seem to want to," Keenan said. "I'm trying to make some other association that is very important. Aha! This man is not a diaper salesman."

"Bravo, Mal. That he is not. He is a policeman. The chief of police, and unless I'm mistaken, another policeman is on his way here with a warrant to arrest your friend."

"Aaaaah, yes. The fuzzz. The fuzz with Roethke in his notebook. The commissar cum dilettante, the better to know me. And one can spell that *k, n, o, w,* or *n, o.* Either way, he is here to know me or no me . . ."

"Not you, Mal. Segalovich. Your friend is suspected of killing that girl."

"Really? I mean, really? That's, oh my . . . I'm afraid my toes are sending me messages. They say the world is spinning very fast and that gravity is very grave . . ."

"Damn you, Mal. Damn you!" Mrs. Keenan wheeled out of the kitchen. Her footsteps could be heard going through the house and then up some stairs. A door slammed overhead.

Keenan shrugged wearily at the sound, then turned to Balzic. "Did I hear her correctly? Or did I miss something?" He giggled. "Do you know what I almost said? I almost said, 'Did I thing some miss,' but I knew that would never do . . . oh, Shazam, Shazam, why don't I ever turn into Captain Marvel?"

"I give up," Balzic said, laughing, "why don't you?"

Keenan took a very deep breath, then another, and said, "I have no idea . . . say, did you say you suspect someone?"

"If I didn't, then your wife did."

"Who? And of what?"

"Anthony Segalovich. Murder."

"Are you serious? Murrr-der. That's impossible. Don't you see, I mean, can't you see—a poet who's in shape is never accused of rape."

"Yeah, well, that might be, but I didn't say anything about rape. I said murder."

"You yes—I mean, yes, but you see, it follows that if he's in shape and he's never accused of rape, why then he would never conceive of murder . . . where was I?"

"You're still right here, Mr. Keenan."

"*Doctor* Keenan. I have not been a mister for some months, or is it years? No matter . . . excuse me, but don't you think it would be wise to discuss this with Tony? I mean, but you should talk with him."

"Okay," Balzic said, standing. "Let's go discuss it with him. Where is he?"

"Follow me," Keenan said, gesturing dramatically, sweeping his arm in a great arc which came to a painful stop when his hand slammed into the refrigerator.

"You sure you can get us there?"

"Certainly," Keenan said, grimacing and opening and closing his hand and wiggling his fingers. He weaved around the corner and led Balzic through a formal, almost Victorian dining room, past a flight of carpeted stairs, and into a cluttered room with a desk, on which sat an old, office-size typewriter, heaps of papers, magazines, and books. Books were stacked haphazardly on a set of shelves which leaned precariously away from one wall, and there were more books stacked on the floor near the desk. There were two chairs, one a Boston rocker, the other a large wooden chair of indistinguishable manufacture, and a short couch.

On the couch, sitting with his shoulders slumped, his large hands hanging between his knees, his head tilted to the left, his eyes wide and red, sat Anthony Segalovich breathing deeply and slowly. His mouth curved up to the right in a half-smile. Without looking at either Keenan or Balzic, he said, "Man, am I skyed. This stuff is wow. Super wow." He made a faint whistle and let his head roll slowly to the right.

"Tony, it's the fuzz," Keenan said, settling uneasily into the Boston rocker.

"You ain't shittin' it's the was," Segalovich said.

"No, no, Tony. Not was. Fuzz."

"Fuzz, was. Was fuzzy. Was fuzzy ever wasy . . ."

Balzic lit a cigarette and looked around for an ashtray. He found one on a small table beside the Boston rocker and balanced it on his knee as he sat in the wooden chair.

"What're you smokin', man?" Segalovich said, focusing momentarily on Balzic.

"Tobacco."

"Ouu, that's bad for you. You can get cancer and every . . . wow, you should've felt that one. That one, that was like, wow, like nuclear . . . hey, man, tobacco's bad. You can get strokes, heart attacks, cancer. You can get cancer of the ass . . . you gotta shit through a hose into a bag and everything . . . hey, Mal, didn't I tell you?"

"Tell me what?"

"What what?"

"What didn't you tell me?"

"I forget," Segalovich said, smiling and rolling his head slowly while staring at something on the braided rug.

"Segalovich," Balzic said, "I guess it's about time I informed you of your constitutional rights."

"Consti-what? Man, I haven't shit in over a week. All I do is throw up."

"No," Balzic said, laughing. "Constitutional rights. Try to read my lips. Con-sti-tu-tion-al rights."

"Oh, them. Yeah, I got them. I got them all over the place. I can pray anywhere I want. I can assemble. I can even reassemble. I can do a whole bunch of stuff, man. I can even speech. Guaranteed."

"Yeah, well that's close but not close enough. So try to pay attention."

"Oh no. Nothin' doin'. I'm not standin' up for nobody. Are you kiddin', man? I'm nailed to this, whatever this is." Segalovich pounded the couch with the flat of his hand.

"'Then try listening carefully."

"Oh yeah. I can do that. Go ahead. Listen something at me and see if I do it carefully. I bet I can do it, man."

"Okay," Balzic said, "in a little while, a state police lieutenant will be here with a warrant for your arrest. The charge—"

"I'm with you so far, man. And carefully, too. Don't forget that, man. Carefully."

"Yeah, I've noticed that," Balzic said. "The charge will be murder."

"Murder? Phew, that's a baaaad rap. That's almost badder than gettin' busted for dealin'."

"A little worse, I think."

"Well, 'sa difference of opinion. So go 'head."

"You have the right to remain silent."

"Silent, man. Wow, that's really, you know, like quiet."

"You have the right to legal counsel, and if you don't know any or can't get one, it's the obligation of the Commonwealth to provide you with one."

"Hey, that's pretty nice of them, you know? You know that, Mal? I mean, providin' me with all that."

"Only if you're unable or unwilling to get one by yourself."

"Hey, like right now, I don't feel like gettin' one, you know? I mean, I couldn't even find the phone right now, you know? I mean, my ass is really tacked to this thing here. I mean, stapled, man."

"Yeah," Balzic said, "I know what you mean."

"Well, my arse is not stapled," Keenan said, getting wobbily to his feet. "And I will call one for you, Tony. The best one I know."

137

"Hey, that's really nice of you, Mal. I mean, no shit. It really is."

"*De nada,*" Keenan said, weaving around Balzic and out of the room.

"Okay, so he's going to call a lawyer for you," Balzic said, "but I want you to understand, clearly understand, that anything you say between now and the time the lawyer gets where you are —anything at all—will be used against you in a trial. Do you understand what I just said?"

"Yeah, man, I can understand that. But do you understand that I'm fuckin' skyed? I'm like up there with the seven-forty-sevens, man."

"That doesn't mean a thing. It doesn't make a bit of difference to a court. Booze, grass—a court doesn't care if it's marshmallows. All I got to testify to is that you said you understood me when I told you your rights. So just between you and me, I wouldn't say anything if I were you. I'd just sit there and enjoy that stuff until the lawyer shows."

"Man, you don't understand," Segalovich said, giggling. "I got nothing to hide. My life's an open book. It's a lousy book. Corny characters, stale plot, bad dialogue, no style, no nothing, but it's open. Just like a shithouse in a state park or someplace. I mean, you *know* people been shittin' there before you. You can smell their stories, man, so you don't sit all the way down. You just sort of go into a crouch and let her plop." Segalovich giggled again. "That is, if you ain't constituted, you can go plop. But if you're constituted, well, tough shit." Segalovich rocked with silent laughter, and then doubled over, rolling back and forth on the couch.

Balzic continued to sit and smoke, watching Segalovich as he sat upright finally, his eyes wet and red, his diaphragm heaving, his face slack. He sat like that for a minute or so, smiling vaguely at some sensation from the marijuana, rolling his head ever so slightly from side to side. Occasionally, he would throw his shoulders back, take a deep breath, and expel it audibly.

"You know," Segalovich said, looking at the floor, "you can never really control anything . . . you can try. You can really break your ass and your brain trying, but you can never really get anything under the kind of control you think you ought to have . . . you know what the fuck I'm talkin' about?"

"I think so," Balzic said.

"I mean, all the time I spent in the gyms, man, all those hours and weeks and years. All that time, man, on the side horse, on the high bar, the parallel bars, vaulting, working on the free exercise, working the still rings . . . all those hours. All those exercises, all those weights I lifted, all those isometrics I did . . . all that to control my body, man. And for what? All because my old man almost made somebody's Olympic team about a thousand years ago . . .

"Ain't that something? I mean, really. All that to learn control, to learn when to get your hips under, your legs together, your toes pointed, the exact moment when to take off and when to start your shoulder turning . . . all that because a guy I can't even remember used to do it. All that because the broad he married, the one he screwed to pop me out, all that because she thought I should do it because he would've wanted me to do it . . .

"And you know, for a long time, man, I really believed I should be doing it because I really believed in it. I mean to tell you, man, I really ate that crap up, just scarfed it up. I thought, yeah, baby, this is really where it's at, this is really the way to control things, really control things. Get so good at those things, man, you could make your body do damn near anything. And all the while, man, it wasn't my life. I was doing it and really diggin' it and really bein' good at it, and I wasn't in control of nothing. No, man. It was my old lady was in control. All the time. She was in charge of my whole life . . .

"I'd be in a meet, man, and there she'd be. She wouldn't have to tell me she was going to be there, man. I could feel her there. I swear she breathed different, and I could hear her breath-

139

ing in the stands. And when I'd fuck up, when I'd miss a move, start it too soon or come off it a fraction too late, I could hear her breathing change.

"And then she'd start to shout, man, and carry on. She'd start shouting, encouraging me. A one-woman cheering section. The better I got, the louder she got . . . and then she'd start anticipating me, man. Yelling at me when to start my next move, what to look out for, what mistakes I could make . . . it was fuckin' embarrassin', man . . .

"That last time, what a circus . . . it was an AAU meet, and I was on the rings. There was, like, two events to go, and I'm so far out front in points, I'd have to break a leg to lose, you know? But I got started wrong on those fuckin' rings. Man, those fuckers just started swayin', man, and I couldn't get them stopped. A foot in each direction, and I just could not get those bastards still . . .

"I was going to go from a handstand right into an iron cross, two strength moves in a row. Lots of points . . . but goin' into the handstand I almost went over the top and the goddamn rings were swayin' worse than ever. I mean, I was having a real bitch holding two seconds up there. It was like two minutes . . .

"And I came down too fast. My feet went way out in front. Christ, I arched my back so hard I pulled something in it, just trying to keep my ass under . . . I go into the cross, and the place is quiet, man, the way it always gets when people see somebody goin' wrong. They get quiet, man, 'cause they're really watchin' to see if the guy can pull it off. And there I am, swayin' like I'm on a fuckin' trapeze, countin' the seconds—you got to hold it for three—and my old . . ." Segalovich started to laugh hard so that it became difficult for him to talk. ". . . and my old lady is down out of the stands, man, and she's praying. Praying, man. She's saying, 'God, don't sway. God, please don't sway. Please, God, don't sway.' And you know what?"

"No, what?" Balzic said.

"I felt like I got hit by lightning, man. I mean it. Like fucking lightning. There I was, two seconds into the iron cross, waiting for the third second to pass, gruntin' my ass off, goin' nuts 'cause I can't get those rings still, and there's my old lady, praying. It was the sequence that got me, man. First it was, 'God, don't sway.' Then it was, 'God, please don't sway.' And then the clincher: 'Please, God, don't sway.'

"And there it was, man. In the third second, it hit me. Like lightning, I knew, man. I knew! I mean, it was so fuckin' corny, but it was perfect. You can't write that kind of stuff, man. You can't make a story out of it. You can't make poetry out of it. It's too fuckin' corny. I mean, there I was, man, crucified doin' an iron cross, and there was my old lady down there prayin' for me, prayin' *to* me, man, to satisfy somebody I didn't even know who was God around our house . . . like lightning, man, I was Jesus. I mean, I wasn't, but I was! I actually knew what it felt like to be up on that cross waitin' to die, man, listening to the women prayin' for him to be what nobody can ever be. What nobody can be, man. Nobody."

"What's that?"

"Perfect, man. Nobody can be that. I mean, I know what a perfect performance on the rings might look like. Might. But nobody ever does it. Nobody ever has and nobody ever will . . . but there was my old lady down there, tryin' her ass off to turn me into the son of God . . . 'Please, God, don't sway' . . . and all because that bastard was dead and I was all she had. . . ."

"What did you do?"

"I just started to cry, man. Just bawl. And then I just dropped down out of the cross, man, and I started to swing, back and forth, just like kids do in a park. I was swingin' so hard, I was fuckin' near goin' over the top. And then I started to laugh . . . you should've seen the people, man. They were goin' bananas trying to figure out how to get me down off those rings. The judges, man, the coaches, they were all running around like wild, man. And my old lady, she's screamin' at me. 'Please, God, Anthony, stop it.' Over and over and over. Christ, it was funny. . . ."

"How did they stop you?"

"I don't know. Next thing I knew I was in a hospital some-where. Pittsburgh, I think. I don't even know. They had me so fogged up with Thorazine, man, I didn't know what my name was. . . ."

Keenan came in then and said, "Attorney Louis Margolis will be here within the hour. He advised me to advise you, Tony, to say absolutely nothing until he arrives."

Segalovich listened to Keenan and then shook his head and laughed. "Hey, Mal, no shit. How come everything you say got to sound like the Gettysburg Address? I mean, really, man, all you need's a beard and a top hat."

"What do you mean by that?" Keenan said.

"What do you mean by that?" Segalovich mimicked him. "Now what the shit do you think I mean? Everything you say, man, you say like you're running for Congress. That's the way you sound, man. Like you're giving a position paper or a news conference or some goddamn thing. Like everything you say is going into a briefcase which is gonna get handcuffed to some-body's wrist and wind up in Istanbul or Helsinki or some fucking place."

Keenan took several very deep breaths and squared his shoulders. "In view of the fact that I have taken it upon myself to obtain counsel for you, Tony, and especially in view of the seriousness of the charge against you, I think it's about time you began to take an altogether different attitude—"

"There you go again, man. Another fuckin' speech."

"As I was saying, I think it's about time you began to assume the attitude apropos the situation, which attitude it seems would be one of the most practical realism."

"Oh, I am, man, I am. I have never had a more realistic attitude than I have right now. I mean, I've leveled off, man. Super Jay, the joyous Jamaican, has got me up to twenty-seven thousand feet, and I'm locked into automatic pilot. I got time to look around and survey the crew, see if everybody's in order, and, man, you're as out of order as anybody I've ever seen. And the reason you're so out of order is 'cause you spend your whole life trying to get out of order. Man, you're the only guy I know who's made a career out of being disorderly in an orderly way. You're full of shit, man, precisely because you got diarrhea, if you know what I mean." Segalovich started to laugh, but his face was no longer slack and his eyes no longer vague. Either the marijuana was starting to wear off or else he had reached an interval of lucidity on his way to another of giggling, seemingly disjointed indifference.

Keenan, for his part, was standing as though prepared for military inspection. His chest was out, his heels together, his thumbs resting on the seams of his trousers. "This is not the time for acrimony," he said solemnly. "You are in serious trouble. I am befriending you. This is not, most definitely not, the time for acrimony."

"Aw, for crissake, man, sit down," Segalovich said. "You keep standing there like that, you're gonna rupture yourself or something . . . 'not the time for acrimony,' Jesus. Befriending me, shit. All you ever did was finish the job my old lady started, you know that? Between the two of you, my old lady and you, you two fuckers got me crazy . . . she wants to turn me into a chimpanzee, and you want to turn me into a chimpanzee that can type . . . still rings and sestinas, the horizontal bar and heroic couplets, the side horse and satire, free exercise and free verse . . . is it any fuckin' wonder I'm doing giant swings inside my head? And all the time tryin' to figure out how I'm goin' to dismount? I should've killed you two . . . what the fuck'd I have to kill her for? Come on, Doctor motherfuckin' Keenan, tell me why. You're so goddamn full of announcements, pronouncements, affirmations . . . 'The universe announces yes, who am I to profane the universe by announcing any less,'—ain't that your fuckin' story, Doctor Keenan? What the hell are you a doctor of anyway? Doctor of Philosophy, shit. Doctor of sick ideas, is that what you are? Tell me something, doctor of sick ideas—d'you ever cure one yet?"

"Tony," Keenan said evenly, "I would adivse you to say no

more. I am advising you of this because if you continue to speak as you are, you will only succeed in getting into greater difficulty than you are."

"Greater difficulty than I am?" Segalovich howled with laughter. "Man, how much difficulty could I be in! You don't understand nothing, man. Nothing! I could split your head open with an ax and pour in some real information, only you got so much shit backed up in there, none of it would filter through. The joke is, we're the same, you and me. I'm constipated in my ass, you're constipated in your brain. You haven't had a new idea since Christ was a carpenter. The bigger joke is you know it. You've known it all along. That's why you're a fucking poet, man, instead of a man who writes poetry. Any asshole can be a poet. *Be* one. But write it? Uh-uh, no way. Man, that takes work. You got to sit down at the machine and get the words on the page, man. Anybody can walk around makin' fuckin' announcements he's a poet. But when you sit down at the machine and look at that blank page, man, that's like standing under those goddamn rings, waiting for somebody to lift you up so you can take hold and do it, man. *Do* it!

"All the talk in the world about keeping those rings still won't keep them still. Just like all your bullshit about being a poet don't get any words on the page . . .

"And I believed you! I actually believed you . . . this is all a bad joke, man. One box inside another box. I believed my old lady, my old lady believed in my old man, she believed in me, I believed in you. And you—you told me I could be a poet. I should've known right then from the way you said it. I could *be* a poet, you said. Shit, man, I can't even write a simple goddamn story. First this happened and then that happened. I can't even do that. Now go ahead, ask me how I know I can't. Go ahead. Either one of you. How about you, cop? You probably the only one really wants to know anyway. The doctor of sick ideas here wouldn't understand."

"How do you know?" Balzic said.

"Because I tried, man. Because I tried over and over and

144

over. And you know whose story I was tryin' to write?"

"Janet Pisula's?" Balzic said.

"See there, Keenan? The cop knows more than you ever will." Tears filled Segalovich's eyes. "The cop knows, and you know what he knows? He knows I couldn't even tell how a girl got so scared of living she wanted to die. You know how many different ways I wrote her story, man? I lost count, that's how many. Because no matter which way I wrote it, it came out wrong. All it was was words. All words, just words . . .

"And you know what finally came to me? There was nothin' but words on those pages about her because there was nothing in me to put on those fuckin' pages. All I knew was she was like me. Something got in her head that somebody else put there. She didn't have a life. She'd been dead for years. All I did was make her stop breathing. . . ."

"Is that why you went there?" Balzic asked.

"Hell no. I went there to get some bread she owed me."

"But we found a lot of money in the room."

"Hey, you just asked me why I went there and I told you. I didn't say anything about taking any money. When it hit me, I mean, when I saw it . . . shit, money was the last thing in the world that made any difference. What good was fifteen bucks going to do me? What good is fifteen thousand going to do me right now? Fifteen million . . . man, you only need money when you got some tomorrows coming. . . ."

"You didn't even ask for the money, did you?"

Segalovich shook his head. "What for? I wanted to see what was inside her—can you understand that? That's what I really went there for. I wanted to find out how come she was dead. So I could write it, man. I mean, when somebody's dead and they're still walking around, it's a goddamn story, you know? But how the fuck do you find out?"

"You might've tried talking," Balzic said.

"Goddammit, man, that broad never talked! She never said one more word than she had to, and half the time you couldn't hear that." Segalovich heaved his shoulders in a deep sigh.

"When I used to go there to do her papers for her, she'd have the assignment written down, and she'd just hand it to me. Then I'd sit down and write it and I'd try to show her what I was doing, you know? So she might learn a little something for herself, you know? But I never knew whether anything I said was getting through."

Balzic thought for a moment. "Is that—that last time—is that what made you try to make love to her?"

"You're too much, man, you know that? Too much," Segalovich said, shaking his head. "How did you think of that?"

"Well, it looked pretty obvious. She didn't have anything on except her panties. There wasn't any struggle. You had to've at least started with that in mind."

Segalovich's shoulders sagged. "Yeah, that's the way it started out. For the dumbest-ass reason in the world. I went in my head from trying to get inside her head to find out why she was dead to getting in her to see if maybe she was still alive and I was too dumb and too blind not to see it. I thought maybe I could feel it. Like, shit, I don't know, like maybe my body could feel something my head couldn't think. I mean, hell, there was a time when I could make my body do damn near anything. Maybe it could even think. . . ."

"But it didn't work," Balzic said.

Segalovich gave a snorting, self-deprecating laugh. "That's got to be the all-time understatement of the world, man. The all-timer to end all-timers. 'Cause that's when I found out I was dead, man. I couldn't feel a thing. All the while she was undressing, man, I couldn't feel a single motherfuckin' thing. All I remember is I started to shake. Just shake all over. And then that fuckin' line of Roethke's Keenan is always quoting jumped at me. 'This shaking keeps me steady. I should know.' That jumped at me and it had a hammer in both hands. It just started pounding on my head . . . I could hear Keenan, just like he was there, reciting it . . . and then my mother was breathing funny in the stands, I could hear her like she was there. And there was this broad right in front of me, this dead broad with her nipples as round as round could be, and all I could think of was those fuckin' rings, and, man, so help me, that brassiere was the same color, the exact same goddamn color as the gloves I used to wear . . .

"The next thing I knew she was saying something about I was him. She just kept saying it, over and over. 'You're him, you're him, you're him,' and I was asking her, who am I? Who am I supposed to be? But all she said was the same thing, over and over. And I knew it was important. I mean, really important. Like if she'd only tell me, then maybe I could go somewhere and write her story and get it right and get it out of me. But I couldn't get it out of her. She wouldn't say who I was or who he was or why I was him . . .

"And then, my head just zipped out on me. Zip-zip, gone. And there she was, man . . . all I did was lay her down real easy, like, as though, like I was trying not to hurt her. Can you imagine that? I just strangled the fuckin' broad and I'm laying her down easy 'cause I don't want to hurt her. . . ."

"What did you do then?" Balzic asked.

Segalovich shook his head. "I don't know. I can't remember a thing. Nothing. All I know is I was here, heaving my guts out in the bathroom upstairs."

"You don't remember how you got here?"

"Nothing. I don't remember how or when or why. I was just there one minute and the next minute I was here, that's all."

"What about the paper?"

"What about the what?"

"The paper. That blank sheet of paper."

"Man, I don't know what you're talking about."

"There was a blank sheet of paper on her stomach. You had to put it there."

"Man, I'm telling you, the last thing I remember doing was laying her down real easy. That paper you're talking about, I don't know anything about any paper. And I'll tell you straight, man, this fuckin' Jamaican, you cops ought to use it. If it gets everybody else the way it gets me, you guys ought to find out about it, 'cause I can't lie when I got this shit in me. I see the lies startin' in the back of my head and runnin' around and gettin' close to my tongue and then I just see them goin' back where they started from.

"Like a minute ago, one started. I was going to tell one about how it's everybody else's fault that I killed that girl, Keenan's, my old lady's, my old man's, everybody's. It was one of those lies some jackoff Ph.D. in sociology or psychology would've come up with. Like I didn't have any choice. Like given the givens, man, somebody like me would just naturally wind up killing somebody . . . statistical determination. Freudian determination. Calvinistic determination, whatever the fuck you want to call it. But that was a bullshit lie, man. I killed that girl all by myself. I killed her 'cause she was me. 'Cause I didn't have the fuckin' guts to kill myself . . .

"And you know what she said, man? Right when I was doing it? She said, 'Please.' Yeah. Not, 'Please don't.' No. She said, 'Please.' . . . poor, dumb fuckin' broad. She couldn't write either. . . ."

Segalovich stood then, momentarily lost his balance, but steadied himself by holding onto the arm of the couch for a few seconds. He straightened slowly and said, "Come on, cop. Take me wherever the fuck you're gonna take me. I stay here any more, I'm going to throw up all over Keenan's typewriter, and he wouldn't appreciate that. I mean, he'd say throwin' up was also part of the affirmation of the universe, but I still think it'd piss him off."

Balzic stood and started to lead Segalovich out of the room, but stopped short of the doorway and said to Keenan, "Listen, when that lawyer gets here, you tell him we'll be at Troop A Barracks and we'll wait for him so he can be at the arraignment, okay?"

Keenan seemed not to hear.

"Uh, Dr. Keenan, d'you hear what I just said?"

"I'm sorry. I was—I was. Yes, I was, that's what I was."

148

"Yeah, well, did you hear what I said about the lawyer and where we'll be?"

"Yes, I heard. It just took a moment. I was thinking of something."

Segalovich faced Keenan. There were tears in his eyes. "Mal, I hope you do think of something, man. I really do." Then he turned to Balzic and said, "Let's go, okay? Only one thing."

"What's that?"

"No handcuffs, okay? I couldn't stand that. I couldn't stand to have those things on me, you know?"

"I know," Balzic said, leading him through the house and onto the porch where they met Johnson coming up the steps.

"This him?" Johnson asked.

Balzic nodded. "Keenan called a lawyer for him, and I told Keenan to tell the lawyer we'd wait for him up at your place."

"You mean we're not going to have him alone?"

"We don't need to, Walk. Not that way. He'll tell you everything you want to know. Maybe a couple things you don't want to know."

"He confess?"

Balzic nodded. He was going to say something, but was interrupted by Segalovich's laughter.

"What's funny?"

"I was just thinking, man," Segalovich said. "The first thing I want you to know, it's not funny. I'm just laughing 'cause I don't feel like crying. But what I was thinking about was my old lady got a scrapbook about this big." He held his hand about three inches apart. "Filled with pictures and clippings, all about me. I was just wondering if she was gonna cut this out of the paper too, you know? I mean, she was always saying she was saving the last couple pages for when I finally made it, whatever the fuck she thought that would take. But what I was laughing about, man, all of a sudden it just came to me. I mean, now I know why they call them scrapbooks, you know?"

"Yeah," Balzic said, "I see what you mean."

Johnson took hold of Segalovich's elbow and led him down the steps and to his cruiser. Just before he opened the door, he called back to Balzic, "You coming?"

"Nah. I'll catch you in about a half-hour or so. I got to go talk to my wife."

"Something wrong?"

"Not yet," Balzic said, going to his own cruiser, "but there's going to be if I don't go talk to her. I got to tell her her brother's turning into a dirty old man and I don't want him around my daughters. I been putting it off for a couple years, but right now I suddenly got the feeling this is the time to say it."

"Well, if that's what you have to do," Johnson said, shrugging.

"It is," Balzic said, getting into his cruiser and turning the ignition. He watched Johnson drive off, then turned around in the alley behind the Keenans' house and headed for home.

He found Ruth in the kitchen and he told her as gently, as kindly as he could what was bothering him about her brother. Though it settled nothing about their spending a weekend in her brother's cottage, and though much of what he said made Ruth angry, he was glad he had not wasted any more time figuring the right way to say it. In the morning, he was very glad for that.

AFTERWORD

If anonymity is the art of taking up space without making a place for oneself, K. C. Constantine has, to this point, practiced that art rather well. There are, after all, four novels by Constantine, with another two on the way, and yet he has been virtually invisible. He does not appear in any of the standard catalogues of crime. He is even missing from John M. Reilly's massive compilation of over six hundred twentieth-century writers of crime and mystery fiction. A somewhat random visit to five public libraries and two university libraries in any section of the country would probably reveal not a copy of his books. He has been forgotten in the bookstores. To be sure, his name rests, mute in its card tray, at the Library of Congress, and Allen J. Hubin, bibliographer extraordinaire, has tersely noted that Constantine exists, listing the four published books with the simple statement behind the name, 'Pseudonym.' Constantine wrote his books, all for the Saturday Review Press / E. P. Dutton, apparently in a sustained outburst of creativity between 1972 and 1975, and then dropped from sight. (At least these are the encompassing dates of publication, though Constantine may well have been at work long before 1972.)

In itself such anonymity is not remarkable, and especially not so in the world of detective and mystery fiction. Such books tend to be ignored by the more serious reviewers, are shipped off to remote bookstores in small print runs, and after a period of withering upon the remainder shelves, are to be encountered thereafter only in those places that specialize in books that smell of must: the reading rooms of New England country inns in winter, the book barns that open up on Martha's Vineyard and along the California coast to cater to the Summer trade, and in the various paperback book dealers and secondhand shops that cling to a precarious existence on the fringe of universities or embedded in the sex-and-fun quarters of our larger cities. Constantine, however, cannot even be encountered in this trinity, for not one of his four books made it to a paperback reprint. To me, at least, he was unknown until two years ago, when in just such an open-beamed barn I stumbled across, for ninety-five cents, *The Man Who Liked to Look at Himself,* and thinking the title worth the risk of less than a dollar, dust jacket intact and all, carted him off with me in a bundle of higher expectations to Cape Cod.

If such a disappearance is not unusual, it is on occasion wrong. Wrongful results ought to lead one to look for causes, and the apparent neglect of K. C. Constantine is, upon examination, also markedly surprising. First, the man writes exceedingly well, though not always (then, who does?). Second, the books were published by a respected press, were slim and inexpensive, were marketed through a book club as well as in the most usual manner, and had at least better-than-average dust jackets designed by Roy Kuhlman. Third, they were well reviewed. The first book, *The Rocksburg Railroad Murders,* published in 1972, attracted the attention of the equally pseudonymous Newgate Callendar, who declared it to be 'one of the most sensitive crime novels of recent years'; the railroad murders carried 'a tremendous wallop.' *Publishers Weekly,* not given to critical exegesis to be sure, thought the plotting and characterization were absorbing, while Sergeant Cuff in the *Saturday Review* praised the 'personable characters' and asked for more books by the same author.

And so Constantine did as he was asked, and the next year coughed up *The Man Who Liked to Look at Himself.* This is, I think, his least-good book, though he feels it to be one of his two best. Given that I discovered him through the book I like least, I think that it is the book's suggestion of clear competence and ability to understand people at their worst, rising above even singularly unpleasant subject matter, that has caused those scholars of crime fiction, Jacques Barzun and Wendell Taylor, to select it for inclusion in their new crime-fiction library, which is to cover 1950 to 1976. This second book was unpleasant in a rather special way, and perhaps it put readers off. Reviewers appear to have ignored it, and in subsequent books the publisher chose to say nothing about its existence except for a listing on the page always reserved for 'other books written by' the author at hand. All of the books have something to do with sex, for they are about life, and all see sex plain: while it brings pleasure, it equally often brings pain, and lust too frequently is more powerful than love, especially where poverty intervenes. The man liked to look at himself having sex, alone or with others, and mirrors not being sufficient, he took to filming his pleasures. The sensation the novel induces is not uplifting, for it is rather like the shock of coming upon some particularly unattractive couple rutting in the bushes just outside one's living room window. It's all too close to home, too real, too distant from sex as implied by slick advertising or seen in company watching Bo Derek make herself available in the movie *10*. Perhaps the reader felt stained. In any event, it appears that he did not come back for more.

There were two more books, however, for Constantine was still developing as a writer, working away at night and after hours on weekends, fully occupied at a job on the fringes of the working-class life he described. Constantine's is an authentic working-class tone; indeed, this is so in his speech as well as in his writing, making one feel that Studs Lonigan is on the other end of the telephone line, and that each sentence has been dug out of the bituminous coal around Rocksburg. Yet one may be permitted some small doubts about this tone, for in the third book, *The Blank Page* (which I regard as Constantine's best), we encounter Theodore Roethke, one of our less accessible poets, and a carefully realized sense of a small-town, small-time, struggling yet valuable college. One feels the author knows the town, the college, the people, from inside, and that Roethke was chosen because that poet, in suicide and in words, had something personal to say to the author. *The Blank Page* is naturalism in the American mode, certainly better in almost any sense of the word save one than *Maggie, Girl of the Streets*. The sense protected by *save one* is, of course, that Stephen Crane went on to win fame by writing a work of undoubted genius, while Constantine, in another time and another place, and plying his craft within another genre, has not yet attracted the attention of the critics who determine such matters.

Those critics who paid attention liked *The Blank Page*. The *Library*

Journal, a bit viciously, remarked that 'the academic world is horrifyingly accurate' at Conemaugh County Community College; *Newsday* recognized that the book was not isolated by telling its readers that Mario Balzic, Constantine's series figure, was getting better with each installment; others agreed that the book was by far Constantine's best. He seemed back on the track. The *Boston Globe* reviewer even said, inexplicably in hindsight, that Constantine 'was one of the most talked about mystery writers on the American scene.'

Well, this seems not to have been so, or there would be no need for this Afterword, and K. C. Constantine would have continued his pace, a book a year, unfolding the human relationships in his ethnically mixed American community (Poles, Ukrainians, Russians, Hungarians, Serbs, Croats, Slovaks, southern Italians, Irish, some Greeks, about as many blacks as Irish, a few Jews, a few Protestants, no blond and blue-eyed Nordics: this is the Rocksburg Constantine describes). Actually I cannot recall anyone having ever talked about Constantine, and this last year when I queried two dozen or so intense mystery fans at the annual festival of dread organized by the New York City bookstore Murder Ink, and held at the Goreyesque Mohonk Mountain House, on what they thought of Constantine, they replied to a man, woman, and child, 'Who?' To be sure, readers in Boston who had liked George Higgins's *Friends of Eddie Coyle* ought to have been talking about Constantine, and maybe they were, but talk is cheap and books cost money.

And so appeared the fourth episode in the life of Mario Balzic: *A Fix Like This.* Constantine was certain that his writing was getting better with each book, he felt a sense of genuine progression, and he was taking on with the *Fix* a tougher problem than he had before, tougher in theme and tougher as a challenge to his writing. He was certain he had a winner, and he still considers this his best book, though it plummeted without a trace, little reviewed, little purchased. Discouraged, Constantine stopped publishing, though he did not stop writing, with other plots bubbling up in him, other figures in his gritty small city in western Pennsylvania requiring his rather special kind of cruelly observed compassion. His fifth Balzic novel, *The Man Who Liked Slow Tomatoes,* is scheduled for publication by Godine at the same time as this volume.

I do not know who K. C. Constantine is, though we have now corresponded and have talked on the telephone. Having broken the odd pseudonym here and there, and being as happy to invade the privacy of

154

the next person as anyone, I had set about in pursuit of Constantine. His books provide an abundance of clues: the knowledge of Italian and eastern European mores as practiced in the United States; the acquaintance, rendered glancingly, with the police, with schools, with the press, with the way machine shops and small-time insurance agencies work; the intimate ear for the conversation that takes place in unfashionable bars in dying industrial towns that are the outriders to the larger industrial cities, where neon signs spew Schlitz in the window and the cardboard coasters are used over and over again. When I inquired, his publisher was helpful, if discreet: Constantine wished to remain alone; his books had not sold as well as they and he had hoped; no one appeared to know him at the publishing house, where young voices on the telephone cheerfully told me that they would look various matters up in the files and get back to me. In time they did, remarking that there didn't seem to be any more books in the pipeline, and that they had no address for Constantine, only the name of his agent. The agent, as all good agents are, was cagey but agreed to forward a letter. I suggested that my quarry call me at a number that was not my own, rather than writing, since letters bear postmarks, and somewhat to my surprise one night, crickets humming outside the window, Constantine called to ask what I had in mind.

An article about his books, I said. He was flattered but felt that he'd rather not. We talked, and Mario Balzic and Mo Valcanas, that never-sober lawyer, and Father Marrazo, full of odd sentence constructions behind which I heard concern for others, were all on the line with us. He had been thinking about writing again, he said, and the call would get him to do so with a more determined purpose. His wife talked to me, and she was pleased. I decided to wait on the article until there was a new book, to herald the return of a unique talent. Constantine declined to identify himself and spoke of liking his privacy. Somewhere along the line we decided his name was Carl, or Karl, or that I could say that it was, and we left it at that, my passion to find out who lurked behind this carefully concealed Trevanian gone, the blank page to be left, in respect, blank.

But one cannot quite fail to speak of a good thing when one sees it. I mentioned Constantine in a column in the *New Republic*. I put *The Blank Page* on my personal list of favorite modern detective stories in a small book on that subject, and Constantine was spotted by some who then asked me who he was. I didn't know, and still don't, and have decided that it doesn't much matter whether I do or not. I was reading the *Rocksburg Railroad Murders* again, rather idly looking for further clues to the locale, having decided that the references to western Pennsylvania were red herrings, that Shippensburg, or even Chambersburg, or just possibly Altoona, was Rocksburg, when I received a note from Constantine. He was writing again, he had a new book nearly finished, and though he wasn't sure he had anything in particular to thank me for, he wanted to anyway. Soon came a Christmas card with a very un-Christmassy message, and I knew that this tough, gritty, clear mind was at work on Chief Balzic again.

Then one day I found myself lecturing in Pennsylvania, and the urge to see Altoona, and the site of the Johnstown flood, and Frank Lloyd Wright's Falling Water, and Friendship Hill, where Albert Gallatin had lived, outside Marion, and to drive through Clairton to think again about why I had so liked *The Deer Hunter* as a film (dreadful book to follow!) while so many critics had discovered within it a racism I thought not there — this composite, unstructured urge, rambling like all urges, came over me, and I set out in a rented car to explore this chunk of truly American America. By loops and whorls I was in Aliquippa, Beaver Falls, New Castle, Slippery Rock, Butler, New Kensington, McKeesport, Washington, and across two borders to Weirton in West Virginia (where *The Deer Hunter* was actually filmed) and Steubenville in Ohio. When I dropped the car at the Pittsburgh airport to return home, one more itch to see a chunk of America well scratched, I knew I had been to Rocksburg.

And so the decision to launch the *Godine Double Detectives* with K. C. Constantine, still anonymous, no fuller name entered behind that pseudonym on library cards by our most assiduous of detectives, still writing and getting better, not all in one smooth acceleration, but in bits and pieces, here and there, with this page and that paragraph, getting better all the time.

For the point of this series is to bring back into print neglected authors in detective fiction, authors who know how to construct a plot as honest as those towns, authors who have contributed to the development of detective fiction, grouping their work in ways that will throw light on the serious side as well as the fun side of why we read such fiction and how it tells us about who and what we are. Books by different authors, though set in the same locale, that show us a city, a place, through different eyes; books, again by different authors, on a common theme, of capital punishment or vengeance or 'the flaw in the crystal' of the apparently perfect man, that show us the variety of life; books, by different or the same authors, as with Constantine, that hold a mirror up to society, showing it plain, candid statements in the demotic speech of our time.

Constantine's first book, *The Rocksburg Railroad Murders,* began with two different titles. I have the original typescript before me, the odd typo surviving, here and there an altered line in the manuscript tightening up the already compressed, realistic dialogue. The book was to have been called *Half Remembered Faces.* Here was a book about how the past caught up with people, about a man who didn't think it funny to write on a blackboard with chalk so that it squeaked, making an angular ugly sound. Out on the macadam roads of America, washed clean by rain, people were destroying each other for little reason, or no reasonable reason at all, wiping the slates clean. But the title wasn't right, certainly, for the book, for it was sentimental where the style was consciously flat, toneless, conveying emotion less by voice than by color, and the color itself mostly gradations of gray. The town was the real character in the book, each of the human voices simply pieces of a larger chorus, out beyond Evanko's Bar and Grille, where Balzic took his quick cold one. So the manuscript went to the publisher with an alternate title, *The Rocksburg Murders.* This seemed to fit the sounds and sights of this town where one could feel the potholes in the street even before dropping axle-deep into them, gravel on the windshield and muddy spray of rain over the wheels, just right, just so, the dialogue a bit stiff, the work of a writer with a good ear whose fingers needed to limber up on the typewriter yet. Somewhere along the road someone decided that *Railroad* ought to be added to the title for any one of a half-dozen reasons at which one might guess and probably be wrong, and the first book was before us.

The town, not the railroad, remained the subject. Here was a place where many different Americans, of different ethnic backgrounds, had been working out their complex code of life, a mix peculiar to small-town, ethnic, blue-collar America. This was not Ross Macdonald's Santa Barbara, or Ed McBain's Isola, or even Hillary Waugh's Stockford, Connecticut. The town was too small and poor to be Michael Lewin's Indianapolis, too ethnic to pass for the small corrupt cities in Illinois and Florida where Hammett and Westlake and Queen and John D. MacDonald lifted the lids. Constantine has a gift for colloquial sociology. Others have been said to have this gift: Harry Kemelman's Rabbi David Small tells us quite a bit about Barnard's Crossing, in Massachusetts, but the place is too obviously a suburb of Boston, itself too unlike Pittsburgh to provide a similar setting. A. B. Guthrie's Midbury, in Montana, is real enough, like the small town in the same state where James Welch tells us of *The Death of Jim Loney*. Still, *New Yorker* cartoons to the contrary, the dimensions of the land out there are very real, and all small towns are not alike, and Constantine's town is special because it is Rocksburg, Pennsylvania, and not Rockford, Illinois, or Rockport, Indiana, or Rocky River, Ohio, or even Rockwood, Pennsylvania. The sentimental might say that Constantine's Rocksburg is a special place; it isn't, it's simply real, and in being real, it is different from the next small town, whatever dwellers in large cities might think, just as the next small town is in turn different from the next again. From the turnpikes all wheat fields and all small towns may look alike, but Constantine knows no turnpikes.

Nor did Janet Pisula. She wasn't going anywhere, just as many people in the small towns — and the large cities — of America aren't going anywhere. She might have done, brain damage and all, shy as she was, but she wasn't and didn't. Balzic understands, and Constantine captures the language, the feelings that pass for thoughts, the sounds of words one encounters on so many college campuses today. If one doesn't punctuate every sentence with a liberal sprinkling of 'you knows' to drive the argument forward into further nothingness, with 'like mans' to be oldster-hip, with excretory and copulative verbs that eject the little meaning and penetrate the tiny, tiny womb of self-knowledge of so many of those who are at college to find themselves, one does not know the language of the campus any more than a Wall Street lawyer could talk at ease with the drunks in Evanko's. There are no turnpikes here, and Balzic is not on a fast track.

The track he is on is authentic Americana. Balzic finds more than one blank page at the local junior college. There are, in the local priest, the competing state troopers, the elderly mother, the wife and daughters, plenty of pages that bear the imprint of a writer who looks at what he sees, and tells us. I hope he is going to go on telling us about Rocksburg in many more books to come.

ROBIN W. WINKS